To Catch a Queen

Also by Shanna Swendson

The Enchanted, Inc. Series:

Enchanted, Inc.
Once Upon Stilettos
Damsel Under Stress
Don't Hex With Texas
Much Ado About Magic
No Quest For The Wicked
Kiss and Spell

The Fairy Tale Series

A Fairy Tale
To Catch a Queen

To Catch a Queen

Shanna Swendson

NLA Digital, LLC

Production Manager: Lori Bennett
Cover art by Kirbi Fagan.
Cover design and book design by Angie Hodapp.

ISBN 978-1-62051-139-8

Uneasy lies the head that wears a crown.
—William Shakespeare, *Henry IV, Part II*

One

Michael Murray ducked under the crime scene tape his partner held up for him and asked the uniformed officer at the scene, "What've you got, Milton?"

"Dead body. You'll have to wait for the ME to know if it's natural causes or not, but it *is* weird."

"Define weird." Michael's threshold for "weird" had shifted radically in the last couple of months.

"See for yourself." Milton gestured toward the body lying sprawled in the grass nearby.

At first, Michael didn't notice anything obviously out of the ordinary. Then again, he didn't consider fairies and magic to be all that strange, these days. It was his partner, Marisol Lopez, who spotted the anomaly. "Well, they do say that disco is dead," she quipped.

That's what was strange. The body looked like it had fallen through a time warp from sometime around 1977. It wore tight white bell-bottom trousers and a shiny shirt with a huge collar. The clothes looked new, but the body didn't. Michael guessed that the dead man was in his sixties, old enough that he might have worn these clothes back in the heyday of disco when he was of an age to hit the town for a little Saturday-night fever.

"This stuff isn't coming back in style, is it?" Michael asked Mari.

"God, I hope not," she replied, then winced. "Sorry. I guess I owe a dollar."

"I'll just stand over here where the lightning bolt won't hit me." Michael had given up trying to talk his colleagues out of teasing him for his goody-goody reputation by charging a fine for swearing or irreverence in front of him. At least it meant the precinct got a free lunch every so often when they emptied the penalty jar.

Michael leaned closer over the body. The dead man looked aged, but not weathered, and his skin was so pale that either he was religious about wearing really good sunblock or he hadn't seen the sun in decades. Even his hands were free of liver spots. His hair was white, but worn in a longish, feathered style that matched his wardrobe.

"He looks scared," Mari commented as she, too, studied the body. "And not just 'Ay! My heart!' scared."

"Detectives!" Milton called out. Michael looked up to see a few uniforms struggling with a man dressed similarly to the dead man. He looked to be about the same age, with the same lack of weathering. "We just found this guy hiding in the bushes over there. Think maybe they're connected?"

Michael and Mari went over to the captive, who looked nearly as frightened as the dead man. "Please, let me go back!" he babbled. "I'll be good, I promise! Let me back in. I don't want to stay here. I don't like getting old."

"What's he talking about?" Mari asked.

"No telling," Milton said. "I don't smell booze on him. Actually, he smells pretty good for a guy wandering through the park and babbling."

"Sir, do you know that dead man over there?" Michael asked.

The man's eyes filled with tears. "He's my brother."

"I'm sorry for your loss. Did you see what happened to him?"

"They made us leave." His voice broke. "We were happy,

but they sent us away, and then we got old." His eyes went wild—wilder—with terror. "Are they still coming after us?"

"He may not be drunk, but I bet a tox screen comes up with something," Mari muttered.

"Should we take him in?" Milton asked.

"Yeah, at the very least he's a person of interest, and we probably need to get him some medical attention," Michael said. He had a funny feeling, though, that the tox screen would come up clean. There was something about this man that seemed familiar, an aura he could barely detect. When he slipped his hand into his pocket and clutched his keychain, the aura became stronger, almost a halo.

"Is something wrong, Rev?" Mari asked him.

"You mean other than the dead body?"

"The dead body is all in a day's work. You look troubled."

He rubbed his shoulder. "My old PTSD is acting up again."

"You should get that looked at. But while you have your flashback, or whatever, I'm gonna take a look around. Let me know if you need a hug or a slap."

"Will do," he replied, his voice already trailing off because of what he'd just noticed. The park around him was full of fae creatures, but he was getting used to seeing that. What caught his eye was another man sitting with his back against a tree. Milton and his buddies had walked right past him without noting a potential witness. Michael squeezed his keychain again and the closer contact with the laminated four-leaf clover in the middle of it showed him the reason why. It was a fairy not even bothering with a human glamour. In fact, he looked like he was barely able to conceal himself from humans. Not that most humans would have recognized him as a fairy if they'd seen him.

Real fairies weren't the cute winged creatures of little girls' Halloween costumes. They looked more or less human—both more and less. They were too beautiful, too ephemeral, and too odd to be truly human, with the kind of coloring that didn't occur in nature. And that was just what Michael could see. He had a feeling that even with his enhanced senses, he couldn't see down to the heart of what they truly looked like.

Pretending he was looking for clues on the ground, Michael made his way over to the fairy and crouched beside him. "So, what's your story?" he asked. "I take it you have something to do with those two." He gestured with his head toward the body and the man who was being put in the back of a squad car.

The fairy blinked in surprise. "You see me?"

"Four-leaf clover. And I've spent a little time in the Realm. I'm friends with the queen."

That got a reaction. "I've done nothing wrong!" the fairy insisted frantically. "I don't deserve exile. You must tell her majesty."

"Exile? The queen cast you out, and those men?" That didn't sound like something Sophie Drake, the current queen of the fairy realm, would have ordered, Michael thought. She hadn't shown any signs of forcing anyone out. In fact, Michael was getting a little frustrated with her about that. On the other hand, the fairy looked terrified, which was common in people who'd dealt with Sophie.

"Her men did, under her name. The humans had to go, as did others who refused to swear fealty." He jerked, startled and whipped his head around like he was looking for pursuers. "They're still after me," he said in an anguished whisper as he clutched at Michael's arm. "And I am so weak in daylight."

Michael would have said the fairy was paranoid, but he sensed something malevolent. It wasn't visible to the naked eye, so none of the nearby police had noticed, but Michael felt it, and he wasn't armed against the fae. He hadn't thought it necessary in daylight. Glancing around to make sure no one was watching him, he reached into his coat pocket and brought out the half-eaten sandwich from his interrupted lunch. "Please accept this offering," he said, holding the sandwich out to the fairy.

The fairy accepted it greedily, without thanks, unwrapped it, and gobbled it up. Then he suddenly stood and whirled, emanating a flash of something that looked like an almost-visible sound wave. The sense of threat dissipated, and the fairy ran away without a word to Michael.

Michael took a moment to catch his breath and had just risen to his feet when Mari approached.

"Find something?" she asked.

Since she didn't mention the odd man Michael had just been talking to or the brief magical battle, he assumed she hadn't noticed any of it. "I thought I saw something on the ground, but it was nothing."

Her phone rang, and he took advantage of that opportunity to place a phone call of his own. Turning his back to his partner and walking a few yards away, he found the number in his directory. As usual, the call went into voice mail after three rings. "Sophie, it's Michael Murray. I have a question for you," he said after the tone. "And no, it's not about Jen, though that deadline *is* getting awfully close. I'm working on a case that may fall into your Realm. That's the one with the capital R. Call me, please."

He didn't hold out much hope, unless he'd piqued her curiosity enough to get her to stop dodging his calls. Maybe her sister would be able to reach her, he thought. Just then, his phone rang, with Emily Drake's name on the caller ID. He shook his head as he took the call. Those Drake girls really were uncanny.

"Hey, Emily, what's up?" he asked.

"I was wondering if you could look after Beau for me. I probably won't make it home between the matinee and the evening show, and I might go out tonight. I don't want to leave him there alone all that time."

"No problem. I'll stop by and get him when I get off work."

"Thanks, you're a lifesaver."

"It's funny, but I was just about to call you. Have you talked to Sophie lately?"

"We mostly exchange voice mails. But she hasn't forgotten you. She *is* working on it."

"I know." He'd found the baked goods left on his kitchen table several times a week, noticed the missing wedding photo with a note left in its place. He had evidence that Sophie was still around. He just never saw or spoke to her. "But that's not why I wanted to talk to her. I'm working on a case that falls into her area of expertise, and I wanted to pick her brain."

"Homicidal ballerina?"

"No, her other area of expertise."

"Huh. But I wouldn't be surprised if one of those bunheads went postal. They're pretty highly strung. If you can't reach Sophie, maybe you could talk to Amelia and Athena. They probably know as much as Sophie does in that area."

"Good idea. Thanks. And how are you doing? I hardly see you anymore, and you live right below me."

"Well, you know, being a superstar keeps me busy." He'd have bought that, considering that she was Broadway's latest sensation, but her tone was a little too bright. She sounded like someone working hard to fake a normal good mood and overshooting the mark by a mile. That worried him. He'd promised Sophie to keep an eye on Emily after her sojourn in the fairy realm, and he didn't think one could break a promise to Sophie Drake and escape lightly. He'd just recovered from one critical injury. He didn't want to sustain another.

"Okay then, but take care of yourself, and let me know if you need anything other than dogsitting. If you talk to Sophie, ask her to call me."

"Will do!" As he ended the call, he made a mental note to leave Sophie a message suggesting she check on her sister.

"You okay, Rev?" Mari asked, startling him out of his thoughts.

"Why wouldn't I be?"

"You look a little pale."

"And you sound like your mother."

"Ouch, that's mean. But seriously, are you okay? Do you need to sit down and take a break?"

"I'm fine. Back to one hundred percent, cleared by the doctors and all. You don't have to worry about me."

They started heading toward the car. "Oh, but now that I've seen you bleeding and gasping for breath, the light fading from your eyes, there's no going back. You'll always be helpless and vulnerable to me."

"Helpless, vulnerable, and armed," he warned. "You know, if you went through the same thing I did, it would be a real bonding experience for us as partners. I could arrange that if you keep this up."

"Yeah, but you'd try to counsel me and save my soul before you pulled the trigger," she said, opening the passenger door of their sedan for him.

"I did that *once*. And it worked," he shouted while leaning across to open the driver's side door as she came around the car.

"And that's why you'll always be the Right Reverend Saint Michael," she said, sliding into the driver's seat. He braced himself as she took off and joined the flow of traffic. She was a native New Yorker who navigated the city streets like a veteran cabbie, so he never bothered asking to drive.

"So, whattaya think about this case, Rev?" she asked, expertly steering around a stopped bus and ignoring the symphony of car horns that followed her maneuver. "Murder or natural causes?"

"I suspect this is going to turn out to be a case for the fashion police, not us." At least, that's what it would look like to normal people if it turned out to be what he thought it was.

"Still, you've gotta love finding a geezer in disco gear in Central Park. I wonder if any clubs are doing a seventies night tonight. I'm suddenly in the mood for that. Want to join me?"

"No thanks. Not really my scene."

"You know, it wouldn't hurt you to get out. You're only an old married man on paper."

"It wasn't my scene when I was single. And I do have plans. I won't be sitting at home alone."

"Yeah, I bet you've got a really rocking Bible study going on."

"Something like that." He couldn't help but smile at the thought of how she'd react if she knew what he did have planned.

TWO

Maybelle, Louisiana
12:20 p.m. (Central Time)

Sophie Drake was on her way down the stairs when her phone rang. She paused to look at it, saw Michael Murray's name on the display, winced, declined the call, and dropped the phone in her purse. "I'm working on it," she muttered as she continued downstairs.

The coast seemed to be clear. She stuck her head into her grandmother's room, saw that she was asleep, and nodded silently to the nurse before heading toward the kitchen. She had to suppress a groan when she saw her mother there, between her and the back door.

"And where are you off to?" her mother asked.

"I have some errands to run on the way to work." Before her mother could come up with any questions, Sophie kissed her on the cheek and made for the door. It was true, technically. She'd just neglected to mention where the errands were. She was far past the age when she should be expected to account for her comings and goings to her mother, but it was easier than the scene that would result if she refused to explain.

She threw her dance bag into the front seat of her car, drove a mile down the road, and pulled off onto a dirt trail into the forest.

She parked in a small clearing, took her bag, veiled the car with a glamour, and opened a gateway into the fairy realm—her Realm.

Sophie was still getting used to the idea that she was queen of the fairies, thanks to a distant ancestor who left the throne to become mortal. When the Realm needed a queen again, Sophie found herself on the throne, due to her blood and the knowledge passed down through generations. Until a couple of months ago, she'd been little more than a frustrated ballet teacher and a small-town society queen bee. Now she was the fairy queen and an enchantress on top of it. That was why she gave her mother excuses. This wasn't the sort of thing that was easy to explain.

Her gateway took her to the gardens of a palace—her palace, she supposed, since that was where her throne and crown were. But she didn't live there and had no desire to do so. In fact, once she'd fulfilled a promise, she doubted she'd come back, other than to make enough of an appearance to remind the fairies who she was.

Not that it was a bad palace. It was luxurious beyond imagination, as long as she didn't look too closely. The throne room doors opened for her and she entered the vast space. The ceiling soared above her, the tall, narrow windows cast light on the marble floors, and far ahead stood the silver throne she'd won with her blood.

She spared a passing glance for the servant scrubbing the floors. Maeve's golden beauty had dimmed somewhat, and Sophie would have felt at least a little bit bad for her if Maeve hadn't been the reason for all this trouble. Maeve didn't even look up from her work, but the other courtiers and servants all stopped at Sophie's approach and bowed. There seemed to be fewer of them than on her last visit. She wasn't sure how many of them were bound to the palace because of consuming enchanted food or drink there, since Maeve was the only one she'd seen drink, but it made sense that those who weren't bound would drift away once they realized the palace wasn't going to become the hub of power and social life in the Realm.

Most of the courtiers went back to what they were doing after she acknowledged them, but Sophie was gratified to see that one remained, smiling eagerly, like she was truly glad to see Sophie. She appeared to be a couple of years younger than Sophie and was much taller, but she still looked like she could be a distant relative. They had similar coloring, with reddish hair, fair skin, and blue eyes (half blue in Sophie's case). That was what had got Jennifer Murray into this situation, when she'd been mistaken for Sophie's sister and kidnapped to bait a trap for Sophie. "Your majesty, you've come back to us!" she said.

"Sophie," Sophie corrected automatically. "And, yes, I want to have another of our chats." She waved away the fairy man who hovered at the woman's side and hooked her arm firmly through her elbow to lead her out of the throne room and down a hallway to a modest bedchamber. "Now, Jennifer, let's have tea," she said, once they were inside with the door closed.

"Emma. My name is Emma," the woman corrected stubbornly.

"No, it's not, and you haven't even been using that name very long. Before you met my sister, you'd forgotten your name entirely. Your name is Jennifer, but people close to you called you Jen." Ignoring Jen's pout, Sophie took a thermos from her bag and poured cups of tea, then opened a small tin of cookies. "Here, drink your tea," she said, her tone turning the invitation into an order.

Sophie made sure Jen drank at least one full cup of tea and ate several cookies. She thought while observing the other woman that it seemed to be working. Jen looked more human, more substantial after consuming the human food. If only her mind were changing, as well. Sophie noticed Jen's gaze straying to the photo sitting on the table. It showed Jen in a bridal gown and veil next to a tall, dark-haired man in a police dress uniform. "Do you remember him now?" Sophie asked gently.

"I remember he was in the market, and he came to help take Emily home," Jen said, but Sophie was sure she was lying. Jen had a touch of fondness in her eyes when she looked at the photo.

"He's your husband. He misses you. Don't you remember marrying him?"

Jen's face softened further. "I—I don't know," she whispered, her voice distant. Almost as though she was channeling a spirit from the ether, she said dreamily, "It took him three tries to get the wedding ring on my finger, his hands were shaking so badly. I thought he'd drop it." The faintest trace of a smile crossed her lips. "He's so brave about things like murderers and criminals, but a wedding terrified him. His brothers teased him about being afraid of commitment, but I think he was scared because he takes commitment so very seriously."

That he does, Sophie thought to herself. It was a rare man who'd remain faithful and keep wearing a wedding band nearly seven years after his wife's disappearance. But she didn't dare speak out loud. She didn't want to break the spell. This was what she'd been working toward for the past two months. She'd never be able to get Jen out of the Realm if she didn't want to go, and Michael was the one thing that might make her want to leave.

"I wonder what he thinks of me," Jen asked, her voice cracking.

"He wants you back home with him," Sophie said. "I could take you to him." She held her breath, waiting for the response. Was this the moment of truth?

"I—I don't know," Jen stammered, looking away. "I don't think I can go."

"I could help," Sophie said gently, leaning forward and placing a hand on Jen's wrist. Jen seemed so close that it wouldn't take much to push her in the right direction, just a little mental nudge. It was so tempting. A few months ago, she wouldn't have thought twice about it—wouldn't even have realized she was doing it. She just took it for granted that people did what she wanted. Then she'd learned that her other notable ancestor had been the enchanter for whom the fairy queen left her throne, and that one of his legacies was the ability to bend things to her will. Now she felt acutely conscious of the effect she had on people.

No, it wouldn't be right, she decided. The only way this would work was if Jen decided of her own free will. How much free will she actually had while in the fairy realm was another question entirely, but Sophie was fairly certain that the magic that might allow her to return to the real world wouldn't work if she hadn't truly made the decision on her own. It might be worth looking into, just in case. She was running out of time and needed to cover all possible angles.

"You don't have to worry about that today," she said lightly, lifting her hand from Jen's and pulling away. "Think about it, though. Try to remember Michael. I could bring you more pictures." Unfortunately, that would mean talking to him in person. She didn't feel bad about taking something that was in plain view on a bookcase, but she drew the line at rummaging through his apartment when he wasn't there.

"No, this is enough," Jen said, her eyes straying to the wedding photo. "I remember this."

"You could remember more." The urgency in Sophie's voice surprised her and seemed to startle Jen, and Sophie forced herself to dial it down a notch. She was so close that it would be a shame to sabotage her own efforts by scaring the poor woman. She took a deep breath and let it out slowly before nudging the tin of cookies across the table. "I've got to go now, but you can keep these. Have one whenever you like, and if you want more, I can bring some." They were her very best recipe, and she'd never met anyone who could stop at just one. She hoped they'd be enough to tempt someone accustomed to fairy food. Maybe if Jen ate them regularly instead of just during Sophie's visits, it would help.

Jen looked up at her like she knew there was something she was supposed to say, but then her eyes clouded. "You're welcome," Sophie prodded, adding, "It's okay to thank me. I'm human, so I don't have issues with that." She gave a little laugh that she hoped didn't sound as fake as it felt. "In fact, I'm from the South, so I *expect* to be thanked. A written note wouldn't be entirely out of place. Now, I'll drop in on you tomorrow, if I can."

"Th–thank you," Jen whispered, choking out the unfamiliar words.

"You are so very welcome," Sophie said, fighting to dampen her enthusiasm. She felt like jumping in triumph. In fact, she did so as soon as she was well clear of the palace. For the first time, she started to allow herself to believe that she might actually pull this off. Then she immediately felt a pang of regret that she brutally brushed aside. She paused for a moment to collect herself before opening a gateway and stepping through.

She came out into a wooded area within Central Park in New York City and stopped to take her jacket out of her bag and put it on, since it was cooler here than back home or in the Realm. The biggest perk so far from being queen of the Realm was the ability to travel within the Realm to anywhere else in the world. That had done wonders for expanding the boundaries of her life. Once her cell phone had a chance to connect to the local network, she checked it and made sure she had just enough time to get to her professional-level ballet class.

Three

The bell over the door jingled as Sophie entered the little basement antique shop. "Why, this is a surprise!" Athena Abercrombie said when she saw Sophie. "Amelia! Sophie's here!" she called toward the back of the shop. In deference to the upcoming holiday, the tiny old woman wore a sweatshirt with a giant jack-o'-lantern appliquéd on the front. "It's funny, I was just talking about you with Detective Murray. He called us with some questions."

"Oh, lovely," Sophie said, her smile feeling tight.

"Come, now, he's a perfectly nice young man, and he knows you're doing all you can to get his wife back," Athena soothed.

Sophie hoped that the red flush she felt spreading across her face would be excused by the fact that she'd just been walking outdoors on a crisp fall day after taking a strenuous dance class, but no such luck. Amelia Abernathy, Athena's sister, joined them and picked up the conversation as though she'd been there all along. "You know, dear, it's *him* falling in love that would jeopardize our efforts to rescue Jennifer," she said. "You falling for him doesn't matter."

Arching an eyebrow, Sophie sat in one of the bentwood chairs by the table in the corner. "I'm enchantress and fae. If I want him to fall for me, he will. I may have a lot of self-control, but the fae aren't known for resisting temptation, and I'm still learning to use my enchantress powers. There's a risk that if I want something, I could will it to happen without even realizing what I'm doing." She shook her head. "No, it's safest if I just avoid him for now and not encourage any little crush I might have developed."

Athena's face softened, and she reached over to pat Sophie's knee. "So you *are* in love with him."

Feeling her face grow warmer, Sophie looked down and slipped off her shoes to flex and stretch her feet. "I wouldn't go that far. I hardly know him. Maybe it's just that I finally got away from my hometown and met a man who's not a dancer." She straightened, absently tucking one foot under her, and said with great resolve, "It doesn't matter, because nothing is going to happen and I'm going to get his wife back for him in the next couple of days, and besides, my position in our little trio rather precludes that kind of relationship for me for the time being."

She was currently serving as the "maiden" in the "maiden, mother, crone" trio of enchantresses, thanks to having had so little life of her own that she still counted as a maiden after the age of thirty. She'd barely noticed that aspect of life passing her by until a night spent holding a grief-stricken, semiconscious Michael Murray had awakened her long-dormant libido and left her with a raging and very inconvenient schoolgirl crush. She hadn't yet written "MM+SD=true love 4ever" on the cover of her notebook, but otherwise she was belatedly living her teenage years suddenly and all at once. Next thing she knew, she'd be screaming her head off at boy band concerts.

"I'm sure you've got it all under control," Amelia said in a way that made Sophie feel like she was being humored. "You're close to getting Jennifer out, aren't you?"

Sophie sighed as she gratefully took the cup of tea Athena handed her. "I think so. She seems so very, very close. Today, she even remembered her wedding to Michael." She tried to will away a pleasant little frisson at the mental image of Michael's hands shaking too badly to properly put the ring on Jen's finger. It was so *adorable*. "I was wondering, would there be any benefit to giving her a tiny nudge? I know it wouldn't work to put her under a compulsion and force her out, but she seems to already be heading in that direction. It wouldn't take much pushing at all, and we're running out of time."

The sisters exchanged one of their glances that made Sophie wonder if they could communicate telepathically. "It's never come up," Athena said at last. "But then, I haven't found any stories about enchantresses or other fairies freeing a fairy captive. Religion seems to work in some stories. Do you know if she's religious?"

"Michael is, and he's a minister's son, so I'd imagine she's at least not hostile to religion. Thanks, I should have remembered that. The Lord's Prayer comes up in a few of the stories, but I've never been sure if they're inspired by true events or are meant as morality tales—knowing your prayers could save your life, so learn your prayers, and all that. It's worth a shot the next time I see her." She pulled her foot out from under her and felt around on the ground for her shoes, preparing to leave, but Amelia cleared her throat.

"There's something else you need to know," Amelia said, her face and voice grim enough that Sophie automatically tensed. "There may be an impostor queen. If you had a message from Detective Murray that you've ignored, that's what it's about. He called us about a case that turned out to be someone who'd been forced out of the Realm after decades in captivity."

"Ouch," Sophie said, wincing.

"Exactly," Amelia said. "There was a fairy nearby who claimed they were cast out of the Realm by the queen. Detective Murray was sure that wasn't you."

Sophie tried not to sigh wistfully and grin like an idiot when she said, "Well, at least he gives me the benefit of the doubt." Then she did sigh, but wearily. "And that's one more item for my to-do list, but I'll deal with it next week."

The sisters exchanged a glance. "There's more," Athena said

with a wince. "Detective Murray is worried about Emily. He thinks she's acting strange, like she's trying too hard to sound normal."

Sophie nodded. "Lately, she's been avoiding me as badly as I've been avoiding Michael. Something must be up. I'll check on her." She glanced at her watch. If she got another teacher to cover her first class, she could meet Emily after the matinee and still get back in time for the rest of her schedule.

As she left the shop, Sophie reflected on the irony of trying to reunite the man she loved with his wife and fighting to keep a throne she'd never wanted. When would she ever get to fight for something she wanted for herself?

Four

Emily Drake reveled in the applause as she took one last curtain call. She'd always lived to perform, but never more so than in the last couple of months. Only when she was onstage did she truly feel alive. But the applause eventually died, and the last members of the audience trickled out of the theater. Still, she hated to leave the stage. She stood there for a long moment after the curtain fell for the last time, until her friend Olivia gave her a nudge.

"Getting a bit greedy with the curtain calls, are we?" Olivia teased. "You'd better hurry and change before the crowd at the stage door gets ugly."

"Ugly?" Emily asked as she allowed Olivia to steer her toward the wings.

"They're waiting impatiently for you to make an appearance. You've got them eating out of your hand. You're on fire. Say, you aren't taking secret music lessons from some scarred guy who lives in the basement, are you?"

Emily twitched. "Why? What makes you think that?"

Olivia paused, frowning, and stared at Emily for a long time. "Are you okay?"

"What makes you think I'm not?"

"You're a theater geek and a *Phantom of the Opera* joke just flew right over your head."

Emily shook her head. "Oh, sorry, now I get it. It's funny, really." She held still while the sound tech removed her body mike. "I'm just off in la-la land, I'm afraid."

"You've been spending a lot of time there lately."

"Well, it's not like I have time to take a real vacation. Not that I'm complaining about eight shows a week. It beats not working."

One nice thing about being a star was not having to share a dressing room with the rest of the girls in the chorus, so she was able to ditch Olivia and get some peace while she removed her stage makeup, took down her hair, and changed into her street clothes,. She put on enough ordinary makeup to make herself look vibrant instead of drained and pulled her red curls back in a scarf before putting on her jacket, throwing her bag over her shoulder, and heading to the cast exit.

She paused for a moment before opening the door, bracing herself for the crowd that would be waiting outside. The surge of applause that hit the moment she opened the door gave her a lift, so she was able to smile and wave enthusiastically, even though she felt like she was watching an old movie on faded film stock. It wasn't quite black-and-white, but the colors had washed out to the barest tint.

There was one person in the crowd who stood out in sharp contrast, like fully restored Technicolor. Her strawberry blond hair seemed to burn, and her odd eyes, one blue and one gray, were bright enough for their color to be visible even at this distance. The blue eye was a vivid blue, and although Emily wouldn't have thought gray could be bright, the gray eye had a silver gleam. Emily didn't understand why the crowd was so focused on her when Sophie was standing right there, so radiant that it was impossible to look away from her.

Emily signed a few *Playbill*s as she worked her way through the crowd to her sister, who shone like a beacon against her drab surroundings. "Hey, this is a surprise," Emily said, hugging Sophie and making a concerted effort to look as normal as possible. If Sophie thought she had reason to worry, there was no telling what she might do, and she usually went for the nuclear option at first strike.

"I was in town to take a class, and I got Deb to cover my first class in Maybelle, so I thought I'd stop by before I headed back. Do you want to grab a bite? I'm starving."

"I don't have a lot of time between shows, but I'll join you for coffee." Emily draped her arm across her much-shorter older sister's shoulders as they headed for the nearby diner Emily and her cast mates frequented. "You know, one nice thing to come out of all the fairy stuff is you being able to just stop by like this. I've missed hanging out with my little big sister."

She knew Sophie was worried about something when that description didn't get the usual reaction out of her. But what was she worried about? Had Michael said something? No, he'd said Sophie wasn't taking his calls. Maybe it had nothing to do with her. She decided to pretend that was the case so she wouldn't look like she was hiding anything.

Once they were in the diner and seated, Emily ordered coffee and Sophie ordered a soup, salad, and sandwich combo with a cup of tea. "I thought ballerinas didn't eat," Emily joked.

"When you take a class, walk all over the city, and open a couple of portals between worlds, you work up an appetite," Sophie said dryly. "And I still have to teach a couple of classes tonight."

"I don't know how you do it. Just doing a show every night and taking a couple of classes a week is about all I can manage, and I'm not even putting up with Mama and looking after Nana. How is she, by the way?"

"Mama or Nana?"

"Either. Both, I guess."

"Both are pretty much the same." Sophie sighed and rubbed her temples, and for a moment she looked like an overwhelmed young woman with way too much on her plate instead of like an almost invincible fairy queen. "I hate to put Nana in a home, but she's reaching the point where she needs more care than we can give her. And then a part of me wants to do it because it means I can get out of there, and I hate myself for that."

Emily reached across the table and patted her sister's hand, then squeezed it, unwilling to let go when it was the strongest physical sensation she'd felt in at least a week. Lately, her senses had been so dulled that it was like living inside a cotton ball, and being around Sophie was like having the cotton stripped away. "You've done so much, more than anyone else. Look at me, I left the state. I bet Mama's driving you crazy."

"She's treating me like a teenager, even though I'm the one more or less running the household. She seems to know something's different, even if she doesn't realize I'm ruling the fairy realm."

The waitress brought the tea and coffee. Emily dumped two packets of sugar into her coffee, took a sip, and added two more packets plus a package of artificial sweetener. Finally, she could almost taste the sweetness. She looked at Sophie over the rim of her mug and realized that Sophie had noticed. Of course she had. She noticed everything. It would have been easier if Sophie had remarked on it because then Emily could have responded and made some excuse, but since Sophie said nothing, responding would only make matters worse.

"I talked to Michael today," Emily said, picking a topic sure to put her sister on the defensive. "He said he's been trying to reach you."

Sophie focused on swirling the tea bag around in her mug. "I know. He called Amelia and Athena, and they told me." It was hard to tell, because from Emily's perspective Sophie was already glowing, but she seemed to glow brighter. "There are some things I'll need to look into for a case he's working on." Yep, she was definitely glowing brighter. Emily thought she knew why Sophie was dodging Michael. *Well, whattaya know,* she thought, resisting a smile. Sophie was human, after all. Mostly.

Sophie wasn't the type to remain on the defensive for long, and she struck back quickly. "How are *you* doing?" she asked.

"I'm great!" Emily said, then realized she'd probably said it a bit too brightly. "Why do you ask?"

"Because I'm your sister and I haven't seen you in a couple of weeks. It's not that odd a question. Then there's that ordeal you went through a couple of months ago that was partially my fault."

"How was that your fault?"

"I should have seen it sooner."

"Oh, get off the cross. We need the wood."

In spite of herself, Sophie smiled. But she got serious again very quickly. "I did notice that you moistened the sugar in your cup with a little coffee. I thought I was the one with a sweet tooth. Are flavors seeming dull to you? That's a common effect of time in the Realm, but I would have thought you'd be better by now."

Emily tried to come up with an explanation, but everything sounded lame even before she said it. "It's nothing," she said with a shrug. It was actually driving her crazy, but at the same time she was performing at a level she never could have imagined before her visit to the Realm, so it was a trade she was willing to make. She didn't even want to contemplate what might happen if Sophie insisted on fixing her and ruined everything.

Sophie's meal arrived, and that paused the interrogation. Emily launched into a diversionary campaign, telling Sophie anything she could think of about backstage shenanigans, that afternoon's performance, Beau's quirks, and Michael's recovery. She noticed her sister glowing a little more brightly when that topic came up. "You might not even recognize him," Emily said, enjoying Sophie's discomfiture. "No sling, and he's even put some healthy weight back on so his face doesn't look so hollow anymore."

"That's good to hear," Sophie said primly, but the intensifying glow surrounding her gave her away.

Emily took mercy on her sister and changed the subject. "How are you holding up in real classes?"

"I thought I was still in pretty good shape, but the first few weeks were brutal. It's getting easier, though, and I've had a couple of people talk to me about auditioning for companies. There's even a choreographer who wants me for a showcase he's doing."

"That's awesome! You should do that."

"I'm not sure I could take a job here without looking too suspicious. Surely Mama would notice if I quit my job and was still gone every night."

"You have got to get out of that house, Soph. Seriously."

Sophie set out cash for the bill and gathered her belongings. "I can't quite yet, but there are times I consider staying in the palace overnight. What do you think Mama would say if I told her I had a boyfriend in Shreveport and was spending the night with him?"

"What's she gonna do, kick you out so she's stuck taking care of Nana by herself?"

"It *is* tempting to test her."

They walked together out to the street. "I'd better get back to the theater," Emily said. "It was great seeing you."

Much to her surprise, Sophie stood on tiptoes to hug her. Sophie wasn't usually much of a hugger. "Be good," she said, releasing Emily somewhat reluctantly and waving as Emily walked away. Emily felt a great sense of relief when she rounded the corner and her sister couldn't study her any longer. She had no idea how well she'd pulled that off. Was she safe a little longer, or would Sophie be on her case?

Five

The Theater District
6:15 p.m.

Sophie normally preferred to walk such a short distance, but she didn't have a lot of time, so she raised her hand and added a tiny extra dose of intention. A second later, a cab stopped for her. She got out at the park entrance on Columbus Circle. The instant her feet hit grass in a place that wasn't surrounded by people, she created a gateway and stepped through, coming out in front of what looked like a small forest hut. She pounded urgently on the front door.

A moment later, a tall, silver-haired fairy opened it. "Your majesty," he said.

"Sophie," she corrected, resisting the urge to roll her eyes. She might be in the throes of a crush and had her mother questioning her comings and goings, but she didn't have to act like a teenager. "May I come in, Eamon?"

He stepped back. "It's your Realm. You don't need to ask."

"I'm being polite." She followed him into a library that couldn't possibly have fit into the small hut. He gestured her toward an overstuffed chair in front of a blazing fire. She didn't wait for him to sit before she asked, "Have you seen Emily lately?"

He sat and leaned back in his chair like he was relaxing, but he gripped the chair's arms. "I have seen her," he confirmed, "but I do not know if it has been lately."

She held back an exasperated sigh. Fairies and their inability to perceive time were enough to drive someone who lived by a rigid schedule mad. "How does she seem to you?"

"I've never been around a human returned from the Realm, so I do not know how to judge."

"Does she seem better, worse, strange?"

He narrowed silvery eyes in thought. "I thought she was getting better. That is why I have seen her less often. Our plan was for me to help wean her from all things fae, including myself."

"Yes, that was the plan," Sophie said. "But I don't know if it worked. She may be worse now than right after she got back. It seems to me that she's craving sensation, that our world is losing color and flavor to her. I think she's under a kind of thrall. There's a trace of magic on Emily, and I think it's holding her to the Realm."

"Maeve must have put chains on her to keep her bound," Eamon said. Sophie was a little alarmed at how worried he looked, as though he truly cared. She still hadn't reconciled herself to the idea that her sister had formed a friendship with a fairy—never mind that she and her sister had some fairy blood, themselves.

"I think she might even be aware of it, but she doesn't seem to want to do anything about it." She leaned back in the chair. "And I don't know what to do. But I'm afraid she might do something stupid or crazy in order to feel something." She hated to make this next request, but she didn't feel like she had any choice. A fairy might be the only person other than herself who could handle this situation. "Do you think you could keep an eye on her?"

"I can do so at night."

"That's when I'm most worried. But in case you need the extra strength…" She took the remaining bundle of cookies out of her bag. "Please accept this offering."

His eyes lit up. Eamon was awfully fond of humanity, as could be seen in his huge library of human literature and his old-professor wardrobe. He was as much of an oddball among fairies as he was among humans. He'd developed a particular taste for human food, which gave fairies power to function in the real world when offered as a gift, but which was poisonous otherwise. "I will do what I can for her, your majesty," he said fervently, taking the cookies from her.

"She'll be at the theater tonight."

"I will go to her there."

She stood and picked up her bag. "Then I'll leave it in your capable hands." It went against her Southern-bred manners not to say "thank you," but that was taboo among fairies. Eamon was enough of a human-phile for him not to mind, but she didn't think it was a good habit to start in the Realm, even if she was the queen.

That reminded her... "Have you heard anything about a queen forcing captive humans out of the Realm?"

"You wouldn't do such a thing."

"I know *I'm* not doing it, but apparently someone is."

"I'm afraid I'm out of the loop—that is the right way to say it, isn't it?"

"Yes, it is." Eamon's grasp of human slang wasn't always so accurate or timely. He was as likely to use hot expressions from the twenties as today. To him, it was like last year's buzzwords.

"I have been avoiding the courts."

"Oh well, thought I'd give it a shot. I'll check in on you later. And try not to let Emily know I sent you. I don't want her to think I'm suspicious."

Though she was pretty sure Emily knew she realized something was wrong. The thing that bothered her was that Emily wasn't asking for help. What could be worse than being so chained to a magical world that you couldn't live properly in the real one?

Once she was outside Eamon's hut, she decided to make one more stop before leaving the Realm. While she was here, time didn't have to count in the outside world, so she might as well make the most of it. Forming the mental image of a clearing in the woods, she stepped out and found herself in a space that looked like a ruined temple, with fallen or falling pedestals surrounding a marble floor.

The wind blowing through pine branches had a musical quality that sounded perfectly natural until one listened for a while and discerned melody and rhythm.

She knew Tallulah would expect her to dance before they spoke, and she might not even appear until Sophie had paid the price for an audience, so since she was already dressed for class, she removed her cover-up and put on her slippers. She paused to listen to the music of the trees before she picked up the subtle beat and began dancing.

It came as a surprise when she heard the sound of applause. She came out of a turn to see a tall, flame-haired fairy with a gauzy dress floating around her. "You wanted to speak to me?" Tallulah said.

"Yes. Do you know anything about putting humans under a thrall to tie them to the Realm?"

"I know about it."

"Do you know who's done it to my sister?"

"She is not my affair."

"Do you know how to break such a thrall?"

"Why would I? It is something that affects humans, not fae."

Trying not to show her growing frustration, Sophie asked, "Then who would?"

"You need to ask those in your world."

"The enchantresses?"

Tallulah made a dismissive gesture. "This is not enchantress magic. You need a fairy doctor or a wise woman—a human touched by the fae, with fae knowledge."

Sophie shook her head in confusion. She'd thought those were just folklore, ways to explain people who knew a thing or two about herbs. "They exist? Here and now?"

"I do not know. I do not frequent your world. You would find them on the boundaries between worlds, in places where they intersect."

"Like the markets?"

"Yes, the markets would be a good place to look for them."

"You wouldn't happen to know when or where the next market will be?"

Tallulah gestured, and a small, wild-looking fairy appeared from among the trees. "The next market?" she asked. He ran back into the trees. "My people seldom venture out, so he will have to ask around."

Sophie started to ask how long that would take, then remembered that any answer would be meaningless. This was why she could never live in the Realm. She'd go mad surrounded by people who didn't understand time.

"I'm surprised your ancestor's knowledge hasn't given you the answers you seek," Tallulah said.

Had it? Sophie hadn't thought of accessing the former fairy queen's knowledge that had come with the crown. It wasn't like searching a database, though. If she needed the answer to something, it usually just came to her. "Nothing has come up," she said. "Either she was like you and it wasn't something that concerned her, or it must have come up after her time. I understand how the Realm works, but I don't know about this sort of thing." She tried a little mental digging around and came across all kinds of information that applied to human abductions, such as how to make a changeling to leave in place of a captive. If she ever needed to kidnap someone, she was ready, but she still didn't know how to free anyone.

The little fairy returned. "The market will be tomorrow night, at the angel fountain," he said, slightly out of breath.

That would be cutting it close, Sophie thought. She assumed that "angel fountain" meant Bethesda Terrace. Now she had to hope wise women still existed and that one would be there and have the information she needed.

She thought of one more thing to ask Tallulah. "Do you know of anyone claiming to be queen, who is casting out human captives?"

The expression on Tallulah's face told her that the mere question was offensive. "I do not insert myself into affairs."

"You practically blackmailed me into taking the throne," Sophie reminded her.

"That was setting things right and restoring the Realm. Since then, I have stayed away from the other factions." She whirled around, sending her layers of gauze flying, and returned to the trees.

Sophie couldn't decide if the lady was protesting too much or if she truly was insulted.

At any rate, it didn't look like she'd get anything else out of the now-departed fairy, so Sophie changed shoes and put on her cover-up, then opened a gateway for home, latching on to the anchor she'd set to return her to the place and time she'd left. She stepped out of the gateway near where she'd parked her car. She paused to synchronize her watch with the car's dashboard clock before driving to the ballet studio.

As she drove through the small town, she had the same feeling of a great weight upon her that she felt every time she returned from the Realm or from any other place she reached through the Realm. Each time, it became harder to return, but she had responsibilities here that she couldn't just abandon.

Still, after taking a class with professionals and dancing for the fairies, it was a real letdown to return home and lead a roomful of little kids in basic exercises.

Six

Central Park
9:00 p.m.

It was thoroughly dark, the lampposts spilling pools of light onto the path with utter darkness between them, but there were still walkers and joggers out. That made the odds of running into a fairy slimmer. On the other hand, Michael and Beau didn't stand out from the crowd. Nobody seemed to find it strange that a man was walking a dog in the park, even at night.

They'd have found it a lot stranger if they'd known what he was doing. He hardly spared a glance for the ordinary people, but he paused in those gaps between pools of light and tried to unfocus his eyes enough to see what was hidden.

So far, the fairy activity appeared to be minimal, just a few of the tiny things that lived in the bushes. There were no signs of a major gathering that implied a market or revel that night, but it was early still. If there were a market, the bubble of space between this world and the Realm wouldn't form until midnight, so the fairy folk who existed in this sphere wouldn't be trooping toward the market until much later. He didn't want to risk missing anything, so he wasn't yet ready to give up for the evening.

If he were totally honest with himself, he'd have to admit that he had no idea what he thought he was doing. He knew where Jen was and what was happening to her, and Sophie and the two enchantresses were working to find a way to get her safely out of the Realm, in spite of her long captivity and the fact that she'd consumed fairy food and drink, which often prevented a return to the real world. It was unlikely that he, a relative novice to all this, would stumble upon the solution by himself while searching for fairies in the park.

But he had to do *something*. He wasn't sleeping much, anyway, and he might as well be out searching for news of his wife instead of tossing and turning. At least when he came back after one of his long nightly walks, he was tired enough physically to get a few hours of good sleep. If he stayed home, he barely closed his eyes and had nightmares when he did so. There was always a chance that he'd find some critical piece of information, and he wasn't sure he'd be able to live with himself if they failed and he knew he hadn't done absolutely everything he could.

Tonight, though, he had another purpose. He was working a case of his own. It was a chance for him to repay Sophie for everything she was doing for him. She wouldn't be able to investigate this herself, since it was unlikely that anyone would say anything about a fake fairy queen to the real one.

They'd just reached a dark patch between lampposts when Beau growled—a serious growl, not his usual mildly irritated at being awakened from a nap growl. "What is it, buddy?" Michael asked softly, then felt like an idiot. The dog wasn't likely to supply specifics. His own senses on high alert, he detected a menacing vibe, like he'd felt in the park that morning.

A terrified scream rang out nearby and before he knew what he was doing, he was rushing in the direction of the scream, his cop instincts to run toward trouble kicking in. Only after he'd run several steps did he notice that he didn't feel any tug on Beau's leash. The dog was running with him, which put his senses on even higher alert. The enchantresses had told him that animals had keen instincts when it came to the fae, and Beau's experiences in the Realm made his instincts keener than most.

Another cry rang out, and this time it sounded like a name. A woman's voice, shrill with desperation, cried, "Daithi! Daithi!" There was no answering call, and then there came another wordless cry of terror.

A figure came hurtling out of the darkness toward Michael, and his hand went instinctively to the weapon on his hip before he saw that it was a woman fleeing as though she was in fear for her life. She saw him just before she reached him and pulled up short with a gasp of fright.

"It's okay, I'm a police officer," he said, holding his hands up reassuringly.

She looked behind her, like she was afraid something was chasing her, then she turned to Michael and said, "Where's Daithi?"

"I don't know. I haven't seen anyone else," Michael said, trying to keep his voice calm and soothing. In the dim light, he couldn't see her well, but he got the impression she was in her late thirties—too old for the prom dress she wore.

Both of them gasped at a noise coming from behind her. He reached to grab her and pull her behind him as he stepped forward. Beau barked a warning. Michael wasn't sure whether to go for his weapon or for the iron nails in his pocket. "NYPD. Stop right there!" he shouted in his best cop voice as he grabbed a handful of iron. He figured that anything that still came at him after that warning probably wasn't from this world. Most common criminals would have run the other way, taking the chance to escape.

The noise came closer, and he prepared to hurl the iron that would repel any fae, but the woman chose that moment to collapse against him, sagging on his left arm. He struggled to hold her upright while the sense of approaching menace grew ever stronger.

He smelled smoke and turned to see a burning torch waving nearby. The flames cast his surroundings into sharper darkness, so he couldn't see who wielded the torch. He didn't think it was whatever was threatening them, though. That was confirmed when a voice near the torch said, "Oh, be gone with you. This isn't your place." Almost instantly, the sense of menace retreated. The torch went out, leaving him momentarily blinded while his eyes readjusted to the darkness.

He was fumbling for the little LED flashlight in his jacket pocket when the voice he'd just heard said, "You let that woman go, young man."

"If I let her go, she'll fall down," he said, looking around for the source of the voice. "I'm not hurting her. I'm a police officer. I'd show you my badge, but I've kind of got my hands full. I was just about to call an ambulance."

"A hospital won't be able to help her," the voice said, drawing closer. Now he could see that it belonged to an older woman, sturdy and stout, pushing a battered shopping cart piled with belongings. A still-smoking bundle of branches was propped in the child seat at the front of the cart. A couple of months ago, he might have thought she was just another bag lady, but there was something about her. He suspected that if he grabbed his clover keychain, he'd see what the difference was.

"I know," he said, adjusting the woman in his grasp into a more comfortable position. "But if I can find out who she is I might be able to find her family, and that might help."

"It might," the bag lady conceded as she came close enough to examine the unconscious woman. She placed a gnarled hand on the woman's forehead, frowned, and said, "But first we'd better revive her. Do you have any human food or drink on you?" She asked the question matter-of-factly, as if she didn't expect him to find it at all odd.

"I have a candy bar."

"That'll help, but first we need to get some liquid into her. I've got some juice." Returning to her cart, she pulled out a blanket and spread it on the ground, then gestured to Michael to bring the woman over. Michael scooped the limp woman up into his arms, her knees draped over one arm and the other arm under her shoulders. He felt a slight twinge in his right shoulder and realized that although he was mostly back to normal, the muscles that had spent weeks resting while his arm was in a sling weren't quite up to carrying women around. Fortunately, it was only a few steps. The bag lady helped him lower the woman to the ground.

Beau waddled over to settle himself on the blanket next to the woman as the bag lady retrieved a bottle from her cart. She knelt beside the woman, gently lifted her head, and spilled a few drops of juice between her lips. A moment later, the woman blinked, moaned, and stirred, and the bag lady gave her more juice. When she was able to sit up on her own, the bag lady gestured impatiently at Michael, and Michael handed her the candy bar. He had to bite his lip to force back a smile when he realized who the bag lady reminded him of: She was essentially Sophie Drake forty years later. She had that same air of taking total control of a situation and acting like she expected everyone to know what was going on.

When the woman had swallowed half the candy bar, she blinked, returning to her senses. "Where's Daithi?" she asked plaintively.

"Who's Daithi?" Michael asked.

"He was my friend. He stood up for me when they came for me. I thought they sent him out with me."

"Who's they?" Michael tried to keep his voice gentle, but he couldn't help feeling some urgency.

"We can talk about that later," the bag lady said as she placed her hand on the woman's forehead. Her eyes fluttered closed, and the bag lady lowered her back to the blanket. "Some rest should do her good," she declared. "I doubt we'll get much sense out of her until she's had a chance to get acclimated." Turning to Michael, she said, "I'm Mrs. Smith. Don't ask if that's an alias because I won't tell you. I didn't know we had one of us on the police force."

"One of us?"

"Touched by them."

"I'm not really—"

"Yes, you are," she interrupted. "I can see it. And you *can* see, can't you? You know what's happening?"

"I've had some dealings with the Realm," he admitted. "But mostly I can see because I've got a four-leaf clover. And I've been elf shot."

She raised an eyebrow. "Elf shot, and you're still walking? You're *definitely* one of us."

"I was with people who knew what to do. But apparently it has lasting effects."

She laughed in a way that was almost a cackle. "That it does, Officer…" Her voice trailed off in a question.

He realized he'd never introduced himself. "Oh, sorry. Detective Michael Murray."

"And what brought you into dealings with the Realm, Detective Murray?"

"It's a long story. And you, do you do this sort of thing a lot?"

"It's my job. They picked me for it. In the old days, they'd have called me a wise woman." She cackled again.

"She's been cast out of the Realm, hasn't she?" he asked.

"Looks like it. If she'd been rescued, it might have gone better, and she wouldn't have been alone. Sounds like her fairy friend was cast out, too. And I bet our friends back there, the ones I scared off with my burning rowan, were driving them out."

"Are you seeing more of these lately?"

"Why do you ask?"

"I had a case this morning of a pair of brothers who must have been there a long time. One didn't make it."

"Yeah, I suppose I have seen more returnees in the past month or so. It may have something to do with the new queen on the throne. She may have a new policy."

"It may be related to there being a new queen, but I'm pretty sure it's not her policy."

"How are you so sure about that?"

"I know her, and she's actually human. Mostly. She also knows that just kicking people out is a bad idea. She's willing to help get captives back home, but she's a lot more careful about it."

"Ah, you're the queen's champion," Mrs. Smith said with a nod.

"I don't know that I'd put it that way."

"Are you here tonight on her behalf?"

"No."

"Then why are you here? This is my territory, you know."

"I'm looking for someone. I have no interest in your territory. I'm no wise person or champion, or anything else. I'm working a case and looking for clues, and I'm trying to find someone. That's all."

"You just keep telling yourself that. You're neck deep, whether you know it or not."

Now Michael had another question for Sophie or the enchantresses. He hoped that this hadn't become some kind of lifelong responsibility. All he wanted was to get Jen back and then go back to pretending that all of this fairy stuff belonged in storybooks. But while he had Mrs. Smith here, he might as well see if he could learn something. "Does human food work to reintegrate them?"

"Fairy food traps them, so it makes sense, doesn't it? It helps ease the way."

"Should I call someone for her?" he asked, gesturing toward the sleeping woman.

She paused, thinking, for some time, then shook her head. "If you're right that the queen isn't behind this, then maybe we'd better wait and see if the queen is willing to take her back. That's probably best for her."

"But what about her family? They'll want her back. They'll at least want closure."

"As long as she's like this, they won't really have her back. Have you ever seen someone who's returned from the Realm?"

"Actually, I have. I've been there, myself."

"You knew better than to eat or drink, didn't you?"

"Yeah," he admitted.

"Then it's not the same. Someone who's gone native doesn't do so well back in the human world, not without a lot of help from the likes of me. It's not just a case of going home and going back to normal." She gave that cackling laugh again. "I'd bet you haven't gone back to normal after your trip, even without eating or drinking."

"I don't really have any urge to go back there, though. I'd be fine leaving it all behind me, and I will, just as soon as—" He cut himself off before he said too much.

He should have known she'd be too shrewd to miss it, though. "As soon as you find that person you're looking for?" She made a sound that was somewhere between a snort and a short, sharp bark. But when she spoke again, her voice was softer, gentler. "Who'd you lose?"

The cop in him thought better of telling her anything, since he didn't know for certain that he could trust her. But he needed to talk, and she seemed to know something about this. "My wife," he said. "She was taken seven years ago, almost to the day, in what turned out to be a case of mistaken identity."

"You know this for sure?"

"I've seen her in the Realm."

"You didn't bring her out then?"

"She didn't want to go." Realizing how that sounded, he hurried to add, "But she wasn't herself. She didn't remember who she was or who I was. We knew better than to just take her then. It's something that has to be handled delicately. I know she has to want to go, of her own accord, and my friend's working on that. I'm just worried that she'll be cast out before she's ready. And I'm also worried that she won't be ready before we run out of time."

"Your friend the fairy queen's helping you?"

He nodded.

She gave another snort. "Yeah, that's not gonna work."

"Well, if the queen of the Realm can't do it, then who?"

She laughed long and hard at this, rocking back and forth in mirth. "You!" she barked between laughs, reaching over to poke him in the chest with a gnarled finger. "I can't believe your queen doesn't know this. Then again, it's not like the fairy queen ever really wants to know anything about letting her captives go. I bet she knows all the things to do, all the rituals, but she's completely missed the key common element."

"And what would that be?"

Her grin exposed yellowed and missing teeth. "It's the oldest cliché in the book, but it's true, which is how it became a cliché. If only those hack writers knew they were getting it right." She paused for a brief cackle. "Love, of course. In the stories about people being rescued from the fairies, they do all kinds of things to free them, but it's not about *what* they do. It's about who's doing it and why. It's always the people who love them—who love them enough to go through all that nonsense. Jumping through the magical hoops is merely a way of proving your love."

"So if you get taken by fairies and no one loves you, you're out of luck?"

"It doesn't have to be romantic love. It can be the love of a parent for a child, a child for a parent, a brother, sister, friend—anyone who's willing to take on a seemingly impossible ordeal for you. And if you don't have anyone who loves you in any way, well, then maybe you're better off with the fairies, living it up and forgetting your old life."

Michael thought that explained how Sophie had been able to save Emily. She may have known all the right things to do, but it came down to the fact that she'd been willing to do anything to save her sister. Did that mean he'd failed in not even trying to save Jen? A flash of anger at Sophie flared up in his chest. She'd talked him out of trying. If it hadn't been for her, he might have had Jen home with him by now.

But no, he hadn't been up for an ordeal of any kind at the time, and he'd read enough to know that trying and failing could have doomed Jen forever. He was ready now, though. "What—" he began, but his voice failed him and it only came out as a rasp. He cleared his throat to get the lump out of it and tried again. "What do I need to do?"

"The ordeal usually presents itself when the opportunity arises, so the main thing you need to do is get to your wife. It's the right time of year for that, when the barriers between worlds are thinner than ever." It was actually even easier than that, he thought, assuming he could get Sophie to talk to him enough to know he needed her to get him into the Realm. "But there are a few things you could try to initiate your own ordeal and give yourself an advantage."

She paused for a long time, and he wondered if she was waiting for him to get out a notebook and take notes. "Such as?" he prodded.

"I'm thinking! This hasn't been as big a part of my job as it used to be in the old days. Someone goes missing today and they think serial killer or going off the grid, not stolen by fairies, so no one tries to get their loved ones out. Even a hundred years ago in some places, they'd have been coming to someone like me for help. You're my first."

She leaned over to check on the sleeping woman, got up and went to her cart, rummaged around, and came back with another blanket and an old notebook with a water-stained cardboard cover. She tucked the blanket around her patient, then sat cross-legged, pulled a small flashlight out of the pocket of her baggy sweater, and started reading the notebook. Michael forced himself to wait patiently and resisted the urge to pull his weapon and order her at gunpoint to tell him what he needed to do to save his wife.

He was starting to suspect she was delaying just to mess with him when she turned off her light, closed the notebook, and said, "Okay, here are a couple of things that usually seem to work." She held up one knobby finger. "One: Ransom her. Buy her freedom. But money or gold won't work. It has to be something more valuable than that."

"Diamonds?" he guessed.

"Nope. Valuable in terms of personal cost to you. But it still has to have value to them. What you give can be a simple memento. It gains value as you trade it for something that means something to the person you're trading it to, and so forth."

"Like that thing where someone started with a paper clip and traded until he ended up with a house?"

"Something like that, only the challenge will be to figure out what you have that's valuable to you that will be even more valuable to someone else."

"Whom do I pay? The fairy who took her lost power, and the queen is okay with letting her go."

"You'll figure that out when you get there. The point is that you're willing to pay. You may even be in a situation where you can offer something as a gift, then they're obligated to give you anything—

or anyone—you ask for in return." She held up two fingers. "Two: You prove yourself worthy of her. Usually, that has something to do with bravery, cunning, faith, even sacrifice. The trick there is that you can't create the situation. You just have to recognize it and take advantage of it when it arises by doing what you have to do. You got that?"

He nodded. He knew he was willing to do anything. He just hoped he'd be capable and that he'd get the opportunity.

She guffawed. "Oh, don't look so grim, Detective. The fun thing about dealing with the fairies is that it's perfectly okay to cheat, find loopholes, and use trickery. In fact, that's where the cunning comes in. If you find an easier way out, that means you've proved yourself smarter than they are." She grew solemn again and reached out to clasp his hand. "But there's always a final test, one of wisdom, which is different from cunning. You'll have to make a choice, and you'll have to make the right one. It's never the easy one." She held on to his hand a moment longer, and he could feel the rough calluses on her palm abrading his skin. Abruptly, she released him and got to her feet. "Help me get her into my cart."

While he was assessing whether he could lift the woman from the ground, an eerie howl nearby made his flesh crawl. He didn't think there were wolves in Central Park, and after the earlier incident with whatever Mrs. Smith had scared away he had a feeling that this was something much worse than wolves. That was confirmed when Mrs. Smith instantly tensed, then rushed to her cart, grabbed the torch, and relit it with a lighter pulled from her pocket. The sudden light blinded Michael, but he sensed the presence of a group of people circling them.

Once his eyes adjusted to the torchlight, he realized that the newcomers were fae. These fairies looked wild, savage even. They wore the wispy clothing seemingly fashioned from spiderwebs and leaves that many of the other fairies he'd seen favored, but they also wore jewelry that looked like it had been fashioned out of human bones. In his police career, Michael had come across a few cases with skeletal remains, and he recognized the finger bones strung together around the neck of one of the fairies. He didn't even want to think about where those bones had come from.

The dancers began chanting, their voices melding into a strange harmony that didn't fit into any musical scale he'd ever heard. He had to strain to make out the words. At first, he thought it was in some other language, but soon he was able to make out words in English—or did the magic that allowed him to see the fae also allow him to understand them?

"The night of the hunt draws near," they sang in a low monotone, "and we will ride again. You'll know what it is to fear, when the Wild Hunt rides again." Their song grew wilder and their dancing more frenzied as they continued. "Again, again, the Wild Hunt rides again. The earth will tremble and blood will flow when the Wild Hunt rides again."

They leapt and whirled like dervishes. Some of them took turns rushing toward the torch, daring each other to come closer and closer to the tongues of flame. Michael glanced toward Mrs. Smith, but whether he sought guidance or reassurance, he didn't know. She glowered at the dancers and held her torch steady, but she made no other moves. He thought he detected fear in her eyes, though.

The dancers noticed the unconscious woman and moved toward her. Michael instinctively stepped in front of her and said, "Leave her alone."

One of the fairies faced Michael. "Oh, one of them, are you? You don't scare me."

Michael went for his gun, but decided against it. Discharging his service weapon would mean paperwork. Instead, he slid his hand into his jacket pocket. Grateful that he was up-to-date on his tetanus shot, he maneuvered a few of the iron nails in his pocket between his fingers so their points would protrude when he made a fist, the way they taught women to carry their keys in self-defense classes. He took a step toward the fairy, easing his hand out of his pocket but keeping the nails hidden.

"Your kind isn't welcome," another fairy said. "You'll suffer most of all when the Hunt rides."

Michael wished he knew more about this Hunt because as it was, his response was limited to "will not." Instead, he smiled enigmatically and said, "Are you so sure about that? How do you know where you'll end up when you face the Hunt?"

The fairy took the bait and moved toward Michael, his fists raised. Michael struck first, driving an iron nail into the flesh of the fairy's upper arm. He was surprised by how easily it went in. He released the nail as the fairy howled in pain, then whipped around to lash at the fairy coming at him from the side. He scraped that one along the jaw and continued the swing to hit a third, driving that nail in.

The screams of pain made his hair stand on end. They were clearly inhuman and spoke to some primitive part of him that wanted nothing more than to run, but he stood his ground. The fairies' screams were soon not the only sounds. Beau barked and snarled, and Mrs. Smith lunged at the attackers with her torch.

Like most bullies, these fairies were quick to flee when their targets fought back and did damage. Soon, Michael, Mrs. Smith, Beau, and the unconscious woman were alone again. Mrs. Smith turned to Michael. "Well done. I see you know a thing or two. Do you always carry iron?"

"These days? Yeah."

"Keep it up. Now we'd better all get out of here in case those yahoos come back with friends. Get her into the cart for me."

Lifting the sleeping woman from the ground was more difficult than catching her after a faint had been. He'd finished physical therapy, but he still needed a little time in the gym. He got the woman settled onto the piles of blankets and pillows inside the cart in a way that didn't look too uncomfortable. Mrs. Smith blew out her torch with an impressive gust of breath, put it in the cart's child seat, then picked up the blanket from the ground and draped it over the woman. As she tucked in the corners, she said, "What hunt were you talking about?"

"They were chanting about some Wild Hunt that's apparently going to ride again and make us all afraid."

She looked up at him, her eyes wide. "You understood that?

You really have been touched. And good timing, too. If the Hunt's going to ride again, we'll need all the help we can get. Most everyone these days will have no idea what to do."

"*I* don't know what to do," Michael said.

"You know about iron, which is more than most. If the Hunt's free to ride, that means things might be getting ugly in the Realm. You'll need to get your wife back, pronto. There's a market tomorrow night at Bethesda Terrace. You'll find what you need there, maybe even a way into the Realm. Good luck. You'll need it." Before he could ask any questions, she trundled the cart away, walking like she didn't have the weight of an entire person in there.

"Okay, that was odd," Michael remarked to Beau, who snorted in what sounded like agreement. "I wonder if she's right." The hope welling in his heart was almost overwhelming. For the first time in seven years, he had an actual plan.

⌒Seven⌒

Every time Emily stepped on the stage, she feared she'd lose her mojo. Acting and singing were largely about feeling, so how could she do either properly when she was so numb? She wasn't sure she could go on living this way. Throughout the evening show, she found herself wishing she'd told Sophie everything and asked for her help.

And then she'd sing one of her numbers and be met with roars of applause. That reminded her she now had the power to hold an audience's hearts in her hand, to make them feel whatever she wanted them to feel. She could make them laugh or cry, and she could make them love it. Ever since her time in the Realm, the house had been packed for every performance. Some people were even addicted, lining up for standby tickets every night. It was like the kids who'd repeatedly flocked to *Rent* in its heyday, something no one would have expected for a musical based on a Jane Austen novel. No one realized that it wasn't the musical itself that had this effect, but rather its star.

Or maybe they did realize it. Emily's agent had a list of producers wanting Emily to star in their shows as soon as her current contract expired. There had already been two musicals written just for her. Never in her wildest dreams had she imagined such success. It had taken her seven years in New York before she'd had the stroke of luck that let her step into a title role as an understudy. Would she have had her current level of stardom if she hadn't been kidnapped by a fairy and been changed by the experience, or would she have only stayed in the role until they hired a bigger name or closed the show? She couldn't help but fear that if her current success had been about her, it would have come far sooner. Even the notoriety from her brief disappearance didn't explain all her fame.

When she thought about it that way, it was a no-brainer. Would she really give up such abilities just so she could taste and feel again? It wasn't as though she was selling her soul. She'd known the risks when she took a drink in the fairy realm. At least there was some upside from it.

As the big finale came to an end, she noticed something different in the theater. Normally, she couldn't see anything of the audience other than a dark blur beyond the stage lights, but one person near the back glowed. Had Sophie stayed for the show? The sellout wouldn't have stopped her if she'd wanted in. But no, that wasn't the same glow as Sophie's. Emily's pulse quickened at the thought of who it might be.

This time, she didn't linger after the curtain calls. She hurried to change into street clothes, then rushed to the stage door. Even in the throng of fans and flashing cameras, she spotted him, shining silver and unmistakably fae in spite of his old-professor human glamour.

She automatically signed autographs as she made her way through the crowd to Eamon. She barely held off throwing her arms around him. There were too many cameras in the vicinity. She settled for standing in front of him and saying, "It's been ages since I've seen you. I was afraid you were avoiding me."

"I thought it best that I taper off our acquaintance to allow you to readjust to this world." He paused, then added softly, "It doesn't seem to have worked."

"But why reappear now? Did you miss me? Oh, wait, let me guess, Sophie sent you."

He didn't confirm or deny it. "I thought you were getting better, but your senses are dulled, are they not?"

After glancing around, she said softly, "This really isn't the place to discuss it." She slid her arm through the crook of his elbow. "Come on, I need a drink."

She didn't know if it was his magic that got them away from the stage-door crowd or if it was the appearance of the actor who played Mr. Knightley, who was quite the hunk with a glorious voice (it was a pity about the offstage personality), but soon they were heading down the street, unmolested by fans.

Although she normally avoided that kind of place like the plague, she dragged Eamon to one of the touristy chain restaurant/bars on Times Square. It would be impossible to talk safely in a quieter place, but noise and crowds would mask any conversation. Besides, if she had enough stimulation, she might feel a little more alive.

She ordered two of the brightest, fruitiest-looking drinks on the multipage cocktail menu and solemnly presented one to Eamon as a formal offering. She didn't know what real-world alcohol would do to a fairy, but his kind sure knew how to drink in their own world.

"So, what does Sophie think's wrong with me?" she asked, after taking a sip of a laser-red drink and finding it disappointingly bland. Even the bite of the alcohol was subdued.

He choked after swallowing a sip of his own drink. She patted him on the back until he could breathe again. Blinking tears out of his eyes, he gasped a couple of times, then said, "She believes you are under some kind of bond or thrall." He put his glass down on the bar and grabbed her hand. She couldn't help but yelp out loud at his touch. It was so startlingly real. And cold. Nodding, he added, "And I concur."

He moved to withdraw his hand, but she clutched it desperately, unwilling to let go and lose the sensation. "This is something different from the effects of being in the Realm and drinking the Kool-Aid?"

"I am aware of no beverage served in the Realm called Kool-Aid."

Trying not to roll her eyes, she said, "You know what I mean. This is different from that?"

"I believe so. When did it begin?"

She downed the rest of her drink and signaled for another. "Well, let's see…I was kind of in a haze for the first few weeks after getting back. I was on fire onstage, but everything else was dim. Since I only felt alive when I was performing, I threw myself into it. That was when my career just exploded. They stopped talking about looking for a permanent lead, and I got all kinds of buzz. Then I started feeling better about the rest of my life. Not normal, but not in the same kind of fog. I seemed to have hit a plateau a few weeks ago, where I wasn't getting any better. At least, not that I noticed. Then last week I started going downhill, to where I am now. I'm not as foggy as I was when I first got back, but I am kind of numb. I think I'd be begging you to take me back to the Realm so I could feel something if I didn't have the show. That gives me a huge fix. So, Doc, what's the diagnosis?"

"Why haven't you said anything to your sister?"

Her new drink arrived, and she swallowed half of it before saying, "She has enough to worry about with the deadline for getting Jen back coming up. It'll be seven years in just a couple of days, and that's the cutoff." The swirling colors in his mercury eyes bored into her, and she added sheepishly, "And I was afraid. I was doing so well in my work that I didn't want to lose it. I didn't *want* to be normal again."

"Have you considered that your success may have been because it was the only time you felt truly alive, so you threw yourself into your performances?" He visibly braced himself, took a drink, then took her hand again and said earnestly, "You will never be entirely normal, Emily Drake." His voice was a little husky, but she wasn't sure if that was because of emotion or the effect of the alcohol.

Feeling a little flustered herself, she said, "You almost make that sound like a compliment."

"You have fae blood. Of course you're not normal."

"I've had fae blood my whole life, but my career didn't start working until all this happened to me."

"I thought it happened just before. That was how I found you, after all."

"So even if you'd never grabbed me, that would still have been my big break that made me a star?"

"Perhaps not to the same extent, since you would have had no reason to push yourself as hard as you have."

The bartender slid a fresh drink in front of her. It was just as tasteless as the last one, but at least she was starting to feel like she was *supposed* to be numb. "I guess that means that the key to acting success is to perform like it's your only reason for living." She raised her glass in a toast, drained it, and signaled for another.

"I do wonder where these bonds came from, as I am certain they were not there before," Eamon said, staring at her like he was analyzing her aura. "Perhaps it has something to do with that impostor queen."

Even as tipsy as she was, Emily snapped to attention. "What impostor queen?"

"There are people being cast out of the Realm, supposedly by the queen."

"Sophie would never do that."

"Exactly."

The bartender provided a new drink just in time. "Oh, great, I get to be a hostage again," Emily groaned before taking a big gulp.

"That is a possibility."

"You know, this is the last thing Sophie needs to worry about right now, since she's got to save Jen. I don't know that she really wants to, but she's being all martyr-like about it and just wanting Michael to be happy. Blech." She mimed gagging. "So don't tell her, okay?"

"She is the one who told me."

Emily signaled for the bill and handed her credit card to the bartender. "Then she's gonna have to learn to delegate. She needs a council, or an army, or something."

"She should know she has us at her disposal."

She paused in signing the credit card receipt to look up at him. He was growing fuzzy and wobbling in a strange way. It occurred to her that downing a number of strong drinks on an empty stomach after hours of performing might not have been the best idea.

"Why don't we go back to your place?" she asked, surprising herself.

"My place?"

"Your library. It's cozy there." She ran a finger along his jawline. "We could snuggle by the fire and think of how to help Sophie."

"I don't think so. We will go to your home."

"Works for me." She slid off the barstool and took a moment to get her legs under her before she dragged him out of the bar. She hailed a cab, and they settled into the backseat. He looked equal parts terrified and fascinated, and she realized this was probably his first ride in a car. She hoped there wasn't enough iron in the car to poison him.

When they left the cab in front of her building, she found herself wanting to run toward the park, where she knew there were entrances to the Realm. He took her hand, distracting her with his touch. That could work, too, she thought, then said, "Why don't you come inside?"

"I plan to."

Her pulse quickened and her breath grew short. "You could stay the night."

"That is my plan, as well. I don't want you going out again in this state."

Grinning to herself, she ran up the front steps. She had to release his hand to unlock first the front door, then her apartment door. Once they were inside, she threw herself at him, kissing him for all she was worth. He kissed back for a moment before pulling himself together and stepping out of her grasp. "I do not think that would be a good idea now, Emily."

She grabbed his hand and reveled in the coolness of his touch. "You thought it was a great idea the last time."

"The circumstances have changed."

Still gripping his hand, she tugged him toward the daybed. He was tall, but as insubstantial as his kind tended to be, so she was able to drag him with her. "Come on, I know you're different, but your people aren't good at resisting temptation." With one final yank, she pulled him onto the daybed with her.

For a moment, she thought he'd melt against her, but he resisted. His voice husky, he said, "Your sister would kill me."

"What business is it of hers?"

"She is my sovereign. You swore an oath to her, as well."

"I thought that was just for show."

"If it worked, then it wasn't just for show."

Annoyingly, tears welled up in her eyes. "I need this, please," she whispered.

He shifted so that he held her against his shoulder, like he might hold a child who'd awakened from a nightmare, and he stroked her hair gently. "It would be ungentlemanly of me because I believe you are el stinko."

In spite of herself, she burst out laughing. "I don't think I've heard that one in a very long time."

"It's wrong?"

"It's a bit archaic." With a sigh, she settled against him. "But yeah, I think maybe I am el stinko. Blotto. Wasted. Drunk off my ass. Three sheets to the wind."

"What do sheets and wind have to do with inebriation?"

"I have no idea. I'm too drunk for etymology. I should know better to drink like that without eating." She'd feel better in the Realm, she knew it, and if it hadn't been for his solid grip on her, she'd have gotten up and gone. His stroking gradually lulled her into relaxation. It wasn't what she wanted, but it was better than she'd had in weeks.

She wasn't aware of falling asleep, but when she woke he was gone and daylight was streaming through her window. Cold, she reached for a blanket and paused with it halfway over her body, suddenly conscious of the soft, fuzzy texture. She pulled it up to rub against her cheek.

Soon, she noticed other things—the taste in her mouth, the scent of Eamon on her pillow, the sound of traffic outside. The sense of being muffled was gone almost entirely. She leapt out of bed and into the bathroom, where she squirted toothpaste into her mouth, only to spit it out a second later when the mint was more than she could take.

"I don't know what you did, Eamon," she muttered to herself, "but baby, I owe you one."

Eight

Maybelle, Louisiana
Thursday, 7:00 p.m.

"Look up, Madison!" Sophie shouted as a group of girls in black leotards and pink tights did grand jetés diagonally across the studio. "Watch your arms, Cameron! Flapping them won't get you any higher." When the last group had reached the corner, she clapped her hands and said. "Good job. Now, everyone to center for révérence." She led the class through an abbreviated set of flowing stretches, ending in a deep curtsy. Rising from the curtsy, she clapped again and said, "Great class. Thanks, everyone."

The teen girls in the class applauded halfheartedly as they exchanged puzzled glances. This was Sophie's last class of the day, and she never ended on time. She'd changed into street shoes, wrapped a jersey skirt around her waist, and put on a sweater while the girls were still pulling on cover-ups and changing shoes. Since the studio was still open, she didn't have to wait for them to leave, so she hurried out to her car. The market wouldn't start until midnight in New York, but that was only four hours away, and she had a fairly elaborate plan to explain the fact that she was likely to be out all night.

As soon as she got home, she ran upstairs and took a shower.

Afterward, she put on heavy tights and dance trunks. Instead of a bra and slip, she wore a filmy dance dress with a snug camisole lining. She never knew what currency she might have to pay for information or favors, so she needed to be prepared to dance. Over her dancewear, she put on a knit wrap dress that fit snugly through the body before swirling into a full, calf-length skirt.

Into her copious tote bag she threw an old pair of pointe shoes, a small iron skillet, and the cookies she'd made earlier that day. While she finished doing her hair and makeup, she used the electric teakettle she kept in her room to brew tea for filling her thermos. She had sandwiches and apples in her room's dorm-sized refrigerator. With any luck, her mother would have no idea that she was prepared to survive a couple of days and even keep another person alive.

Then it was time to test her cover story. "I'm getting together with a friend," she said as she passed the living room on her way out. "I'll probably stay over in the city instead of coming home late, so don't worry about me." That was all true, and was it her fault if her mother thought the city in question was Shreveport rather than New York?

"I'm assuming this friend is female," her mother said icily.

As a matter of fact, the friend from the New York class she'd made plans with *was* a woman, but something in Sophie snapped, and before she even thought about what she was saying, she said, "Is that any of your business?"

Her mother's mouth hung open in shock. Sophie had never gone through a rebellious teenage phase, so that might have been the first time she'd ever sassed her mother. Finally, her mother said, "While you're under my roof—"

Sophie cut her off. "But it's not your roof. Technically, it's still Nana's. When she passes, it'll be mine. I'm not living here as your dependent. I'm living here to help you. If you decide you don't care for the way I'm living my life, you're welcome to tell me not to come back under 'your roof,' but then you'll get to deal with everything I've been taking care of for you. Now, if you'll excuse me, I'm running late for dinner."

She made her exit while she was still riding the adrenaline high and before she found herself backtracking and apologizing. It was a sign of just how shocked her mother was that she didn't manage to react before Sophie made it to her car. Sophie forced herself not to look in the rearview mirror as she drove away, lest she have second thoughts. She was shaking with disbelief about what she'd just done, but it was high time, she told herself. Her belated teen phase did have some good points. Now, if only she could get over that foolish crush.

She went through her usual routine of parking her car, hiding it, and opening a gateway. Once inside the Realm, she immediately opened another gateway that took her into Central Park, and finally breathed a little easier with a sense of freedom. After pulling a belted wool jacket out of her bag and putting it on, she headed to the restaurant where she was to meet her colleague. Her mind, though, was already on that night's market.

Nine

The Theater District
11:15 p.m.

Emily changed quickly as soon as she came offstage. As far as she could tell, she hadn't lost her mojo when the spell on her had broken. The house was still full and she still had to do multiple curtain calls. She could hear Sophie's voice in her head, telling her that magic had nothing to do with it, it was all her and she had just needed the chance to shine and be noticed. Maybe her mental Sophie was right. And if the crowd outside the stage door was a little smaller, it was because it was a Thursday night.

She signed a few autographs and smiled for photos as she made her way to the street and hailed a cab, making a mental note to put a car service in her next contract, assuming that it didn't all go up in a puff of magical smoke. If the cabbie thought there was anything odd about her asking him to take Central Park West on the way to her apartment, he didn't say anything.

She kept her eyes peeled for unusual activity around the park. Since Halloween was a huge fairy holiday, she was pretty sure there'd be a market soon, and that would be a great place to investigate this phony queen. Sophie might not be ready to delegate, but that didn't mean others couldn't volunteer to help. The real queen couldn't very well scope anything out about the impostor, and any information she could glean would only help her sister.

The area around the park didn't look too different. She wasn't sure what she was expecting, but there weren't any hordes of strange people streaming into the park. She was about to direct the driver to take her home when the cab stopped for a light and a man with a dog on a leash crossed the street. It was Michael and Beau, and Michael wasn't dressed like he was just taking the dog out for a late-night pit stop, but rather like he was going on a casual date, and he carried a messenger bag over his shoulder.

She threw a few bills at the driver and said, "I'll just get out here, thanks. Keep the change."

She had to run to keep Michael in sight. He moved like a man on a mission. As they went deeper into the park, the level of activity increased, and she could see the faint trace of aura that told her these people were fae—that sense hadn't disappeared when the bonds had broken.

Michael stopped on the bridge overlooking Bethesda Terrace, and she hung back, reluctant to let him see her. Was he meeting Sophie, or was he on some mission of his own? Then not too far away, she noticed Athena and Amelia. "The gang's all here," she muttered to herself. This night could get really interesting.

Ten

Central Park
11:55 p.m.

Michael stood at the balustrade overlooking Bethesda Terrace and checked his watch one more time. His pulse quickened with anticipation. The first time he'd seen one of these markets, he'd had no idea what was happening. He'd tried to rationalize an entire festival materializing out of thin air in Central Park. Now that he knew the truth, he braced himself for the shock.

One more check of his watch showed that he still had a couple more minutes. Others were starting to gather in the area. He was sure most of them were some kind of fairy folk, but now he knew there were more humans in on the secret. A stirring in the waters of the lake on the other side of the terrace startled him, then he realized that there were people in the water—using the term "people" loosely, of course.

Beau, who'd been slumped against the railing, came to attention and stood, so Michael checked his watch again. It was almost time. He held his breath, and while he waited, the terrace suddenly transformed.

This market was bigger than the ones he'd seen before, like

the difference between the regular greenmarkets and the Christmas markets held around the city. The terrace was packed with brightly colored booths. The only empty space other than the narrow aisles between rows of booths was a dance floor near the edge of the lake, beside which a small band played.

The market was already crowded with folk who'd come from the Realm, and the more earthly fae who'd been gathering flooded down stairs and paths into the market. Beau started walking, joining the flow of the crowd, and Michael came along behind the dog.

When he reached the first of the market stalls, he put his hand in his coat pocket and felt for the little angel figurine. It was a pewter version of the fountain in the middle of the market. Detective Tanaka had given it to him when Michael started his training to be a detective, continuing the joke begun during Michael's patrol days when someone had realized that St. Michael the archangel was the patron saint of policemen. Michael tolerated the good-natured teasing and had a box full of angel figures, magnets, and postcards that had landed on his desk or in his locker over the years. This one was the most meaningful because it had been a sign that the senior detective had accepted him. He hadn't realized just how important it was to him until he contemplated giving it away.

But what would be a worthwhile trade for it? Not food or drink, which eliminated about half the stalls. He'd brought human food with him, either to sustain himself or use as payment while in the Realm. Fairy food was unlikely to do him any good.

On second thought, he realized he shouldn't be looking at the stalls, but rather at the vendors. His trade would only have value if he got something they valued, and they wouldn't be selling anything personally meaningful to them. He walked slowly through the market, glancing at the fairies and other beings staffing their booths. None of them appeared to be wearing anything that looked like it might have great sentimental value. Then again, would anyone guess that his most treasured item of clothing was his first NYPD sweatshirt, now faded and tattered?

On his second pass through the market, he noticed a woman

selling small sculptures that looked so lifelike that he halfway suspected they weren't sculptures at all, but rather enchanted beings frozen into position. In this place, that wasn't entirely out of the question. Her booth was nearly empty of shoppers, and he thought that was causing her some distress. Her eyes darted back and forth as she watched people approach and pass by, and all the while, she absently stroked the shawl around her shoulders. It might have been woven from spider silk, it was so filmy, but the colors were more intense than anything in nature, and they seemed to shift. Even if he didn't need to use it to buy Jen's freedom, it would make an excellent welcome-home gift, he thought.

Her eyes lit up when he approached her booth, and he felt bad for not being a real customer—that was, until she said, "Get your own brownie here, sir. You can release him when you need his services, then put him under enchantment and out of the way again when he's done his work."

"That's not really something I want right now," he said, suppressing a shudder. "But I was admiring your shawl."

She glanced down at it and ran a hand along it. "Yes, my first brownie made this for me."

"What do you want for it?"

"It's not for sale," she said, wrapping it tighter around herself. "Does this look like a clothing booth?"

With a surprisingly strong pang of remorse, he took the figurine out of his pocket and held it out to her in the palm of his hand. "Would you perhaps be interested in this?"

"Ooooh," she breathed, her eyes growing wide as she leaned down to look at it. "How did you ever enchant one of those?"

He started to correct her mistaken impression but thought better of it, instead closing his fist around the figure and pulling it away. "Trade secret," he said vaguely. "But I might be willing to trade for your shawl."

"May I see it again?" she asked eagerly, almost greedily. He opened his fingers just long enough for her to get a glimpse, then closed his hand again. She shut her eyes, and her face showed her internal struggle before she whipped off the shawl and thrust it at him. He handed her the figure and hurried away from the booth before she realized that there was no enchantment on the angel figure—at least, not that he knew of. He couldn't take that for granted any longer.

He pulled back on the leash when Beau got too far ahead of him. In this crowd, he didn't want to trip anyone. A moment later, he saw why Beau was so eager when he glimpsed red-gold curls in the crowd. How had he not noticed Sophie earlier? At least, he thought it was Sophie. He craned his neck to see around and between the people in front of him. She was shorter than most of the fairies here, but as slightly built as she was, she still looked more substantial, more real, and that made her stand out in the crowd. Meanwhile, as bright as her hair was in the regular world, it was dim compared to the unreal hues the fae folk sported.

He eased up a little on the leash to let Beau follow Sophie. He wanted to see what she was up to at the market. She paused every so often to speak to the people working the booths or to passersby, but mostly she kept moving like she was looking for someone. What surprised him was how little attention she got. She was the queen of these people, and he couldn't imagine the queen making an appearance in such a public place without causing a bit of a stir. When he'd been with her in the Realm, everyone seemed to know at first glance exactly what she was.

Frowning, he put his hand in his pocket to grab his clover keychain and took another good look at her. Nope, there was nothing there. Should there have been? He'd barely seen her in months, and in those rare times he hadn't bothered to look with his enhanced sight to see if there was something magically different about her.

She did have a bit more of a glow about her than an ordinary human, but she wasn't wearing a tiara not visible to the naked eye, or anything like that. If there was something about her that said "queen," she must have hidden it, the fairy equivalent of a movie star wearing dark glasses and a baseball cap.

But he knew what she was, and she was just what he needed.

He closed the gap between them before loosening Beau's retractable leash. "Go get her, Beau," he murmured, and the dog trotted forward to circle around her. When he was certain there was no way she could dodge or escape him, he said, "Hello, Sophie. We need to talk."

Eleven

Bethesda Terrace
Midnight

When the marketplace magically appeared on Bethesda Terrace, Emily couldn't help but squeal and clap her hands in delight. It was so magical, like something out of a dream.

It also looked real and vivid. The spell that had seemingly trapped her in a gray haze might have been broken, but the world still wasn't what it once had been to her, and she was beginning to wonder if it ever would be. This place, though, had all the color and life of the Realm, everything she'd missed since her return. She didn't want to go back there, not forever, but it was good to get a little dose of it.

All around her were bright colors, intense smells, lively sounds. She imagined that if she were to eat or drink anything, the taste would be amazing, but she knew better than to try. That was why she was in this mess in the first place.

Fortunately, there were enough people around and there was enough noise that Michael didn't seem to have heard her squealing. He was so fixed on whatever he was after that it apparently hadn't occurred to him that anyone he knew might be there.

She joined the others heading down the stairs into the market. Then, through a gap in the crowd, she saw strawberry-blond curls floating gracefully, barely moving, as though the person wearing them was gliding. "Oh crap, Sophie?" she muttered. It was going to be a challenge keeping a safe distance from four people.

A band was playing a lively jig that made her toes tap, and she wanted more than anything to join the dancing, but she wasn't here for fun. Maybe when all this was over, she could come to a market on her own time.

She couldn't resist reaching out to touch the silk floating from one booth. It slid through her fingers like cool liquid. The next booth sold a spicy drink, and she could detect the spices from where she stood—cinnamon, cloves, and something utterly alien. Her mouth watered, but she reminded herself that it was risky. She didn't know if the usual Realm rules applied to this place, so she didn't want to take the chance.

A familiar silvery head on the next aisle made her smile, and she glanced around to make sure none of the people she knew were watching her before she ran to greet Eamon. "I was hoping you'd be here," she said, hugging him.

"I am somewhat surprised that you are," he replied, not releasing her after belatedly returning her hug.

"I thought I'd do some research into the impostor. But the enchantresses, my sister, and Michael are also here. It's a party."

"Have you found anything useful?"

"I just got here. You?"

He glanced around. "This market seems small. There must be activity elsewhere."

"This is small?"

"For this market at this time."

"What else might be happening?"

"Whatever it was, I was not invited." He frowned at her. "Are you sure it is wise for you to be here?"

"Oh, you mean the bonds and potential hostage thing? All better. Check me out and see for yourself."

He studied her for a moment, his eyes widening. "That does seem to be the case," he said.

"You mean you didn't do it? I woke up this way after you left."

"I had nothing to do with it."

"Maybe they realized I was too well-guarded to take this time."

"Perhaps. But I am still concerned about the impostor queen."

She hooked her arm through his elbow. "Let's do some investigating, then."

Twelve

Sophie's first instinct was to flee. She even tensed her muscles, preparing to spring forward, but she felt Beau's leash against her ankles. If she tried to run, she'd only do an ignominious face-plant, and Michael was already too close for her to make a clean escape. "Traitor," she muttered to the bulldog before she plastered a smile onto her face and turned to Michael.

Then she completely forgot any witty comeback she might have had prepared because he looked really, really nice. Emily was right, he did look much healthier than he had the last time she saw him. She hadn't realized just how ill he'd been then until she saw the contrast with the way he looked now. He was fair-skinned, but there was a big difference between the gray pallor he'd had before and the light pink of tonight. He still had lean features, but he was much less gaunt than before, and his clothes fit him far better, like he'd gone back to the weight he'd been when he bought them. Under a classic khaki trench coat he wore dark jeans and a sweater that looked touchably soft in exactly the same mossy green color as his eyes. *Snap out of it, Sophie,* she told herself sternly.

She noticed that he was holding a diaphanous shawl that had to be of fae manufacture. What did he want with that? She doubted he was doing some early Christmas shopping at the fairy market. Pulling her wits about her, she quirked an eyebrow and said, "That's a lovely shawl. The color really brings out your eyes."

Her remark threw him off balance enough that instead of saying whatever he was confronting her about, he glanced quizzically at the shawl, as though he'd forgotten all about it. He shoved it into his messenger bag.

While he was momentarily discomfited, she took advantage of the opportunity to put him on the defensive. "What brings you here tonight?" She mentally kicked herself for asking a stupid question. She, of all people, should know what he was doing. She was mostly surprised that he'd known to be here. She'd made sure he couldn't follow her to the market this time by staying away from anywhere he might be. Then she made the mistake of remembering the last time, when she'd hauled him home, nearly unconscious, and held him through the night until he recovered from the shock and pain. If her thoughts showed on her face, this could get awkward.

"You know what I'm doing here," he said, closing the gap between them. The crowd was too dense for her to back away and maintain a comfortable distance.

"Not really," she shot back. "At least, I don't know what you think you'll accomplish. You weren't going to do something foolish like try to get into the Realm and get to Jen, were you?"

His expression told her she'd struck home, but he looked defiant rather than guilty. "And what are you doing here?" he asked.

"I'm working on it."

"Don't you think I should be brought into the loop on that, seeing as how it affects me directly?"

"I've got it under control," she insisted, glancing around for an escape route. He was awfully close now, close enough that the green in his dark eyes was so vivid that it drew her hypnotically, and that was dangerous.

"Care to share some details? Like a status report so I know

what you've been doing? And then I can tell you what I've found, which is pertinent, which you'd have known if you'd been willing to *talk to me.*"

He sounded truly angry, and his eyes flashed with fury. She understood why he was angry, but she couldn't tell him why she'd been avoiding him. That would only make matters ten times worse. She could just imagine his reaction to hearing that she hadn't been telling him what she was doing to return his lost wife because she was afraid she was falling in love with him and even more afraid that she could make him fall in love with her, which would ruin all chances of saving his wife, and she had to avoid him for both their sakes. "I'm sorry," she said simply, not bothering to make excuses. "What do you have to tell me?"

He deflated a bit, as though he'd been prepared for her to fight back and didn't know quite how to deal with a calm response. Reaching out to take her arm, he said, "Let's talk. There's got to be someplace quieter around here."

She allowed herself to close her eyes and enjoy the sensation of him holding her arm as he led her away from the center of the market. Then she gave herself a mental kick and opened her eyes to see that he was leading her around the fountain to the edge of the lake, where there was a low wall. There were still people here, and naiads in the lake itself, chatting with people leaning over the wall, but there was far less hustle and bustle. She settled herself on the seat built into the wall, arranging her skirt just for an excuse to distract herself. The setting was a little too magical and romantic to share with an unobtainable man she found irresistible. Beau flopped down, leaning heavily against both their legs.

She was surprised to see that Michael, too, seemed to need to gather his thoughts. He glanced around and took a couple of deep breaths, as though he was trying to decide where to start. Finally, he just plunged ahead. "Okay, so like I told you in the *many* messages I've left for you, people are being cast out of the Realm, supposedly under orders of the queen, which I figure you're not doing."

"Of course not. I do plan to try to return any captives who

want to get home, once I figure out a way to do that. But just kicking them out is awful."

"Well, I've been out looking, in case Jen is one of those who gets kicked out. She'd need all the help she can get, I figure."

Sophie shuddered at the thought. She hadn't even considered that possibility. "That's a good idea," she admitted. "I take it you didn't find her."

He shook his head. "No, not yet, and I've had help looking." He swallowed, like he was preparing himself to admit something that he was still struggling with. "It seems my experiences have changed me a bit. It's not just the clover that lets me see things. They keep saying I've been touched."

"Oh," she breathed, catching herself before asking why he hadn't said anything. For all she knew, he'd been trying to tell her for the last couple of months. "That must be…interesting for you." His clover would have let him see the major things when they were right around him, but once he'd been elf shot and had spent time in the Realm, a whole new world would have become visible to him.

"That means I've met people," he continued. "There's a woman out in the park I would have said was a bag lady if I'd seen her a couple of months ago. Now, though…" He shrugged and shook his head. "She claims to be a wise woman, someone with fairy knowledge. She was helping the outcasts."

She couldn't hold back her gasp of surprise, and without realizing what she was doing, she reached over and clutched his hand. "That's what I'm here looking for. I think I've been looking in the wrong places for help. The fairies don't know how to undo a connection to the Realm because it's not something that affects them. We need to talk to the people on the outside who work with fairies. I didn't know wise women still existed."

"Apparently, they do." He seemed to be a little uncomfortable with this admission, not quite meeting her eyes, so she suspected there was more to it than he was telling her at the moment. Then she realized she was holding his hand and released her grip, but it turned out that he was holding on to her, so she couldn't pull away without jerking her hand out of his. She resolved not to enjoy it. He squeezed even tighter and leaned toward her. "She told me how to free Jen. I know how to save her. That's why I'm here. Sophie, it has to be me. I'll need your help, but you can't do it without me."

She wanted to smack herself on the forehead. "Of course! Redeeming someone always takes love. Why didn't I think of that? I'm sorry. I should have realized sooner." He'd relaxed enough that she was able to ease her hand out of his grasp. She didn't feel comfortable discussing his love for his missing wife while holding hands with him. Her equilibrium returned the moment she was no longer touching him. Feeling a lot steadier, she said, "I don't suppose she told you specifically how?"

"Apparently, the task or trial arises when it's time, but she had some ideas for how it should go." He gestured toward the corner of shawl peeking out of his bag. "I might have to buy her freedom, and she thought that trading things of value until I had something her captor values might come up. So, I got a start on that. Though I don't know if it will work, since it doesn't seem like she has a captor now, with Maeve out of power."

"Maybe it's not so much a ransom as it is a gift for Jen. Think of it as wooing her all over again. You did it once before."

"Yeah, but the last time I wasn't competing with the fairy world. She was a struggling actress and I was a guy with a steady job."

Oh, he was so much more than that, but she didn't think this was the time to give him a flattering ego boost. "I'm sure that's not the only reason she married you."

He stared at her so intently that she felt her skin prickling under his glare. "So, now what do we do?"

She knew he wouldn't accept "I don't know" for an answer, but she *didn't* know, and she didn't know what to do about it. For once in her life, she was utterly without a plan or an answer, and all her newfound power was useless. "We go with your plan. We get you into the Realm and see if you can free Jen." Funny, it sounded like her voice, but it wasn't the sort of thing she'd imagined she would say. In fact, it went against her every instinct.

No, actually, it had been her instinct speaking. What it went against was the part of her that resisted instinct, that tried to be rational about everything, even the things that weren't at all rational. She was magical in multiple ways, human and fae. Maybe she should listen to her instinct.

As surprised as she was about her decision, he looked even more shocked. "Seriously?" he asked, an eyebrow arched skeptically. "You're not just messing with me?"

"It's all I've got right now. Don't tell me you've changed your mind."

He was already on his feet and tugging at her hand. "Not at all. Let's go."

She let him pull her to her feet. Beau grunted and shifted position as he lost his backrest.

A shout from the other side of the market caught their attention, and they turned to see a wave of oddly dressed fairies swarming down the stairs into the market. Sophie was used to the wild fae, but these looked like cartoon images of savages, wearing necklaces of bones. "Oh no, not these guys," Michael said with a groan. Sophie turned back to look at him. "I ran into them the other night. They're bad news."

The invaders proceeded to demonstrate that by running wildly through the market, upending booths and knocking people over. As they ran, they sang something that sounded like "Again, again, the Wild Hunt rides again."

"*This* is the Hunt?" Sophie asked, speaking mostly to herself. "It's a night early. And I thought it would be more impressive."

"I think these are fans of the Hunt," Michael said, not taking his eyes off the invaders.

Sophie hated being the fairy queen, and she normally preferred to let the Realm rule itself, but she couldn't stand by and allow it to descend into anarchy. She started to head for the fray, but Michael caught her arm and held her back with an iron grip. "These are my people. I have to do something," she protested.

"They're just schoolyard bullies. You can help more by getting your Realm under control."

Soon, it didn't matter that he was holding her back because the savages were running toward them. "My impostor must be getting rid of her rival," Sophie suggested, instinctively throwing up a magical barrier to hide and shield them.

"It might be me they're after," Michael said. At their feet, Beau growled.

"What did you do to piss them off?"

"It involved some nastiness with iron nails."

"Nice." Though she was torn about running from a fight, Sophie made a decision. "Let's get out of here. I need earth to open a gateway."

She ran along the lake, dragging him with her by the grip he kept on her arm. The melee at the market was so loud, she couldn't tell for certain if they were being pursued, but she felt it safest to act as though they were.

She shivered at the sense of altered reality as they passed the marketplace boundaries and returned to the ordinary world. If Michael had encountered the savages in the park before, she didn't think the boundary would hold them, so she kept running. As soon as they reached a reasonably sized patch of earth, she pulled Michael off the path.

"Now what?" Michael asked.

"I open a gateway."

"Just like that?"

"I'm the queen. I have the keys to the Realm."

With a thought, she opened the gateway. She could feel it, but she could tell from his expression that he didn't realize anything had happened. "Okay, now I'd better have some physical contact to get you through." She held her hand out to him, and he took it.

"What about Beau?"

"I don't actually know how it applies to animals, but he leash seems to work."

"Maybe you'd better take him, just in case." He passed the leash handle over to her.

"Shall we?" she asked when they were all settled.

He gave a determined nod, then hesitated. "We're not stepping into something scary, are we?" His free hand went to the holster on his hip.

"Scarier than what's after us?"

He nodded, swallowed, and said, "Okay, let's do this."

She stepped forward, with him following a split second later. They came out into the twilight world of the Realm, facing the vine-covered wall of what used to be a palace.

"Oh no, not again," Sophie groaned.

～Thirteen～

The Marketplace
1:00 a.m.

Eamon pulled Emily into a sheltered space between two booths at the first sound of angry shouts. "What's happening?" she asked, straining against his grasp to try to see.

"I know these fae. It's best to keep out of their way. They are very bad news."

Both of them winced at the crashing sound when the intruders flipped over a nearby booth. "Don't they have security here?" Emily asked.

"There is a truce in effect at the market. Security should not be necessary."

"Yeah, well, obviously it is."

They had to dart from their hiding place and run with the crowd fleeing the violent gang when the chaos drew closer to them. Emily looked around for her sister. Next to Sophie was probably the safest place to be in just about any fight. But she didn't see any sign of Sophie. She did spot Amelia nearby and grabbed Eamon's arm to lead him in that direction. The enchantresses might be the next best thing to Sophie.

Athena was with her sister in an odd island of calm. She

reached out a hand and drew Emily and Eamon into their charmed circle. "What is this?" Amelia demanded of Eamon.

"They come from the Borderlands. They are not welcome in the Realm itself. But I have never seen them do anything this bold. They usually only prey on the helpless who have no other recourse."

"And what are you doing here, Emily?" Amelia asked, sounding like a stern teacher scolding a naughty pupil.

"Just scoping things out," Emily said with a shrug. "I thought I might pick up some intel on the impostor queen for Sophie."

"Do you think that's wise?" Athena asked.

"I'm all better, really. Whatever Sophie or Michael told you about my condition, it ended this morning, like *that*." She snapped her fingers for emphasis.

"We'll discuss this later," Amelia said, returning her attention to the chaos at the market.

From the safety of the enchantresses' magical bubble, Emily watched the intruders. "They seem to be looking for someone—or maybe something," she mused aloud. The violence and destruction were more focused than if they were merely trying to intimidate people, she thought.

"But who, or what?" Amelia asked.

"Sophie?" Emily suggested. "If they work for the impostor, they might want to get the real queen out of the way."

"We should do something," Athena said. "They're talking about the Hunt."

"The Hunt?" Eamon asked, his eyes darkening to the color of tarnished silver.

Amelia listened for a moment. Emily strained her ears, trying to make out words in the intruders' song. Soon, she did pick up on a boast about the Hunt riding. She wasn't sure what that was, but it didn't sound like it was going to be a happy, fun time.

"If they're associated with the Hunt, that could threaten our world, which puts this in our jurisdiction," Amelia said firmly. "Come, Athena. You two, stay out of the way."

When she first went to work in the sisters' antique shop,

Emily never would have imagined the two eccentric old women as formidable, but she'd learned that they kicked some serious ass. Now they threw magical fireballs that drove the attackers away from their prey and herded them all together in the middle of the market. Once the other market attendees noticed that their tormenters were under attack, they joined in. Emily couldn't help but wish she had a bit of Sophie's power so she could take part in the battle.

Either the thugs had accomplished what they came to do or hadn't anticipated this much resistance, because soon they'd fled the market, some running up the stairs and others heading down the tunnel under the park road. When they were all gone, Emily and Eamon joined the enchantresses. Athena was grinning in triumph, but Amelia looked worried. "This is not a good sign," she said.

"What's this Hunt, anyway?" Emily asked.

"It's a legend," Athena said.

"It is no legend," Eamon said somberly. "But it has been a very long time since the Hunt has ridden."

"The legend tells of a great procession of fae, usually on Halloween night, and it was considered misfortune to cross their path," Amelia explained.

"Supposedly, thunder was the sound of their horses' hooves," Athena added. "Some legends say they're ghosts."

"They are fae," Eamon said, "but no fae you would want to encounter."

"And now this is going to happen here?" Emily asked.

"If it happens, it may happen everywhere," Amelia said. "They could ride in and out of the Realm, all over the world."

"Why now? Does this have anything to do with the impostor?"

"It is possible, if this is something the impostor suggests or allows," Eamon said. Emily could tell just how serious this was from the look on his face. He was scared, and fairies didn't scare easily.

"So we need Sophie," Emily concluded. Getting Jen Murray back was important, but the fate of the world could be at stake. She scanned the marketplace, which now looked like nothing had happened. The magical merchants had managed to clean up quickly and had returned to business as usual. She didn't see any sign of her sister or Michael. "Where is Sophie?"

The sisters joined hands and closed their eyes. "She isn't here," Amelia reported.

"She went home?" Emily asked.

"I don't think she's in this sphere," Athena said.

Emily's heart leapt into her throat. "They took her! And I guess they got Michael, too." She clutched at Eamon's arm. "They've got my dog!"

ᴄᴏFourteenᴏᴄ

"You aren't going to have to win the throne again, are you?" Michael asked Sophie as the two of them stared at the vine-covered walls of the palace. "At least you know how to do that."

"No, I don't think so," she said absently, sounding like she'd barely heard his question. Abruptly, she turned to him. "May I have your keychain, please?"

Under other circumstances, Michael might have questioned such an odd request, but Sophie wasn't the capricious type. If she asked for something, she had a good reason, so he handed it over.

"Now what do you see?" she asked him.

He was about to say that nothing had changed, but when he turned to Sophie to say so, out of the corner of his eye he saw the palace without its veil of vines. When he looked straight at the palace, it looked as vine-covered as ever, but whenever he started to look away, it shifted. "I don't think the vines are really there," he said hesitantly.

"That's what I thought," she said with a satisfied nod, handing his keychain back to him. "It's a glamour aimed at fairies. It still affects you a little because you were elf shot, but I was hoping that without the four-leaf clover, you might see past it."

"Someone's trying to hide the palace from people in the Realm," he concluded. "Why?"

"We've got a false queen out there who won't be able to sit on the throne or wear the crown. She'd want to hide the real things to make the scheme work. But that's not our priority right now." She took off walking toward the palace, striding so rapidly that he had to hurry to catch up with her, even though she was nearly a foot shorter than he was.

He almost ran into her when she stopped abruptly. "Oh, that is not right," she muttered.

"What is it?" he asked. Instead of answering, she put her hand out, and a faint glow appeared around it. She pushed like she was testing an invisible barrier, and the glow pulsed.

"So it's more than just imaginary vines," he concluded.

"Someone's locked me out of my own palace," she said, indignation competing with shock in her voice. "They put up their own shield outside whatever spell was already there."

He didn't think that sounded good for Jen, but refrained from saying so because he was pretty sure she was well aware of that fact. He also resisted the impulse to ask what she was going to do about it because he knew she'd do it if she knew.

She studied the barrier for a moment, frowning, then turned and walked in a different direction—along the barrier, Michael assumed. Beau paused to lift his leg against it, and that was when Michael could see for a fact that there was something invisible keeping them out. He followed Sophie as she tracked the circumference of the barrier.

"I have an idea," she said. "It's folklore-appropriate, so it just might work."

They'd walked almost all the way around the castle when they reached a wall that wasn't covered in vines. Sophie reached out a tentative hand and was able to turn the handle of a door set into the wall. She let the door swing all the way open so they could see inside what looked like a kitchen yard. There was a well, a small herb garden, a vegetable patch, and a few outbuildings. Some chickens roamed, but there weren't any people, fae or otherwise. At the back of the yard loomed the palace.

"Okay, it looks like they did leave this part unguarded," Sophie said, leading the way into the kitchen yard and toward a door in the palace. "They must not have expected a queen to know how to get to the kitchen."

The door was shut, but Sophie opened it with a touch. As they entered the kitchen in the bowels of the palace, Michael couldn't help but wonder why they bothered to even have a kitchen in a world where everyone could just conjure up what they wanted. He supposed it was the appearance of it all. What was the point of being a ruler without servants?

Not that there were any servants here. The place seemed deserted. "This is odd," Sophie said. "Normally, there are at least a few brownies here." Raising her voice, she called out, "Hello?"

"You obviously aren't the kind of queen who avoids the kitchen," Michael remarked.

"I've explored the palace," she said with a shrug. "You never know when you'll need to know your way around."

There was a rustling sound, and Michael looked down, expecting to see mice scurrying across the floor. Instead, several small, wizened creatures were crawling out of cracks in the walls. They bowed when they saw Sophie. "Your majesty!" one of them said. "You are safe."

"Why wouldn't I be?" Sophie asked, pulling back on the leash when Beau tried to sniff at the creatures, who cowered away from him.

"Something happened here, and we hid," another of the creatures said. "Now everyone is gone."

"Everyone?" Michael asked, alarmed.

"What happened?" Sophie asked.

"There was noise. And it got dark. And we hid." The little thing was shivering now, and it huddled with its colleagues.

"We'd better check upstairs," Sophie said. "Keep yourselves safe."

"We could prepare you a meal, your majesty," one of the creatures offered, but not very enthusiastically.

"That won't be necessary," Sophie said as she headed toward the door.

Michael lost count of how many flights of stairs they went up before Sophie opened a door and they emerged in a long, seemingly endless corridor. Sophie went straight to one of the hundreds of doors on the corridor and knocked sharply. "Jennifer? It's Sophie," she called out. When there was no response, she shrugged and said, "Well, it is my palace," before doing something to the doorknob that made the door slowly open. She pushed the door open wider, then paused to look back at Michael. "Brace yourself. She might be a bit resistant to your presence."

Unfortunately, he was used to that. So far, Jen had generally refused to admit that she knew him. Even so, he steeled himself and took a deep breath before following Sophie into the room.

It was the kind of bedroom he expected to find in a palace, with a canopied bed, wing-backed chairs in front of a carved marble fireplace, and a dressing table fit for a princess. It was also uninhabited, unless Jen was hiding under the bed. "Jennifer?" Sophie called out. Michael bit his tongue to keep himself from calling out, as well. That might just drive her away.

When there was no response, Sophie handed Beau's leash to Michael, knelt by the bed, raised the bedskirt, and peered underneath. "I had to be sure," she remarked as she stood and brushed off her skirt.

He glanced around the room. It looked to him like the sort of room Jen would like. In fact, if they'd had the space, this was exactly how she'd have wanted to decorate their bedroom. The familiar wedding photo sitting on a table was like a punch to the solar plexus, taking his breath away. "Is there anywhere else she might be? Somewhere else in the palace?" he asked.

"Let's find out." And she was off, leaving the room and heading down the corridor. Before following her, Michael grabbed the photo and stuffed it in his bag, then jogged to catch up, Beau puffing at his heels.

"Are you going to order a search party?" he asked when he came alongside her.

"Something like that," she said vaguely.

The corridor led to the throne room, which he remembered from his last visit. The vast room was almost entirely empty. The sole occupant was a woman scrubbing the floor. "What are you doing, playing Cinderella?" he whispered to Sophie. "I never pictured you as the wicked stepmother type."

"Before you get too sympathetic to her plight, that's Maeve, the one who kidnapped your wife and held her all these years, even though Jen wasn't the person she wanted. And I didn't trap her. She trapped herself."

"Oh, well, in that case, scrubbing floors is too good for her," he muttered.

Sophie went up to Maeve and loomed over her. The fairy woman looked up, brushing a stray strand of golden hair off her face. "Your majesty," she said, injecting a tiny dose of arrogance even into her deference.

"What happened here?" Sophie asked, gesturing around her at the empty room. "Where did everyone go?"

"How am I to know, since I can't go with them?" Maeve said. "They simply left."

Sophie opened her mouth as if to issue a retort, but paused and apparently thought better of it. She whirled and returned to Michael. He refrained from asking what they'd do next, since that was pretty obvious, and Sophie had a dark look on her face that made him want to stay on her good side.

"Well, apparently the impostor has also stolen my courtiers," she said, glowering. "Not that I wanted or needed them, but I would have liked to keep Jennifer safe."

"Where do you think she is?"

"I don't know if I can locate her from here, but I may be able to see who she left with." She spun and strode rapidly toward the dais. Michael gave a little tug on Beau's leash as he moved to follow her. The dog grunted once before getting back to his feet and coming along.

The ornate crown of the fairy realm sat on the seat of the

throne, the throne and crown encased in a shimmering, translucent dome. Sophie stood in front of the throne, facing the room, and held out her hands. Michael took an involuntary step backward when the room filled with ghostly figures.

"This is what it usually looks like," Sophie said. "Though the people are somewhat more substantial." With a sidelong glance and a slight smirk, she added, "But not much."

"There's Jen!" he said, pointing. He wanted more than anything to go to her, but he reminded himself that it wasn't real. Even in this ghostly form, she looked more like the wife he remembered than the woman he'd seen on his last visit to the Realm. Whatever Sophie had been doing, it must have been working.

"She's there with her usual friend," Sophie remarked. "I think she'll be safe as long as she's with him."

He nodded even as he felt like he was being stabbed in the gut at the sight of his wife with another man. "How long ago was this?" he asked.

"I don't know. Time is funny here, and it doesn't correspond to our time. But it was the last occasion when there were people in this room. This is a kind of echo of their psychic energy, for lack of a better term."

"And you can do this how?"

She sighed. "To be honest, I'm not entirely sure. I just do it. I didn't even know I knew how to do it until it came to me, so I'm assuming it came with the crown. I don't even know if I can do it anywhere else." She waved a hand, and the people moved in double time, like a film being fast forwarded. She slowed the image back to real time when all the people clustered in front of the dais, listening to someone speaking.

Both Michael and Sophie turned to see an image of a tall, white-haired woman standing beside them, clearly orating. "Can you get sound on this thing?" Michael asked.

"Unfortunately, I don't think so."

The woman, apparently having finished her speech, moved down the dais steps and through the crowd toward the front doors of the palace. The crowd, including Jennifer, streamed after her like a wake. "Hmm, I guess Maeve was the only one who fell into the trap of the feast," Sophie remarked.

"What do you mean?"

"Remember the banquet table laid out here? Eating or drinking would trap someone in the palace, just as eating or drinking in the Realm traps you here. I know Maeve dug into the feast, but I didn't see whether anyone else did. It's a pretty common trap in stories. I thought most of the courtiers stayed because they had to, but apparently they wanted to."

"What about that woman in the image? Do you think she's the impostor?"

"I think that's Niamh. She and her consort, Fiontan, have their own court. It's as good a place as any to start looking for Jen." She headed down the steps, but he called her back.

"Won't you need your crown?"

"I'm probably better off staying incognito."

"But to defeat the impostor, won't you need to prove you're the queen?"

"I'm not worried about that at the moment. It'll be easier to sneak in and get Jen without drawing attention to myself."

He hated himself for what he was about to say, but he knew he'd hate himself even worse if he didn't say it. "I think this impostor queen is a bigger priority. You saw those lunatics at the market. If she's stirring up something like this Hunt, that could threaten our world. We have to stop it."

"The deadline for Jen is tighter. I can deal with the impostor once Jen is safely out of the way."

"If this impostor is kicking people out of the Realm, Jen might be sent out, and I've seen what that looks like. It's not pretty. I'd rather her be safe here than losing her mind out there. Once everything's okay, we can get her home."

She regarded him for a long moment, and he thought her eyes might have grown just a little brighter—with tears, or magic? Then she gave him a tiny smile. "It might not be an either/or situation.

We could find Jen and the impostor in the same place. At any rate, I don't know that bringing the crown to the impostor would be a good idea. It's safe here, but if someone vanquishes me and takes it, they might become the rightful wearer, and then we really *would* have a mess. I've got the power of the queen, whether or not I have the crown, and here no one can get to it. Even if someone manages to vanquish me, they'd have to find the palace, get inside, and break the barrier to get the crown."

"Okay, then, you know what you're doing. Lead on."

He and Beau followed Sophie down the dais steps. It seemed like a mile between them and the doors, but finally they were there. Sophie gestured at the giant doors, but nothing happened. Scowling, she stepped forward, put her hand on the handle, and leapt backward with a yelp. She tried again, and shook her head when the doors remained shut.

Michael went to put his shoulder against the door. "I know a thing or two about getting through doors," he said, but she pulled him back.

"Trust me, you don't want to do that."

"So we're trapped in here?"

"There's always the kitchen. Come on."

He could have used a rest and maybe a snack, but he wanted out of this place, so he followed her through the heart of the palace down to the lower level. The door through which they'd entered was closed, and Sophie's gesture didn't open it. Michael nudged her aside and gave it a good kick, but it didn't budge and a shock went up his leg.

Sophie put her hands on her hips and glared at the closed door. "Okay, *now* we're trapped," she said.

Fifteen

Emily tried not to panic. Even if Sophie had been kidnapped by the creepy fae gang that thought this Wild Hunt was a great thing, the ones she needed to worry about were the fairies. Sophie was probably more dangerous as a captive than as an enemy in open warfare. The last person to take Sophie prisoner was currently a slave in the fairy queen's palace, and that happened before Sophie had much practice using her magical powers. Sophie loved both Michael and Beau, and she wouldn't let anything happen to either of them.

That didn't make it much easier for Emily to wait for the enchantresses to assess the situation and make a decision. "If we went now, we might be able to catch them," she said to Eamon.

"We do not know where in the Realm they might have gone," he told her somberly without turning his eyes from where the enchantresses and a couple of fairies who must have been guards or security officers were attempting to interrogate a prisoner.

The prisoner ignored their questions, instead singing an eerie song to himself. "Again, again, the Hunt will ride again," he sang, occasionally interrupting the song for a shrill giggle.

When the waiting grew too much for Emily, she stalked over to the enchantresses, grabbed Amelia's arm and said, "We need to help Sophie."

"Her disappearance may have nothing to do with this," Amelia said, her voice tight, like she wasn't sure she believed it herself. "She and Detective Murray were likely to go into the Realm tonight, no matter what, to find Jennifer."

"Well, even so, she's going to need help. Saving Jen, finding and stopping this impostor, and making sure this Hunt thing doesn't happen are a bit much to take on all at once, even for Sophie. You said this was your jurisdiction." She gestured toward the prisoner. "Let's do something, then. I know I don't exactly qualify for Sophie's role in your magical trio, but I can still help."

"That may just be tradition," Athena said. "We don't know if virginity is actually a technical requirement. In the old days, they may have assumed that any adult woman would be married, and motherhood would be inevitable without reliable birth control methods, so any unmarried woman might work as a maiden."

Even in the tense situation, Emily couldn't help but smile. "I meant that I don't have Sophie's magical powers."

Athena flushed crimson. "Oh, dear, apologies for the assumption."

Emily really had to fight to keep from laughing. "So, let's go into the Realm." She turned to Eamon. "That would be your part in this. You can take us, can't you?"

"It is possible. But are you sure it is safe for you?"

"Safe? Not likely, given the impostor and the Hunt. But I'm not jonesing for the Realm, if that's what you mean. I'd rather not go, but my sister's in there, and she needs my help. Look what she did for me."

He addressed the enchantresses. "You agree with this?"

"This is our job," Amelia said with a nod.

"Where in the Realm should we go?"

That was a real stumper. On her last visit, the Realm had been a dream—or nightmare—landscape that shifted and twisted around itself. It was impossible to map, and that made it impossible to know where to go. But thinking about her last time gave her an idea. "What about the free fae?" she asked Eamon. "Wouldn't they be most resistant to a ruler?"

"That's who we usually work with," Athena said, nodding. "Their agenda fits most closely with ours."

"I know of some common gathering places," Eamon said.

"Then what are we messing around for? Let's go!" Emily said, grabbing his hand.

"Not so fast," Amelia said. "How prepared are you for an extended time in the Realm? Do you have food or other supplies?"

"Oh, right," Emily said, resisting the urge to swear. Eating or drinking could trap her in the Realm, and she didn't want to go through that again.

"We have some weaponry and herbs, but we'll at least need water," Amelia said. "We have supplies at the shop."

Emily bit her tongue before blurting that it would take too long. Their shop was almost at the river, and cabs would be scarce at this time of night.

Athena turned to Eamon. "Do you know of a gateway in Riverside Park?"

"Yes, there is one."

"Then you'll come with us. You may not be able to go into the shop, but we won't take long."

The four of them trooped out of the park, and Amelia apparently had the same knack as Sophie for summoning a cab out of thin air. Emily waited outside the iron-laden shop with Eamon while the sisters gathered supplies. He hadn't even made it to the steps before he started shaking and sweating.

"You think I'm nuts, don't you?" she asked him.

"Plumb loco," he agreed with a smile. "But I do not believe you are wrong. If there is an effort by any ruler to subjugate the fae, the free ones will resist. They are also more likely to have human mates who might be targeted."

"Human mates? You mean captives?"

"Not every human in the Realm went unwillingly or stays

unwillingly." He glanced away from her. "Fae and humans do often find love with each other."

"And I guess they'd have to live in that world. The Realm's not too bad for humans if you don't have anything to lose here, but this world would be rough for a fairy."

He didn't comment on that, and the sisters came out of the shop a moment later, laden with bags. Eamon and Emily took the two largest bags, and the party set off down the street toward the river.

"This is where Sophie would come in handy," Emily remarked as Eamon sought the gateway. "She just goes into the Realm from anywhere."

"Sophie is queen of the Realm," Eamon said absently, his attention focused on his task. "I do not have her power." He grinned abruptly. "Ah, here it is."

They all held hands and stepped forward. Emily felt something shift. She remembered the sensation of falling between one step and another from the last time. She hadn't realized that she'd closed her eyes until she opened them and saw that she was in a different world.

They'd gone from the middle of the night to a strange eternal twilight, but without a visible sun. The colors were so intense that they brought tears to Emily's eyes, and the sound of distant music wafted through the air, like there was some kind of cosmic Muzak being played.

"We should probably head toward the music," Emily said. "Wherever music is, that's where fairies will be." She was a little surprised by how much she wanted to reach the music so she could dance to it. Maybe she wasn't quite as cured of the fairy craving as she'd thought. Or perhaps it was just that she was a professional dancer and this music was very danceable.

The party began heading in that direction. Amelia and Athena appeared in awe of their surroundings, which Emily found amusing. They knew so much, but they didn't have a lot of experience with actual fairies in their Realm. Eamon also looked out of place here in his old-professor attire, even if he was the one native to the Realm.

They hadn't been walking long when another sound drowned out the distant music—something that sounded like a military marching cadence. That was unusual in Emily's admittedly limited experience in the Realm, and a glance at Eamon confirmed her suspicions. He was looking around anxiously. A squad of fae men in medieval-looking military livery appeared, and as soon as they spotted the humans, they headed toward them at an alarmingly rapid pace. Emily started to run, but in a heartbeat she and her party were surrounded, with no way out.

"More humans," one of the soldiers said with a sneer. "Corrupting our Realm, are you? Well, enough of that!"

Sixteen

The Palace
Soon Afterward

Sophie was glad that Michael didn't ask the usual useless questions that tended to come up in this sort of situation, like "We're trapped?" or "How can we be trapped in your palace?" Instead, he stayed quiet and let her think, not even asking her what they could do. If she needed any additional reason to love him, that was one right there.

But this was no time to contemplate the merits of a man who was off-limits to her. She needed to find a way out of here. It came back to the crown, she was fairly certain. The first step anyone in her position would take would be to put on the crown that gave her control over the palace. Maybe that was what her unseen opponent wanted, for her to take the crown out of its protective bubble. That meant that option was off the table unless she got desperate.

"Is there anyone Beau could kiss?" Michael asked with a wry grin. A kiss from Beau, as Sophie's mortal protector, had already broken one spell.

"Nobody's asleep," she said, and then she laughed out loud. "But you are a genius. A sleeping spell may be just what we need."

"You're not planning to wait for a handsome prince to come rescue you, are you?"

"I'm a queen, not a princess. But I have a feeling whoever trapped us is in here with us, hoping I'll get out the crown and make it ripe for the picking. So if I knock out everyone in the castle but us, it might break the spell holding us, or at least weaken it while the caster is unconscious."

"You don't need the crown for that?"

"I don't think so. We're at the root of the palace, so it shouldn't take much to spread it upward. I'll exempt us, but I'll need contact to do that. Can you pick up Beau and put him on the table here?"

While he shifted the grunting bulldog, she mentally ran through the information that had popped into her head. She placed one hand on Beau's back and took Michael's hand with the other, took a deep breath to center herself, and reached out to the palace around them.

The air grew heavy. Even though she was in control of the spell, she felt weariness spread over her, and Michael's eyes blinked. Beau yawned, but that wasn't unusual behavior for him.

She waited several minutes before saying, "I hope that does it. Let's try the door." Reluctantly releasing Michael's hand, she went to the kitchen door. Much to her relief, the handle turned. "It seems to have worked. Let's get out of here."

He put Beau back on the ground, and they hurried out of the kitchen, through the kitchen yard, and out of the palace enclosure. From the outside, the barrier of vines was still visible, which meant that the magic creating it didn't require constant maintenance.

"I don't know how long that sleeping spell will hold, so we'd probably better get going," she said, taking off away from the palace.

"I take it we're going to pay this Fiontan and Niamh a visit," Michael said, matching his stride to hers.

"Do you have any other ideas?"

"No, that would be my plan. I guess you know where to find them."

"Not at all."

"Then where are we going?"

"To find someone who does know. Directions are tricky in the Realm. Maps are all but useless. You almost have to know where you're going in order to get there." She stopped and turned to him. "You do remember the rules, right? No eating or drinking anything they give you, no direct thanks. If I tell you to do something, do it without arguing because you can bet I have a good reason for it. They can't tell an outright lie, but that doesn't mean that what they tell you is the truth. They may not be answering the actual question you asked, or they may be leaving out something important. Try to avoid owing them any favors. It's best to do something that forces them to owe you something."

"Like being kind to animals and old people."

She smiled. "Exactly. We're lucky that you're a third son because that means that situation is likely to come up."

"You make it sound like this is going to be dangerous."

"It is. There's a reason this isn't a popular vacation spot for humans."

"But you're the queen of this place."

"One more rule: Don't ever mention that unless I've brought it up. If you're the impostor, what's the last thing you'd want around?"

"The real queen. So you want to stay under the radar. I was wondering about that at the market. It's like you're using some kind of cloaking spell."

She raised an eyebrow. "You can see that?"

"Sort of. It's hard to explain. It's not bad that I can see these things, is it?"

"No, I don't think so. But it is interesting." Very interesting, indeed, if being touched by magic had left lingering effects.

"What's our first step?"

"Find someone to do a favor for so we can make them give us directions. Keep your eyes open."

·Seventeen·

Elsewhere in the Realm
Meanwhile

Emily kept her cool by imagining what Sophie would do. If Sophie were ever captured, she'd give the impression that it had been part of her plan and her captors had been foolish enough to fall into her trap. So, Emily kept her head held high and looked coolly down her nose at the fairies holding them prisoner.

The captors hadn't threatened them yet, merely forced them to march. Emily figured the worst-case scenario would be getting booted from the Realm. If they were lucky, they'd be taken straight to the false queen.

A glance to her side told her that Amelia and Athena were behaving in a similar way and showing no fear, though instead of looking cool, they were regarding their surroundings with rapt fascination. Only Eamon seemed concerned, and Emily realized that exile for him might actually be deadly. Getting booted really would be a worst-case scenario.

The one thing she hadn't counted on was rescue—at least, not until Sophie knew something had happened to her.

One moment, the forest through which they walked was eerily

silent. The next, the air was full of shouts and battle cries as a wave of fairies rushed toward them, appearing seemingly out of thin air. They wore the natural-looking clothing of the wild fae, and they'd blended seamlessly with the surrounding trees.

One of them grabbed Emily's hand. "Come with us," he said, pulling her along with him as he ran. After noting that the others in her party were also being led, she joined him in putting on some speed. She didn't know yet if she could trust the new people, but they didn't seem to be holding them at sword-point yet, which she considered an improvement.

She wasn't sure how long they ran before they reached a denser section of woods and their guides slowed. Amelia and Athena must have been in remarkably good shape for their age, since they were less out of breath than Emily was. She wondered if it was magic or if they'd been doing aerobics since the eighties. One guide shouted a phrase in a musical language Emily didn't understand, and a voice from within the trees responded in the same language.

A gap appeared in what had appeared to be a dense stand of woods. Their guides ushered them through the gap, which closed behind them. Inside the walls was a great encampment of fae. Tents clustered around cooking fires, and a wild music skirled through the air, as always in any gathering of the fae.

The fairy who'd been guiding Emily gave her party a slight bow and said, "You are welcome to find sanctuary here among the others who would be exiled."

"Everyone here is on the list to be kicked out?" Emily asked in dismay. There were hundreds of people, and most of them weren't human.

"We've managed to catch most before they are ousted. Others come to us before the queen's guards reach them."

Emily opened her mouth to say that those weren't really the queen's guards, but Amelia caught her wrist and squeezed hard enough to make her gasp instead of speaking. "We'll just sit over here beside this fire, if you don't mind," Amelia said, maintaining her grip on Emily as she led the group to sit in a cluster.

"We'll learn more if they don't know what we know," Amelia hissed once they were all seated. "They already seem to trust us."

"But they don't know anything or they'd know the queen they're hiding from isn't the real one," Emily protested. "If we could convince them that the queen is an impostor, we've got the makings of an uprising, right here."

"You want to start a rebellion?" Athena asked, her eyes wide.

"The free fae live in constant opposition to rule," Eamon said. "It would not take much to make them rebel. The difficulty would be in getting them to follow orders well enough to complete an uprising." He glanced around at the camp. "Though I must say, they're surprisingly well organized here."

"I think they'll do okay if they're fighting for a common cause," Emily said. "We just need to stir them up and make them eager to fight instead of hiding."

"You believe we could do this?" Amelia asked.

"I spent six months in the chorus of a touring production of *Les Misérables*. I think I know a thing or two about stirring up a rebellion."

"As I recall, that rebellion wasn't too successful," Amelia pointed out.

"That was France," Emily said with a shrug. "The important thing is that if you do that show right, you have the audience ready to march out of the theater and take over the world. That's what I know how to tap into."

"How would you prove that the queen is an impostor?" Eamon asked.

"Couldn't you back me up? You've met the real queen, and you know she wouldn't do this."

"They would have no reason to believe me," he said, and there was a mournfulness in his voice that struck her. She'd noticed that he didn't participate in any of the fairy courts and knew he was considered among the free fae, but he didn't fit in with this crowd. Was he an outcast among his own people? She made a mental note to find a way to bring that up in some less fraught time.

Athena sat watching the camp for a while, then said, "If they know where to find this queen, and if we could convince them to take us there, all we'd need is to find Sophie and bring her there to show who the real queen is."

"And how do you propose we do that?" her sister asked.

"Singing and dancing work as currency, right?" Emily said. "I can start earning their trust that way, get them all singing some stirring songs, and soon we should have our army." In her head, she imagined the camp full of fairies marching around to "Do You Hear the People Sing?" but she knew that was likely just a fantasy. It couldn't possibly be that easy, but it was the only plan she could think of at the moment. It didn't seem like it would hurt to try, at any rate. Her only other option was waiting in this camp until someone else decided to do something.

She stood and headed toward the center of the camp. When Eamon joined her, she felt a surge of optimism. The music was wildest there, and she listened for a while before easing her way into the group of dancers. She was a professional in her world, and she'd learned a thing or two on her last visit to the Realm, so she hoped she'd do well enough to catch their attention.

She was really surprised when Eamon joined her. His stuffy professorial appearance gave the impression that he wouldn't be into dancing, but he was fae, after all, and that seemed to put music and dance in his blood.

Soon, the two of them were spinning madly in the center of a circle as a group of fae clapped in rhythm. As though reading each other's minds, the two of them came gradually to a halt, and then Emily raised her voice in song, belting like she was trying to hit the upper balcony.

Eighteen

Michael hadn't seen much of the Realm on his last visit, but he didn't think it had been this empty. Was it the particular area or was something else was going on?

"Is it always like this?" he asked.

"Like what?"

"Empty. Deserted."

"Not that I've ever seen. But the market is in progress, and there's a big holiday for the fae coming up, so there might be some kind of revels."

"So they're not all in hiding from the terrifying new queen? The fake one, I mean."

He thought he detected a trace of a smile before she answered. "I suppose that's also a possibility. Let's head for the trees over there." She pointed toward what looked like the edge of a wooded area. "I usually find small gatherings among the trees. They don't tend to like wide, open spaces. And we may as well let Beau off his leash. They don't have leash laws here, and I doubt he'll stray too far from us."

"You're sure he won't just lie down and refuse to go with us if we don't drag him?"

"Trust me. I have an idea."

"You think he'll bloodhound some fairies for us?"

"Something like that. Maybe."

They walked in silence for a few more minutes, Beau ambling just a few feet ahead of them. The silence reached a point where it became uncomfortable, so Michael said, "We haven't talked in a while. How are things with you?"

She turned to look at him, raising an eyebrow. "Really, you want to catch up now?"

"Why not? What else are we going to do while wandering aimlessly through fairyland? Or do you need to meditate?"

"Things are great with me," she said with obviously forced cheer. "My grandmother's getting worse and I may be forced to kill my mother if she doesn't get off my back and stop treating me like a teenager. My sister seems to be under a weird thrall to the Realm. And I'm going to have to make some big decisions soon about what I really owe to other people and what I can do with what may be my last chance to live my own life. And how are you? Probably just about as peachy as I am, huh?"

He winced and felt bad about nagging her about Jen. She had a lot going on without his problems. "Yeah, I see your point. On the bright side, I'm back at work and have two good arms again."

"You're better?" she asked sincerely.

"Not really one-hundred percent yet, but I count as 'well.' I need to rebuild some strength and stamina, but I'm functional now. It doesn't even hurt anymore."

"That's good."

"As for you being overwhelmed, well, if we succeed today, that'll be one less thing for you to worry about."

She turned on him. "No ifs. Don't even start thinking that way. I can understand bracing yourself for failure, but I need you to believe wholeheartedly, to want to succeed with every fiber of your being."

Taken aback, he raised his hands in mock surrender. "Sorry. I mean when. *When* we succeed. Is that better? And I do want to."

"I know," she replied softly, not quite looking directly at him.

Beau trotted ahead when they reached the edge of the woods, like he'd caught the scent of something. "This looks promising," Michael remarked.

A moment later, Beau returned to them, a squirming figure in his mouth. "Beau, no!" Sophie cried out. She pointed at the dog and firmly said, "Sit!" Kneeling beside Beau, she gently cradled the figure in her hands while saying, "Let go, Beau."

One of the small creatures that dwelt in the undergrowth of the forest sat in her palm. It was as close to the kinds of fairies seen in storybook illustrations as anything Michael had yet seen in the Realm, with clothes made of flowers, but it was hideously ugly. "My lady, I owe you my life," the fairy said, sketching an awkward bow. "Whatever I can do for you, I will. I will slay dragons for you."

Visibly fighting back a smile, Sophie said, "That won't be necessary, but I could use directions to Fiontan and Niamh's court."

"I have never been there myself, but it lies over the river, in the valley between the great peaks." He pointed beyond them, where the tops of two mountains were visible over the trees.

Sophie placed the fairy gently onto the ground. "Be well," she said. It bowed once more, and after a wary glance at Beau it scampered off into the underbrush. Once it was gone, she gave Beau a scratch behind his ears. "Good boy," she crooned.

"Did you train him to do that?" Michael asked.

She looked up at him and grinned. "You spend a lot more time with him than I do."

"I've never managed to get him to fetch anything for me. It's usually the other way around."

"I think he just has a sense for these things. Supposedly, animals' instincts are better than humans because they don't know what they're not supposed to be sensing. They just take it as it comes. Beau seems to be particularly good at it, though."

He stared off at the distant mountains. "I guess we have to walk to those mountains."

"Not now that we know where we're going. We'll need Beau's leash again." He held it out for her, and she pulled the hook down to clip it onto the dog's collar. She stood, brushing off her skirt, and held her hand out to him. "I know a shortcut."

He took her hand and waited to see what happened. When she closed her eyes, he did so, as well. She squeezed his hand to signal him, and she strode forward with her. He had the strange feeling of moving a great distance with a single step. He took a moment to be sure he was standing firmly before opening his eyes to find that they were practically at the foot of the mountains that had been so distant a mere moment ago.

"Wow, that's handy," he said with a low whistle. "Now what?"

"Now we need to find more detailed directions. Or else we can wander until we stumble upon their court. From what I've seen of these fairies, we can look for the kind of castle where you might expect to find Dracula."

"Appropriate for Halloween. Too bad we forgot our costumes."

"I can take care of the costumes. And I will, when we get there."

"Costumes?" he asked, alarmed, as they began walking, normally this time.

"You have to fit in. Haven't you ever wanted to play *Lord of the Rings*?"

"When I was in junior high, maybe."

"Don't worry. It'll just be glamour."

"No tights, though."

"Don't worry, no one you know will see you."

He didn't find that reassuring, but he had a feeling she was messing with him, so he didn't rise to the bait. When they'd walked a while longer, he thought he heard a rustling in the vegetation nearby. "Do you hear something?" he asked softly.

She turned around to scan the surrounding trees. "Maybe."

"There's no wind."

"No."

"Do we get ready for a fight?"

"Well, we kind of *want* to run into someone," she reminded him.

"Good point."

"But keep your guard up."

Beau growled, which didn't help his nerves. Something was out there, and he had no way of knowing how friendly it was or could be persuaded to be. If they were lucky, Fiontan and Niamh's sentries had caught them and would take them to their court. When being captured was a best-case scenario, it was hard to know just how vigorously to defend themselves.

Michael's hand instinctively went to the gun on his hip as the rustling sounds in the nearby trees grew stronger. "Show yourselves," Sophie called out.

About a dozen fae who looked like something out of a Robin Hood movie stepped out of the shelter of the trees. Every one of them was armed, most with bows and arrows, a few with swords. Michael wasn't sure he and Sophie could fend them off, even with Sophie's magical abilities.

"Humans!" one of the fairies said. "You have saved us some effort. We were going to cross into the other world, but you have come to us." He gestured with his sword and two of his people went to Michael and Sophie, binding their wrists with ropes.

Michael glanced at Sophie, silently asking if she was going to do anything. She gave him a reassuring nod as the fairies prodded them forward. The fact that Beau wasn't putting up a fight made him feel better. Maybe this wasn't a total disaster. She probably had a plan. He sure hoped so.

Nineteen

It turned out that rousing theater songs were just as effective with fairies as they were with audiences in the real world. There was something about these songs that stirred the heart, and soon the fairies were marching around, shaking their fists or waving scarves over their heads. When Emily was sure that they were one upturned wagon away from building a barricade, she climbed onto a bench and shouted, "Why are we letting them make us live like this?"

The singing died away as the fairies turned to look at her. She felt momentarily self-conscious, but plunged ahead, playing the character of fiery revolutionary to the hilt. "No true queen of the fae would treat her people like this," she said. "Why should she be allowed to exile us? Has any queen before treated us this way?" She didn't know the truth, but she figured the enchantresses would have known something, since their traditional role was maintaining a balance against the fae and their rulers.

A few of the fae shook their fists, and that began to rally some of the others. Emily felt a surge of encouragement. "Do you want to live like this forever, herded into hidden camps? You are the free fae! You should be running unbound, you should be with the ones you love." To emphasize this point, she reached down to pull Eamon up onto the bench with her and kissed him thoroughly. She suspected she'd have better luck if they thought she was just another human in love with a fairy than if they knew she was here for the purpose of stirring up trouble.

If she had a little fun along the way, well, that was a bonus. Kissing Eamon was like nothing else she'd experienced. His lips were cool and dry rather than warm and moist, but something about the cool sent tingles through her body. It was like making out with someone who'd just brushed his teeth with extra-minty toothpaste.

Eamon didn't seem at all shocked by her actions. Either he'd figured out what she was up to or he was enjoying himself. Possibly both. When Emily made herself surface for air, she noticed that there was also a kiss-a-thon happening in the audience. She hadn't realized how many humans there might be in the Realm. On her last visit, the humans she'd seen had been captives or slaves. Even if the captives had gone native and adjusted to their new lives, they hadn't given the impression that they were truly where they wanted to be.

But these people seemed to be there voluntarily. They'd found love among the fae and didn't appear to mind the fact that they couldn't leave. She'd spent so much time trying to get back home that she'd never considered anyone might want to stay. She supposed it depended on what they had waiting for them at home—or, more likely, what they *didn't* have.

"We must stop this!" she shouted, raising her fist in the air. "We must be free!"

"What foolishness is this?" a voice cried from within the crowd.

"The only foolishness I see is the free people of the Realm hiding in the woods," she said.

A fae woman with her arm around the waist of a human man stepped forward. "What can we do against our queen? At least here we're safe. If we act, we could all be exiled, and not all of us would survive that." She wore what looked like a Victorian party dress, and Emily realized with a shudder what would likely happen the moment this woman left the Realm.

"But it isn't your queen who's doing this. That's the problem," Emily said.

"This is the truth," Eamon added, speaking up for the first time. Emily turned to him in surprise and saw that he'd removed many of the human factors of his glamour. Now he shone silver, and she was reminded that he really was an alien being. "I have met the true queen. I served as a scribe to the last true queen. This is no queen, no royal order."

"If we can get rid of the impostor, we'll be safe, I promise," Emily said. "I can't tell you why or how I know this, but I do. We'll be okay. We just have to make a stand and stop it."

Hundreds of skeptical eyes faced her, and she was unsure what else she could do. She appreciated the risk they took in listening to her, but she didn't know a way to prove that what she said was true.

Then she got an idea. "I had a love, then she was lost," she began singing. It was the song that had won the kingdom for Sophie, the song that contained the information needed to enter the palace and win the throne, passed down for centuries by the last queen to her human descendants.

There must have been something in the song that they recognized as truth, even if they'd never heard it before. She finished the song and let it ring in the ensuing silence before saying, "You see, I know. I was there when the new queen was crowned."

"What do you propose we do?" someone in the crowd asked.

"First, we need to find the impostor. Does anyone know where she's holding court?" No one spoke up. "Who would know?"

"The ones carrying out her orders might," another fairy suggested.

"Okay, the guards, right. They should be easy enough to find."

There was a titter of uncomfortable laughter in the crowd, and someone called out, "Yes, but they don't take their prisoners there. They exile their prisoners."

"But maybe they'd lead us to the impostor if *we* took *them* prisoner." Emily thought for a moment, putting together the pieces of a plan. "We'll serve as bait, an obvious couple tainted by outside influences. We'll need some fighters lurking to grab the guards when they come for us, and then we can get them to take us to the queen. Once we know the situation, we can decide how to proceed and send a message to the rest of you. That way, we're not putting the whole group at risk. Do I have any volunteers for the raiding party?"

Emily held her breath, afraid there would be none, but several hands went up. She couldn't help but grin in relief. "Awesome!" Turning to Eamon, she said, "What do you say we go get ourselves captured again?"

Twenty

As she and Michael were marched deeper into the mountainside forest, Sophie had to wonder if perhaps they should have put up a fight. She could tell by the worried glances Michael kept throwing at her that he was wondering the same thing. Beau was the only member of their party who was perfectly content with the status quo. He trotted happily along on his leash. If he hadn't wanted to go with these fairies, they'd have had to drag him.

She studied their captors and found that she had to agree with Beau. Aside from the weapons and the ropes, they didn't seem all that menacing. They'd made no threats, had caused no harm. Their attention was more focused on their surroundings than on watching their captives for potential escape attempts. Sophie imagined that she could easily unleash her powers on them later if she needed to, but for the time being she preferred to remain incognito.

They reached a cabin that blended so well into the landscape that it looked like it had grown rather than being built. In the Realm, that was a distinct possibility. Two of the fae entered first, then the others gestured for Sophie and Michael to enter. Michael had to duck to get through the doorway.

It took a moment for Sophie's eyes to adjust to the dimmer light inside, and then she saw that this modest cabin was like Eamon's hut, which had a vast library inside. They were in the great hall of a manor house. Light came from torches set into the walls and from a massive fireplace at the end of the hall.

Michael shot Sophie a surprised look, and she remembered that he'd never seen Eamon's place, so this phenomenon was new to him. "This would come in handy in New York real estate," he muttered with a wry grin. "I don't suppose you could hook me up."

"I don't know if it would work in our world, but I could give it a shot. Wouldn't people wonder about it, though?"

"I'd settle for enlarging the bedroom and closet. Not many would see that."

"This way," one of their captors said, interrupting their conversation. He led them to a giant four-poster canopy bed whose curtains were pulled back to reveal a fairy woman lying against the pillows, her head rolling back and forth in agony.

"My goodness, she's in labor," Sophie breathed.

"So?" Michael asked.

"Fairies are immortal. They don't exactly have to repopulate. Births are incredibly rare."

"You will bring the child into the world," the leader of their captors said to Sophie.

"They kidnapped us to play midwife?" Michael asked.

"Supposedly, they can't give birth on their own. They need humans to deliver babies," Sophie said. "That's one of the reasons humans are kidnapped in folklore."

The fairy stepped forward and removed the rope from her wrists. She rubbed her arms absently as she tried to think of what to do. The closest she'd come to childbirth was watching *Call the Midwife* on television. She didn't even like holding babies. "Let's see," she hedged, trying to keep her uncertainty from showing, "I guess we need hot water and towels." They always needed hot water and towels for deliveries on television and in books, though she wasn't exactly sure why.

Michael edged closer to her. "I take it you've never delivered a baby before," he whispered.

"And you have?"

"Several, actually."

She turned to look at him in surprise. "Seriously?"

"I'm a New York cop. You may have noticed that traffic doesn't always flow quickly in our fair city, and babies usually aren't willing to wait. Whatever emergency personnel can get there in time handle the delivery."

"Do you think you could do this?"

"I don't know if it's any different for fairies, but if it's not the backseat of a cab, it'll be a step up over what I'm used to." He paused, glancing around at the waiting fairies, then said more softly, "I'm guessing this would count as a huge favor."

"Oh yeah," she said, equally softly. "This is a once-in-a-lifetime thing, even for them." She raised her voice to address the fairies. "This is your midwife," she said, resting her hand on Michael's shoulder. "He's quite experienced."

"I don't know if I'd go that far," he muttered, but she silenced him with a glare.

They removed the bonds from Michael's wrists, and he put down his coat and bag before checking on his patient. Sophie dropped Beau's leash, and the dog immediately headed to the hearth, dropped to the fire-warmed stones, and started snoring. "What do you need me to do?" she asked Michael warily.

"Sit by her head and play coach," he ordered. "I'll need that hot water and some cloths or towels eventually." Sophie forced herself to focus on the matter at hand rather than swooning over Michael taking charge of the situation.

She settled beside the woman in labor and took her hand. "It's going to be okay," she said soothingly.

"How long has she been in labor?" Michael asked, but he got blank looks in response.

"Fairies," Sophie explained. "They don't really do time."

"Oh, right. Well, are the contractions close together or far apart?"

Before anyone could answer, the woman cried out and contorted in pain. Michael noted the time on his watch as Sophie squeezed her hand and stroked her hair. When the contraction passed, Michael said, "Okay, let's take a look." As he pulled the covers away from the woman's legs, he glanced up at Sophie and said, "You know, this is easier when I've got a doctor or paramedic on the radio."

"But you know what to do, right?"

"I know the basics, but if there's anything odd, it would be nice to get some feedback or coaching."

"I'm not sure a doctor would be much help here."

"Though I'm pretty sure 'odd' is guaranteed." The woman writhed again and Michael checked his watch. "Not long now," he reassured the mother-to-be, and Sophie squeezed her hand. "This is usually when I start hearing sirens in the distance," he remarked. He took control of the room, barking commands to the other fairies, to Sophie, and to his patient.

Sophie had never seen him at work in professional mode, and now she wished she could have avoided it because it really wasn't helping her situation. Although she liked being in control, she had to admire strength in other people, and this was just adding to her already-long list of reasons to admire him.

Once things started happening, they happened quickly, and Sophie became too busy playing birth coach to notice much of what Michael was doing until she heard an unearthly high-pitched squall and turned to see Michael holding a bloody, messy, twisted little creature. He was staring at it like he'd just brought an alien into the world.

"It's too young to maintain a human glamour," Sophie told him softly.

"Then I'm going to assume it's healthy and this is what it's supposed to look like." He handed the infant over to one of the other fairies and instructed them to clean it while he dealt with the rest of the process. "To be honest, I'm just guessing here from what I've observed," he said as he worked. "Usually the paramedics take over about now. How is she?"

Sophie laid a hand on the mother's forehead. It was cool to the touch, but she didn't know if that was the normal chill of the fae or a sign of shock. The woman's eyes were closed, but her chest rose and fell. "She seems to be alive."

The leader of the fairies stepped up and moved Michael out of the way. "You have done what was needed. The birth was a success." He gestured another fairy forward with a basin of water for Michael to wash his hands. While Michael cleaned up, the fairy continued, saying, "We will now escort you back to your world."

Sophie slid off the bed and went to his side. "Actually, you can escort us to the court of Fiontan and Niamh. That's where we were headed when we were so rudely interrupted."

The leader balked. "That would not be appropriate."

"Oh, really?" Sophie asked, keeping a smile plastered on her face but adding iron to her voice. "By my calculation, you owe my friend here a life debt. A little escort to the place we were going anyway is nothing. You'd still owe him a debt, to be called in later." When the fairy hesitated, she added, "Is a new life of so little value to you? You were fortunate to have stumbled upon a human who actually has some experience in this."

The fairy was clearly not happy, but he gritted his teeth and bowed toward Sophie and Michael. "Very well, then. Do you wish to leave immediately, or do you need rest and refreshment?"

Sophie glanced toward Michael, who looked drained. "We'll take a moment, but we have our own refreshments."

She picked up both their bags and nudged Michael toward some chairs by the fire. He sank wearily into a chair, and she poured him a cup of sweet tea from her thermos. "Good work back there," she said softly. "We were lucky that you knew what you were doing."

He drained the cup and handed it back to her. "What would have happened if things had gone badly?"

She refilled the cup. "They'd have probably killed us. Or tried. I wouldn't have let them."

"You'd have introduced them to their queen?" he whispered with a smile.

"Something like that." She opened the tin of cookies and held it out to him before taking one for herself. "But I didn't have to. And now you've secured us safe passage the rest of the way."

They finished their snack and Sophie put the containers back in her bag. They gathered their belongings, woke Beau and gave him some water, and faced the leader. "We are ready to go now," Sophie said firmly, not giving him a chance to argue.

He selected two of his men and gestured them forward. "These two will escort you on your way, though I warn you that humans are not welcome in Fiontan and Niamh's court, other than as slaves."

"Oh, we're old friends," Sophie said. "We met at the queen's court. Now, if we could be going…"

They headed at a brisk pace toward the mountains. Both Michael and Sophie had to pause to put their coats on because it was considerably cooler here. Although steep, the path was relatively easy. Their guides made no effort to make conversation, and Sophie wasn't comfortable chatting with Michael in their presence.

She wasn't sure how much time had passed before they rounded a bend and saw the castle situated on a crest between two peaks. "Wow, you were right. It does look like a place Dracula would live," Michael said. "I take it Fiontan and Niamh were the Goth types at the battle where you were crowned."

"Yes, that was them."

"And I left my black nail polish at home."

"I think this is closer to the authentic variety—you know, sacking Rome and all that."

"Even more fun. You know the most interesting people."

The castle had appeared distant, but they reached it in no time. Their approach was somewhat hampered by a seemingly endless procession of fairies making their way down the road that led to the castle's drawbridge. Sophie thought this was an opportune time to create a glamour so they fit in with the crowd. She decided to make it so that Michael wouldn't see it, then also erased it from her own vision because the dark robes suited him a little too well.

"We can make it from here," she told their escorts. "You have fulfilled your duty."

They bowed, then one of them handed a small embroidered cloth to Michael. "The debt is not discharged. This is how you may call upon our master again."

Sophie was gratified that Michael merely bowed in return and resisted the urge to thank them. He tucked the cloth into his bag as they merged into the procession.

"We kind of stand out here, don't we?" he said.

"I took care of it. To them, we blend."

"Care to share how we look?"

"A lot like everyone else. No tights."

"This looks like the happening party of the year. You think Jen might be here?"

"They seem to have left the palace at the same time Jen disappeared, so it's a good place to start looking. It would be like them to decide they were the rightful rulers."

"And they're having a big party."

"Could be a coronation ball," she agreed.

"What do you do if it is them?"

"We get Jen away, break the thrall, and then I worry about challenging them."

"What if they've got her disguised?"

"I think you'll know her, regardless." Unwelcome tears welled in her eyes as she said it. How ironic that one of the things she loved about him was his pure devotion to his missing wife. She really did know how to pick attainable men.

"They're not going to be checking invitations, are they?" he asked when they'd crossed the bridge and were nearing the door.

She craned her neck and rose on tiptoes to try to see around the people ahead of them. "It doesn't look like it. No one's pausing at the door."

They passed through the doorway, went down a passageway, and emerged in a vast hall that was too large even for the castle they'd seen from the outside. Fiontan and Niamh sat on thrones at the head of the room, attended by numerous servants bringing them food and drink.

Michael clutched Sophie's arm as he scanned the crowd. "Do you see Jen?" he asked.

Twenty-One

The Realm
Later

Acting "natural" had to be the hardest thing to do, Emily thought as she and Eamon wandered through the area where they were most likely to be caught by the fake queen's guards. If you were acting, then by definition you weren't being natural. Faking "natural" required going deep into character and creating the illusion that there was nothing artificial about the situation. Maybe that's what her problem was: She hadn't done the necessary work to prepare for this role.

"What's our backstory here?" she asked Eamon.

"Backstory?"

"How we got to this point."

He turned to her, his eyes wide with alarm. "Are you having difficulty with your memory?"

"No, I'm fine. But we're supposed to be acting here, and if we aren't convincing, this plan isn't going to work. To be convincing, we have to know who we are and how we got here. Otherwise, we might as well be waving giant 'Bait!' signs." She thought for a moment, then said, "Okay, how's this? You fell in love with me from afar when you were exploring my world, and you brought me with you to show me your world."

He nodded, quite seriously, and his eyes darkened as he said, "Yes, that is what happened."

She hesitated for a moment, unsure if he was agreeing to her idea of a backstory for their roles or saying something different entirely. He looked so earnest, but then he always looked pretty earnest. It was one of his more endearing qualities. In the theater world, she didn't meet too many genuinely earnest people. And if he really meant what he said, what did it mean? This didn't seem to be about acting anymore.

She was so flustered by this train of thought that it took her a couple of tries before she could properly form words and make them come out. "So now you're showing me your world, trying to convince me to stay here forever with you."

"The impostor queen will not allow that. And your sister would find a way to kill me if I kept you forever."

Okay, so he didn't understand acting. And did that mean that what he'd said about falling in love with her was true? "It's a lie, a ruse. You don't know that the queen will keep us apart, and in this scenario the real queen isn't my sister. I'm just a normal human."

"No one would believe you were a normal human."

"Then an exceptional human, which is why you fell in love with me."

"Yes," he said, nodding, his voice soft, and his eyes sending shivers through her whole body. Yikes, he really did mean it, didn't he?

She fought to maintain the pretense that this was just about the ruse. "So if you weren't worried about my sister, and you wanted me to stay with you, what would you do?"

He thought for a moment, then waved his arm in an arc over his head. Silver sparks trailed his hand, fluttering to the ground around them in a shower of flower petals. The petals made a musical tinkling sound as they fell. It was kind of cheesy, but Emily couldn't help but be at least a little captivated by it.

"Do you have this kind of magic in your world?" he asked her.

Putting herself in character and making herself forget for a moment about her sister and the enchantresses or about stage special effects, she looked up at him with what she hoped were starry eyes. Actually, she was pretty sure her eyes were starry, and it had nothing to do with acting. "Oh, that's so wonderful," she sighed. The remaining silver sparks reflected in his eyes. Or maybe they came from his eyes. She wasn't sure. She just knew she was tilting her head and leaning toward him, and he was bending and leaning toward her, and then their lips met and she forgot about acting. Maybe it wouldn't be so bad to stay here, forever young, forever together, making beautiful music and magic.

A harsh voice shouting, "Halt by order of the queen!" ruined the moment and reminded Emily why they were there. She opened her eyes and moved away from Eamon to find that they were surrounded by guards.

Remembering to play her role, Emily said breathlessly, "The queen? What's this about?" She forced herself not to look toward the nearby trees where their allies lurked.

"I have no business with the queen," Eamon said, also playing along. "Why does the queen care what I do?"

"The queen is purifying the Realm. Those who are tainted must be cast out," the guard said, gesturing at them with his spear.

Any day now, Emily thought, and a split second later the free fae burst from their hiding places and surrounded them. The enchantresses emerged and used their magic to immobilize the guards. The free fae confiscated their weapons.

"Now, let's have a little chat," Amelia said. "You speak on behalf of the queen. Have you seen this queen?"

"Only from a distance," one of the guards said with great reluctance, like the words were being pulled from him.

"Do you know where her palace is?" Amelia asked.

He seemed to fight with every fiber of his being until at last he said with a tone of defeat, "Yes."

"Good. You will take us there."

He fought even harder before he began walking forward, slowly and reluctantly, along with his colleagues. "Well?" Amelia asked her allies when they didn't immediately fall into step.

"We will take one of them," one of the free fae said. "He may be useful." Amelia nodded and did something that must have released his compulsion. The free fairy took him away. The rest of the party followed the other captives.

Emily kept her focus ahead of her. She suddenly felt very self-conscious with Eamon. She knew she liked him and found him attractive. She'd known he had some kind of fondness for her. But that little scene they'd played had felt a little too real for comfort, and she still couldn't tell if he'd meant the things he'd said. She hadn't been sure his kind even felt love the way humans did. Then again, he wasn't an ordinary fairy. He'd read far too many human books, including, as she recalled, a number of paperback romance novels that had been left behind on park benches. Had he figured out the acting thing just in time, or had he been telling her the truth?

Not that it mattered, she told herself. They lived in different worlds, and while there was some appeal to the idea of remaining young and pretty forever, she had a life in her world she had no interest in giving up. The Realm was fun in small doses, but she thought it would get boring after a while, and she'd seen what became of humans who went native in the Realm. It wasn't for her, and even if she could get Sophie to let her in for brief visits, what kind of future would she have with a man who never changed, even as she aged?

No, best to get her mind off that particular track and focus on the task at hand: Getting the impostor off the throne so Sophie could take care of things.

Twenty-Two

Fiontan and Niamh's Hall
Soon Afterward

Michael had to admit that these surroundings were closer to what he'd expected of the fairy world than anything else he'd experienced thus far, based on the cramming on fairy tales he'd done after his last adventure. He could imagine the evil stepmother queen reigning over this assembly while Sleeping Beauty slept in one tower and Rapunzel was imprisoned in another. He hoped Sophie knew what she was doing in magically disguising them because to him they stood out like the proverbial sore thumb.

He was used to being one of the taller people in any group, so it was disconcerting to be at eye level with or shorter than most of the people in this assembly. Even without a magical disguise, Jen would fit right into this crowd. Like so many of these women, she was tall and had bright hair. Unfortunately, that made it difficult to spot her, if she even was here. The pointy, veiled hats many of the women wore didn't help matters. As he studied the crowd, he reflected that he'd been lucky she hadn't insisted on something like this bash for their wedding reception.

"Can you spot the humans in a bunch like this?" he murmured to Sophie. "That would probably narrow it down."

"Not without drawing attention. An enchantress wouldn't be welcome, and if I use much fairy magic, it would give away who I am."

She rose on her tiptoes to scan the crowd. "She's your wife—what do you think she'd be doing in a place like this?"

Reluctantly, he said, "She'd be dancing. But that doesn't narrow it down much." Almost everyone was dancing—not gyrating to the music or waltzing, but moving in intricate patterns of rows or circles, kind of like square dancing or the Virginia reel they used to do in PE class.

"Then we dance," Sophie said. "The benefit of this kind of dance is that you end up running into just about everyone along the way."

"That's fine for you," he protested. "You're a professional. If you want to give away the fact that I'm a clumsy human, putting me on a dance floor is a good start."

"Oh, this isn't really dancing. All you have to do is follow the pattern, and that's easy enough to figure out."

He wasn't so sure about that. Everyone was flitting about gracefully. He'd have happily stayed with Beau, who'd flopped against the wall next to the bags they'd set down and closed his eyes, but Sophie grabbed his hand and dragged him to the end of a row of couples.

The dance consisted mostly of moving forward and backward. Then they moved diagonally, switching partners, and he found himself facing a svelte woman whose hair shimmered with a greenish tint. When he looked at her out of the corner of his eye, he thought her skin had a similar tint, with the texture of fine scales.

They changed partners again, and now he saw what Sophie meant about getting to investigate everyone in the room. He gradually moved down the line, but none of the women he danced with were his wife. At the end of the row, he faced Sophie again. "No luck," he mouthed to her. She nodded and guided him to the adjacent pattern.

The music was lively enough that he was almost getting into it—not that he planned to take this up as a hobby when he got home unless Jen needed it to stay happy in the real world, and not that he'd ever admit to his colleagues that he'd done anything like this. Just thinking about Mari ever hearing about it made him shudder.

It took him a moment or two to figure out the pattern of this dance, but he caught on before he had to leave Sophie for his next partner. Toward the end of the line, he thought he spotted a willowy redhead, and he had to force himself to stay with the pattern until he reached her rather than rushing forward. He mentally practiced all the suave "Fancy meeting you here" lines he could give, but by the time he neared her, he was sweating and shaking like a kid at his first school dance. When at last she became his partner, he saw immediately that it wasn't Jen. He wasn't even sure why he'd thought she might be. His disappointment was so bitter that he had to force himself to carry through instead of leaving her alone on the dance floor.

At the end of this dance, he pulled Sophie to the edge of the hall. "I'm not sure she's here," he said. "If she were, she'd definitely be dancing."

Sophie barely seemed to be listening to him. She kept her eyes focused on the crowd, and a slight crease had formed between her eyebrows. On Sophie, that was an indication of serious anxiety.

"What's wrong?" he asked.

She turned to look at him like she'd almost forgotten he was there. "I was wondering where this court came from. Weren't they more or less wiped out in that battle? We didn't see this many people leaving my palace. And not everyone is garbed appropriately. Some of this is the room's glamour. I think they're recruiting to rebuild their court."

"Do you think this is the false queen?"

"Apparently they're not known for loving humans, so I could see them purging the Realm. But I don't think they'd be playing supreme ruler in their own court. Everyone knows they didn't win the throne, and it would be obvious that nothing has really changed for them."

"So, maybe a challenger, but not the impostor?"

"I don't know." As though by conscious effort, she shed that concern. "But that's not why we're here."

She started to drag him back to the dance floor, but he resisted, shaking his head. "I need to catch my breath." They made their way back to the sleeping Beau, where she retrieved tea and snacks from her bag. Beau woke up enough to accept a dog biscuit from Michael's bag and a dish of water.

While Michael drank his tea, he watched the constantly flowing crowd. The more he saw, the more every woman seemed to morph into Jen, to the point he was afraid he might not even recognize the real one if he came face-to-face with her.

The white-haired queen rose from her throne and moved down the dais steps. It reminded Michael of the image he'd seen in Sophie's palace. "Could she recognize us?" he asked.

"I think I've got us under a good enough glamour to fool her," Sophie said, but he noticed that she stayed next to the wall instead of moving back among the dancers, even though they'd finished their snack. Michael realized he was holding his breath to see what the woman would do.

He didn't get a chance to find out.

Every door in the hall and on the galleries above flew open suddenly with a loud bang, perfectly in sync, so that the sound of the slam surrounded them. Light flooded into the hall through the doors, so bright that it had to be enhanced. The music continued for a few bars longer before it petered out, leaving the hall in stark silence.

The ball's attendees shaded their eyes against the harsh glare and peered at the doors. The rulers returned quickly to their thrones, as though staking their claims. The king was the first to break the silence. "Who dares intrude on our revels?" he boomed.

Silhouettes of armed men appeared in each of the doorways. The silhouettes solidified into soldiers who came marching in a seemingly unending stream into the room. Archers surrounded the hall on the gallery, and men with spears and swords blocked the doors. One man with a brightly colored feathered crest on his Roman-style helmet marched straight up to the dais. He stood tall and proud, not so much as bowing his head toward the two fairies seated on the thrones.

"By order of the queen, you are ordered to report to her palace to pledge fealty," the soldier said.

"I'll do no such thing," the ruling woman snapped. The soldier raised a hand and a rain of arrows fell from the gallery, narrowly missing the thrones, like a knife-throwing circus act.

"You will, you and all your court. Your loyalty is to the queen now. There is no need of courts."

"I think this is our cue to get out of here," Sophie whispered in Michael's ear. He glanced down to see that she had both their bags and coats. She handed him his. "We don't want to get caught up in this, so I think we need to be elsewhere, fast."

"You can do that?"

"I think so. We saw Jen leaving with Fiontan and Niamh, so she's very likely here, and once everyone else is gone, we'll have a chance to search."

The soldiers were already rounding up the guests. The rulers put up a fight. The result was the kind of chaos that made a good diversion. Unable to believe what he was saying, Michael said, "But if we go with them, we'll find this impostor queen."

"That's not my priority. We've already had this argument, and as you'll recall, I won. We're going to find Jen, and we can't do that while we're captives, so we'd better get out of here while we still can."

She took his arm and pulled him toward what looked like a servants' entrance, one of the few places where there were no soldiers. He didn't resist at first because his heart was in total agreement with her. He didn't like the idea of being anyone's captive, and he wanted more than anything to find Jen.

But his head fought back. Hating himself for it, he said, "We've got to stop that impostor. This is too big a chance for us. There's no guarantee that we'd find or save Jen if we got away, but if we stop the impostor, that makes Jen a little safer, wherever she is, because she won't just be cast out. We still have a little time."

She looked up at him, regarding him like she was reading his soul. "Are you sure?"

"No," he admitted, "but I don't think I could live with myself if we didn't do this. The whole Realm's at stake, and possibly even our world—there's that Hunt thing. It's all bigger than my one problem."

She watched him a while longer before nodding. "Okay." With a smile, she added, "And if it makes you feel better, this kind of sacrifice is exactly the sort of thing that might count toward winning her freedom."

"See, there you go," he said with a grin of his own that he had to force. "You know I'm right."

Knowing he was right didn't make it any easier to let the soldiers herd them into the group being driven out of the castle.

Twenty-Three

Their captive guide slowed his pace, and the free fairy escorting him prodded him in the back. "Keep going," he ordered.

"We're almost there," the captive shot back. "Can't you see that the trees are thinning? We're almost out of the forest and on the plain."

"So?" Emily asked.

"The plain is where the palace is."

"There is no palace on the Great Plain," Eamon said.

"You just couldn't see it because it was hidden until the new queen won her throne," the captive argued.

"I was a scribe in the palace in the days of the last queen," Eamon said, his voice mild, with no hint of argument in it. "The palace was not on the Great Plain. Are you sure you have the right palace?"

The captive faltered momentarily, shook his head, and said, "It is where the queen is."

With a sly smile, Eamon asked, "Are you sure you have the right queen?"

One of the free fae who'd gone ahead gestured to them. "It's here! The palace!"

"Really?" Emily said, rather surprised.

"We were expecting to find a palace," Athena reassured her.

They reached the end of the tree line and found themselves on a rise overlooking a vast plain. On the plain sat a fairy-tale castle straight out of Disneyworld, all gleaming spires and parapets. Surrounding the castle appeared to be most of the population of the Realm, gathered in an epic campout. Brightly colored pavilions with pennants streaming from their peaks were scattered around the field, with thousands of people among them.

From a distance, it looked festive. The sound of sprightly music carried up to their vantage point, and there were people dancing, as usually happened when the fae gathered. But Emily noticed the glint of armor on men who rode the perimeter of the gathering, and she doubted they were there to protect the attendees.

"We will send back for our forces," the free fae leader said. He took three long strides, and then he suddenly seemed to be a hundred yards away. Another step, and he vanished into the distance.

"What's that?" Amelia called out, and Emily turned back to look where Amelia was pointing on the plain. It looked like a dark snake was winding its way down a distant hill and heading toward the castle. A moment later, it was much closer and it became clear that it was a procession of people.

"It appears to be Niall and Orla's court," Eamon said.

"You can see that far?" Emily asked.

He turned to her. "Of course."

"Impressive. I don't suppose you have X-ray vision, too?"

"Alas, I am not capable of seeing through solid objects," he said, sounding quite serious, but she thought his eyes might be twinkling. "My distance vision, however, is excellent."

As the procession drew closer, Emily could make out more details, and she could spot the tuxedos on the men. When they reached the edge of the encampment, guards guided them into place and widened the perimeter to surround them.

"They must be bringing in the courts to pay fealty to the fake queen," Eamon remarked.

"The queen is not fake!" their captive insisted.

"Yes, she is," Emily said. "I've been to the real palace, and this isn't it."

A cloud of dust rose on the outside of the camp, swirling in the air and circling the gathering. It looked like horses running down a dirt road, but the plain didn't seem all that dusty. When the head of the dust cloud faced them, Emily caught a glimpse of red eyes and flaming hooves. "That is the Hunt," Eamon said, tension in his voice.

"That's what they're going to unleash on our world?"

"Only if they're successful," Amelia said firmly, "and we are here to stop them."

"We need to find a way inside that perimeter," Athena said.

"Getting *in* doesn't seem to be the problem," Emily said as she watched the glint of armor and weaponry circling the crowd in the wake of the Hunt. "They seem a lot more concerned about anyone getting *out*."

"Still, we don't want to be conspicuous as we enter," Athena said. "We aren't likely to be successful if it's obvious that we're here to stop the impostor, and a party as small as ours that's not being escorted by guards would stand out."

"And if we march in with our army, that might be a little obvious," Emily said, nodding in agreement.

"There's another procession coming," Eamon said.

Emily couldn't see anything, not even the dark snake, for several minutes. Finally, she saw something that was more of a mass. The guards herding these people would probably have had more luck with cats. At the center of the group was a statuesque redheaded woman. "Isn't that the woman who made Sophie take the throne?" Emily asked.

"Yes, it's Tallulah," Eamon said with a nod. "I cannot imagine that she would come willingly. If the free fae had anything resembling a queen, it would be Tallulah."

Tallulah's people vexed the guards by swarming around them and then melting into the gathered crowd. The guards gave up herding them and focused on Tallulah. They didn't bring her to any of the camps, instead escorting her into the castle itself. Emily hadn't noticed if Orla and Niall had received similar treatment, but Tallulah was so tall and her hair was so bright that she was easy to track.

"Something's coming!" one of their free fae allies called out in a whisper, and they took cover behind trees. They were just in time as another great procession suddenly appeared out of the distance and marched right past them.

The medieval attire of this group told Emily that this was likely Fiontan and Niamh's court. The first time she'd seen them, their procession had struck fear into the hearts of the free fae. Now, though, they were captives. Their court seemed larger than Emily remembered. She'd thought that most of the courts had been decimated in the recent war for the throne, but this court must have gained some adherents. Perhaps the fae had seen them as the best bet for standing up to this terrifying new queen. If so, they had miscalculated.

Then Emily noticed a pair of figures that didn't fit: a tall, dark-haired human man and a small woman with strawberry blond hair. With them was a red-and-white bulldog on a leash. Emily barely stopped herself from calling out, "Beau!" Instead, she tugged on Eamon's arm and pointed. "It's Sophie and Michael, and they've got my dog. He's okay!"

"Joining them would be a good way to get into the castle area," Amelia suggested.

"And be taken prisoner," Emily pointed out.

"Only if we let that happen. And we won't. Come on."

Amelia and her sister blended seamlessly into the procession. Emily glanced at the free fae leader, who shrugged and said, "I will wait for the army, and we will await your signal."

"Okay, then," Emily said. "Are you up for this?" she asked Eamon.

"Always."

They slipped through the trees until she spotted Sophie again, then fell into step beside her. "Why is it that every time I run into you in the Realm, you've managed to get yourself captured?" Emily asked.

Her sister's surprised reaction made Emily wish she'd thought to have her camera ready. It wasn't a reaction she got to see very often.

Twenty-Four

Sophie nearly lost her footing when she turned to see her sister. "Emily? What are you doing here?" she hissed.

"We thought you'd been taken by those Hunt groupies, and you had my dog with you, so we came to rescue you. But then we got captured by the guards and rescued by the free fae, and then I talked them into resisting the impostor, we captured one of the queen's guards, and got him to take us to the fake palace. While some of our people are bringing our army here, we're infiltrating the crowd around the palace. What've you been up to?"

"We weren't taken. We simply chose that as an opportune moment to head into the Realm," Sophie said as she tried to parse the flood of information her sister had just relayed. "We're perfectly okay and have everything under control."

"And yet you appear to be a prisoner."

Sophie couldn't resist raising an eyebrow. "At this moment, so do you. We came along as a way of finding the fake palace. What have you seen here so far?"

"They seem to be gathering the whole Realm. We've seen a couple of courts marched in."

"They must be planning to present the fake queen publicly. But why bring the rulers who were present when I took the throne? They'd be able to point out the impostor."

"They seem to be taking the rulers somewhere else when they arrive."

"That makes sense," Sophie said with a nod. Emily caught her eye and tilted her head ever so slightly toward Michael. Sophie shook her head, and Emily sighed. Michael wasn't looking too good, and Sophie was worried that he was regretting his decision. It had already been a long night, and she suspected he wasn't quite as recovered as he claimed. They might have had Jen home by now if they'd stayed behind at Fiontan's castle.

They left the tree line and followed a winding path down the slope to the plain. Michael slipped on some loose rocks, and Sophie instinctively reached out to catch him, holding his arm to steady him. "I stand out like a sore thumb around all these people with fairy grace," he said ruefully.

"Just be careful. We won't get far if you break an ankle."

He wasn't looking at her, though. He stumbled again because he was staring into the distance rather than watching his footing. "What the heck is that?" he asked, pointing.

Sophie looked where he'd indicated to see a dervish of wind, sand, flame, and glowing red eyes approaching. "That is the Hunt," Eamon said.

"They seem to be working security for this gig," Emily added. "And maybe this is the staging area for whatever they have planned when the queen gives them the go-ahead."

"And I thought their groupies were bad," Michael said with a grimace. "We *really* need to stop this." He directed the last sentence at Sophie with a meaningful look, as if to make it clear that he knew he'd made the right decision.

The Hunt passed, and now they approached a phalanx of armored guards whose ranks parted to allow the procession to enter the grounds. Guards guided their group to one of the last empty spots. Ahead of them, Sophie noticed that Fiontan and Niamh were being escorted away, and she made a snap decision.

"Y'all stay out here and see what you can learn," she said to Emily as she handed over Beau's leash. "We'll see if we can find where they're stashing the rulers. The rulers know me, so if I can get them to say something about the impostor, that might help."

Before Emily could protest, Sophie took Michael's arm and said, "Come on." As they walked, she changed their glamour so that they looked like another pair of guards in the party. That allowed them to enter the castle unchallenged.

She'd expected them to head into the dungeons, but instead they went up a long spiral staircase into what appeared to be the tallest tower. At the top, the leader of the guards put on heavy gauntlets before unlocking a cell door. Another guard shoved Fiontan and Niamh inside. They shouted protests as the guard hurriedly relocked the door and stepped away with a sigh of great relief. He peeled off the gauntlets as he and his colleagues moved toward the stairs. Sophie quickly moved to stand on one side of the cell door. She caught Michael's eye, and he stepped into place on the other side. The guards didn't quibble one bit about leaving them to stand watch.

"An iron cage. They're serious," Sophie murmured.

"No wonder they wanted out of here," Michael replied, his voice barely audible.

Sophie mentally counted until she reached the number of steps she'd noted on the way up before she dropped their guard glamours and turned to look at the lock. She'd become good at unlocking doors with her enchantress powers, but this thing refused to budge.

"No luck?" Michael asked, watching her struggle.

"None. It seems to require an enchanted key. Sorry about that," she called into the cell. It was hard to tell in the darkness how many prisoners there were, as they all crowded as far away as they could get from the iron holding them prisoner. She conjured a ball of light at the same time Michael switched on a flashlight.

She recognized Niamh and Fiontan, and she assumed the couple in 1930s attire was Niall and Orla, based on Emily's description. There were a couple dressed in the flounces of the

Georgian period and a pair right out of a Jane Austen movie. And then there was Tallulah.

"There you are, little one," Tallulah said with a smug smile. She moved forward—not as far as the bars, but much farther than any of the others.

"I take it you were expecting me," Sophie said. By this time, she knew better than to be at all surprised by anything her former mentor said.

"I hoped you might do your duty."

Sophie resisted the urge to roll her eyes. Instead, she addressed all the occupants of the cell. "Most of you know that any queen being crowned here is an impostor because you saw me take the throne and the crown and bring the real palace back to life. Summer returned to the Realm when I wore the crown. If you, as the leaders of your courts, refuse to bend the knee to an impostor, that may prevent any false coronation."

"You are willing to declare yourself in front of the Realm?" Tallulah asked, and Sophie knew she was being tested.

"I'm the rightful queen, aren't I?"

"I don't see a crown," Niall remarked from back in the cell. "You could be any human girl with a trace of fae blood. Look at you, standing so close to iron."

"I'm also part enchantress," Sophie argued. To be honest, the iron did make her a little uncomfortable, but it was so pervasive in modern life that she was used to the feeling. It just wasn't the poison for her that it was for a full-blood fae. She turned to Tallulah. "You know who I am. You practically forced me into this."

"I do know who you are, but I also know that the masses will require some proof before they will rise up against an impostor. You will need your crown."

A shiver went down Sophie's spine as she realized what was likely going on. "No, I don't think so," she said softly, shaking her head. "That's what they want. This isn't about crowning a fake queen. It's a trap to take the crown. No other queen can be crowned while the crown is safe. But the moment I get that crown in a position where it can be taken from me, that makes it possible for someone else to be crowned legitimately."

"If you're the true queen, you'd be able to defend the crown," Orla commented.

"Bringing that crown here would be the dumbest move since someone decided to go alone to check out that noise in the basement," Sophie argued. "It's a trap with a giant sign with neon letters blinking 'trap, trap, trap' at me. Oh, honey, do you really think I'm that stupid?"

Tallulah took another step closer to the iron bars. "You can't defend a crown you refuse to wear, and if you won't defend your crown, perhaps you don't deserve to wear it. You can't expect your nobles to recognize your rule and stand up against an impostor if you aren't willing to show yourself to be the true queen. The crown will make it very clear who is the rightful queen."

Sophie glared at Tallulah. "Seriously, you're not going to back me unless I bring the very thing everyone wants to get their hands on right into the place where someone's scheming to get it?"

"I trust your ingenuity, little one." With that, Tallulah returned to the shadows at the back of the cell.

Sophie stood there for a moment, clenching and unclenching her fists. Every instinct she had said that this was a very, very bad idea, but she didn't see any other way out. Tallulah was right; she couldn't expect the entire Realm to bend the knee to her and turn away from an impostor just on her word.

In frustration, she adjusted the dampening glamour she'd been using to hide her true nature and let her power shine. "How about this? Does this convince you?"

A few gasps from the shadows rewarded her, but Tallulah's voice said, "The crown will show the difference between the true queen and the impostor. An impostor will not be able to wear the true crown, and you must have the true crown to show that the fake is truly fake."

Sophie whirled away from the cell and headed down the stairs. A soft clumping sound on the steps behind her told her that Michael was trying to catch up with her. "I don't want to hear a single 'I told you so,'" she warned him.

"Neither of us knew the situation at the time," he said diplomatically. "What are you going to do?"

"I guess I have to go get my crown," she snapped. "Getting out of here may be the hard part. Otherwise, I can get to the real palace easily, and now that I know where this palace is, I should be able to get back. Just tell the others what's up, okay?"

He caught her wrist. "Wait a second, you aren't going to do this alone, are you? Weren't you just saying it's a trap?"

"How much help do you really think you'll be?" she asked, then instantly regretted her spiteful tone.

"I'm another pair of eyes and ears. I'm a third son. I'm now apparently some kind of wise person." He patted his bag. "And there's someone out there who still owes me a big favor. At the very least, I'm experienced cannon fodder."

That made her smile in spite of herself. To tell the truth, she wanted him along, for all the wrong reasons. It would be one last chance to spend one-on-one time with him before he was reunited with his wife, and although she was fairly certain she could handle whatever came her way, she'd learned that it was nice not to have to go it alone. But those weren't good reasons for dragging him into the kind of danger she knew she'd face. Just getting away from this castle could be deadly.

And so, reluctantly, as soon as they reached the bottom of the stairs, she adjusted her glamour to make herself look like a guard once more and lost herself in the crowd.

Twenty-Five

Emily glanced around, wondering how her sister had disappeared so quickly. Beau strained at his leash for a moment and grunted once, but then he came back to Emily and flopped down at her feet. "Oh well, at least she has Michael with her," she muttered.

"I believe she gave them a glamour. That is why you don't see them," Eamon said.

"And that sounds like a good plan for us," Amelia said. "What do you think would be least obtrusive here, Eamon?"

"Something not human. The impostor doesn't seem to care for humans in the Realm."

"In that case, perhaps it would be best if the glamour came from you. Our work might show as human magic."

"It would," he said with a nod. He held his arms to his side, palms facing forward. After a moment, he dropped his arms.

"I don't see anything different," Emily said, investigating her own hands and squinting at the others.

"I thought it best that we still be able to recognize each other," Eamon said. "The glamour will work only on the fae. Other than myself, of course."

"Now what's the plan?" Emily asked.

"We need information," Athena said. "We don't have any idea who this queen is or if she has any agenda other than taking the throne."

"Isn't putting herself out there like this a risky move?" Emily asked. "I mean, when Sophie took the throne, there were practically fireworks. You could tell. Everything changed."

"That would be easy enough to fake," Athena said.

"Yeah, but why hasn't anyone done it before now? The throne's been empty for centuries."

"I'm not sure anyone would have believed it if there had not already been reports of a new queen being crowned," Eamon said. "We can feel the change in the Realm, so someone who steps forward to take credit for that may be credible. Before, we knew the Realm was still dying."

"And this dog-and-pony show" —Emily gestured at the festive gathering around them — "is their way of sealing the deal."

"We do need more information," Amelia said. "Perhaps we should split up, move through the crowd, and see what we can learn by listening. What do the fae think of these developments? Are any of them here willingly? Do they want a queen? Do they plan to support her? Is there any real opposition?"

"So, you two and us, meet back here in an hour?" Emily checked her phone. "I have three in the morning, New York time. Wow, and I'm not even sleepy. But we'd better get back to our world before the Friday-night show. One mysterious disappearance may have helped make me famous. I'm not sure I could get away with two."

Amelia checked the diamond-encrusted gold watch on her wrist. "My watch says the same as yours. We will meet you back here at four."

As the enchantresses moved away, Emily knelt and gave Beau a scratch behind the ears. "Come on, buddy, wake up. Time to go." The look he gave her when he opened his eyes almost made her feel guilty for interrupting his rest. With a deep grunt, he pushed himself to his feet, gave himself a shake, and looked back over his shoulder as though to ask her what the holdup was.

She let the dog lead the way. Sophie had said he had good instincts about this sort of thing. He wasn't the only dog at this gathering, so he didn't make them stand out. The other dogs were strangely uninterested in him, not that Emily minded. Breaking up a fairy dogfight wasn't what she had planned for this mission.

"You know, I'm not sure that performing *Les Mis* for this crowd will make much of an impact," she remarked to Eamon. "I'd need a megaphone." She looked up at the palace and added, "But that balcony would be perfect for doing *Evita*. I bet that's what they have planned. They might crown the queen and put her on the throne inside—or pretend that's what's going on—and then bring her out on that balcony to show off to the masses. Boom, instant credibility in a Buckingham Palace photo-op."

"I have read the *Playbill* for *Evita*," Eamon said with a solemn nod. "That does seem to be an appropriate scenario."

From what Emily could tell of the crowd, she didn't get the sense that most of these people were unhappy about being there. As with any gathering of more than two fairies, a massive party had broken out. There was music and dancing, and even if they'd been marched here at spear-point, they were having a good time now.

They approached a circle of dancers, and Emily handed Beau's leash and her bag to Eamon. "Back in a sec," she told him over her shoulder as she moved toward the dancers. It was easy enough to slip into the circle and join them. They treated her as one of their own. She took that to mean that her glamour was working and her dancing skills were up to fae standards.

The dancers stopped, laughing, when the music ended. "What do you think's going on here?" Emily asked the dancer next to her.

"You don't know, either?" the fairy woman asked, her brilliant green eyes narrowing.

"I just know we were marched here, but it seems odd to force us to attend a revel."

The woman laughed in a way that reminded Emily of church bells. "It does seem that an invitation should have sufficed." She gestured at the palace. "I suppose it has something to do with the lost palace being found again. The Realm has come back to life, and we should all celebrate."

"Yes, that is worthy of celebration," Emily said, struggling to keep a straight face. She really should have taken the time to develop a character for this escapade. That would have made it easier to be sincere and in the moment. "But doesn't it seem strange that such an obvious palace remained lost for so long?"

"Perhaps it was hidden by enchantment until the true queen was drawn to her throne."

"Perhaps. Let's just hope she provides a feast appropriate to the occasion."

Emily made her way back to Eamon. "It sounds like you were right," she reported. "They're just assuming that everything's okay because the Realm came back to life. So Sophie's really going to have to come up with something good."

She jumped at the sound of not-too-distant thunder. Did the Realm have storms? If so, all these people out here were in big trouble. For a moment, she wondered if someone had just royally pissed Sophie off, but then she saw the approaching dust cloud that signaled the arrival of the Hunt. She unconsciously reached for Eamon as Beau growled and backed up against their legs.

This close, she could see more detail, and it was even more terrifying. The cloud wasn't actually dust. It seemed to be made up of hellfire smoke that glowed with a reddish haze. The smoke formed shapes of horses with fiery manes and tails and eyes of glowing embers. At the horses' feet ran doglike beasts, also with glowing eyes. The riders on the horses had stag horns on what she hoped were helmets, but which she feared might be their actual heads. Instead of glowing, their eyes looked like black holes that bored into the dark heart of the universe.

Something made a whining, keening sound, and she thought at first it might be Beau, but then realized was herself. She was utterly paralyzed, unable to run away, speak, or move.

When the smoky hell cloud passed, it was as though a great weight lifted. She almost felt that she would have floated into the sky if she hadn't been holding on to Eamon. A glance at the nearby fae showed that they seemed to have had a similar reaction. They were all moving slowly, as though they were waking from a dream. The crowd was utterly silent for several minutes before some musician played a tentative chord and others gradually joined in the song. Another moment later, the dancing resumed, like nothing had happened.

"Wow, that was intense," Emily said when she was sure she had the breath to talk.

Even Eamon looked a little pale and shaken. "Yes," he agreed in a weak whisper.

"I'm guessing that would be reason number one that we have to stop this impostor. This kind of thing isn't good for the people of the Realm, and we definitely don't want to unleash them on my world."

They went back to walking through the crowd. Emily kept her grip on Eamon's arm. She wasn't sure what protection he might be against the likes of the Hunt, but his presence was reassuring. She was looking around for the next group they might be able to infiltrate and question when a guard appeared in their path.

"What are you doing here?" he demanded.

Twenty-Six

It only took Michael a second to realize that Sophie was gone and one more second to grab his clover keychain so that he could see past glamour and spot that she'd disguised herself as a guard. She was moving quickly, but he had longer legs, so he caught up to her easily and grabbed her elbow. "Just what do you think you're doing?" he asked.

He got the impression from the look in her eyes that she'd forgotten for a moment his ability to see through magical disguises, but she recovered quickly. "You know exactly what I'm doing."

"I'm not letting you do it alone."

"I can move more quickly without you."

He tilted his head to the side, regarding her skeptically. "Really? I don't recall slowing you down much. I've been pretty useful so far, and can you afford to leave a third son behind when going on a quest in fairyland?"

"I never should have told you about that," she said with a sigh. She resumed walking, but since she didn't try to ditch him again, he figured that meant she was okay with him joining her.

They made it out of the castle and through the crowd. As they neared the perimeter of the encampment, everything went silent. The silence was followed by the sound of thunder that soon sounded more like hoofbeats from hell. "The Hunt must be making their rounds," he said, forcing his voice to sound more calm than he felt.

"Turn around, quickly. Don't look at them," she said, her voice so taut with urgency that he didn't even think about questioning her. Once they'd both turned their backs, she explained, "I'm not sure our glamour would work on them, and the last thing I need right now is to be outed."

When the thunderous sound had passed, along with the ensuing total silence, they turned back around. Sophie and Michael hurried forward while everyone else was still regathering their wits.

The guards must have assumed that the passage of the Hunt had served to maintain the perimeter for the moment, for there was a big enough gap to slip through, and soon they were on the path leading up to the forest.

Both of them paused to catch their breath. "This queen is obviously bad news, if those are her henchmen," he said.

"Oh, I think they may come in handy. I'll have to bend them to my will." He wouldn't have been entirely surprised if she'd been serious, but he caught the faint twitch of her lips that told him she was joking.

"It would take you about half an hour before they were wearing flowers and running around doing good deeds."

"I don't know. They're pretty nasty. It might take a whole hour." She held her hand out to him. "Ready?"

He took her hand and braced himself for a journey. "Ready."

They stepped forward together, arriving outside Sophie's palace. It was still veiled with the illusion of vines. To him, nothing looked different, but he glanced at Sophie to see her staring quizzically at it. "What's wrong?" he asked.

"I don't know if 'wrong' is quite the right word. That barrier spell seems to be gone, which should make things easier because we can get to the crown without climbing all those stairs."

"Maybe your sleeping spell was stronger than you realized and whoever cast the spell is still out," he suggested.

"Or they want to make sure I get the crown out of here, which just proves that I'm right about this whole thing being a trap." She moved forward, pulling him with her by the hand he'd forgotten she still held. He caught up to her quickly. After about three strides, she dropped his hand. "Oh, sorry about that," she said. "I didn't mean to drag you around."

"Don't tell me you got me confused with Beau."

"Of course not. You're much taller."

"And I don't snore nearly as much."

She quickened her pace enough that he had to lengthen his stride to keep up with her. He'd never figured out how a woman nearly a foot shorter than he was could outwalk him so easily, even when he was more or less in good health. His partner Mari was a tall woman and a fast walker, yet he never found himself lagging behind her.

While he was contemplating this, they reached the main doors to the throne room, and Sophie threw them open with a casual gesture without breaking stride. The throne room was as deserted as it had been on their last visit, and Sophie blew through it on her way to the dais.

She stopped just in front of the throne and stared at it for a long while, her hands on her hips like she was challenging or scolding it. Finally, with a deep sigh, she made a gesture that removed the shimmering dome that covered the crown. She picked up the crown and held it for a moment.

"Are you sure about this?" Michael asked softly.

She turned to look at him as though she'd forgotten he was there. "No," she admitted. "Do you have any better ideas?" She sank onto the throne the way she might collapse on the sofa at the end of a long day, almost as if she was unaware of what it was.

Even if she didn't realize it, the throne seemed to. The changes were subtle—the silver shone brighter, the light in the room was stronger, and Sophie herself had a radiance about her. If he looked at her out of the corner of his eye, she appeared to be wearing royal robes, and she had the image of a crown resting on her head although she held the actual crown on her lap.

She must not have noticed these changes or his reaction to them, for she just kept talking, apparently thinking aloud. "It's got to be a trap. They need the real crown for credibility, but they can't get their hands on it while it's still here."

"Would anyone else be able to wear it, even if you brought it there?"

With a wicked grin, she asked, "Care to find out?" Then she shook her head. "I don't think so. The throne literally ejected Maeve when she tried to take it. I wouldn't want to be the impostor who dared to put on this crown. It might even be fatal."

Figuring that if she was going to rest, so could he, Michael sat on the top step of the dais, at her feet, and turned to look up at her. "Then what's the point of bringing a crown there that would only point out the fraud in an extremely unpleasant way?"

She lifted the crown, holding it against the light, and stared at it for a while. "I think they might want to win it from me—like if they take it from me in some kind of challenge or battle, it becomes theirs."

"No figuring out and following an impossible riddle and then using your own blood to prove your worth?"

"That was to pick up an unclaimed crown. I don't know if rightful inheritance comes into play after that."

"If she had to constantly be on guard against others trying to challenge her, no wonder your ancestor retired to marry an enchanter and become mortal."

"No kidding. And if it's going to be like that for me, I'd as soon retire, myself. But I could never leave the Realm in the hands of whoever these people are, or anyone like them. That wouldn't be any good for anybody. But I wonder if this kind of thing was all that common."

"Couldn't the crown tell you that? It wasn't in that download you got?"

She shook her head. "I don't recall anything about fighting to keep the throne. Things seem to have been pretty stable." Wincing, she raised the crown and placed it on her head. If things changed when she sat on the throne, they were even more different when she wore the crown while on the throne. There seemed to be life in the vast, empty room, even though only the two of them were present, and Sophie radiated sheer power. This was what he'd imagined of her from the way Emily used to describe her formidable older sister. He felt like he should be kneeling before her, even as she lounged casually in the silver chair.

"No, this situation seems entirely unprecedented," she said after a while. "Which makes me think that either *I'm* missing something big or *they're* missing something big."

"Wasn't it that fairy who got you into this who insisted you get the crown?" He barely stopped himself from adding "your majesty" to the question, she was that regal.

She leaned forward, resting her elbow on her knee and her chin on her fist. "Yeah. That's what has me confused, and it's the only reason I went along with this plan that I'm still certain is a trap—for someone, at least. If she practically forced me to take the throne, surely she wouldn't demand that I do something that could risk losing it."

"Maybe she's right. You can't hold a throne by hiding out. The final step to really winning it is defending it."

Looking down at him with eyes that were bright with unshed tears, she said, "That's what I'm afraid of. And the irony is, I don't even *want* this throne." One tear slipped from her eye to trickle down her cheek. "What if I have to stay here to hold the throne, if it's the power vacuum from me being an absentee ruler that allows things like this to happen?"

He didn't have a reassuring answer to that. "What would you do if that's the case?"

She sat up straight, looking more regal than ever. "My duty, I suppose." With a bitter laugh, she added, "It's not like I have much of a life to give up—no husband or kids, no real career. Not even that many true friends I'd miss who'd miss me."

He remembered what Mrs. Smith had said about those who didn't have anyone in the outside world who loved them enough to be able to rescue them and wondered if it applied to a fairy queen, as well. The last one had been saved from her throne by love. Could someone save Sophie? Almost without thinking, he asked, "Wouldn't your grandmother be next in line for the throne?" It was a second or two later before the thought really clarified. "I know she probably wouldn't be fit for the crown, but if you're going to get technical, you'd be her heir, wouldn't you?"

Sophie's eyes went really wide. "Ohhhhh," she said, drawing the sound out. "I suppose so." Then she shook her head. "But she's old and ill."

"Isn't this place some kind of fountain of youth?"

"You don't age while you're here. I don't know if it reverses aging."

"Even if you have fairy blood?"

"I have no idea. But it's rather beside the point right now. It doesn't matter which one of us is the true heir to the throne if we can't hold on to it."

"If you give the impostor a real public trouncing in front of the entire Realm, that should solidify your power, I'd think," he suggested. "It's entirely possible that the reason no one has taken the crown in a challenge is that the crown gives you enough power to prevail over anyone."

She smiled, and the entire throne room grew even brighter. "Let's hope so!" she said with great feeling. She removed the crown, placed it in her bag, rose, and drifted down the dais steps.

Shaking his head at being left behind yet again, Michael hauled himself to his feet and went after her. He caught up with her when she stopped dead still in front of the massive front doors. "Is something wrong?" he asked.

"You know, if someone wanted me to get this crown so they could snatch it, would they wait for me to get it back to the fake palace?" she asked.

"Probably not. You're thinking there's an ambush on the other side of those doors?"

"Very likely."

"So we head back to the kitchens?"

"Don't you agree?"

"Yeah. But I think it would help if we could arrange a diversion, too."

"Good thinking. Come on." He wasn't sure what she meant by agreeing with him only to abruptly turn around and walk away, but then she bellowed, "Maeve!" Her voice had the ring of magical authority to it, and the person being ordered would have no choice but to obey. Sure enough, it was only a matter of seconds before the beautiful, golden-haired fairy came running into the throne room.

She didn't look at all happy about it. "You summoned me, your majesty?" she snarled, sarcasm heavy in her tone.

"I need you to do something for me," Sophie said, a funny little smile flickering across her lips. "First, we need to fix you up." She gestured at the fairy, whose hair turned a slightly more reddish color. Her servant's uniform transformed into a dress like Sophie's. Sophie surveyed her handiwork. "Hmm, you're too tall, but I don't think anyone's paying that much attention to me, so I think you'll do. Now, wait for my signal, then open the front doors and walk out."

"You're giving me permission to leave the palace?"

"Not the grounds. Walk until you can go no more and are drawn back into the palace. Do whatever you want or need to do if anything happens while you're out there."

Maeve looked truly baffled, which Sophie seemed to find amusing. "That is all? Just walk out?"

"And do what you need to do while you're out. Yes, that is all I require of you." Michael got the impression it took all of Sophie's willpower not to laugh out loud at this.

"How will I know your signal?"

"Trust me, honey, you'll know it when you see it."

Sophie was still snickering under her breath as she and Michael headed down the stairs to the kitchen. "You're using her as a decoy?" he asked.

"I know!" she said with an uncharacteristic giggle. "It's so deliciously ironic. She got us into all this because of her bid to be queen, and now I'm making her play queen as a diversion." With a soft sigh, she added, "At least I'm getting to have *some* fun."

The little creatures in the kitchen burst into a flurry of activity when Michael and Sophie emerged from the stairwell, but Sophie waved them aside. "Sorry, just passing through. Keep up the good work." Once she and Michael were outside, she said, "I suppose when I'm here on a permanent basis, I can make them deliriously happy by eating all the things they offer me. It's not like it will matter if I can ever leave the Realm again." Her voice sounded bravely resigned, like she was bracing herself for a suicide mission.

"Would it work that way for you?" he asked.

"I imagine so. I'm mostly human, and I doubt the crown makes that much difference." They reached the wall of the kitchen yard, and Sophie raised one hand to eye level. A glowing ball of light formed in her palm. She moved her hand, batting the light away, and it flew up and into a window of the palace. After about thirty seconds, she said, "Okay, that should do it. Let's go."

He opened the gate in the wall, then they joined hands and ran through it. He wasn't sure when the transition happened, but he soon realized they were no longer near the palace but rather were moving at great speed through a forest. He had the strangest sense that they were being chased. Sophie gave his hand a hard squeeze and stopped abruptly, pulling him back. Whoever was chasing them flew past, and as soon as they were gone, she stepped off in a different direction. Michael experienced the increasingly familiar sensation of traveling great distances in a single step.

But they didn't arrive at the fake palace or at any other place that looked familiar.

"Where are we?" Sophie asked, saying out loud what Michael was thinking.

"Where were you trying to go?"

"The fake palace. I must have been too distracted and blew past it. Well, here we go again, and be ready for a trap."

They took another great step, but the palace was still nowhere in sight. The only thing that resembled their intended destination was the mass of uniformed members of the queen's guard, who were quite taken aback by the sight of two humans arriving suddenly in their camp.

"Drat! I must have pictured the wrong thing," Sophie muttered.

"Well, you were expecting a trap," Michael replied.

Before Sophie had a chance to whisk them away, the guards surrounded them. "Halt in the name of the queen," their leader said. "All humans must be ejected from the Realm, lest they pollute it with their impurity."

Twenty-Seven

Outside the Impostor's Palace
A Moment Later

While Emily was still too shocked to speak, Eamon replied without missing a beat, "We're here to greet our new sovereign, of course."

The guard looked at them for a moment, blinking in confusion. "The Hunt sensed humans among us, and her majesty does not tolerate that."

"Of course not," Eamon agreed earnestly. "If I see a human, I will be sure to report it. We wouldn't want to sully the queen's triumphant day."

"You do that," the guard said with a snarl before turning and stalking away. Emily didn't release the breath she'd been holding until she could no longer spot him in the crowd.

She turned to Eamon. "Good save. But I swear, I could see your nose growing with every word."

He frowned and reached up to feel his nose. "It appears to be the same size as always, and I am not using a glamour that extends my nose."

"Okay, looks like not every book made it to your library. But what do you think he meant about the Hunt ratting me out?"

"They may be able to see past glamour. I was able to keep the guard from seeing your true self, but we may have no such protection against the Hunt."

"I vote we stay well away from the Hunt."

"Agreed."

Emily had to nudge Beau back to his feet before they could continue their exploration of the encampment. She wasn't sure how Michael and Sophie managed to have such adventures with the bulldog in tow. She'd have blamed it on Sophie being Sophie if the same thing didn't tend to happen with the very human (as far as she knew) Michael.

She bumped Eamon's shoulder with hers. "All kidding aside, that was pretty sharp back there. I was sure we were doomed, and you were cucumber-cool."

"Ice-cold," he agreed, his silvery eyes twinkling with amusement. "I am one cool cat."

"I think that means something different, but I guess it still works."

The guards were now moving through the throngs—still looking for the rogue humans the Hunt had sensed? They brought a few individuals out of each group and moved them toward the palace itself. As far as Emily could see, they were all fae, so it wasn't a human roundup.

As she watched, she suddenly had a desperate longing to go into the palace. It was like the yearning she'd had for the Realm a few days ago. She grabbed Eamon's arm to anchor herself. "We need to find the sisters," she said.

"Yes, they should be warned about the Hunt."

"That and I'm getting another one of those strange urges. I don't think I'll ever be happy again unless I get into that palace."

He turned to look at her with great alarm. "Is it like before?"

"Well, I can still see colors, hear sound, smell things, and presumably taste, but this world does seem a teeny bit flatter than before, and I'm sure it would be much better in the palace."

He placed his hands on her shoulders and gazed at her. "It may be the same spell," he said with a nod. "We should find the enchantresses."

Releasing her shoulders, he caught her arm in a firm grip and cut a path through the crowds almost as well as Sophie might have, heading unerringly to the two old women.

Amelia checked her watch when they approached. "You're back early."

"This can't wait," Emily said.

"You should avoid the Hunt when it passes," Eamon said. "They appear to be able to see past glamour, and they are aware that there are humans present."

"Yeah, and we have to get inside that palace, as soon as possible," Emily added.

Twenty-Eight

Sophie had expected to have to defend her crown against the usurper. She hadn't expected to be kicked out of the Realm by the impostor's guards because she was human. The impostor had already managed to establish quite the bureaucracy if her various factions of minions were working at cross-purposes. In other circumstances, it might almost have been funny, but she really did not have time for this nonsense.

"You're making a big mistake," she said, figuring it was only fair to warn them.

One of them moved forward to grab her, and she instinctively released Michael's hand so she could generate a shield and fend off the guards. The wave of magic sent him and his colleagues reeling backward. "What trickery is this?" a guard asked.

"Have you considered that it's not a trick?" she asked. "Obviously, you have me mistaken for a human. I'm willing to forget your error if you'll let us go on our way."

She thought for a moment that it might work, but then the lead guard gestured at Michael. "You may go, but he must leave the Realm." He raised a slightly slanted eyebrow. "Unless he also has hidden fae abilities."

"He's a wise one," she said, reaching for something that might hold sway.

"They do their work in their own realm."

"Unless they're needed here. He's here to deliver a baby."

That took them by surprise, and they glanced at Michael with something that looked almost like respect. "Has the baby been delivered?" the lead guard asked.

"Yes," Michael said. "Mother and baby are healthy. At least, I think they are."

"Then his duties are done and he must leave."

"I'll take care of escorting him home," Sophie said, taking Michael's hand again.

"We will see to it that he leaves," the guard insisted.

"He belongs to me." *I wish,* she added mentally.

"Human servants are no longer permitted in the Realm. They corrupt us."

The guards closed in, and Sophie calculated the odds. She wasn't sure she could fight them off all at once while protecting Michael. It was possible that her fairy queen powers could trump all of them, but this wasn't the time to test the limits of her abilities. On the other hand, maybe it wouldn't be such a bad idea to start turning the false queen's minions against her, and if she turned this one group, there would be that many fewer guards available to throw Jennifer out of the Realm while Sophie was busy dealing with the impostor.

With a deep breath and long, slow sigh, she dropped all the veils she'd put up against her identity and let her royal glory show. The guards took a step back, but they didn't seem to grasp what she was showing them. Then again, she reasoned, how could they, if their only experience with fae royalty was with an impostor?

She was still trying to think of what her next step should be when the ground around them seemed to come alive with light. Hundreds of tiny voices speaking in not-quite unison cried out, "My lady! Your majesty! You honor us with your presence!"

Sophie couldn't help but smile. Her little friends, the smallest and, when seen up close, ugliest residents of the Realm, had come to her rescue yet again. They'd helped her win her throne in the first place, and now they just might be key to helping her keep it.

The guards looked at the ground, then back at Sophie. "What is this?" the lead guard asked.

"*They* seem to have figured it out," Sophie said, trying hard not to sound too smug, although that was a real challenge. For the finishing touch, she took the crown out of her bag and placed it on her head.

In case there was any doubt, Michael knelt before her and brushed his lips across the knuckles of the hand he still held. That took her breath away for a moment, until she forced herself to snap out of it and noticed the glint of mischief in his eyes.

The guards took the cue and fell to their knees. "Forgive us, your majesty," the leader said. "But how can this be? You are not at your palace."

"The queen at the palace is an impostor, and that palace is a fake," Sophie said, trying to ignore the tingling that lingered on her hand from Michael's kiss. Fake kiss, she reminded herself. "I am on my way to oust her from her false throne and declare myself before the Realm."

"How may we serve you, my lady?"

"Tell me what you know. Have you seen this so-called queen?"

"No, my lady. We receive her orders from our commander."

Sophie glanced at Michael. "Hmm. That makes me wonder if there even is a queen."

"They're planning to crown someone," he said.

"Maybe that's what the trap is—get the real queen, and get me under their thumb somehow."

"What would you have us do, my lady?" the lead guard asked.

"Could you reach any of your colleagues and let them know they're serving an impostor?"

The leader glanced at one of his men, who stood, took a few steps, and then disappeared in a blur. "The word will spread."

"The rest of you should come with me to the palace." With a glance at Michael, she added under her breath, "Maybe showing up with bodyguards will make it harder to spring the trap." She gestured for the guards to rise, but before they made it to their feet, shouts rang out from the surrounding woods.

Wild fae streamed from among the trees, surrounding them. "Unhand these people," their leader shouted at the guards.

"We're not really being handed," Sophie muttered to herself as she tried to figure out the new situation. She knew the wild or free fae were opposed to the idea of any overall ruler of the Realm, but she'd hoped that being a hands-off ruler who merely served to keep the Realm alive would keep them from opposing her. Naturally, they'd be against the kind of queen the impostor was proving to be. "It's okay," she said out loud, holding out her hands in a calming, appeasing gesture. "They're helping us. They're not kicking us out."

More of the free fae had arrived, and now they had a chance to take stock of the situation. Sophie could only imagine how it looked to them. She was radiating royal glory and had the queen's guards and the wee ones kneeling before her. She quickly tamped down her royal aura, remembering too late that she still wore the crown, which was a dead giveaway.

"It's the queen!" one of the free fae shouted. "Take her!"

Sophie grabbed Michael's hand and shouted to the guards, "Meet at the palace." Sending a surge of enchantress magic at the nearest free fae to scatter them, she made for the gap that formed in their ranks and tried to envision the grounds around the fake palace as she ran.

She wasn't sure where they ended up. It didn't look at all familiar, and the guards were nowhere in sight. One thing she was sure of, however: The free fae had followed her.

Twenty-Nine

"Why would you want to go into the palace?" Amelia asked.

"I imagine that's where the action will be," Emily replied.

"She's under a compulsion," Eamon said firmly.

"A compulsion?" Athena said with a horrified gasp. "What kind?"

"The same thing that was happening to her earlier, when she felt compelled to enter the Realm," Eamon said.

"This was why you were behaving oddly?" Amelia asked.

"Yes, but I got better," Emily insisted. "It went away entirely. Until now. But think about it: Once the queen comes out here, it's a done deal. She's been crowned. She'll just be having the Buckingham Palace balcony moment out here. We need to get inside. They seemed to be picking people to go into the VIP area. I'd bet my compulsion would get us on the guest list. Someone must want me in there."

"Which is a very good reason for you *not* to go in there," Amelia insisted. "They may want to use you in some way. Remember how Maeve used you against your sister?"

"How do you plan to stop this impostor from out here?"

"That is your sister's job."

Athena glanced around. "Funny, we haven't heard from Sophie in a while."

"I'm sure she's okay," Emily said. "And she'd need us to get in position. Maybe that's where this compulsion comes from."

"It doesn't." Eamon snapped. "This has no trace of Sophie in it."

Emily noticed one of the guards moving through the crowd nearby, picking out people, presumably to go into the palace. She moved away from the group and put herself in the guard's path. His gaze flicked past her, then he stopped and turned. "You," he said. "With me."

Putting on her best Sophie impression and dialing her charm up to maximum, she said, "Can my friends come, too? I don't want to leave them."

"Bring them along," he said, clearly too busy to be bothered.

Emily gestured to the others. "Come on!" When they hesitated, she said, "I don't think he's going to let me back out, and you don't want me going in there alone, do you?"

Eamon was the first to join her, dragging a reluctant Beau. The sisters looked at each other, shrugged, and came along.

Emily's heart pounded with anticipation, and it swelled with the joy of coming home at last as they approached the towering arched doors of the palace.

⁂Thirty⁂

The Forest
A Moment Later

Sophie wasn't prone to panic, but she figured if ever there was a time for panic, it would be now. She desperately needed to get back to a place she'd left when she needed to retrieve something, but obstacles were popping up to keep her away. If she were barefoot and wearing her nightgown, she'd be living out her most common recurring nightmare.

The free fae fighters closed in on Michael and Sophie. She could feel the magic coming from them and knew her enchantress trick wouldn't work again. "So, now we have our little queen," one of the fae said with a sneer.

"Sorry to disappoint you," Sophie said with all the bravado she could muster. "I know everyone expects me to be taller."

Michael stepped in front of her, his bulk eclipsing her entirely. "This isn't the queen you're looking for," he said. "Don't you see that she's with me, a human? The queen who's been causing you problems would never tolerate me. This is the true queen, the one who brought the Realm back to life." He dug in his satchel and came up with the favor the earlier fairies had given him. "Here's proof—

not long ago, I delivered a fairy baby. How often does that happen here? Would it have happened if the rightful queen hadn't taken the real throne?"

Sophie was glad that he was facing away from her and couldn't see the glow she was sure was spreading across her face. She forcibly told herself that he wasn't praising her out of adoration, but as a very clever way of making a case that might get them out of this fix alive. He really must have done his homework, she thought, if he'd managed to associate the renewed life of the Realm with new birth. Even she hadn't made that connection, though it did make sense. She sighed at the realization that there was yet another reason she was obligated to actually hold that throne.

Reluctantly, she stepped out from behind Michael and said, "I know you don't want a queen, and I understand why. To be honest, I don't *want* to be a queen, but the Realm needs someone on that throne if it's to stay alive, and you're better off with me than with this impostor who's actually trying to rule. I won't make anyone bow to me, so long as you leave me alone and harm no one else."

She glanced around the circle of warriors, trying to gauge their reactions. Most of them appeared hard and cold, unmoved by her and Michael's arguments, but she thought she saw a softening in a few of them.

Michael placed a hand on her shoulder, and Sophie tried not to flinch or lean against him, even as his light touch took her breath away. "She won that throne through trials and by blood," he said. "I was there. I saw it. She had the knowledge of how to do it and the right bloodline because she's descended from the last real queen. You need her."

"And if I get rid of this impostor, you'll barely notice me unless you drop by the real palace, which you're welcome to do," she added.

Two of the warriors lowered their weapons on one side of the circle. Two more bowed their heads slightly. Their leader, however, didn't falter at all. "We want no ruler. We answer to no one," he said. "Since you are human, you may leave the Realm, but you must never return."

"Yeah, and then be ready for lots more impostors who'll be much heavier-handed than I am," Sophie snapped, losing patience. She tried to judge the ones who didn't seem to be in line with their leader. Was it merely moral and philosophical support, or would they actually help her?

She made eye contact with the two who had lowered their weapons and hadn't raised them again even when their leader spoke up. They met her gaze, held it, and nodded ever so slightly. She wasn't sure what they had planned, but she felt fairly certain that they would help her with whatever she did.

Reaching to take Michael's hand in a show of unity with him, she said, "You can stand with me or against me, but you won't force me out of my Realm."

While the leader of the opposition was opening his mouth to reply, she generated a magical flash and a smokescreen before tugging Michael toward her likely allies. They made a hole for her and turned to fight off any who tried to follow Michael and Sophie. She prepared to make a long stride into the distance, but wasn't quite sure where to go. Of all the places she knew in the Realm—which wasn't too many, as she hadn't explored widely—she didn't know of any that were guaranteed to be safe. In desperation, she took them to the ruined temple where she danced for Tallulah.

The clearing was deserted, which was a good sign. Before their pursuers could catch up to them, she opened a portal to the outside world, in a place she knew well. She pulled Michael through the portal just as the free fae caught up with them.

They emerged in a chilly park in the hours before sunrise. That had been a slight miscalculation. She'd forgotten how late it was in the year, but she only knew one place farther east well enough to open a portal, and it was enough farther north that it probably still wouldn't be daylight.

"Where are we?" Michael asked, keeping up with her as she ran through the park toward the sound of traffic.

"Hyde Park, London," she said.

"London?"

"I was trying to find a place where it wouldn't be night. It's a bad time of year for that, unfortunately."

She didn't have to look over her shoulder to know that the fae had pursued them through the portal. Instead, she focused on running. It was early, but the city was already waking up. When they reached a street, she searched for landmarks. "Yes!" she cried out when she saw the Hyde Park Corner tube station ahead. "We should be able to lose them in there," she said, dragging Michael along with her.

"I don't know about you, but I don't carry British currency with me on my usual nights out in New York," he said.

She shot him a withering look. "Seriously? Do you remember who I am?"

"It's hard to forget when you're wearing a crown."

"Oops, right." She pulled the crown off and shoved it into her bag. "I don't think I can pass for Duchess Kate."

"And I don't think she wears a crown except for special occasions. Or ever takes public transportation."

She didn't bother looking to see if their foes were still pursuing them as they headed into the station. It would be the rare fairy who could handle even the escalator ride. Eamon would love it, but he'd need fortification, and she wouldn't put him on a train even with a basket of cookies.

A wave of her hand got them through the turnstiles. "We'll only need to go one stop," she told Michael once they were on the platform. "There's another park, and there I can get us elsewhere in the Realm. It's an easy walk, but I figured we'd lose them in here."

"I still can't believe I'm in London," he said, gazing around with a dazed expression.

"Barely. You'll have to come back sometime and see the sights. This time, though, I want to minimize the amount of time we spend outside the Realm so we have more flexibility for our return time when all this is over." She sighed. "But I would have loved to have a proper cup of tea."

She still hadn't spotted any fae in the station by the time a train arrived, so she felt somewhat less harried when they got off at the Green Park station and went aboveground. Her main concern was finding where to go within the Realm. She was running out of places she knew, and she'd had no luck getting to the one place she really wanted to go.

"I guess I might as well give it another shot," she muttered as she started to open a portal in the park.

"Getting to the fake palace?"

"Yeah. Every time I've tried, I end up somewhere else."

"What are you picturing when you're navigating?"

"The fake palace."

"Maybe that's why it's not working. You have to go someplace real."

"Could be, but I'm not sure how much of the Realm is real. Fiontan and Niamh's castle may be no more real than that palace. The only thing more fake about it than any other place may be the fact that it's said to be the home of the true queen."

"If it's new, then maybe it hasn't settled into the fabric of the Realm. Maybe you should picture somewhere nearby, like that rise overlooking the valley."

"Hmm," she said, nodding to herself. "That could be it. How did you suddenly become an expert on the fairy world?"

"I was a geeky kid who read too many fantasy novels, and I've been doing my homework since our last adventures. Of course, applying fantasy-novel logic to the real fairyland may not work, but it's not like we have a lot to go on."

"Let's give it a shot," she said. When she'd completed the portal, she took his hand, and together they walked back into the Realm.

And right into an ambush.

Or was it? The armed men facing her wore the uniforms of the queen's guard. Sophie didn't know how much time might have passed in the Realm while she and Michael had been in London or how long it would take the message to spread, but there was a good chance that she had allies among this bunch. She pulled herself up into a regal, defiant posture and let her royal glory show. "The tales you have heard are true," she said. "I am your rightful queen, not that impostor in the fake palace."

When they didn't react, she remembered that she'd put the crown away. She took it out of her bag and placed it on her head. They didn't respond in quite the way she expected, though. A few of the men in the back ranks fell to their knees, then quickly rose again when they noticed that no one else had knelt. A moment later, the leader knelt, glancing at his men with a clear signal. They all dropped to their knees, almost in unison.

"My queen," the leader said, bowing his head. "Allow us to escort you to your palace."

"I don't really want to go to my palace," Sophie said. "But I would appreciate an escort to the impostor's palace." Under her breath, she added, "Maybe *you* can get me there."

"I don't like this," Michael whispered.

She glanced up at him. "Why?" It wasn't a challenge, but rather an earnest request for information. His instincts were good, and sometimes he had even clearer sight in the Realm than she had.

"Let's just say that I wouldn't holster my weapon even after these guys put their hands in the air. I think their reaction was more calculated than spontaneous."

"So, trap?"

"Mm hmm."

The leader of the guards stood and said, "Now, if you will come with us, my lady."

Sophie grabbed Michael's hand and said, "Run."

Considering that her Realm navigation skills had been failing her lately and that she kept stumbling into yet another ambush, she decided against trying to make great strides across the Realm. Instead, she threw up a barrier behind them as they ran. She wasn't sure how long it would hold the guards, but it might keep their backs free from arrows.

But she wasn't the only one using magic. A thicket of thorns sprang up ahead of them. Sophie didn't break stride as she blasted a path through them. "Seriously?" she remarked. If the guards believed she was the real queen who needed to be kept away from the impostor, they didn't seem to appreciate the power she had over the Realm.

She and Michael made it through the thorns, which she allowed to grow back in her wake. Let their pursuers get caught in their own trap, she thought.

She pulled up short, though, when they reached the edge of a great canyon. There was no bridge in sight, no obvious way across. They were cornered, unless she could think of something. She wasn't sure she had enough faith in her magical powers to create a bridge or fly the two of them across.

"It's not real," Michael said. "It's illusion."

"Are you sure?"

"Look at it out of the corner of your eye." She tried that, and there was the faintest image of ground over the chasm, but it didn't look solid to her. "I think it's a trick," she said, shaking her head.

He squeezed her hand. "Close your eyes and trust me."

She looked up at him, meeting his eyes. He looked utterly sincere, and she knew he wasn't suicidal. But still…

The guards were closing in on them, her barrier having dissipated and the thorns having been obliterated. She nodded at Michael, but she didn't close her eyes. Instead, she focused on him as he stepped out onto what appeared to be nothing. It still looked to her like they were walking on thin air, but her feet were striking solid ground. Soon, she developed the confidence to run, but she didn't release Michael's hand. A mad part of her brain felt like he was the one giving them something to walk on, and if she released him, she'd fall.

In spite of the feeling of something beneath her feet, she couldn't hold back a sigh of relief when they reached ground she could see. "Hold on a second," she told Michael. When he stopped, she released his hand and held her arms out in front of her. She controlled the Realm, and the impostor's people had best not forget it. The canyon may have been an illusion to her, but she reshaped the landscape so that it became real.

"That might slow them down a little," she said as she and

Michael resumed walking. She wasn't quite sure what to do now. She'd failed in every attempt to reach the fake palace. Maybe she could go back to the real one and find a way to make a big splash there.

She'd just reached for Michael's hand to take them there when he stumbled and said, "Ow!"

"Are you hit?"

"By something. It stings. It's not like the last time, though. I can still move."

She looked over her shoulder and found that they were still being pursued. Of course a canyon wouldn't be much of an obstacle to magical beings. "Can you run?"

"I'll manage."

He actually kept up pretty well, which gave her hope that any injury was superficial. Obstacle after obstacle arose, all of which she dealt with so easily that she couldn't help but wonder why they bothered.

"You know, I think I've had this nightmare," Michael said between pants.

"You too?"

"Yeah, and in the dream, I never got where I wanted to go."

"This is real, though."

It took her a few minutes before she noticed that it was getting darker. The Realm didn't have day and night in the traditional sense, just a constant state of semi-twilight. If the light was changing, something was wrong.

The trees around them were different, no longer really trees, just twisted shapes. There was something familiar about it, but it was Michael who recognized it first. "We're in the Borderlands," he said.

"You know about the Borderlands?"

"That's how we got into the Realm the last time, since we didn't have a fairy queen to make a portal for us. We crawled through a hole."

The Borderlands were the places where the Realm was physically joined to the human world. It was a kind of no-man's land, and neither human nor fae were truly safe from its denizens.

"We need to get out of here," she said. "Most of the things that live here don't answer to me."

That was when the soldiers leapt out from behind the twisted tree trunks. *This* was the trap, and they'd let the other soldiers chase them right into it.

She tried every magical trick she knew, but her powers were weaker here on the edge of the Realm, which was probably why she'd been herded here. She switched to her enchantress magic, but she knew less about it, so it was less reliable. The fae magic that came with her crown was pure instinct. Enchantress magic took training and practice to use for anything on this level.

Michael was doing his part, scattering iron, which kept the attacking fae at a distance, but the two of them were badly outnumbered. To make matters worse, something was dropping out of the sky at them, little things that clutched at her clothes and hair and nipped her skin with tiny, sharp teeth. Next to her, Michael brushed them off himself while muttering, "I hate these things."

Just when Sophie was starting to despair, the area grew lighter, not because of anything shining from above, but because of a glow rising from below and taking to the air. The little creatures had arrived, and they were swarming against the Borderlands dwellers. That freed Sophie and Michael to concentrate on the soldiers. They couldn't get close enough to the humans to use swords, thanks to Michael's iron, but some of them had spears. She threw up the best barrier she could, but it didn't seem to hold up well unless she concentrated on it, and concentration was difficult with so much going on around her.

"Sophie!" Michael called out, and she whirled just in time to see a spear flying straight at her. He pushed her aside, but didn't quite get out of the way in time, so it grazed his arm.

She rushed to see if he was injured, but something held her back—a silver chain that had wrapped itself around her waist. She couldn't free herself from it, and it was drawing her back toward whoever held the other end. She'd encountered something like this before, so she quit fighting and instead turned to run at the person holding it, creating slack in the line. She was readying herself to leap at the soldier on the other end when another chain caught her, bringing her to the ground.

As she fell, the crown came off her head and rolled along the ground. She reached for it with both her hands and her magic, but one of the soldiers swooped in and grabbed it. A split second later, all the soldiers disappeared, along with the crown and the silver chains.

⁓Thirty-One⁓

Inside the Fake Throne Room
Meanwhile

Emily had to admit that this throne room was far more impressive than Sophie's. Sophie's had potential, but it was mostly empty and lifeless. This was more what a royal throne room should look like, which, she supposed, was the point.

It actually looked a lot like Sophie's palace, she decided as she studied her surroundings. The impossible proportions of the room were similar, and the tall arched windows were almost identical.

"Whoever created this has seen the real palace," Amelia said, confirming Emily's suspicions.

"Look at the throne," Athena said.

It was far away, so Emily couldn't see much more than a glint of silver. But it did look a lot like Sophie's throne.

"I believe it may be an illusion," Eamon said, squinting at it.

"Yes, it is," Amelia confirmed.

The big difference between this room and the real one was the celebration taking place in it. Bright banners hung from the ceiling beams, sprightly music played, long banquet tables were loaded with festive food and drink, and flowers were on display everywhere, spilling from vases and spiraling in garlands down every pillar. Sophie would say it was too much, but really, was it possible for there to be "too much" at a royal occasion in fairyland?

The other big difference from Sophie's palace was the number of people present. Granted, Emily had only been at the real palace immediately after it was reawakened by Sophie taking the throne and in the aftermath of a war, so she'd hardly seen it at its best, but she couldn't imagine that a palace occupied by an absentee queen would ever be the site of such a revel.

Every court in the Realm appeared to be represented. There were a few fairies in the midcentury Doris Day attire that had been favored in Maeve's old court. A lot of fairies were dressed in medieval finery right out of a fairy-tale book. There were also some dressed in 1930s glamour, in Regency attire similar to the costumes in Emily's show, in Victorian finery, and in elaborate Georgian confections. About the only thing missing was the austere look of the Puritans. Emily allowed herself a moment of amusement from imagining that as the look for Sophie's court, but then there wouldn't be nearly enough pastels or floral prints for her.

All of these people were talking, dancing, or availing themselves of the food tables. Even if they'd been brought there against their will, they didn't seem to mind too much now. They'd forgotten whatever protest they might have made while indulging in the party.

"I don't see anyone who might have been at the real palace," Amelia said as she craned her neck to scan the crowd.

"They would have locked them up," Emily said. "They wouldn't want them giving up the game." She searched the crowd for a familiar strawberry blond head, but the throngs were too dense for her to spot any one person who would have been shorter than anyone here. Where was Sophie? She needed to have those rulers free and able to denounce the false queen.

"Do you think something happened to Sophie?" Emily asked Eamon. "You'd think there'd have been a sign of her by now. Like an explosion or a riot." A thought popped into her head. "We should go looking for her now that we're inside the palace."

"Is this that compulsion again?" he asked.

"No. It's different." Actually, it came from the same place in her head, but she knew it was the right thing to do, and if she told him it was at all like the compulsion, he wouldn't let her go. Could she help it if she was being forced to do something she'd want to do anyway?

She started to head off to the other end of the throne room, but something held her back. The resistance was linked to her hand, and she looked down to see that she was holding Beau's leash, and the dog had stubbornly planted himself on the floor. "Come on, boy," she said, but Beau just glared at her. She tried handing the leash over to Amelia and Athena, but they shook their heads.

"I believe your dog is sending you a message," Athena said with a smile.

"But we need to find Sophie!"

"What good would you be able to do for your sister, who is an enchantress with the power of the entire Realm at her beck and call?" Amelia asked.

"Whatever drew her into the palace is drawing her in deeper," Eamon said.

She shot him a glare to let him know she thought he was a traitor, but he was looking at her with such tender concern that it stunned her. He really did care. For a moment, she forgot about the urge pulling her elsewhere in the palace. "Do you really think I might be in danger?" she asked him softly.

"You're in the Realm. Anything you can't explain is a potential danger." She started to protest, but he distracted her by putting his arm around her shoulders. He was probably trying to keep her from going anywhere, but it made her feel cherished. She wasn't sure what to make of all this. Maybe it was part of whatever spell was being cast on her.

Just as suddenly as the compulsion had come upon her, it was gone. The feeling was so surprising that she might have lost her balance if Eamon hadn't been holding her. "Wow, that's weird," she said. "It's gone, like that, just like the last time."

"Do you still think it's a good idea to head deeper into the palace to look for Sophie?" Amelia asked, a slight smirk on her lips.

"No, not really. But I do wonder where she is."

"She knows what she's doing," Athena said with a reassuring pat on her arm.

"But we should be doing *something*. If Sophie hasn't freed the other rulers to come discredit the impostor, maybe we can."

"What do you mean?" Eamon asked.

"I don't know, maybe a whisper campaign? See if we can raise some doubts, get people to question the situation?"

Athena grinned and clapped her hands with great enthusiasm. "Oh, that would be fun!"

"But we should be careful," Amelia put in with a tiny glare at her sister. "We don't want to get hauled away as subversives."

"Keep moving," Emily suggested. "Don't hang around in one place too long."

"You and I should join the dancing," Eamon said. He sounded very sincere, but there was a glint in his silvery eyes. Without a word, she handed Beau's leash and her bag over to Athena and let him sweep her onto the dance floor.

The dancing reminded her of the Regency dances in her show, which meant the pattern wasn't too hard for her to figure out. Even better, it allowed her to interact with every man in the line, and Eamon could do likewise with the women. In the first section, while they were still dancing together, she said, "You know what to do, right?"

"Raise doubts."

"But keep it subtle."

The section finished, and she moved down the line to her next partner, who bowed to her as she curtsied. "I'm a little surprised by all this pomp, aren't you?" she said when she stepped toward her partner and took his hand. "Obviously, the queen's been on the throne for a while, so why a coronation now?"

The dance took them a step apart for a moment, and when they rejoined to walk in a circle he said, "What do you mean?"

"I mean, what use would the real queen have for all this? Isn't the throne won through trials and blood?" With that, she was handed over to her next partner, where she started again. It was hard to tell if the whispers were having any effect, but at least she felt like she was contributing something to the effort.

When she rejoined Eamon, she asked, "How did it go?"

"They are a bunch of empty-headed ninnies who care little about who is on the throne as long as they are invited to a big party," he said with great disgust.

"So, not so great?"

"Perhaps I have planted the seeds of doubt, but I'm not sure they'll remember anything for long."

"I don't know how things went for me, either. Would they even care if there was proof that this was an impostor?"

"Not as long as it doesn't interrupt their fun."

He sounded so bitter that it was almost funny. She grinned as he spun her in a circle. "Why don't you tell me how you really feel?"

"I thought I did." Before she could explain that she was being sarcastic, he smiled and said, "Now you see why I like humans."

"We've got our share of empty-headed ninnies. More people vote for TV singing competitions than for Congress, so maybe we're not too different."

The dance ended, and they joined a different group, repeating the same process with similar results. "I wonder how the A-sisters are doing," Emily asked when they finished that dance. "And I wonder if it's doing any good at all."

The sound of trumpets rang through the throne room, and Emily figured they'd find out soon enough.

Thirty-Two

It took Michael a moment or two to realize he didn't have anyone left to fight. He spun around, looking for enemies, but the soldiers were gone, and it seemed like the little fairy creatures had driven away the Borderlands things.

He was surprised to see how far Sophie was from him. He'd thought they were fighting back-to-back, but she was a good thirty feet away, sitting on the ground and looking stunned.

"Sophie, are you okay?" he asked, running to her.

She turned toward him, her eyes wide with shock and horror. "They got the crown." Her eyes flashed with anger. "I knew this whole thing was a bad idea."

He knelt next to her and squeezed her shoulder. "There's always the chance that the crown won't do anyone any good. It wasn't the fake queen who took it from you, so I don't see any way she'd be able to wear it. She wasn't the one to defeat you."

She leaned into his hand for a moment, as though taking comfort in the touch, then abruptly flinched away. "Maybe, but the fact remains that I was sent to get the crown so I could prove my position to the fairy rulers, and now I don't have it. What do I do?"

"It looked to me like you were doing a good enough job of playing queen, regardless of what you had sitting on your head."

"I hope you're right." She blinked rapidly, fighting away tears. After a couple of deep breaths, she seemed to have herself more under control. With a frown of concern, she asked, "Are you hurt? I thought I saw you get hit, and you were hit when we were coming here."

"*Something* hit me," he said, craning his neck to see the back of his shoulder. "But while it's sore, it doesn't feel bad, not like a gunshot."

She moved to inspect his back. "I can't even find a rip in your coat."

"Well, it is waterproofed. Maybe that repels magical spears, too."

"Maybe. You can move?"

He moved both arms and wiggled his fingers. "It's not at all like the elf shot." She was still frowning, though. "Okay, what are you worried about?" he asked.

"I don't know enough about their weapons. For all I know, something magical did penetrate your clothes and your body without leaving an external mark."

"So I'll be turning into a frog pretty soon?" When she didn't even smile at that, he got a sick feeling in his stomach. "Or is that the best-case scenario?"

She rubbed her temples like she was fighting off a bad headache. "I don't know. I don't know what any of this means. I'm afraid I'm way out of my depth."

That was something he'd never thought he'd hear from Sophie Drake. She didn't strike him as the sort who'd ever be willing to admit weakness. Either he'd won her trust in a huge way or she was at the end of her resources. Or perhaps both. "Is there anyone who could help?"

"I've already talked to Tallulah, and she hasn't been at all helpful. Your wise woman might know what to do about whatever it was that hit you, but she wouldn't know anything about a fairy crown." She rubbed at her temples again, then abruptly gasped softly and looked up at him, a smile spreading across her face, so bright that it almost lit the dark Borderlands. "You're a genius," she breathed.

"I am?"

"You asked earlier about my grandmother being the rightful heir. She had to have learned all the same things she taught me, and she's one generation less removed than I am. There's a chance she might know something I don't."

"How much would she remember?"

"She might be clearer on fairy lore than she is about what happened last week. She's still singing that song she taught me that helped me take the throne, and she doesn't miss a word. If we bring her here, she might revive enough to tell us something."

"Do we have time? They've got the crown already."

"I should be able to do the same trick with time that I do when leaving our world to come here. We can come back to the time we left."

He stood and extended a hand to help her up, but she sprang easily to her feet. Now that she had a plan, she looked a lot more like her usual self, which was reassuring. He didn't want to face the trouble that had Sophie shaky and shocked. "What about your mother?" he asked as he followed her out of the Borderlands. "I guess you can do the time thing so you can get your grandmother back before she notices anything's different."

"Just in case, I'll leave a changeling."

"Isn't a changeling another fairy left in a person's place?"

"Not always. It can also be an enchanted object that looks like the person. That's what often happened when people thought their missing loved one was actually dead or in a coma." Sophie smiled and shook her head. "Funny, not too long ago I was frustrated because my fairy knowledge told me how to make a changeling but not how to free a captive." She reached for his hand. "Ready?"

Instead of answering, he squeezed her hand, and they stepped off together. They came out in what smelled like a pine forest. It was still night, or perhaps very early morning. A soft glow appeared nearby, and he saw that Sophie had conjured up a light. "Ah, that's just what I need," she whispered. "Could you please pick up that log there?"

He bent and lifted a log about eight inches in diameter and nearly five feet long. He rested it on his shoulder, and Sophie nodded in approval before dousing her light. She moved forward confidently, apparently in such familiar territory that she could find her way even in the darkness.

They went another ten or so yards before they were on the edge of the forest, where it gave way to a lush lawn that was still rather wooded, though the trees were more widely spaced. On the other side of the lawn stood a large white house. Michael couldn't see details in the darkness from where he stood, but he got the impression that the house was old and stately. It looked very settled in its surroundings.

"I'll go make sure the coast is clear," Sophie whispered. She ran lightly across the lawn and up onto a small rear porch that looked like it must lead to a service entrance. She easily turned the door handle and slipped inside. He was just starting to worry that she'd run into trouble when she reappeared at the door and beckoned to him.

He focused on stealth rather than speed as he made his way to the house. The last thing he needed was to wake Sophie's mother by stepping on a twig at the wrong time. He'd heard enough of her mother's voice over the phone that he didn't want to have to face that woman.

He entered through a mudroom. Sophie led him through the kitchen and dining room into a large central hall. The faint light from a street lamp outside, coming in through the transom window over the front door, was reflected in highly polished wooden floors. He followed Sophie into what must have once been a formal parlor. Some of the delicate, feminine antique furniture was still in the room, but it had been shoved aside to make room for a hospital bed.

In the bed lay a figure that looked frail, but that Michael suspected held more strength than anyone would guess, based on what he knew of Sophie. In fact, the sleeping woman reminded him of Sophie. She had a similar build and bone structure, and he'd have guessed that her white hair had once been red.

Sophie bent over her and whispered, "Nana? It's Sophie. I need to talk to you."

Sophie may have called him a genius for planting the seed

of this plan, but Michael was starting to doubt that any good could come of this. The old woman looked far too frail to be of much help, and when she opened her eyes, they were so blank and confused that he wasn't sure she knew who Sophie was.

Sophie gently squeezed one bony hand. "Nana, I need your help in the Realm. I'm hoping you know something. You may have told me somewhere along the way, but I don't remember."

Nana blinked, looked momentarily distressed, then suddenly her eyes cleared and she said, "It's about time you remembered you're not the only one in the lineage."

Sophie flinched, but it only took her a second to recover her poise. "I'm sorry, but you must admit, you haven't been that forthcoming for a while. Now, do you remember anything about how the crown works? I won it with the trials, like in the song, but is that the only way for someone to take the crown?"

"Oh, honey, do you really expect me to remember anything useful in my state? You know what you're going to have to do."

"Will taking you to the Realm help?"

She gestured at her ravaged body. "Could it possibly hurt? Now, let's get moving before your mother wakes up." For someone supposedly in the last stages of Alzheimer's disease, she sounded surprisingly lucid, but then Michael guessed that this kind of conversation might have been taken as a sign of dementia by someone who didn't know what was going on. "You, with the log, bring it over here, young man."

Michael set the log down on the bed, against the railing. As gently as he could, he gathered Nana into his arms, carrying her like she was a child. She weighed hardly anything, but he still felt some muscle around her slight bones.

Once Nana was out of her bed, Sophie took a nightgown out of a nearby dresser and slid it onto the log, then rolled it into place where Nana had been lying. The next thing Michael knew, the woman he held in his arms was also in her bed, lying so peacefully and so still that she might have been dead. If he hadn't been holding the real woman, he'd never have guessed that the body in bed was fake.

"Very nice work. You've obviously learned a lot," Nana commented. "I'd love to see your mother when she finds my body."

"Nana!" Sophie scolded. "Besides, I made it so you just look like you're sleeping. That way I can get you back here before Mama even notices."

"You seem to have forgotten to consult me about my wishes," the old woman said frostily.

"We'll discuss this later. But first, we need all the royal help we can get." She waved Michael back the way they'd come in. Nana fell asleep in Michael's arms, and he wondered if her momentary lucidity had been genuine or if it was just wishful thinking on their part that made sense out of what she'd said.

They reached the woods, and Sophie put her hand against his back to guide him through the gateway she opened. When they arrived in the Realm, Nana said to Michael, "You can put me down now."

He set her on her feet, keeping his arm around her shoulders to steady her. Already, he was fairly certain that she was taller than she'd been while lying in the bed. She turned back to him. "Thank you kindly for the assistance." He had to blink in surprise when he saw her face. He'd thought she resembled a much older version of Sophie, but now she might almost have passed for Sophie's mother rather than her grandmother. Her posture was straighter, her eyes were brighter, and her hair was darker, no longer stark white, but a faded red color. "That's better," Nana said with great satisfaction.

She took in the Realm, a smile spreading across her face. "So, this is the fairy realm. Lovely, isn't it? I spent my whole life hoping to see this day."

"You knew it was real all along?" Sophie asked. "It wasn't just a legend to you?"

"I figured it out somewhere along the way, but I wasn't sure what I could do about it. I never saw any fairies, never found a way into the Realm. I knew it would be you when you were a child and told me about dancing with the fairies."

"It would have saved me a lot of trouble if you'd told me then. I might even have been able to save Emily."

Nana gasped. "What happened to Emily?"

"They took her last summer while trying to get to me. Remember, I told you about it? I learned everything about the crown and throne when I was saving her. She's okay now. I hope."

"See, it worked out," her grandmother said, patting her on the arm. "You needed to learn it for yourself." She glanced down at her nightgown. "If it's not too much trouble, can you do something about the outfit? I feel underdressed. I can't bear to be out in public in my nightclothes."

"Do you have anything in mind?" Sophie asked.

"Surprise me." A moment later, Nana was dressed in a pale blue suit, a hat worthy of Queen Elizabeth perched atop her now-styled hair. Nana glanced down at herself and gave an approving nod. She now looked even younger and stronger than when they'd first entered the Realm. It was like the years were falling away from her. "Now that I'm decent, I don't believe we've been properly introduced." Her glance at Sophie may as well have been a direct order.

"Nana, this is my friend, Detective Michael Murray. He's Emily's upstairs neighbor, and he helped us earlier when Emily was taken. His wife is currently a captive somewhere in the Realm. Michael, I'd like you to meet my grandmother, Leonie Drake."

Leonie held out her hand to him, and he shook it. "Pleased to meet you, ma'am."

"Likewise," she replied, sizing him up with steely gray eyes that he had a feeling didn't miss much. Turning to Sophie, she said, "Now, what seems to be the problem?"

"There's someone trying to take over the Realm, claiming to be the queen who won the throne, and I think whoever's behind the impostor has the crown. I don't know how this works. They haven't gone through the trials, so I don't know if the impostor could be considered to have won it properly."

Leonie shook her head sadly and made little "tsk-tsk" sounds. "Oh, honey, I thought you were the responsible one. You lost the crown?"

"I had it ripped away in an all-out fight," Sophie snapped defensively. "But does that count as them really winning the crown?

Would the impostor be able to wear the crown and become the true queen?"

Leonie frowned in deep thought. Her lips moved slightly, like she was reciting lyrics of old songs. Finally, she shook her head. "There's a slight possibility, depending on how involved this impostor was in the scheme that took the crown from you. I wouldn't chance it. I'd say our best bet is to get the crown back before it goes on anyone else's head. That would be for the best for both you and this impostor."

"That's what I was afraid of," Sophie said with a sigh. "Now, we need to get to the palace before the impostor can be crowned."

"You mean go near the palace," Michael pointed out.

He thought Sophie might have blushed slightly. "Yes, that. And maybe without the crown, I won't have so much of a target on my back."

She took his and Leonie's hands. They took three steps together and ended up in a familiar setting: the hill overlooking the fake palace. However, they weren't alone. An army of fairies was gathered there, but they were far more focused on the field below than on any newcomers.

"This must be Emily's army," Sophie whispered.

"What on earth is Emily doing with an army?" Leonie asked. "I'm not sure I'd trust that child with a Boy Scout troop, bless her heart."

"Emily's grown up a lot since you saw her last," Sophie said without taking her eyes off the soldiers. "And I believe this is merely an army she raised. She isn't the one leading it."

"They're on our side?" Michael replied, fighting back the grin at Leonie's remark.

"I hope so. I'm really tired of running." Sophie raised her voice and said, "Excuse me, but are you the free fae working with my sister, Emily?" Some of them turned to regard her, and she added, "She looks like me, but taller, and she's with a fairy named Eamon, who has silver hair. She sings a lot. If you've met her, you'll know just who I mean." She sounded like she was encountering an acquaintance at the supermarket, not addressing an army of otherworldly beings.

"You are Emily's sister?" one of the fae asked.

"Yes. She's down in that crowd, checking things out. I take it you're waiting for her signal to act. Well, I think I'm what you're waiting for."

Unlike most people encountering Sophie, he didn't just surrender to the inevitable and give in to whatever she wanted. "How do I know what you're saying is true?"

With a slight roll of her eyes, she moved her hands fluidly in front of her body, and then she began to glow. No bride was ever as radiant as this. She might not be wearing a physical crown, but she was crowned with a kind of light. The fae moved slightly away from her, though they didn't kneel.

"We want no queen," one of them said, and many of the others nodded agreement.

"Here we go again," Sophie muttered before saying out loud, "You need someone sitting on that throne and wearing the crown if you want to keep the Realm alive, and you're better off with me because I don't want to be there. As far as I'm concerned, you can all rule yourselves, just so long as I don't have to deal with you. Whoever it is down there probably won't be so lenient. She's already kicking the humans out."

That was when Michael noticed something about the gathered army: There were humans among them. They had that slightly off look of longtime human residents of the Realm, like his wife, Jen, had the last time he'd seen her, but they were still clearly human. "She's here with me, isn't she?" he said to the army. "She's helping me, not kicking me out. Speaking as a resident of the human world, I'd prefer her on the throne. The impostor has called out the Hunt. I want to stop her before she unleashes them on my world."

Sophie turned to look at him with surprise, like she'd forgotten he was there. She nodded. "Yes, that's what I want, to stop this. I don't want you to kneel to me or serve me. I just want to keep the Realm as free and alive as possible while keeping the human world safe. Are you with me?"

The leaders huddled, and Michael caught only wisps of

conversation. The occasional voice was raised, then quickly hushed. "What do you intend to do with an army?" Leonie asked her granddaughter.

"March in at the head of it and conquer my enemies?" Sophie said, as though it was painfully obvious.

"It would be awfully conspicuous," Michael pointed out. "And likely bloody." That won him a look of something that might have been approval from Leonie.

Sophie winced. "Oh. You're right. Once you get out the army, it's kind of hard to put it away." With a wry smile, she added, "I know choreography, not military strategy. Something tells me this isn't going to work quite like *Swan Lake*, with everyone going exactly where they're supposed to go, in perfect unison. What would you suggest?"

"Me? I'm no military strategist."

"You're a cop, though, and that's closer than a ballerina is."

"There aren't enough people here to take on the Hunt and everyone else down there," he said after thinking about it for a while. "They could work as backup, but you'll do better at sneaking in on your own."

"He's right," Leonie said. "If you come in with an army, you'll never get into the palace. They'll make a point of stopping you."

"Okay, then we'll sneak in and leave the army here for backup, assuming they agree," Sophie said with a nod. "Or even if they disagree, except then I won't have them as backup."

The free fae finished their huddle and turned to face Sophie. "We will support you. What will you have us do?" the leader said.

"Stay here and wait for my signal. I want to avoid bloodshed if at all possible."

With a smile, the leader said, "We are in agreement with that view. How will we know your signal?"

"Trust me, if I need to signal you, it'll be hard to miss. Now, I'm going to try to sneak in and disrupt the proceedings. Wish me luck!"

She, Leonie, and Michael made their way down the steep path. She held them back just before they reached the plain. "Do you see the Hunt?" she asked.

He looked for the telltale dust cloud, but it wasn't circling the palace. "Over there!" he said, pointing. He didn't see the riders themselves, merely a dark cloud with glowing red points in it. "It looks like they're gearing up to ride out."

"Then we'd best be moving," Leonie said, striding forward.

Sophie followed her grandmother. "I want to be in charge before they take off."

Michael had to hurry to catch up with both women. They slipped into the crowd, presumably hidden in some way, Michael hoped, and moved toward the palace.

The sound of trumpets rang out, seemingly coming from inside, but as loud and clear as if the trumpeters were standing on the outside balcony.

"Sounds like something's about to happen," Michael said.

"We need to get in there, *now*," Sophie said.

Thirty-Three

The crowd in the throne room went quiet at the sound of the fanfare, and they all turned to face the dais in anticipation. The main event was apparently about to happen. Emily clutched Eamon's hand, and he made a path through the throng toward where the sisters stood, Beau sleeping at Athena's feet.

"I'd guess someone's about to get crowned," Emily said.

"But with what? The crown is in Sophie's palace," Athena said.

"So is the real throne," Amelia said dryly. "That doesn't seem to be stopping them. Very few people have seen the authentic item in centuries. How much will it matter?"

A set of doors beside the dais opened, and the fanfare rang out again as a group of richly dressed fae processed onto the dais to stand on the steps. Emily stood on her toes to try to see over the crowd. "Wait a second, it's the rulers, the ones Sophie went to see," she said. "I recognize Fiontan and Niamh, Niall and Orla, and that woman who knew Sophie."

"Wasn't Sophie supposed to be talking to them?" Athena asked. She was also standing on her toes, but she was so tiny it did no good.

"I don't see Sophie," Emily said, a knot forming in her stomach. The last thing an impostor would want at her coronation would be the real queen. What had happened to Sophie? "She'd have been able to fight off a fake, right?" she asked Eamon.

"She is quite powerful and formidable." He surprised her by giving her hand a reassuring squeeze. If he felt the need to console her, that was a bad sign,.

After another short fanfare, the crowd turned to face the rear of the great hall. Emily got the sense that someone was moving through the center of the room. The attendees parted to allow the procession to pass. When it drew closer, Emily saw that it was a group of fairies who looked like young women, but who were probably centuries old. They were dressed something like the fairies in storybooks, with wispy dresses that swirled around them, decorating their shapely bodies rather than really concealing them. Their bright hair streamed down their backs, with garlands of flowers woven into it. The fairy in the center of the group held out a pillow of flowers, upon which rested a crown.

"Is that…" Emily started, her voice trailing off in dismay.

"It does look like Sophie's crown," Amelia said.

"But is it real or a copy, like the throne?" Emily asked.

"I believe it is real," Eamon said, squinting at the crown.

"How did they get it?" Emily asked, her pitch rising along with the panic surging through her body. "Sophie sealed it up. We saw that. No one should be able to get to it but Sophie." Now she *knew* that something must have happened to her sister. Sophie tended to get weird feelings when something bad happened to a family member, but Emily had felt nothing. Why couldn't that gift work both ways? She should know if her sister was in danger.

Athena stood on her toes again and craned her neck to get a glimpse of the procession as it passed by them. "Is that the impostor queen? The one with the crown?" she asked.

"No," Eamon replied, his eyes still on the group of fairies. "These must be handmaidens, here to present the crown to the queen. I wonder how that will work."

"How should it work?" Emily snapped. "They put the crown on her head, then it's a done deal."

"I don't know about that," Amelia said.

"You saw what your sister went through to win the throne," Eamon said. "Do you really think it's so simple as putting on a crown?"

"It could be dangerous for someone who didn't win it to put that crown on," Athena said.

"Then why have it here?" Emily asked.

"They must have some plan," Amelia said.

"Probably a crown switcheroo," Athena suggested. "They parade the real one through the crowd so everyone can see it up close and know it's real, then put a fake one on the impostor's head."

The handmaidens made it to the foot of the dais and stood there. The trumpets sounded one more time, this fanfare longer, louder, and more elaborate than the previous ones. The crowd drew to attention like the trumpets had just played the opening bars of "The Star-Spangled Banner," and a set of doors behind the gallery overlooking the dais opened.

A parade of uniformed guards came through the door, taking their places along the gallery. After one last trumpet flourish, a richly robed woman appeared in the doorway.

She was so far away, it was hard to see much about her, other than that she was tall and had reddish hair. The crowd took a moment to respond with tepid applause that gradually built in intensity and volume. It didn't seem quite as loud as Emily might have expected from such a large group, so she hoped the whisper campaign had done at least some good.

The woman didn't appear to acknowledge the applause. She merely stood totally still. The air around the gallery shimmered, and a great, red-carpeted staircase appeared, curving down from the side of the gallery to the dais. The guards on that side marched down the staircase, each guard taking a position on a step. The remaining guards formed columns on either side of the queen-to-be, marching alongside her as she made her way across the gallery and swept down the staircase.

Her long cloak streamed behind her on the steps. Emily was impressed that she went down the stairs without lifting the hem of her long skirt, but she made it without mishap. Once on the dais, she walked straight to the throne and sat on it.

Finally, Emily was able to get a good look at her, and she gasped out loud.

Apparently, she wasn't imagining things, for Amelia also gasped and blurted, "My word! It's Jennifer Murray!"

✑Thirty-Four✑

The Palace Doors
Meanwhile

Sophie knew she could open the palace doors, but doing that without being noticed was more of a challenge. If she'd had the crown, she'd have flung open the doors and made a grand entrance. Without it, she wasn't so sure she could pull that off. Sure, she could radiate royalty, but would that convince a crowd when someone wearing a crown was sitting on a throne?

Michael tapped her on the elbow. "What about a servants' entrance, like you used to sneak into your own palace?"

"You enter your own palace through the servants' entrance?" Nana asked, aghast. "That's just not done."

"I had good reason," Sophie replied. She worried her lower lip between her teeth as she mulled it over. There was something thematically appropriate about it, the kind of thing that would happen in a fairy tale. On the other hand, Nana could be right. Was that the way for the rightful queen to make an appearance? But if she did it right, no one would know, and they'd never think to look for her entering that way. "I really think that's our best option right now. Let's go," she said.

There was a constant flow of people in and out of a side entrance, and it was easy enough for the three of them to slip in among the others. She gave them the glamour of servants, over Nana's objections, and they joined the line of fairies carrying laden trays up to the throne room.

Another trumpet fanfare sounded while they made their way into the room. Sophie didn't have a chance to look up at whatever was happening until she set her tray on a table. She'd never waited tables, so carrying a tray of fancy food wasn't a skill she'd ever developed, and this was not the time or place for a rookie mishap. When she, Nana, and Michael had all divested themselves of their trays, she adjusted their glamours to fit into the gathered attendees.

Michael suddenly grabbed her arm as some kind of procession moved through the center of the room. She couldn't quite see what it was, but he had a much better vantage point. "It's your crown," he said, bending to speak into her ear.

Nana studied the procession, shaking her head. "That's the crown? It's not quite what I pictured."

"They're not going to be crazy enough to put it on anyone, are they?" Sophie said, turning to Michael in dismay.

"It would serve her right," he said, raising an eyebrow.

"Is that Emily over there?" Nana asked.

Sophie followed her gaze across the throne room. "Yes. She's here with the enchantresses."

"And a fairy, looks like." Before Sophie could stop her, she headed across the throne room, straight for Emily.

"Oh, that's going to be fun," Sophie grumbled. "There's no telling what Emily will say about bringing her here."

"But for the moment, she's out of your hair," Michael pointed out.

"I'd rather keep an eye on her."

Another fanfare rang out, drawing their attention to the head of the room. They watched as soldiers came out onto a gallery, and soon a tall, red-haired woman in royal robes thick with jewels and embroidery came out and stood for a moment. Sophie couldn't see far enough to get any sense of who the woman might be, but strangely, she didn't read as fae. A human? She supposed it made sense if any word at all had spread about the fate of the last queen or of the identity of the new queen. Aside from her height, this woman might fit a rough description of Sophie, so her appearance wouldn't contradict any rumors.

But if the impostor was human, that probably meant she was a puppet, and someone else, likely fae, was pulling the strings. Maeve couldn't leave the real palace, but it could be one of the other rulers who couldn't take the throne when it was known that someone else had won it, but they could rule from behind the scenes if they found a patsy who fit the profile.

The impostor came down the curving staircase and took her throne, and that was when Sophie recognized her. She barely had the chance to realize that it was Jen Murray before she had to leap to hold Michael back from rushing to the dais to reach his wife.

"Not now," she hissed, dragging him further back into the crowd.

"It's Jen!" he protested.

"I noticed. But what do you plan to do, in this crazy crowd when we don't know what's going on?"

His eyes were wild and his breath came in deep gasps, but reason gradually returned to his face, and he nodded. She kept her arm around his waist, just in case. "You're not going to let them put that crown on her, are you?" he asked, his voice hoarse with anguish.

"I won't let them hurt her," she promised.

"She wanted to be a princess. Do you think this was her idea?"

"I think she's being used." It was hard to tell from this distance, but Jen's face was even blanker than it had been when they first discovered her in the Realm. She might not be objecting to the royal treatment, but Sophie doubted she was the one behind the plot. "Let's see what happens," she urged, trying to keep her voice as soothing as possible even as her thoughts churned over this latest development. Had Jen been here all along? If so, the image Sophie had seen in her palace of Jen leaving with Fiontan and Niamh's court must have been faked, probably by whoever had put the various spells on the palace. It had done the trick of distracting her while casting suspicion on the wrong people. But who was the puppet master pulling Jen's strings?

The fairy rulers had been moved from their cell to the throne room and stood on the dais. Sophie thought a silent apology to Tallulah for losing the crown. If only she still had that, she could easily have stepped up and challenged the impostor. Without it, her claim wasn't quite as obvious, and making that claim now might put Jen at risk. Tallulah didn't seem at all dismayed, though. She must have had a plan, but Sophie couldn't figure out what it might be. It would have been nice if Tallulah had shared it with her.

"Who has come here to acknowledge my rule?" Jen said, her voice ringing through the vast chamber. Sophie recalled that she'd been an actress before being abducted by the fairies, and she still had the vocal projection for it.

The captive rulers glanced at each other, their reluctance obvious. They knew she wasn't the real queen, but would they play along? Were they being threatened or under a compulsion? It seemed like a very risky move to have them there.

It was Niall, the one who looked like a character in a 1930s movie, who stepped forward first. Dropping to one knee, he bowed his head and pressed his hand against his chest. "My queen, it is my duty and honor to serve you."

When his consort, Orla, was the next to step forward, Sophie got suspicious. By going first, they'd put all the others in a very difficult position. Either they followed suit, or they called those two out as liars. If Niall and Orla were behind this, that had been neatly played.

The others did all fall in line, taking their turns in front of Queen Jen. Tallulah was last, and Sophie found herself holding her breath. Would she, too, play along, or was she up to something?

Tallulah moved forward to face the throne, but she didn't kneel. She gazed at Jen for a long time until the throne room grew utterly silent in anticipation. Finally, she said, "I do not bow to a queen who hasn't been crowned." She gestured toward the crown being held on a cushion of flowers. "But here the crown is, ready for you. We seem to have done this all backward. Doesn't the coronation come *before* the oaths of fealty?"

Sophie was even more certain that Niall must be the mastermind when he twitched visibly. Obviously, this hadn't been part of his plan. And Sophie had a sneaking suspicion that it *had* been Tallulah's plan. That's why she wanted the crown present.

But there was one thing Tallulah hadn't counted on: the impostor's husband.

Michael wrenched himself away from Sophie and strode forward to stand at the bottom of the dais steps, directly in front of the throne. "This woman is my wife, and I've come to claim her," he declared.

"Oh dear," Sophie whispered to herself. This was about to get very complicated—and very dangerous.

⚪Thirty-Five⚪

Michael hadn't even thought before acting. All he knew was that he couldn't let that crown be put on Jen's head. Beyond that, he had no plan, no idea what to do next.

The woman staring down at him from the silver throne looked like the wife he remembered, but she regarded him like he was a complete stranger. When he'd seen her in the Realm before, she'd been distressed when he said he was her husband. Now, though, she just looked at him with mild amusement.

"You claim me as your wife, do you?" she said. "It's not so easy to take a queen as your bride. You'll have to win me."

Michael went cold as he realized he was facing that challenge Mrs. Smith had warned him about. Unfortunately, he was no better prepared now than he had been then. He'd made one trade of value, and then he'd become sidetracked by everything else that had happened since the market. What would he have to do to win his own wife back? Slay a dragon?

Jen paused for a moment before she leaned forward, smiling slightly. "Do you love me, brave champion?"

Feeling like he was trapped living out a fairy tale, he forced himself to respond in a way that fit the scenario. "With all my heart." His voice broke slightly on the last word.

She rose from her throne, and the air shimmered around her, dissolving her into a blur. The blur resolved into three Jens, all of them identical. "Which of us is the real one?" they asked in perfect unison.

Of course, there would be a test. He had to prove his love for her, and a man who loved a woman should be able to pick her out of a lineup. He didn't think it was fair, though, when they were perfect copies.

He had to fight back a smile when he realized *that* was the trick. Two of them were illusions, and seeing past fae illusions was one of the gifts he'd been stuck with after his previous adventures in the Realm. He ever so casually slipped his hand into his pocket to grab the four-leaf clover keychain so he'd have all the help he could get with this. Jen had given him the keychain long ago, saying he was her lucky charm and he needed one of his own. He doubted she could possibly have imagined how he'd end up using it.

After a blink, two of the Jens faded into nothingness. He walked straight to the one on the right, took her hand, and kissed it. "My lady," he said formally. He hoped he wasn't imagining things or flattering himself when he thought her smile looked genuine. Did she want him to win? Hope rose in his chest, giving him a surge of strength.

What really surprised him was the response of the attendees. They applauded and shouted approval, and he glanced back to see that he had quite the cheering section. He supposed everyone loved a good romance. Then he noticed Sophie standing nearby. He'd forgotten about her in his rush to save Jen, and he could only imagine what she was thinking now. She'd probably kill him when she got a chance, but he didn't care what she did after he got Jen out of this mess and safely back home.

Actually, Sophie didn't look too angry, he thought. She was very pale, and though she stood perfectly still, he could tell she was tense. The vibe he got from her was *don't screw this up*. He had no intention of doing so.

Jen slid her hand out of his grasp, and he realized he'd forgotten to let go. He felt the loss of her touch keenly as she moved back to her throne in a swish of skirts. "Well done, my brave champion," she said as she took her seat, a hint of mockery in her tone, but perhaps a note of fondness, as well. Or was that just wishful thinking? "Now, what have you to offer for me?"

If he'd said out loud what he was thinking, he'd owe the precinct a fortune for the penalty jar. He knew that was going to come up, and he'd utterly failed. He somehow doubted that a fairy-made shawl he'd traded an angel figurine for would hold muster. Otherwise, he had the keychain, about twenty bucks, his sidearm, and some iron nails that he didn't think would go over well as a gift of love.

She gestured toward his left hand. "Is that gold? That ring would do nicely, I'm sure."

He automatically folded his right hand over his left, hiding his wedding band. Without thinking, he said, "No. This ring doesn't leave my finger. It hasn't left my finger since you put it there nearly ten years ago." Well, except for the time he was in surgery and intensive care, but he'd had no say in that, so he didn't think it counted. He wasn't sure if refusing her was the right thing to do—maybe he was supposed to give up anything, including the token of their love, in order to win her. After all, the ring was merely a thing, a symbol, and she was what really mattered. But it felt right. Sophie and the enchantresses had told him that he'd never be able to free Jen if he'd moved on, and the ring was a sign that he hadn't. Out of the corner of his eye, he saw Sophie nodding ever so slightly, so he had a feeling he'd passed a test.

Jen looked vexed for a split second, but then she smiled. "I will not ask for your ring. But surely you have something else of value to give, if you treasure me as much as you say you do."

"Who will I be paying?" he asked, mostly to stall for time. "Am I buying you from someone, or am I winning you with a gift?"

"It is for me, of course," she said. "And I am not easily impressed. I have all this." She gestured at her jewel-encrusted clothes and the opulent surroundings. He couldn't help but smile as he remembered their original courtship. She was the daughter of a wealthy, important man, and he was a cop, still in uniform back then. Although she was trying to make it on her own as an actress without relying on her father's money, she was hard to impress with material goods. He wouldn't have stood a chance if he'd had to buy her affections with gifts and favors. It had been a fancy date if they ate at a restaurant with seats instead of grabbing something from a street cart.

Then he remembered: He had a favor! That counted as currency in this world, and it would be hard to put a price on it. He reached into his satchel and pulled out the embroidered cloth. "This was given to me to signify a debt owed to me," he said. "I delivered a baby. I understand that doesn't happen very often here." The collective gasp of the audience behind him was almost enough to create suction, it was so strong. He got the impression he'd made a good move.

He stepped forward to hand the token to Jen. "Now the favor is owed to you," he said.

She gave a sidelong glance to where the other fairy rulers still stood in a line. He guessed that the guy in the tux was pulling her strings. He'd gone first in recognizing her, and Michael knew for a fact that he knew Jen was an impostor because he'd been there when Sophie won the throne. The tux guy didn't look happy, but the audience was too enthusiastic about this gift for him to get away with making Jen reject it. He nodded slightly, and Jen's eyes went distant for a moment, as though she was listening to instructions on a magical earwig.

Jen returned her focus to Michael, and she granted him a warm smile. He might have been imagining things, but he was sure she looked more like herself and less like the brainwashed shell she'd been when she'd first sat on the throne. Were the bonds on her weakening? Mrs. Smith had mentioned having to show bravery, and he didn't want to think about what that might entail. Maybe that was where the dragon came in.

"This is an excellent gift," Jen said, squeezing the cloth in her hand, then apparently noticing what she was doing and spreading it out carefully on her knee. "You have demonstrated your love and shown how much you value me, but love is not enough to catch a queen. No, my consort must be the bravest champion in the Realm, defending me against all my enemies."

I knew it, Michael thought. He wondered what this was going to entail. He'd had hand-to-hand training in the academy, but taking down a perp as quickly and efficiently as possible wasn't the sort of thing that made for a good show of fairy-tale valor. He had no idea what to do with a sword beyond acting out lightsaber battles with his brothers using cardboard gift-wrap tubes. He wondered if he could get away with pulling an Indiana Jones and just shooting his sword-swinging opponent. He was a really good shot, and that should count for something.

Of course, it all depended on the opponent. Was he going to have to joust against the queen's champion? But no, she'd mentioned enemies. One of the free fae who didn't want a queen?

Jen rose from the throne and came toward him, taking his hands in hers and bringing them to her breast. "My greatest enemy is among us here today. There is a vile witch who would keep me from my rightful throne. Slay her for me and win my heart." She released his hands, ending him off on the mission.

Michael glanced at the tall, red-haired fairy who'd insisted that Jen put on the crown before she'd kneel. Was this the "witch" he was to slay? And how was he supposed to do that? "I'm not really armed for this sort of thing," he said. A split second later, a sword appeared in his hand. "Oh, good," he muttered. Now he just had to avoid making a fool out of himself. And slay a witch.

Jen wasn't looking at the red-haired fairy, though. She was looking out into the crowd, and there Michael saw a woman who looked like the evil queen's disguise in the Disney Snow White movie, the old hag who offered the princess a poisoned apple. She certainly looked evil, but she also looked like an unarmed old woman. It didn't seem very gentlemanly to go after her with a sword.

He glanced at Jen, who pointed at the woman and shouted, "Kill her!"

When he turned back to his opponent, he saw her out of the corner of his eye and realized it was Sophie. To free his wife, would he have to kill his friend?

He stood frozen, unable to act. This situation was utterly impossible. He couldn't kill Sophie, not even for Jen. The human world needed a fairy ruler who wasn't the puppet of an anti-human psycho, so Sophie needed to win. And that meant he'd lost. All that effort to save his wife, and it came down to this.

Sophie hadn't moved, either. She just stared at him with her odd, mismatched eyes, seemingly daring him to attack. He couldn't, though. As formidable as Sophie was, she wasn't his enemy, and she was unarmed. As if reading his mind, she dropped her tote bag and held out her hand. A sword appeared in her grasp. With a theatrical flourish, she spun around neatly and landed in a defensive posture. He suddenly remembered everything she'd said about how dancers were fast, agile, strong, and had excellent balance and great endurance. He might have more upper-body strength when he was at his best, and his significant height difference gave him a better reach, but he had a feeling he was toast if she really fought.

He studied her face for a moment and thought he saw a glimmer of something in her eyes. He knew she'd do everything in her power to help him win back Jen and that she also wasn't going to let fairy politics harm the human world. He was going to have to trust her and hope she trusted him. He let his bag slip off his shoulder and raised his weapon.

⮐Thirty-Six⮐

Emily barely had time to react to the fact that Jen was the impostor queen before Michael stepped up. That meant Sophie was around somewhere. She wouldn't be that far from Michael. Emily just couldn't see her sister anywhere. That had to be either because she was short or because she had put on a glamour. Maybe both. If she was here, the fireworks were sure to begin soon.

But really, *Jen* was the fake? "Oh," Emily said out loud, drawing Eamon and the enchantresses' attention away from the drama on the dais. "I bet I know what that compulsion was about. Whoever's behind this—and I'm betting on Niall—needed a fake who matches Sophie's description. Who better than her sister? I've got similar coloring, and I'm human with fae blood, though it isn't as obvious as in Sophie. They were trying to pull me back to the Realm. When that didn't work, they went with plan B, which is Jen. She got taken in the first place because they thought she was me, so other than the lack of fae blood, she fits."

"And the compulsion to get you into the palace?" Amelia asked.

"Jen may have been resisting, so they needed a backup." Emily returned her attention to the dais, where three Jennifers were facing Michael. "She's going along with it now."

"She may not have much choice," Eamon said. "If she's under the kind of thrall you were under, she may be unable to resist the orders she's being given."

Emily barely suppressed a shudder at the thought of what might have happened to her if Sophie hadn't meddled and sent Eamon to babysit her. She could have been the puppet on the throne, luring her sister into danger.

"Why, Emily Mae, look at you, all grown up." The voice jolted her back to the present, and she turned to find herself facing a stranger who looked oddly familiar. She was a petite redhead dressed in a "ladies who lunch" suit. If it hadn't been so far from Sophie's style, she'd have almost mistaken the woman for her sister. But she seemed older than Sophie, even though she didn't look old at all. The woman smiled, clearly enjoying Emily's discomfiture. "Don't tell me you don't recognize your own grandmother."

"Nana?" Now it all clicked into place. Emily had seen old family photos in which Nana had looked like this, but they were back from when Emily and Sophie's father had been a boy. The last time Emily had seen her grandmother had been at Christmas several years ago, and Nana had been bedridden and barely lucid—nothing like the woman facing her now. "What are you doing here?"

"Your sister needed my help."

"So you got out of bed and came into the Realm?"

"Don't be silly. Sophie and her friend came and got me. And don't worry, we left a changeling so your mother won't know."

Emily wasn't sure how to react to seeing her invalid grandmother looking young again and in the middle of things in the fairy realm. It was hard to decide which thing to freak out about. "So, Sophie popped out of the Realm, brought you here, left a changeling, and apparently made you young and healthy again because she needs help?"

"Exactly. I'm glad you've finally caught up." Nana glanced around the throne room, sizing up the situation. "And I can see why Sophie thought she'd need help. She seems to be in some trouble, and her friend isn't helping matters. I thought we'd discussed not forcing a confrontation."

"The impostor turned out to be his wife, who was taken by the fairies years ago," Emily explained.

"Oh, yes, that would explain his behavior. She mentioned his wife being taken, but I didn't realize *this* was the wife. That rather complicates the situation, doesn't it? Is he a threat to Sophie?"

"I don't think so. They're pretty good friends." Out of discretion, she decided to leave out the part about Sophie being in love with him. Nana would probably figure that out for herself. "Sophie will do what it takes to help him free his wife." She turned to the others. "Can Michael free her, or is all this just for show?"

"There are rules," Eamon said. "If he fulfills the requirements of the trial, she has to be freed. That's how the magic works."

"Which means the trials may be impossible," Amelia said. "That's how the fae like to do things."

Nana cleared her throat and looked very pointedly at Eamon and the enchantresses. "Oh, right," Emily said. "Nana, this is Amelia and Athena. I used to work for them. They're enchantresses. And this is my friend Eamon. Guys, this is my grandmother, Leonie Drake." Nana raised an eyebrow at the introduction of the fairy, but she didn't comment. Emily wondered if Sophie had briefed her on that.

Up at the dais, a sword appeared in Michael's hand. "Now may be the time for your army to make its presence known," Amelia said to Emily. "You should go get them."

"But Michael's here, and that means Sophie is here, too. She has to be," Emily protested.

"What would you do to help them if you stayed?" Athena asked.

That wasn't really a fair question. "Moral support?" Emily suggested weakly.

"They don't need another spectator," Nana said.

"But it might confuse matters somewhat if yet another would-be queen arrives at the head of her army," Amelia put in. Emily looked back and forth among the three women. If they tag-teamed, she was in trouble.

"They were going to use you, so it fits," Athena added.

Emily couldn't help but grin. "I like the way you think. Sophie may kill me, but I'll die having fun." She took Eamon's hand. "Come on. I'll need glamouring up. Y'all watch Beau. Don't let him do anything stupid." Considering that the dog was sprawled on the floor, snoring, there wasn't much chance of anything resembling action on his part, but when Sophie was involved, there was no telling what might happen.

The audience was so caught up in the events at the front of the throne room that it was relatively easy to slip out. Even the guards had moved away from the doors in an attempt to get a better vantage point.

Things were somewhat different outside, where the festivities continued, the gathered crowd oblivious to what was taking place inside. It was probably a good thing the Realm didn't have Jumbotrons, Emily thought. This way, she might stand a chance of having the entire crowd on her side before she entered the palace at the head of her army.

The Hunt didn't seem to be making its rounds anymore, which made Emily wonder what they were up to. But she didn't have time to worry about that. She and Eamon hurried up the hill to where the army still waited.

"Why would your sister have brought your grandmother?" Eamon asked as they walked.

"I have no idea. I guess theoretically she's also in line for the throne, and she might have the kind of power Sophie does. We could probably use the help. But she's way too much like Sophie, so this could make things very interesting."

"She's like Sophie?" Eamon asked warily, and she gave him a grim nod in reply.

"Let's just say that a lot of it seems to be genetic."

"So we should probably hurry to secure the army and return."

"You got it." Although she was tired, she forced herself to walk faster toward the place where the army was supposed to gather.

Fortunately, they were exactly where they were supposed to

be. "Emily!" the leader said when she approached. "We were waiting for your sister's signal."

"You met Sophie?" It must have gone well, since they all appeared to be in one piece.

"Yes, she and her consort arrived here. You didn't tell us your sister was queen of the Realm."

"Now you know how I knew the queen taking action against you was an impostor."

"Should we continue to wait for the signal?"

"Change of plans. Do you think you can glamour up some shiny armor? It seems that the queen needs an army, and it's gotta look good."

✑Thirty-Seven✑

The Dais
Meanwhile

Sophie held her breath as she waited to see what Michael would do. She didn't think he'd actually try to hurt her—he wasn't that desperate yet—but what he did next would affect the plan she was still frantically spinning in her head.

She didn't yet see a way out. She owed it to him not to be the one thing standing between him and his wife. Any temptation she might ever have had to allow him a gallant failure so he'd have to give up on saving Jennifer and move on with his life (preferably with her) was thwarted by the head-to-head nature of this trial. Defeating him would mean she'd never have him, even if he lost Jen forever, because she'd be responsible for the loss. She didn't think he could forgive that.

At the same time, she couldn't allow an impostor to steal her throne and use her rightful position to attack the human world, no matter who that impostor was. It was a no-win situation, and the best she could do was play for time until she could come up with an idea or someone else could make a move.

It felt like ages before Michael lunged at her with his sword.

His eyes telegraphed exactly where he was aiming, so she easily danced out of the way. She didn't think he knew anything about this kind of fighting, but she was sure that not telegraphing his moves in a fight would have been part of his police training. That must mean he was playing along. Her swordplay experience was limited to choreographed stage bouts that were more dance than fighting, but that meant she could make this look good.

She parried his thrust and focused intently on the spot just below his right shoulder, leaning her body ever so slightly in that direction before making her riposte. As she'd hoped, he saw the blow coming and blocked it. She danced back out of the way with a pirouette just for show, avoiding his retaliatory strike and parrying his riposte as she came out of the turn.

The crowd booed, and she realized that she'd been cast as the villain. She could only imagine what Niall—and it had to be Niall—had made her look like. Jen had called her a vile witch, so she probably looked like a suitably evil crone. That would certainly make some of her moves look even more impressive.

She jumped sideways to avoid Michael's next strike, doing a grand glissade that took her legs to a near-split in mid-leap. It would be a terrible move in a real fight, but the amount of air she got looked good. As soon as she landed, she went into a series of lightning-fast chaîné turns. Spinning as she traveled, she came up behind Michael and swung at him. He caught her sword with a backswing.

They stood for a moment, their swords pressed together, and she thought he looked like he was having to work to hide a smile. This was fun, actually. Or it would be, if the stakes weren't so life-or-death and if she knew how to end it suitably. What would happen if she let him win? If she surrendered, they might make him kill her, but maybe she could fake her death. She'd never made herself vanish in a puff of smoke, and this was no situation for trying something new, but she might be able to glamour herself in such a way that she could get out of sight, and then she could still take the crown and prove herself the rightful ruler.

But would that fulfill the magical requirements of whatever

held Jen? To win, he'd have to defeat the witch, as he was ordered. She wasn't sure a faked death or a surrender would count. Since she had no intention of actually dying, faking would be the best she could do. Maybe she could get away with just killing the hag glamour Niall must have given her.

They continued circling each other, doing the occasional thrust, parry, riposte combination. He kept his movements strong and economical, while she put in enough flash to make it look like taunting. Neither of them had drawn blood, and it sounded like the crowd was growing impatient. They were calling out for her head, booing every time Michael swung at her without killing her. When she managed a quick glance at Jen, the would-be queen looked like she was ready for this to be over with. She drummed her fingers impatiently on the arm of her throne.

That meant the fight needed to start looking a little more real. Sophie aimed her sword at the inside of Michael's coat, where the audience couldn't see what happened to it, hoping he got the message. Her jacket was unbuttoned, with the belt undone, so if he just got the tip of his sword inside her jacket, she could make it look like he'd got in a good strike.

He caught on right away, and she loved him a little more for it. Once his sword made it into the depths of her coat, she cried out and flinched before parrying his sword away. Instead of moving gracefully out of reach, she staggered backward, her free hand pressed against her side. The crowd roared their approval.

Sophie forced herself to move more slowly, like she was in pain, when she counterattacked. She aimed a flurry of strikes against his sword, which he easily batted away. Then he left himself open, as though encouraging her to get in a good hit of her own.

No, that's not how this works, she wanted to scream at him. This wasn't about playing fair. She was the villain, the wicked witch, the evil usurper queen. He was Prince Charming. He was supposed to win, not be a gentleman and let her look good.

Then again, it did add a little drama to the proceedings if the hero got at least a bit bloody. Why not give Jen the chance to worry about him? Maybe it would jolt her more back to herself if she thought her husband was wounded. Sophie took the opening he gave her and thrust her sword into the depths of his coat with an evil cackle.

It took all Sophie's willpower not to grin at his response. Jen might have been the actress in that marriage, but he'd picked up a thing or two. For a second, Sophie even wondered if she'd miscalculated and had actually struck him, his look of dismay and betrayal was so powerful. If he'd reached into his coat and brought back a hand covered in blood, she might not have been too surprised.

He staggered quite theatrically, and when he caught Sophie's eye it looked to her like he was fighting not to laugh. She'd never seen him as being such a ham, but then she hadn't spent any time with him when there wasn't an immediate crisis, so while she knew the kind of man he was deep down inside, she didn't really know what he was like on a day-to-day basis.

He pulled himself together with a visible effort and lunged at her. His attack was so ferocious that she had to react quickly to avoid it and barely skittered out of the way. Even though the fight was fake, she was starting to get tired, and he looked even worse. He was breathing hard and a little pale. It was time to end it.

She caught his eye, and when she was sure she had his attention, she closed her eyes in a very decisive way, trying to signal her intentions. He flinched, so she got the feeling he'd read her correctly. She nodded, and the distress on his face was evident as he raised his sword.

She built the glamour in her mind as the sword came toward her. At the last second, she ducked and rolled out of the way as she brought up the illusion that would show the old hag falling to the floor under her cloak. Meanwhile, she threw up another glamour around herself, making herself invisible as she lay on the floor. Michael should be able to see what really happened, but it was hard to tell, the distress on his face was so evident.

The crowd roared, and Michael slowly turned to face them, his sword hanging by his side. Sophie quickly added a glamour of blood to his blade so his victory would look authentic. He acknowledged the audience, then returned his attention to Jen, who had risen from the throne, beaming. She held her hands out to him, and his smile brought tears to Sophie's eyes as he moved toward his wife.

"Michael?" Jen said softly when he came to her, reaching up to touch her husband's face. For the first time since Sophie had known her, Jen's eyes were clear and sharp, like she was finally fully conscious of who she was.

His eyes glittered with unshed tears as he said, "Yeah, it's me."

"Michael, they made me do it," she said, her voice shaking.

"It's okay, I know," he replied, putting his arms around her and drawing her against his body. With a strangled sob, she buried her face against his shoulder. He dropped his sword, letting it clatter onto the floor, as he held her like he would never let her go. It looked like the happy ending of a romantic movie with the hero and heroine happily reunited and together forevermore.

Sophie had to wipe tears from her eyes. She knew she'd lost him, but seeing him this happy made it worth it. This was what she'd set out to achieve, undoing the wrong that had been done because of her. It was amazing that she could hurt so badly and yet be so dizzyingly happy at the same time. So, this was what it was to love, what she'd been missing out on with her oh-so-busy life. Maybe she could find it again, and this time with someone more available.

When the cheering and applause eventually dimmed somewhat, Tallulah broke the spell by stepping up and saying, "This is all lovely, but the fact remains that a queen needs to be crowned here today so we may all kneel before her."

Michael and Jen broke apart enough to turn to stare at Tallulah, he in alarm, she in confusion. She glanced at Niall, as if asking for direction. Michael might have restored her to herself and made it possible for her to choose to leave the Realm, but Niall still seemed to have some hold over her. Surely he wouldn't be crazy enough to make her put on a crown that would kill her, or did he have something else up his sleeve? Sophie couldn't take the chance.

Removing her invisibility glamour, she let her full royal glory show as she rose to her feet. Jen gasped and put a hand to her mouth, Tallulah smiled wickedly, Niall and Orla glared daggers, and the other rulers looked relieved. The crowd close to the dais reacted with a rumble of noise that was difficult to judge, but Sophie was most focused on Michael's face. His relief at seeing that she really was alive was almost palpable, and he gave every sign of rushing to hug her. But then a voice from the crowd cried out, "She's an impostor!"

Sophie followed the sound and saw her grandmother moving through the crowd. Nana didn't seem to be able to see Sophie from where she was, so Sophie suspected she was talking about Jen and didn't know Sophie had revealed herself. But to much of the audience, it looked like she was accusing Sophie of being the fake. Before Sophie could think of a way to salvage the situation, the doors at the back of the throne room flew open with a resounding bang and a radiant figure on a white horse entered, calling out, "This queen is an impostor!"

Thirty-Eight

Emily wasn't sure where the free fae managed to scare up horses or if they even had. She didn't want to think about the possibility that she might be riding an illusion. It felt real enough. Fortunately, she didn't feel the clothes she could see herself wearing because they looked pretty uncomfortable. She'd spent a summer in college playing a member of the royal court at a Renaissance festival, and she had a feeling that the heavy, jewel-encrusted brocade she appeared to be wearing would be even worse than full Tudor garb in July.

But she knew that when you're riding into a palace at the head of an army, you've got to make the right impression, so she'd had Eamon give her the full treatment. She wondered if the camera on her phone would capture the reality or the glamour. It would be fun to have a picture of this.

The reaction of the gathered population of the Realm as she rode down the hill was everything she'd hoped it would be. They didn't know that the queen was inside the palace already, so the richly attired woman surrounded by armored knights arriving at the palace must have made total sense to them.

She raised a regal hand to quiet the cheers that rose as she entered the grounds. "Thank you, my people!" she called out. "It does my heart great good to see you all here. But you should know that I didn't call you to this place. The so-called queen within the palace is an impostor. Will you support me in claiming my throne from her?"

Their roar was very satisfying. Emily couldn't help but smile. Then she remembered that her sister, the true queen, was also inside the palace, and she had no idea what Sophie might be up to. As she kicked her horse into motion to head toward the palace doors, she decided that adding confusion to the situation should help in the short term, since Sophie could definitively prove her right to the throne.

Two of her soldiers went ahead to open the great palace doors, and she rode straight into the throne room. *I have* got *to do a fantasy movie,* she thought to herself as she forced herself not to grin like an idiot about living out this scenario. She wasn't sure if it was happy accident or more of Eamon's handiwork when a beam of light hit her just so, right as she dramatically declared, "This queen is an impostor!"

She kept riding forward, the stunned attendees clearing the way, and she had to fight not to wince when she saw Sophie standing at the foot of the dais in full queen mode, with Jen on the dais and still in her regalia. And not too far away was Nana, looking like a redheaded Queen Elizabeth II in her suit and hat. Oops. Now everyone was going to wonder which queen she meant was the impostor.

Michael, who looked utterly exhausted, stood with his arm around Jen, which meant at least something had gone well—for Michael. Emily glanced at her sister. No one else would have noticed anything was wrong, but Emily knew Sophie well enough to know that her heart was breaking in two. Emily shook her head fondly. Only Sophie would be so noble as to put herself at risk to help the man she loved get back together with his long-lost wife. No wonder she was still single.

Jen's eyes clouded again and she pulled away from Michael. "She is the impostor!" She pointed straight at Emily.

"Am I?" Emily asked. "What about her?" She pointed at her grandmother. "Or her?" She turned to indicate her sister.

Jen looked from Nana to Sophie, and she looked confused. She shook her head and blinked, like she was trying to clear the cobwebs. "I'm not really the queen, either," Jen called out, raising her voice so it would be heard throughout the throne room. "She's the real queen." She pointed at Sophie. "The crown belongs to her."

Niall lost all his suave cool at that. "What did I tell you?" he snarled as he rushed toward Jen and Michael. A blade appeared in his hand, and he brought it down on Jen. Or where Jen would have been if Michael hadn't gotten in the way.

Emily, Jen, and Sophie all cried out at once, and Emily thought she heard other voices. Jen caught Michael as he fell, and Emily saw a flash of metal as Sophie picked up a sword from the ground and ran it through Niall in one fluid movement. Orla lunged toward her husband, but was tackled by the other fairy rulers.

Emily wasn't sure what it looked like when a fairy died. They were essentially immortal, so they didn't age or get sick, but supposedly they could be killed. Niall just vanished, along with the sword sticking through his body. Was that a fairy death, or had something else happened?

But that wasn't Emily's main concern at the moment. She jumped off her horse and ran toward where Jen cradled Michael on the steps of the dais. Sophie was already sitting beside them, and Eamon, Amelia, Athena, Nana, and Beau weren't far behind.

Jen searched her husband for wounds. "I don't understand. There should be blood, shouldn't there? But he's unconscious, and so pale." She stroked his face. "Michael, please, wake up. I'm sorry, so, so sorry. This is all my fault."

"No, it's not," Sophie told her, a reassuring hand on her shoulder. "You got caught up in something far bigger than you know."

Emily knelt by her sister and squeezed her hand in silent support. Sophie was holding it together pretty well, but Emily could tell she was on the verge of snapping. "What is it, Soph? Is there something you need me to do?" Emily asked.

"I think it was a magical weapon," Sophie said, freeing her hand from Emily's after a quick squeeze so she could examine Michael. "No blood, but maybe a curse. He was hit earlier with something similar, so maybe this triggered that spell to make it worse."

"Can you break it?" Jen asked tearfully.

"I don't know. But you may be able to," Sophie replied.

"How?"

"We're in a fairy tale, and he just won your freedom. Kiss him."

In spite of the magnitude of the situation, Jen raised a skeptical eyebrow, like she thought Sophie had to be joking. "Kiss him?"

"You're in the fairy world and your husband is under a curse," Sophie shot back. "Haven't you ever seen a Disney movie? If it doesn't work, I'll think of something else."

"We're working on it," Amelia called out from where she and Athena were digging through their bags and arguing softly with each other. Beau waddled over and plopped down against Michael's legs, nudging him with his nose. Emily figured he'd make a good plan B. She was sure the dog was awfully fond of Michael. His wife was probably a better candidate for a loving kiss, though. Emily had to admit that it would also be interesting to see if Sophie could save him. She certainly loved him enough, but that would open up a whole can of worms and maybe inspire a soap opera or two.

"Okay, if you think it'll work," Jen said. She bent to kiss Michael on the lips.

Emily realized she was holding her breath as they all waited to see what would happen. Sophie might have looked more anxious than Jen did. She'd gone absolutely ashen, tears trickled down her cheeks, and her lips moved in a silent prayer. Emily took her sister's hand again, and Sophie clutched it hard enough to crack her knuckles.

It felt like hours later, but it really was probably only a few seconds before the color started returning to Michael's face. His breathing became audible, and then his eyes opened to meet Jen's. "Hey there," he whispered, and she broke into sobs as she collapsed onto him. He awkwardly wrapped his arms around her.

Sophie's shoulders shook ever so slightly, and she took a few long, deep, shuddering breaths, willing herself back under control. Emily squeezed her hand again and vowed to find someone more available to set Sophie up with, as soon as possible. Pining over a married man—even if his wife was a captive in fairyland—wasn't healthy, especially not for someone with no relationship track record.

"I believe we came here for a coronation," a nearby voice said. Emily looked up to see the tall, red-haired fairy who'd kicked all this off by demanding that Jen put on the crown before she'd kneel to her as ruler. "And we seem to have a candidate as queen."

Moving as though in a dream, Sophie released Emily's hand and stood. "Yes, I claim the throne," she said, sounding amazingly steady for someone who'd been so shaken a moment ago.

"Then you must put on the crown."

Sophie practically floated up the dais steps and sat in the throne Jen had vacated. The fairy gestured toward the handmaidens, who brought over the flowery pillow with the crown resting on it. Sophie took the crown and placed it on her own head.

If there'd been any doubt who the true queen was, it would have been erased by what happened next. When Sophie took the crown in the real palace, it had come to life. Here, the fake palace disappeared, leaving Sophie sitting on a large stone on a grassy mound in the middle of a field. There was no longer a distinction between the fairies inside the palace and those gathered outside, so the entire Realm was there to see their queen.

Although the setting was simpler, it seemed to Emily more authentic, more like the fae really should be. There was something wild about it, under the sky—or what passed for a sky in the Realm—and surrounded by nature. Sophie had dropped the illusion of royal robes and instead wore a simple knit dress with a full skirt that draped over the rock where she sat. Even without the jewels and rich fabric, she radiated regal power.

Every fairy in the valley fell to his or her knees. Jen raised herself to her knees, and Michael joined her after glancing around. Nana raised an eyebrow before gracefully lowering herself. Amelia and Athena were already on the ground, but they adjusted their postures to look more respectful. Beau got up with a deep, snorting sigh, climbed the mound, and settled down against Sophie's ankles. Emily normally would have ground her teeth at the idea of kneeling before her big sister, but this one time it felt right. After all, she'd presented herself as a candidate for queen, and that meant she had to acknowledge the real one or risk looking like a traitor. She knew Sophie wouldn't string her up, but she didn't want to make any bets on what Sophie's more ardent followers might do.

And it did seem like she might have a few fans. The free fae must have been somewhat appeased by the disappearance of the palace, like Sophie was getting rid of the symbols of oppression, or something, because they were kneeling just like everyone else.

Sophie gestured for them all to rise. "I don't ask anyone to kneel to me. I ask only that you keep the peace with each other and with the world above."

She frowned then, or maybe she was squinting in an effort to see in the distance. Emily turned to follow her gaze and saw what looked like a forest fire on the edge of the valley. Even as Emily watched, it grew larger.

"What is that?" Michael asked, speaking for everyone.

From where she lay pinned by the other rulers, Orla cackled. "The Hunt, it rides!"

"Oh dear," Sophie said with a soft sigh.

Thirty-Nine

The Mound
Next

How could she have forgotten the Hunt? Sophie wanted to kick herself. Then again, it wasn't as though she hadn't had other things begging for her attention. She'd managed to help Michael free his wife from fairy thrall, had taken out the person trying to usurp her throne, and had reclaimed her rightful place in the Realm. It would be perfectly understandable if she let a few little details slip her mind. Unfortunately, the Hunt didn't count as a little detail, and it was heading straight for her. If it kept on this course, it would trample the assembled masses and her, probably on its way out of the Realm to menace the human world. She couldn't let that happen.

But she wasn't sure what to do about it. She didn't recall anything in the folklore about fighting or stopping the Hunt, only that looking directly at them might leave one vulnerable to being taken by them to the fairy realm. They were already in the Realm, so that was a moot point, and none of the folklore said anything about what danger the Hunt posed to the fae.

She tried accessing the fairy queen's information to find how they must have been bound in the past, but nothing useful came to mind. Turning to her grandmother, she said, "Nana, do you have any ideas? I know you told me stories about the Hunt."

"Theoretically, they should answer to the true queen of the Realm."

"I guess that's a starting point." Sitting still on her rock, Sophie let her senses extend until she was tapped into the Realm itself, a part of its fabric. Then, with all her might, she thought *STOP!*

The flashing whirlwind didn't stop its advance. "Rats," she muttered to herself. One thing she could do, though, was seal the Realm to keep them out of the human world. She tightened the barriers. Now they'd *have* to stop the Hunt, or else she, Michael, Jen, Emily, Nana, Amelia, and Athena would be trapped here forever, the Realm entirely cut off from the human world, with both sides left the poorer for it.

As the Hunt rode toward them, Sophie began to understand all the legends about it, the reasons people heard it in storms and hid their faces until the tempest passed. The fae gathered in the valley scattered ahead of the thundering hooves and fiery eyes, but the Hunt no longer rode on the ground. They were rising into the sky, looking ever more like a raging thunderhead as light flashed through the dark, roiling clouds. Everyone around her screamed and ducked as the Hunt passed overhead, and Beau whimpered as he burrowed under Sophie's skirts, but she refused to be cowed. She glared defiantly upward, seeking and holding the gaze of the horned leader's fathomless eyes.

Then they were gone, vanished into the distance. Emily rose from her duck-and-cover posture and said, "You've got to stop them! They'll be riding to our world."

"I've closed off the Realm," Sophie said. "I still need to stop them so you can get out, but it's not quite as urgent."

"What about the Borderlands?" Michael asked. "They may not be able to open or use a portal, but could they squeeze through the passages?"

Sophie felt sick to her stomach. "Oh. You're right. They won't be able to ride through as a herd, and the openings will be limited, but they could get through."

"Or they could just blast wider openings," Amelia said, her eyes grim.

"Yeah, we don't want that," Sophie said absently, even as her mind was frantically spinning to come up with a plan. "We need to head them off." Raising her voice, she called out to the army of free fae that had followed Emily into the palace. "Can you track them?"

"Yes, my queen!" a fierce-looking female fairy called out. She was already swinging herself back into her saddle.

"Then go, and leave a trail." The woman nodded, and she kicked her horse into a gallop, disappearing into the distance, leaving a line of shimmering gold behind her. Sophie turned to her friends. "I think I have an idea for how to neutralize the Hunt, but for that I'll need humans with me. I hate to ask all of you to go into battle, but I don't think this will be a physical fight."

"I'm with you," Michael said. Jen clutched his arm and nodded.

"I believe this is one of the reasons I'm here," Nana said, looking like she was ready for war.

"I'm in," Emily said.

"As am I," Eamon said.

"I think I know what you have in mind, and you can count on us," Amelia said, adding with a glance at Eamon, "but this is not a fight you can join, Eamon. It will be difficult."

"You plan to use the ancient weapon of mankind against us: faith," he said. "I am not as weak as others of my kind. I own several Bibles and have even touched them. I do not fear your prayers."

Sophie couldn't help but raise an eyebrow at that. He was a very uncommon fairy. Maybe he and Emily could make things work, if Sophie was right about what was developing between them. But this wasn't the time to worry about that. She addressed the free fae army. "The humans among you have the chance to defend both your adopted home and the world of your birth. Will you join me?"

About a dozen humans stepped forward. "What weapons do we need, my queen?" one called out, his hand on his sword.

"I don't think any blade is going to do much good. What I need is your voice and whatever you might remember from Sunday school, if you were into that sort of thing back in the day."

"How are we going to intercept them?" Emily asked. "They've got a head start, and they're mounted."

"We'll follow the yellow-brick road, of course," Sophie said, allowing herself a smile. She'd never tried to take this many people with her across the Realm in one step, but with the crown on her head sending images and impulses into her mind, she knew she could do it. She had the power of the entire Realm at her disposal. She could see the scout's trail ahead of them, glowing golden, and the direction told her exactly where in the Borderlands it was going. She glanced back over her shoulder at her friends and followers. "Everyone ready?"

Emily picked up Beau's leash and nodded. Eamon squeezed Emily's other hand. Jen clung to Michael's elbow. Nana, Amelia, and Athena were bright-eyed and eager, and behind them, the human contingent of the free fae looked fierce and determined. Sophie actually felt pretty good about this.

She stepped forward on the golden pathway, and two strides later she was in the shadowy darkness of the Borderlands. "Are they here yet?" Emily asked when she arrived.

"I don't think so, but they'll come through here," Sophie replied.

"And you know that because?"

"I'm the queen. Didn't you get the memo?"

Bantering with her younger sister boosted Sophie's confidence, which was good because this place gave her the creeps. The awareness that came with the crown only reinforced how dangerous it was. The eerie silence made matters worse. On her last visit, she would have wanted the creepy noises to stop, but now she suspected the denizens of the Borderlands were silent because they sensed what was coming and had made themselves scarce.

Soon, even the eerie silence would have been welcome. The thunder of the approaching Hunt was more frightening in this setting. And then the chanting began.

"The Hunt, the Hunt, the Hunt will ride again."

"I hate these guys," Michael said with deep feeling.

"Do you still have iron on you?" Sophie asked without taking her eyes off the approaching flashes of red in the darkness.

He checked his bag. "A bit, but there's not much left."

"Make a perimeter."

"Gotcha."

He started with a line ahead of them, then circled behind the group, scattering the nails. Meanwhile, the Hunt had drawn close enough that she could make out the horns on their helmets. "I'm assuming you do have a plan," Emily said. "Care to share?"

Nana answered for her. "We're going to sing hymns, recite Bible verses, and say prayers."

"Yes, that's it, exactly," Sophie said, trying not to be miffed that her grandmother was stepping on her toes. After all, she'd learned what to do from Nana.

"I've heard about stepping out in faith, but wow," Emily said, her voice shaking.

"It's traditional," Athena explained. "Supposedly, one of the best ways to defend yourself against the darkest sort of fae is to use any symbols of the Christian faith. I suppose other faiths work, too, but most of these stories come from Europe, which was predominantly Christian at that time."

"It can be effective against those who have had less exposure to the human world," Eamon added.

"I'm hoping it will be enough to force them to stand down," Sophie continued. "Then I might be able to impose my will on them. Niall must have promised them something or done something to free them from any restraints."

"Wouldn't that have been squashed when Niall died?" Michael asked.

"I don't think he's dead," Nana said. "He's likely still giving orders if they're still acting on them."

Sophie turned to her, wincing at the physical pain that thought gave her. "You mean, this isn't over?"

"Did you see a body? It's probably a diversion," Nana said with a nod. "It's what I would do. You faked a death in your own fight."

"Right," Sophie acknowledged, drawing the word out as she thought. "Then we've got to make this work, and quickly."

"If it doesn't work?" Emily asked.

"Then we're making a last stand."

"Wow, talk about motivation," Emily said with a grin.

The Hunt headed straight for them. Sophie would have told herself to hold her attack until she could see the red of their mounts' eyes, but that was the first thing to become visible. She threw up a magical barrier using enchantress magic, and the other two enchantresses added their strength to it once they noticed what she was doing. "Keeping the worst of the fae out of our world is our job," Amelia said with grim determination.

Sophie turned to her sister. "You've got the biggest voice. How about a verse of 'Amazing Grace'?"

Emily's eyes sparkled. She lived for this sort of thing. She belted out the opening line, and the others joined in. Sophie had never been able to put much power behind her voice, but she was surprised by how strong Michael's baritone turned out to be. She glanced at Eamon and saw that while he looked somewhat uncomfortable, he was holding fast at Emily's side. The choir of the free fae humans gradually joined in behind them, singing the same melody in a multitude of languages.

Sophie might have been imagining it, but the Hunt seemed to be slowing. More details became visible as they stirred up less dirt and smoke. She could see how skeletal they were—the riders, the horses, and the dogs that ran at the horses' hooves. At Emily's feet, Beau growled at his fae counterparts. Emily held his leash tightly, keeping him from going after them.

But the song wasn't actually scripture and was relatively recent. It might not even have been written when the Hunt rode more regularly in the human world. "Does everyone know the Twenty-third Psalm?" Sophie called out.

Michael, the minister's son, started that one. Sophie, Nana, and Emily joined in immediately. Athena and Amelia picked it up. Jen appeared a little more foggy, but she wouldn't have heard it in a very long time. Sophie was really surprised when Eamon echoed them, only a word or two behind. Some of the others also added their voices.

The Hunt slowed even more, and a few of the horses tried to wheel away. Their riders fought to control them. Some of the dogs stopped entirely. It was working. Sophie decided to unleash one last weapon. "The Lord's Prayer!" she called out.

"Which version?" Amelia asked.

"Whichever one you know," Sophie replied. "It doesn't have to be unison."

They only got halfway through the prayer before the Hunt faltered entirely. Sophie gestured for the others to stop. "Do you yield?" she called to the leader of the Hunt.

He didn't speak, but his answer was implied when the Hunt kept moving relentlessly forward until they came up against the enchantresses' shield. Up close, they were utterly terrifying. She'd thought the stags' horns were affixed to their helmets, but they seemed to grow straight out of their heads. Their eyes were like portals into infinity, and the stench of sulfur surrounded them. Every survival instinct Sophie had ordered her to flee, but she forced herself to stand resolutely still, staring down these creatures from the depths of hell. She heard movement behind her, and out of the corner of her eye she noticed some of the others in her group backing away. She didn't blame them. In fact, she wished she could join them, but she stood fast, her friends and family at her side. Beau whimpered once, but he, too, stood his ground.

In a voice she felt in shivers down her back rather than actually heard, the Huntsman replied, "I yield to no one."

"Do you know who I am?" she demanded.

"You are the queen of the Realm."

"I order you to stand down."

"We do not stand down."

Indignation overrode her fear. "Oh, really?" she said. She

sensed Emily edging away from her. Her sister recognized the warning signs, even if Mr. Horn Head didn't seem to. His brains had probably been turned to ashes long ago. "Is it a matter of pride, or did Niall offer you something good?"

It was hard to read expressions on a nearly featureless face, but she thought the bottomless eyes narrowed ever so slightly. "The great lord freed us to resume our rides."

"And what do you get out of the rides?" she prompted.

"Enough of this!" he roared. With a gesture, he threw a ball of flame at her. It spattered against the magical barrier, which weakened enough to allow a few sparks through. The enchantresses countered the fire with ice, and Sophie strengthened the barrier with a gesture, refusing to let herself flinch. She was intrigued by the mention that the Hunt had been freed. That implied that someone—perhaps one of her fairy ancestors—had at one time managed to chain or imprison them. It would have been nice, though, if she had any clue as to how to go about doing that. She wondered if Nana might know, but she couldn't ask for help in front of them without looking weak.

"You take souls when you ride, don't you?" she asked, trying to sound casual and not like the germ of a plan rested on this conversation.

"That is correct," the Hunter acknowledged. "Hunting gives us life."

Mentally crossing her fingers in case her theory was wrong, she said, "If you leave the Realm, you'll die."

The lead Hunter's horse reared, its monstrous hooves pawing at the air in fury. "Do you think you can slay us, little queen?"

"I don't have to. The people outside will take care of it. They don't fear you anymore. They don't believe in you anymore. Heck, most of them haven't even heard of you. They'll see or hear you coming and call it a thunderstorm. They'll have a scientific explanation for it—air temperatures, atmospheric pressure, wind speed, static electricity, the speed sound travels. What happens to the fae without belief?" She felt like she was at a production of *Peter Pan*, but instead of asking the audience to believe in fairies and clap their hands, she was saying, "Don't believe, and Tinkerbell's toast."

She thought the Hunt might be faltering. The flames in their eyes dimmed, and the cloud around them diminished. Behind Sophie, Emily started softly singing "Ave Maria," barely audible, but still enough to seep into the subconscious and possibly even deliver a double whammy.

Sophie moved in for the kill, taking the risk of moving through the protective barrier and facing the Hunt directly. "The time of the fae has all but ended in the world above. The stories they tell children about fairies are cute and funny. Children aren't taught to fear fairies. They dress up like them in butterfly wings and frilly skirts. Instead of running from you, they'd invite you to a tea party."

"Then we will ride within the Realm, where we are still feared."

"I can't let that happen, and I will stop you." She let enough of her royal power show to drive the point home. She wasn't exactly sure how she'd stop them, but she'd find a way, even if she had to lock them in a room and pipe in recordings of church services.

"What will we do if we do not ride?" It was hard to tell since she couldn't read his expression, but she almost thought he sounded a little lost.

"Maybe you should find a more productive use of your time," she said. "What have you been doing since you last rode?"

"We have been confined to the Borderlands—neither entering the Realm nor leaving it for the outside world."

That explained the cultists Michael had encountered. They probably went in and out of the physical entrances to the Borderlands and must have encountered the Hunt there.

A crazy idea occurred to her. It was absolutely insane, but it felt somehow right. "What if I offered you a job? A real job, not just running around terrifying people."

"What job would you have us do, little queen?" The ominous voice dripped with disdain.

"I need a royal guard, some knights to serve the throne and keep peace in the Realm."

"And why should we serve you, human queen?"

"The fact that I'm queen isn't enough?"

He made a sound that might have been laughter, but that made her skin crawl. "We don't serve. We do our will at the pleasure of the ruler."

Sophie felt like she was close to a breakthrough, but couldn't quite grasp the one concept that would turn everything around. It was just *there,* but still out of reach. As she so often did when imposing her will on others, even before she'd realized she was using magic to do so, she tried switching viewpoints. What was in it for them, and how could she get them to see that?

In this case, why would a band of soul-stealing monsters want to become the queen's royal guard and be trapped inside the Realm? Did they actually like all that hunting, or were they just not able to see any other possibility? Maybe if they saw what could be, it would change their minds.

She pictured the ultimate makeover, from hell fiend to Lancelot—change the dark armor to shining silver, add some color in a tabard. The horns might have to stay, but as proud stag horns that looked noble rather than evil. His hideous black horse could be a snowy-white steed, strong and healthy, with eyes like diamonds. She held the image in her mind until it was more real to her than what stood before her, then adjusted reality to fit it.

She knew from the gasps behind her that she'd succeeded. The Huntsman looked like something on the cover of a paranormal romance novel—the kind of hot, not-entirely-human guy who'd fall madly in love with an ordinary human woman. If he had any self-esteem issues at all, maybe this makeover would change his perspective.

"This is what you could be if you served me. Or, rather, if you chose to offer your arms in my service."

He couldn't see himself well, but she could already tell he was carrying himself differently, and the other members of the Hunt were looking at him the way women side-eyed another woman who'd just had a spectacular makeover.

The Huntsman raised his hand, signaling to his colleagues, who moved closer to him. Lights flashed and the clouds thickened, momentarily obscuring them. When the clouds cleared, the leader bowed his head and said, "We will serve you, my queen, if we may all take new forms."

"Agreed. I'm sure things will go much better for you this way." She looked inward, gathered her power, and cast her will outward.

All the riders and horses were transformed to match their leader. The dogs became sleek hounds that looked much healthier and less mean. They approached Beau and went through the universal canine sniffing ritual, then Beau turned back to Sophie, seemingly reporting that the dogs were on board with the changes, too. "There, that's better," Sophie said with some satisfaction. She turned her attention to the Hunt cultists, but they'd made themselves scarce. Apparently, the reformed Hunt wasn't quite as interesting to them.

"Wow, Soph, talk about a makeover," Emily said, moving forward to join her once the enchantresses lowered their barrier.

"That was an interesting strategy," Amelia said, not sounding entirely approving.

"I figured it was better to turn them than defeat them, since I wasn't entirely sure how to destroy them," Sophie said with a shrug.

"Better you than me," Jen said wryly. "I think it would have been pretty much widespread doom if I'd still been on the throne for all this."

"Nonsense," Sophie said. "Remember, the same person was pulling the strings for all of you. The Hunt would have answered to you and made you look good."

"And I'd have sent them out into our world," Jen said. Michael put his arm around her shoulders and gave her a reassuring squeeze. Sophie swallowed the lump that appeared in her throat and made herself turn away.

"Good job, honey," Nana said. "I'm proud of you."

"Now what?" Michael asked.

Without looking directly at him, Sophie said, "Let's get back to the valley. I want to finish this once and for all with Niall. Maybe my new guard will help. Then I'll get everyone home. Emily's got a show tonight, and I'm sure you're ready to get back to normal."

"Yeah, that'll be nice, right, Jen?"

"Home, wow," Jen said softly. She looked a little dazed by the idea, which was to be expected.

Sophie raised her voice and addressed her followers. "Okay, everyone, back to the valley," she said. She reached for Michael and Amelia's hands. Eamon took Emily and Athena, and Michael maintained his hold on Jen. Emily held Beau's leash with her free hand. Nana didn't seem to think she needed any assistance. The free fae humans and the Hunt came behind them. All of them stepped off together, and a few strides later they were back in that wooded area above the valley where the palace had been.

Or still was. It was back, looking exactly like it had the first time they'd arrived in this place.

"Didn't you get rid of that?" Emily asked.

Sophie stared down at palace and tried not to sigh in weariness and frustration. "I thought I proved that I was the real queen, so I don't know what his game is now."

"Maybe he's giving up the puppet idea and putting himself up as a potential ruler," Michael said.

"I guess we'll find out when I show up," Sophie said.

The lead Huntsman rode forward and addressed Sophie. "Would you care to ride, my queen?"

"It would be impressive," she said, raising an eyebrow.

"A good queen should know how to make an entrance," Nana agreed.

"Can you take the rest of our party?" Sophie asked.

"Gladly."

Sophie gestured for the others to join them. The lead huntsman pulled Sophie up to sit sidesaddle in front of him. She was a little unnerved by being picked up by such a creature, but she told herself it was a lift in a pas de deux and comported herself accordingly.

The others were also lifted, the men riding pillion behind warriors. Emily unclipped Beau's leash and let him run with the Hunt's hounds. One of the Huntsmen sounded a hunting horn as they began the descent into the valley. It was a stirring sound that made Sophie's blood sing. Nana's grin told her that it had a similar effect on her. Although they were riding to what was likely to be a major confrontation, for just this one moment, Sophie felt on top of the world.

It seemed far too soon, then, when they reached the palace. Sophie waved at the doors to open them and signaled the Hunt to stop for a moment so that everyone in the throne room would have a chance to see what stood on the threshold. Taking a page from Emily's book, she had the Hunt ride straight into the palace. When they were halfway across the room, she reached out and tweaked the fabric of the Realm, making the palace disappear entirely.

Niall, who'd been sitting on the throne like he owned it, suddenly found himself sitting on a rock in a field, which was much less impressive.

"I can't leave you alone for a minute, can I?" Sophie said, looking down at the fairy.

"You're no William Powell, honey," Nana added. "You may as well give up that act right now."

"And you are no true queen," Niall said to Sophie with a sneer. "You may have fae blood, but it has been corrupted by human blood."

"The blood's been good enough for the crown to work," Sophie said. She gave him a too-sweet smile. "Care to give it a try, yourself?"

"If I won the crown from you, I could wear it.

"That sounds like a challenge to me," Nana said. "How about it?"

Sophie barely refrained from asking her grandmother if the Alzheimer's disease had crept up on her again in the Realm. Instead, she gave her a questioning look.

Nana signaled her rider to move his mount closer to Sophie. "We're both of the lineage. Either of us could wear the crown. It's two against one, and we're the rightful rulers, so how can we lose?"

"Okay, if you're sure about this." Sophie addressed Niall. "You want the crown and throne? I propose a contest. We each suggest three trials. The people choose the winner of each trial and the winner of the throne. If you can prove yourself more worthy of the crown in the eyes of the people, then I will give the crown to you and no longer question your right to rule."

Although she managed to sound perfectly calm and confident as she spoke, Sophie was trembling inside from the enormity of what she'd just proposed. The consequences of failure were dire. Both the Realm and the human world stood to suffer, based on what Sophie had seen of his policies when he was the power behind the impostor.

But, strangely, Sophie felt utterly confident that she could prevail, with Nana's help. She knew in her heart that she was meant to have this throne. In the real world, that wouldn't mean much. Unworthy people were always inheriting or being elected to positions of power. But the Realm was the setting of fairy tales, the place where good won, evil was vanquished, and the most worthy would always win the crown.

Niall pondered for a moment, probably weighing those same considerations. If he was smart, he'd back down, but then again, he wouldn't have come to this point if he hadn't believed that as a true fae, he'd make a better ruler. He smiled and said, "Very well, I challenge you for your throne. Let the contest begin."

❦Forty❧

Michael had to force himself not to cry out in dismay when Niall accepted the challenge. Was Sophie nuts? Of course she was, he realized. She was just the very particular kind of nuts that managed to pull off audacious things no one else would dare try. She waved the Hunt aside, and once the Huntsmen had taken up position around the competitive arena, Michael dismounted and went to help Jen down.

"I don't think this is such a good idea," Jen said, her forehead creased with worry. "I saw what he was doing when he was making me front for him. We can't let him rule the Realm. He was forcing all the humans out, as well as all the fairies who associated with humans." Her eyes strayed to the crowd, like she was looking for someone. She sighed audibly in what sounded a lot like relief and smiled slightly.

He forced himself not to read anything into this and refused to let himself try to find the target of her gaze. "I know. I saw some of the fallout from that. It wasn't pretty."

She turned back to him, her eyes going wide with alarm. "Not pretty? How?"

"It seems that although people don't age in here, the moment they set foot in the human world, their real age catches up to them. If you've been here long enough, it can be fatal."

"Oh." She glanced down at herself, like she was trying to imagine what might change.

He put his arm around her and pulled her to him. "You shouldn't have to worry. Seven years isn't much time, and it's the age you'd be now, anyway." He grinned and kissed the top of her head. "People would think I robbed the cradle if you didn't catch up."

"I've been gone seven years?"

"To the day."

She reached up to touch his temple. "That explains this. You didn't have any gray at all when I left."

"Gray?" he asked, faking dismay.

"Just a hair or two. It looks very distinguished. I suppose I'm responsible for those."

"Only one. I think the thug with a gun can be blamed for the rest."

"You had an arm in a sling the last time you were here, didn't you? I'm sorry, but that time is still a little foggy."

"Yeah, I got shot. But I'm better now."

"I always worried that your job was so dangerous."

"Actually, I'm a detective now, which is supposed to be safer than being a beat cop. I'm not usually the first one on the scene. But this one time, I knocked on a door and someone panicked."

"Is anything else new with you?"

"Very little. I live in the same apartment, and I haven't changed much at all. Things were actually pretty calm until the last few months. That's when I got shot, then Emily went missing, and that's how I got mixed up in all this and found you."

"How did Emily get you mixed up in this?"

"She's my downstairs neighbor. She moved in a few years ago, to the apartment where that girl—oh, you know, the publishing intern—used to live."

She knitted her brow. "Beth?"

"Yeah, that's it. She moved out, and Emily moved in. She sort of adopted me. I think she figured she'd found a good potential dogsitter. When Em went missing, Sophie showed up looking for her, and when I followed her one night, I saw you, and I learned that Hamlet wasn't kidding."

"There are more things in heaven and earth, Horatio, than are dreamt of in your philosophy," she quoted automatically.

"See, you haven't forgotten everything. It'll all come back to you."

"I did make a fetching Ophelia, didn't I?"

"Very. Though I'm still not sure what they were thinking in setting that play on the moon."

For the first time since he'd last seen her back home, she laughed. "Oh, that was a crazy production, wasn't it? But it was a job, even if it was so off-Broadway it was practically in a different time zone." Her smile grew wistful. "And that was the job I was auditioning for when I met you."

"It was the first time I saw you act." His throat grew tight at the memory. The show had been pretty awful, but he still fell in love with Jen while watching her play Ophelia in space.

"Is there anything else I need to know?" she asked, her eyes flicking momentarily toward Sophie.

"I've gotten pretty good at laundry. Not so much at cooking."

"That's not what I meant."

He showed her the wedding band he still wore. "I wouldn't have been able to free you if I'd fallen in love with anyone else. People have been telling me all along that I should give up and move on with my life, but I knew you were still out there, somewhere, and I would find you."

For a second, he thought she was disappointed, but then she smiled. That warmed his heart, assuring him that it had all been worthwhile. "You did find me."

"I had help. It's good to be friends with the fairy queen, and she's been working hard to find a way to get you out of here."

"Yes, she's been visiting me, trying to get me to remember you. I'll have to thank her." She laughed a little. "It's going to take time to get used to that again."

"That 'no thanks' thing is a strange custom. Don't be surprised if Sophie finds a way to change it. She's Southern. Manners are very important to her."

Her attention returned to where Sophie, her grandmother, Niall, and a few fairies were fine-tuning the rules of the competition. "Do you think she can win?"

"I wouldn't put anything past her. She's not just a fairy queen. She's also an enchantress, so she's got two kinds of magic. I don't know about her grandmother, but they've got the same heritage."

Tallulah seemed to be playing referee. She climbed onto the throne stone and motioned for silence. "The challenge for the throne will now begin. Niall, as challenger, has the right of choosing the first contest and will compete first. Niall, what do you propose?"

"I propose a contest of music, one of the arts that define the fae. We will each perform a song."

Emily, who'd come with Eamon to stand by Michael, asked her fairy friend, "Okay, how bad is this?"

"Niall was once a noted bard. Can Sophie sing as well as you?"

"She hasn't had the training I had, so she won't be blasting anyone out of the second balcony, but she's got a pretty voice. I don't know about Nana, but I had to get the genes from somewhere."

Niall conjured up a harp and took a seat on the throne stone. His tuxedo looked incongruous in the setting, but that didn't matter once he ran his fingers lightly across the harp strings. The sound didn't affect Michael's ears so much as it went straight to his soul.

Then Niall started singing. His voice was clear and lilting. Michael would have bet that his notes were so true that he could easily shatter crystal if the crystal was pure enough to be in tune. His song was about lost loves found again in eternal summer, and it tugged at the heartstrings in a way Michael had never experienced. At his side, Jen was sniffling, her gaze straying back to the crowd. Emily was clearly fighting not to show how stirred she was, her arms crossed defiantly over her chest and her jaw set, even as a tear welled over her lower eyelashes. Michael couldn't bring himself to look at the rest of the audience.

Then it was the Drake women's turn. Sophie and her grandmother conferred for a moment before Leonie started singing the old song that had been passed down through generations, a bit of nonsense that turned out to contain the clues needed to claim the throne of the Realm. Michael could see where Emily got her pipes. Leonie's voice was rich and strong. Sophie chimed in on the second verse, adding a descant in her softer, more delicate voice. The two voices blended in an eerie way. It wasn't quite as affecting as Niall's performance, however. If Michael removed his personal bias for the contestants, he'd have to give this round to Niall.

At the end of the song, Tallulah stepped onto the stone again and called out, "All for Niall!" The applause was intense and went on for a while. "All for the queen!" The response wasn't dramatically weaker, but the difference was still noticeable. "This contest goes to Niall. Now, your majesty, what contest do you propose?"

Michael noticed the use of the title—a hint of her loyalties or perhaps an attempt to sway the crowd? "I challenge Niall to a contest of magic," Sophie called out.

"I wonder how this'll go," Emily muttered as the participants wrangled over the rules.

"Your sister has the power of the crown and is an enchantress, as well," Eamon said, as calmly as a television golf analyst. "But Niall is full fae with far more experience."

"That's not reassuring," Emily said, elbowing him in the ribs.

"He is very powerful," Jen said, her voice tight. "Trust me, I tried to resist him, and it was hopeless."

"But Sophie wouldn't have proposed this if she weren't confident, right?" Michael said.

"You have met my sister, haven't you?" Emily said with a wry smile. "She's confident about everything."

Apparently, this was to be a direct magical battle, not a showcase. As the one who proposed the contest, Sophie got first strike. She and Leonie joined hands, presumably joining their powers, and at first they didn't seem to be doing anything. Then Sophie said sweetly to Niall. "Come on over here, hon."

Without hesitation, he walked straight toward the two women and bowed to them before kissing their hands, in turn. Only after he had bowed again did he seem to realize what he was doing. "Yeah, that's the way Soph pretty much goes through life," Emily said with a chuckle. "That explains so much about her."

Niall struck back by hurling a ball of fire at the Drake women, but it exploded harmlessly against a magical shield. When it was Sophie's move, a wreath of flowers covered Niall, pinning his arms against his sides. He had to use his next move to remove the flowers. When he was free, a tiny storm cloud appeared directly over his head, pouring rain on him while whipping him with wind and flashing lightning. He moved the cloud over Sophie and her grandmother, but another shield appeared over their heads, so not a drop of rain touched them.

Tallulah raised her hand. "That's a spell repeated," she said.

"It's a similar concept, being a shield, but it's a different spell," Sophie argued. "The spell to block a fireball isn't the same as the spell to block water. Water would have gone through the fireball shield."

"It's still a shield. This round goes to Niall."

"What? That's not fair!" Emily protested.

She looked like she was about to head out and confront Tallulah, but both Michael and Eamon held her back. "Listen to the crowd," Michael urged. The valley was ringing with boos and jeers. "I think she did that on purpose. She's building sympathy."

"The outcome of these individual tests means little," Eamon said. "It's all about winning over the gathering for the final vote. Tallulah has made a shrewd move to make the crowd favor Sophie." Emily's glare indicated that she didn't entirely buy that, but she quit straining against the two men.

"Niall, your next contest?" Tallulah asked.

He looked awfully pleased with himself when he said, "I challenge you in another of the great fae arts: dancing."

Emily laughed out loud, and Michael grinned. "What is it? Will she be able to compete there?" Jen asked.

"Sophie's a prima ballerina," Michael said.

"Who was trained by fairies," Emily added. "Seriously, she's unreal. If she hadn't been looking after Nana, she'd probably be the biggest ballet star in the world by now. She's older than a lot of pros, but give her a year, and I bet you'll be hearing about her if she even tries to make a go of it."

Niall got to go first. He beckoned to his consort, Orla, and gestured to the group of musicians who'd gathered nearby. A marble dance floor appeared to cover the ground in front of the stone. They started dancing ballroom-style, moving fluidly in unison. "Wow, they've got a real Fred and Ginger thing going on," Jen said.

"I know, right?" Emily said. "I've danced with him. He's pretty good."

"How does that stack up against Sophie?" Jen sounded anxious.

"I guess it depends on what they're looking for, but just wait and see." Michael was glad Emily had taken care of the endorsement because he'd noticed the suspicious way Jen regarded Sophie. She had absolutely nothing to worry about, but him praising Sophie's dancing wouldn't help the situation, and the one time he'd been even slightly tempted by another woman had been the last time he saw Sophie dance.

While Niall and Orla danced cheek-to-cheek, Sophie sat off to the side, putting on ballet shoes and wrapping the ribbons around her ankles. She'd slipped out of her wrap-around dress, revealing that she wore a gauzy short dress under it—some kind of dance outfit, from what he could tell. Once she had her shoes on, she went through some warm-up exercises.

Niall and Orla finished to a nice round of applause. The crowd liked his performance, but they weren't in raptures. The couple took several bows before finally leaving the stage area.

Sophie waited a moment before striding slowly and deliberately out to the middle of the floor and taking a starting position. Beneath her feet, the floor turned to wood. Michael realized he was holding his breath in anticipation. He'd wanted to see her dance again ever since the last time.

The music began, slow and mournful. Sophie's first move was to lift her arm. It was a simple motion, but somehow she made it look like her hand was floating upward of its own accord. She rose to her toes, as though her whole body was being pulled upward by her hand. Then she seemed to be released, drifting back to the ground, her knees bending as her heels hit the ground. Next, it was her right foot that was pulled upward, her knee bending until her toe passed her knee, then her leg extending until her knee practically brushed her shoulder. At the same time, she rose onto the toe of her supporting leg.

She balanced in what looked like an impossible position for a long moment before whipping her body around so that her leg was now extended behind her, her back arched and her arms held in front of her. She made it look easy, but Michael had the feeling that doing those moves required the kind of muscles most people didn't begin to possess.

"Wow," Jen breathed. "That's impressive. I'm sore just looking at her doing that."

"That's nothing," Emily said, grinning.

The music picked up, and Sophie's feet moved with blinding speed as she did quick little turns around the perimeter of the wooden floor. Back in the middle, she did a jig-style step that ended with her jumping back and forth sideways, one leg raised to the side in the air, but coming down so that she landed on both feet. She bent her knees, then rose to one toe, raised her other toe to her knee, and spun around several times. When she lost momentum, she kicked out her leg and whipped it around, amping up the spin. Michael lost count of how many times she spun around. Her hair, hanging loose around her shoulders, flew wildly around her.

She came out of the spin, took a few steps, then jumped, both legs in front her body. She scissored her legs as her body flipped around so that she landed facing the other direction. From there she ran a few steps before leaping, her legs in a full split. She seemed to hang in the air for an impossibly long time before she finally landed, light as a feather.

The crowd roared in approval, and she gave a graceful curtsy. Emily whistled and cheered as she clapped, and Jen was almost as enthusiastic. Michael shook himself out of the spell to clap.

When the applause had died a little, Tallulah gestured for silence. "All for Niall?" she cried out. The response was tepid. "All for the queen?" The roar was nearly deafening. "This contest goes to her majesty."

"Okay, we've won one," Emily said, clasping her hands together.

"By a very large margin," Eamon said. "That was an impressive demonstration."

"Your next contest, your majesty?" Tallulah asked Sophie.

Barely breathing hard, but still a bit red-faced and sweaty, Sophie frowned, like she wasn't quite sure. Before she could speak, Leonie stepped forward. "I call for a game of chance."

◦Forty-One◦

Sophie could barely believe her ears. Her grandmother had never so much as allowed playing cards in the house because cards were used in games of chance. "I thought you didn't believe in gambling," she hissed at Nana when she made her way over to her.

"I don't," Nana replied calmly.

"Then what—" Sophie broke off when Tallulah came over to consult on the form of the challenge. She decided to leave this one to Nana. Presumably, she knew what she was doing. While they talked, she took off her pointe shoes and rubbed her feet, then stretched a bit while she cooled off. She decided to wait until the faint breeze dried her sweat before she put her dress back on.

Nana suggested a game of dice, which was a real shock. She hadn't even been crazy about the family playing Monopoly, even though the money had been fake, because she thought dice made it into a game of chance.

Each contestant threw the dice, and Tallulah declared a winner before they played another round. Nana won every single time. By the fourth round, Sophie started studying what she did. She thought she detected a trace of magic. After the seventh round, Nana was declared the definitive winner. When Nana rejoined her, Sophie accused, "You were using magic to cheat!"

"I told you, I don't believe in gambling. If you know the outcome, it's not gambling."

"But you believe in cheating?"

"In a contest against the fae, there's no such thing. There's only being clever and being more clever. He was also cheating. My cheating was simply more effective."

"Okay, then," Sophie said, barely fighting back a smile. She'd almost forgotten how feisty her grandmother could be, it had been so long since she was really herself. Now she felt fairly certain that bringing her here had been the right idea.

While Niall consulted with Orla about the next challenge, Sophie put her dress back on and tied the belt at her waist, then put on her shoes. Her hair was probably a lost cause after all the spinning about she'd done, but she tried to smooth it back away from her face.

Niall returned to face Tallulah. "I propose a contest of puzzles," he said, smiling so smugly that Sophie was sure he had something nasty up his sleeve. That meant she needed to come up with something equally nasty for him. What was his biggest weakness, and how could she exploit it?

But she didn't have time to come up with her test for him because he was already outlining the rules with Tallulah. Each contestant would pose a puzzle for the other. Tallulah would decide when time was up. Before today, Sophie would have been sure Tallulah was on her side. Now, it was hard to tell. She'd made one questionable ruling against her so far. Either that was part of a greater plan or the fairy didn't care who won.

Niall was practically grinning and rubbing his hands together like a movie super-villain when he approached Sophie. "My test for you is one of character, will, skill, and ingenuity," he said. "That said, I'm sure you'll win, one way or another, because my puzzle offers you two ways to win. Even if you can't solve the puzzle, you may still get what you want—though you must decide what you want most."

"Is this part of the puzzle, or is this just the introductory paragraph?" Sophie asked, fighting to sound calm even as she tried to parse what he'd just said.

"Oh, you're a plain-spoken lady, I see," he said with a patronizing smile that made her want to introduce his teeth to her toes. Too bad she'd already taken off her pointe shoes.

"And you're clearly an aspiring politician."

"You're right, my lady. Enough wasting time." He waved his hand at Amelia and Athena, and suddenly the two elderly enchantresses were bound in silvery chains tied in a complicated knot. "Once the challenge begins," Niall said, still sounding unnervingly pleasant, "the chains will slowly tighten. You must find a way to free your friends." His grin grew wider. "But never fear! They don't have to die, even if you fail. You have a second chance. You can decide if there's something you're willing to trade for their lives."

"Like, say, a crown?" Sophie asked.

"That's up to you. But whether I'll accept your offering is up to me." He glanced at Tallulah and added, "You won't have to time this puzzle. It times itself. And it begins now."

Instantly, Amelia and Athena were pulled closer together by the tightening chain. Sophie darted straight to them, Nana at her side, to inspect the knot. It looked impossibly complicated.

"Hmm, rather Gordian, isn't it?" Nana remarked.

"So you think we can just break it?" Sophie asked. "I doubt there's a blade that would cut through this."

"Not a physical one," Amelia said. The chain went around her middle, and she was doing an excellent job of remaining calm. The much-shorter Athena was in more distress, as the chain pinned her arms to her sides.

"You know, he didn't specify dealing with the knot itself," Sophie mused out loud. "The knot isn't the weak point. What if we all focus on one particular link in the chain?" She reached out and touched a tiny link that, so far, wasn't in physical contact with the two women.

Sophie focused all her magical energy on that link. She sensed the flow of power coming from Nana and the two enchantresses. Her fae magic did little good, but enchantress magic was designed to fight fae magic.

Athena cried out as the chain tightened. It was slipping upward as it constricted and was very close to her neck. The targeted chain began to glow. Risking a burn, Sophie grabbed and twisted it. It broke apart in her hand, and she flung the ends of the chain apart, freeing the enchantresses.

Sophie's fingers didn't start stinging until a moment later. There were blisters on the tips of her thumb and first two fingers. Nana noticed this, as well, and grabbed her wrist before Sophie could follow the instinct to put her fingers in her mouth. "Cold water's what you need," she said.

Athena ran to retrieve her bag and came back with a bottle of water, which she poured over Sophie's hand.

"I believe it's time for your puzzle for me," Niall called out. His voice was as smug as ever, but when Sophie glanced his way, she thought he looked a little alarmed. "Or are you going to forfeit?"

Sophie looked at Nana to see if she'd come up with anything, but Nana shook her head. It was probably unfair to expect much of her, since she'd come out of the fog of advanced Alzheimer's not too long ago, but Sophie was also drawing a blank.

She needed to prey on his weakness, or, if not his personal weakness, then a weakness common to his kind. Looking out at the spectators, where her sister, Michael, and Jen were watching her, gave her an idea. "Jen, Em, can you come over here for a moment?" Turning to her grandmother, she added, "And I'll need you, too, Nana."

She ended up with a row of redheads. No one would get them mixed up because they were all of different heights, had different facial features, different eyes, and different shades of hair color. No human, that was. To the fae, they all looked more or less alike, which was why Maeve's people had grabbed Jen while looking for Emily and why Niall's attempt to put Jen on the throne might have worked, even with fairies who'd seen Sophie as queen.

The difference was in their auras, and Emily's aura had been magically altered to protect her. Sophie went to the enchantresses. "Can you do some temporary aura tweaking on all of us?"

"Of course," Amelia said, sounding almost insulted.

While the enchantresses did their magic, Sophie employed fairy magic to adjust their glamours, putting them all in the images of royal robes. When Amelia and Athena indicated that they were done, Sophie had the group of redheads mingle, mix up, and then line up, their backs to Niall.

Without facing him, Sophie called out, "Can you find my sister in this group?" At her signal, they all turned to face him.

Sophie couldn't remember if Emily had ever been identified to him as her sister, but he must have been the one trying to draw her back into the Realm before he switched to Jen as a backup plan. For most humans, spotting the sisters in the group would have been easy, in spite of the drastic height difference between Emily and Sophie. Their faces were almost identical. Emily often joked about Sophie being her "Mini Me."

But Niall frowned at the lineup. Emily started humming the *Jeopardy* theme under her breath, and Sophie had to restrain herself from shooting a glare at her sister, for fear that a scolding big sister would give away the game.

A soft rumble from the crowd suggested that they were getting restless. At the very least, they were bored and were talking among themselves. Sophie wondered if the boredom would count against her—for coming up with a boring puzzle—or against him— for taking so long to solve it.

Tallulah finally stepped forward and said, "Time is running out. Should we give him a hint? Or perhaps pose an easier question? This will not count as solving the puzzle, but can you tell which of these women is the true queen of the Realm—at least, until the challenge is concluded? If you can find the queen, that might help you find her sister."

Niall pondered for a long time. At last, he pointed to Nana and said, "This is the queen."

"She is in the royal lineage," Tallulah admitted, "so you are at least partially correct. But now, can you solve the puzzle that was posed to you?"

With the air of a man making a wild guess, he pointed to Sophie. "This is the sister." It actually wasn't a bad guess, since Sophie looked more like Nana than any of the others did, but it was still wrong.

Sophie dropped the glamours and stepped out of the lineup. "Sorry. You got the second queen, not the sister."

He turned to Tallulah in dismay. "Is this a trick? They're lying!"

She shook her head. "No, you were wrong. I can verify which is the sister. The queen has won this contest. Your majesty, the next challenge is yours."

It was the final contest, and if the score really mattered at all, Sophie and Nana were ahead. Still, the final challenge needed to be something so definitive that it would make the final vote an obvious choice.

"The next challenge will be a contest of mastery over the Realm," Sophie said as the solution came to her. "After all, the true ruler should be able to sense the power of the Realm and use the fabric of the Realm."

"And how do you propose to test this?" Tallulah asked.

"A race to the real palace and back. Each contestant must bring back a rose from the palace garden." Sophie wasn't even sure why that popped into her head, but the more she thought about it, the more *right* it was.

Of course, she'd need to get there before Niall did, but she thought she could manage that. While Tallulah laid out the task and the rules, Sophie reached out to the sense of the Realm that constantly verged on her awareness. A tweak *here* and an adjustment *there* created a detour or two and a few good obstacles. For good measure, she added a loop, like a metaphysical roundabout with a hidden exit.

When Tallulah gave the starting signal, Sophie grabbed Nana's hand and stepped out for the palace. They arrived across the river from the drawbridge, where Sophie had first seen the palace when it was covered in thorny vines like something out of a fairy tale. "Okay, let's get that rose," she said, heading for the drawbridge.

Nana grabbed her wrist, pulling her back. "Wait. I presume you bought us some time?"

"Of course."

"Good girl. Then I think I should go through the trials for the throne."

"I already did that. That's how the palace woke and the Realm was restored."

"Just in case, I think it's a good idea that both of us meet the requirements. Both of us competed in this contest, and if I didn't really qualify, he might try to use that loophole against us."

"Okay, I guess. It shouldn't take long since I know how it works now." Sophie raised her voice and said, "I call out for your aid again." She hoped the little fairy creatures would be there this time. Turning to Nana, she added, "We'd also better make sure Niall *doesn't* meet the requirements."

"Then maybe we shouldn't have sung the song in front of him."

"That's if he recognizes it for what it is or can figure it out. I gave each verse to Maeve as we went, and she still failed all the tests."

Much to her relief, the ground was soon alight with the little creatures. "Why, they are like in the storybooks!" Nana exclaimed.

"You might not want to look too closely at them," Sophie said with a wince. "But they're very helpful." She sang the relevant verse of the song: "If she can cross not wetting her feet, then she will know the way to my heart." The lights flowed into the river, and a giant lily pad appeared near the shore. "After you," Sophie said.

Nana stepped gingerly onto the lily pad, and a second pad appeared. She grew steadier and more confident as she crossed. Sophie came behind her, and when they were both on the far shore, the lily pads and the lights in the water vanished.

The gate opened easily for them, and as soon as they were inside, Sophie reached out in her mind to cast the spell that would hide the palace. She didn't know how long it would be before Niall got there, and she thought it was only fair that he get the full experience.

They crossed the garden path of mixed stones and shells, the little creatures clearing the way so Nana could follow the instruction not to step on a shell. That brought them to the rose garden. Nana sang that verse softly to herself before picking up an older bloom that was fully opened and darkened to a red so deep it was nearly black. Sophie couldn't help but smile at the sense that Nana was doing all the right things. She supposed she shouldn't have been surprised, considering that Nana was the one who'd taught her.

The hedge opened to reveal the maze ahead. "I suppose I need to complete the maze instead of us just running back with the rose," Nana said.

"I haven't noticed any sign of Niall," Sophie said, looking behind them while also sending out her magical senses. Where was he? Even with the obstacles she'd set in his path, he should have been here by now. He might not deserve the throne, but he was still a powerful fairy ruler centuries older than she was and with far more experience in the Realm.

The maze wasn't particularly complicated, since the song gave the directions: all left turns, aside from one final turn to the right. That brought them to a door. "It will take blood to open it, won't it?" Nana said.

"That's how it worked for me," Sophie confirmed.

Nana ran her thumb across a thorn, then pressed it on the door frame. The door opened, and Nana glanced back at Sophie. "That should do it, then."

"Wait, one more thing. The crown." Sophie had almost forgotten that she still wore it. It was surprising how quickly she'd become accustomed to its weight on her head. She reached up and removed it.

Nana took off her hat so that Sophie could place the crown on her head. When the crown touched her, Nana's eyes glazed over slightly, and Sophie hurried to steady her. She remembered what it had been like when she'd first been crowned. It was like plugging her brain directly into some kind of fae database. She'd been sitting on the throne at the time, so she didn't know if Nana was getting the full experience, including the flashback to the story of their ancestor, the last queen of the Realm, but she could tell that something big was happening to her grandmother. It also looked like the crown wasn't rejecting her. That was a good sign.

Eventually, Nana's eyes came back into focus. It might have been Sophie's imagination, but she was pretty sure she looked even younger. Her hair was darker and redder, almost Emily's color, her eyes were brighter, her skin smoother, and her posture straighter. Sophie had never realized that her grandmother was actually taller than she was. "Your majesty," she said with a smile, dipping a slight curtsy.

"Oh, none of that," Nana said, reddening slightly. "We should get back and win this contest once and for all."

"Not so quickly."

They both whipped back around at the sound of Niall's voice. He stood insolently inside the doorway, a red rose tucked into the buttonhole of his lapel.

If Sophie had spoken, she would have stammered incoherently, so she kept her mouth shut and hoped her glare spoke volumes for her. Her self-control was tested when Maeve joined Niall. "Hello, your majesty," she said, her voice laden with sarcasm.

Sophie was so surprised that by the time she sensed the darkness closing in around her, it was too late to stop it.

∽Forty-Two∽

The Throne Stone
Meanwhile

The fairies might not have had much sense of time, but Emily sure did, and she was getting impatient. Sophie and Nana had been gone far too long, and Emily didn't trust what Niall might do out of sight of the rest of the Realm. Why had Sophie come up with such a silly test? It was like she'd deliberately created her own trap and walked into it.

Emily tugged at Michael's sleeve. "How long have they been gone now?"

He checked his watch. "It's only been about twenty minutes."

"That's way too long, isn't it? Sophie can get entirely across the Realm with a single step, so this thing should have taken five minutes, tops. A step or two to get there, grab a rose, a step or two back, and boom, done!"

"Remember that time is weird here. That twenty minutes on my watch may not mean anything."

"Don't tell me you're not worried."

"I suspect Sophie's up to something, and you know her, she has it all under control."

"I imagine your grandmother is is being qualified to take the throne," Amelia said. Athena punctuated that with a reassuring pat on Emily's back.

"Oh, right!" Emily said, suddenly feeling a lot better. "*That's* what they're doing. They'll want to run through all the tests in that song. And, bonus, if Niall doesn't do that, then he's not up to par. Okay, doing all that stuff might take a little time, even if they already know what to do."

But although Emily now knew what might be taking so long, the rest of the crowd was getting restless. They may not have measured time in the human way, but they did get bored easily. A party had broken out, with music and dancing. In another part of the gathering, there were a few fights going on, with spectators wagering on the outcome. On the other side of the field, a big group was playing a game that looked like a psycho cross between baseball and rugby. If the royal contestants didn't return soon, their kingdom would have forgotten why they were there. Emily wondered if that would help or hurt Sophie's claim.

Michael was the next one to grow anxious. He checked his watch again and said, "Now it's been half an hour. That's more than long enough. I don't think it took this long the first time around when there was a battle going on and Maeve was using you as a hostage."

Although Emily had been all for being zen about it, the moment Michael admitted to being worried, she was ready to jump. Turning to Eamon, she said, "You need to take us to the palace. Sophie might need help."

He paused, considering. At last, he said, "It has been a long time, I believe, and I am concerned that neither has returned."

"Awesome. So, who's with me?"

"We'd better come," Amelia said. "If they're in trouble, they'll need magical support."

Emily turned to Michael. "You in?"

She could read the conflict in his eyes. He was worried and probably would have insisted on going at any other time, but he'd just found his wife and stood with his arm around her. She didn't look at all happy about the idea. "I'm not sure how much help I'd be," he said. "Maybe I'd better keep an eye on things here."

"Yeah, that's probably a good idea," Emily said. "What if they come back the moment we leave? Which, knowing Sophie, is entirely likely."

He still didn't look too happy, but he did look relieved. "Okay. Be careful," he said. "She'd kill me if I let you go into danger."

"Yeah, she's probably had her fill of rescuing me." She handed over Beau's leash. "You can dogsit." The sleeping bulldog didn't even seem to notice he'd changed hands.

Eamon was already holding Amelia's hand, and Amelia held her sister's hand. Emily took her spot on Eamon's other side, and as soon as their hands were clasped, they all stepped off.

It wasn't the quick trip Emily expected. There seemed to be a sideways step, and for a moment she felt like they were walking in circles, but when the long stride ended, they were right in front of the palace. "What was that?" she asked when she caught her bearings.

"I believe I fell into one of your sister's traps," Eamon said. "Once I noticed it, I was able to untangle it, but she initially detoured us to the other side of the Realm."

The palace looked pretty much the same way it had the first time Emily saw it, like Sleeping Beauty's palace while she was asleep, thorny vines obscuring everything. "Shouldn't the vines be gone if they succeeded?" Emily asked, now starting to feel fully justified in her worry.

"The vines appear to be your sister's work," he said after staring at the palace for a while. "She may have tried to block Niall's way."

"Oh, then that's a good sign," she said, but she was still worried. Something about all this felt wrong.

They were on the right side of the river, though, so they didn't have to worry about lowering the drawbridge or getting through the gate. They just needed to get through the throne room doors, which was going to take some work, since vines were blocking it off. That was if they wanted inside. If Sophie and Nana had been going after a rose, they'd be in the garden.

"How did you get in the last time?" Emily asked the enchantresses.

"We followed your sister," Athena said.

"But you went in through the garden, right? Do you think you can do it again?"

Instead of answering, Amelia took off around the edge of the river that acted as a partial moat. There was a small pedestrian gate next to the closed drawbridge. Vines twined around the gate's metal bars, but Amelia cleared those with a wave of her hand. The gate unlocked easily, as well. "Enchantress magic doesn't seem to be blocked at all," Amelia said.

Emily didn't wait to discuss the finer points of magic. As soon as the gate opened enough for her to pass through, she ran. The rose garden should be straight ahead, as she recalled. It was right where she remembered it, nearly head-high bushes laden with roses that perfumed the air.

But there was no sign of her sister or her grandmother. She ran around the rosebushes, making sure no one was lying on the ground behind any of them. By this time, the others had caught up. "They're not here!" she cried out.

"Maybe they went back already, like you told Detective Murray," Athena suggested hopefully.

"No, something is wrong here," Eamon said. His eyes had gone a steely gray, which gave Emily the impression that he was worried, indeed.

"Okay, then, what would they have done next if they were working their way through the song?" Emily said, thinking out loud. "How does that stupid song go?" She hummed the melody to herself, but while she could remember most of the verses, she couldn't remember the right order.

"After the rose garden, there was the maze," Athena said. "I believe the opening was about here." She pointed to the wall of greenery ahead of her. "But the last time, it had already been opened."

"And, like last time, we're not worried about winning a crown. We just want to get there," Amelia said. She raised her right hand, pointed her index finger, and blasted a hole through the greenery to reveal the maze. Next, she blasted a path straight through the middle of the maze. They all ran through, coming up to the last hedge, which remained intact. Amelia held them up there. "We should perhaps get a better sense of the situation before we forge ahead," she whispered.

She and Athena stood still, their eyes closed and their hands held palm-up out in front of them. They looked to Emily like they were calling up spirits from the ether. She glanced over to Eamon, ready to make that joke with him, but he, too, appeared to be in a magical trance. Emily strained her ears and tried to peer through the leaves. Now would have been a good time for any latent magical powers she might have to kick in, she thought, but she didn't seem to be accessing anything but her ordinary human sensory input.

"I don't sense them," Amelia said after a long moment, her voice sounding strained.

"Me, either," Athena chimed in.

"I know only that something is as it shouldn't be," Eamon said.

While they were getting mystical, Emily found a slightly bare spot in the hedge—probably from where Amelia had blasted it the last time—and through it she spotted two figures lying on the ground. "Oh my gosh! There they are!" she hissed at the others, gesturing for them to join her, even as her stomach knotted with tension. She didn't think motionless bodies were a good sign.

She was ready to rush out of the maze and go to Nana and Sophie when a pair of legs came into view. Looking through the narrow portal through the hedge, she had to change her angle to move up from the figures on the ground to see a face, and then she had to bite her tongue to keep from blurting, "Maeve!" out loud. Instead, she whispered, "Maeve's there, too. She must be in on this, that double-crosser."

"She must have been left behind to watch them," Amelia said.

"Which means Niall's probably already on his way back to the stone," Emily said. "There goes this contest. Good thing we're already ahead. Or would this count as cheating? Is there a form of cheating so blatant that it would disqualify anyone in a fairy contest?"

·

"I am afraid the contest is hardly our biggest worry at the moment," Eamon said, "not if the queens have been incapacitated." He frowned for a moment and said, "I will confront Maeve. That should serve as a distraction that will allow you to neutralize her." He didn't give them a chance to argue with his plan before he moved around the last hedge to exit the maze.

Emily bit back an anxious cry of, "Eamon!" just before she ruined any element of surprise he might have had. It was almost as nerve-wracking watching him in danger as knowing her sister was in trouble, and that was a revelation. Those kisses had apparently not just been acting on her part. She had a lot to think about when all this was over.

She heard Maeve's voice say, "Eamon, what are you doing here?" and forced her attention back to the matters at hand.

"I hadn't seen you in your court," Eamon said.

"I have no more court," Maeve spat.

"Oh, that would explain why I couldn't find it," Eamon said, sounding remarkably casual, like he'd just bumped into Maeve while aimlessly wandering around. He was playing up his absentminded professor persona, as though he really had been so out of the loop that he'd lost track of her current situation. Emily had to reassess his acting ability once more—and what did that mean for those kisses?

"I never should have had you find that girl for me," Maeve said. "She brought me nothing but trouble."

"Didn't you accomplish your goal in luring her sister?"

"My goal was to win the throne," Maeve snapped. "That did not go as I planned it. But I will have it soon anyway."

"Oh?" Emily couldn't see him well through the bushes, but it looked like Eamon was standing with his hands in the pockets of his tweed jacket. Eamon wasn't really a casual guy, ever, but Maeve didn't seem to have noticed that he was acting out of character.

"Yes. I've made plans and alliances, and as you can see, I've had my revenge on that usurper who took my rightful throne."

That sent Emily's heart into her throat. Were Sophie and Nana lying there dead?

"I was wondering about that," Eamon said, still sounding way too nonchalant. "It seems an odd place to take a nap, but as much as I've read about humans, I still don't understand them. So I suppose you did something to make them fall asleep here?"

Emily glanced back at the enchantresses, hoping for some reassurance, but they were busy conferring with each other on a plan of attack. Emily didn't want to interfere with that, so she returned her attention to the strange scene playing out between Maeve and Eamon.

"Soon the court will come here, after Niall is named the rightful ruler, and I will be his consort as reward for my assistance in defeating his enemies," Maeve gloated.

"I thought Orla was his consort," Eamon said.

"She lacks the proper ambition to rule at his side."

"That would take a lot of ambition," Eamon agreed amiably. "And with that much ambition, why stop at being a mere consort?"

The enchantresses motioned for Emily to stay where she was, then they eased their way out of the maze, splitting up to come at Maeve from both sides. Eamon had managed to gradually shift position as he talked to Maeve so that she had to turn her back to the maze to continue facing him. That allowed the enchantresses to sneak up on her. Before she could react, they hit her with a spell that dropped her where she stood.

Emily didn't wait for Maeve to hit the ground before she rushed out of her hiding place and fell on her knees beside her sister and grandmother. Much to her relief, she found strong pulses in both of them. "I think they're just under a sleeping spell," Athena reassured Emily as she knelt beside her.

"Then maybe we should have brought Beau with us," Emily said, forcing a smile. *Or Michael,* she added mentally.

"Oh, this isn't a kissing kind of spell," Athena said. She was already digging in her bag, searching for something. "This one?" she asked her sister, holding up a vial.

"That's probably the best to start with," Amelia said after bending to peer at the vial.

Athena uncorked the vial, and the scent of whatever was

in there wrinkled Emily's nose and brought tears to her eyes. The enchantress waved it in front of Sophie and Nana, then the two sisters held their hands out toward each other and murmured something under their voices. The air crackled with energy, like a summer storm was approaching.

Sophie's eyelids flickered first, and she stirred like she was having a bad nightmare. Nana moaned softly, but barely moved. Emily gripped her sister's hand and urged, "Come on, Soph, wake up. That jerk's probably stealing your throne even now."

That was when she noticed that Sophie was no longer wearing the crown. She had been wearing it when they left, hadn't she? Nana wasn't wearing it, either, but her Queen Elizabeth hat was gone. "Guys, we've got a problem: Niall must have the crown," she said to the others.

"We don't have time to be delicate, then," Athena said, her jaw set with determination. She pulled another vial out of her bag and added, "You might want to hold your nose for a second. This one can be rather pungent."

Considering what the last one had smelled like, Emily decided not to risk it. She took a deep breath, held it, and pinched her nose as Athena uncorked the bottle. This time, she barely had to wave it in front of Sophie before Sophie sat straight up, her eyes wild with the air of someone who'd awakened abruptly while in the throes of a nightmare.

"Where is he?" she demanded.

"He's gone, probably back to the valley," Emily told her, then winced as she added, "And it looks like he took the crown with him."

Nearby, Nana woke more gradually. "That potion is vile," she remarked, rubbing her nose.

"It never fails," Athena said, returning the corked vial to her bag.

"How big a head start does Niall have?" Sophie asked.

"He was gone before we got here, so at least ten minutes," Emily said. "But you can probably get back there soon enough, and you're still ahead even if he wins this one."

Sophie started to get up, and Eamon gallantly offered her his hand to assist her. It was a sign of how rattled she was that she accepted it instead of just bouncing up on her own. Once Sophie was up, he helped Nana rise.

Sophie was already on her way into the palace. Emily rose and rushed after her. "Don't you need to get back there to finish the contest?"

Without breaking stride, Sophie said, "If he wins mastery of the Realm, he wins, even if he did cheat. So I need to win this one definitively."

The others had entered the palace and were following them, but Emily kept up with Sophie. "And how do you plan to do that?"

Sophie grinned. "I'm taking the contest to my turf."

⤳Forty-Three⤳

The Throne Stone
Meanwhile

No sooner had Emily and the others left when Niall returned, striding down the hill into the valley, a rose in one hand and the crown in the other. Michael noticed that he hadn't tried to put on the crown yet, which meant there was still hope. If he'd truly defeated Sophie to take it from her, he wouldn't have hesitated.

"Oh, my opponent hasn't returned yet?" he asked far too nonchalantly as he approached the stone. He handed the rose to Tallulah with a gallant bow. "I believe this was the object of the quest, and I seem to have won the race." He acted as though he was surprised to find the crown in his other hand. "I also have brought this, which the queen seems to have misplaced. I can wait awhile before I put it on. Ceremony is important, after all."

A flash of anger and dismay crossed Tallulah's face ever so briefly, but she very quickly schooled her features to act like she wasn't worried at all. "We have yet to see the full outcome of this contest," she said.

"Wasn't the contest to get to the palace and bring back a rose?" Niall asked, his eyes wide and innocent—unnaturally so. He looked like one of those paintings of kids with big eyes that were probably meant to be cute, but that gave Michael the creeps.

"We have to determine the origins of this rose and what you did to obtain it," Tallulah said. "You could have taken a rose from anywhere."

"But where did I get this?" he asked, brandishing the crown.

"That is not proof of mastery over the Realm."

"It's proof of mastery over the queen, which is the same thing." He drew closer to Tallulah, standing so that he was almost nose to nose with her. She didn't flinch in the slightest. "I know she's your favorite, but you're going to have to call this one for me."

Before Tallulah could answer, there was a strange wrenching sensation. For a long moment, Michael lost track of where he was. He couldn't see or hear anything, and he felt detached from reality. It was similar to what happened when Sophie crossed the Realm in a step or two, but more disorienting because he wasn't traveling. He knew he was standing still. His feet weren't moving, and they never lost contact with the ground, but he felt like he was suddenly in a different place.

When the blur of his surroundings resolved and came into focus, he found that they were back in the palace—the real one. It looked more like he'd expect a palace to look because now it was far from deserted. He, Jen, Tallulah, and the fae rulers were arranged around the dais steps. The throne room was full of the other attendees, and the doors and windows were all open, revealing the rest of the gathering on the palace grounds, where they could also look inside.

At the head of the room, Sophie sat on the throne, her sister and the others arranged around her like courtiers. Sophie gave the little smile that Michael had learned meant someone was about to get eviscerated. "There, that's better," she said sweetly—too sweetly, her voice full of steel magnolia honey. "I realized that I designed this test badly. What does *crossing* the Realm really say about one's mastery of it? So I brought the Realm to me." She handed a rose to Emily, who took it to Tallulah. "Here's my rose, and there's a whole garden of them out there."

"This is an interesting development," Tallulah said, barely concealing a smile. "While the test was presented in terms of a race, the point of it was to demonstrate mastery of the Realm. Niall won the race, but who can argue that transporting the residents of the Realm by rearranging the Realm itself demonstrates the kind of mastery none of us could achieve?" She turned to Niall. "Unless you would like to try?"

Michael hadn't seen a fairy redden with rage, but Niall showed that it was possible. "You're bending the rules to suit your favorite," he accused.

"Then perhaps you should show us how you won the race," Tallulah suggested.

Sophie nodded ever so slightly to Eamon, and a moment later a blond fairy in a maid's uniform rushed to Niall. "You won!" she cried out, throwing her arms around him. "Now we will rule side by side!" Only when she pulled back to see his reaction did Michael recognize Maeve. Next to him, Jen stiffened. Jen had been Maeve's captive, and Maeve had kept her, even after realizing she wasn't the woman she sought.

Niall looked even more distressed than Jen at Maeve's appearance, though probably because his consort was coming toward him with a glare that made everyone present take a step back. "You were going to rule with *her* at your side?" she asked, her voice icy in spite of the storm raging on her face.

"No!" he cried out, trying to shrug his way out of Maeve's embrace. "She must have misunderstood. I just needed her help to get into the palace."

Now Maeve was outraged. "You were using me? You *promised.*"

All the while, Sophie leaned an elbow on the arm of her throne and watched as if she was enjoying a particularly juicy soap opera. She'd clearly engineered the situation for maximum dramatic impact. The fairies in attendance watched with equal relish. They knew a good scene when they saw it, and they laughed out loud. The laughter didn't sit at all well with Niall, who tried to distance himself from both the women he'd wronged, even as he glared at the crowd.

"The test was to manipulate the Realm, not a person," Tallulah said with barely restrained glee. "You may have won the race, but you did not win the contest." A cheer rose from the assembly, and Sophie allowed herself a slight smile of triumph.

"But I have the crown!" Niall shouted, raising it over his head. "How did I get that, if not by besting the queen?"

"If you believe you won that crown fairly enough that it and the Realm will accept your rule, feel free to put it on," Sophie said, still with that honeyed tone that implied she was seriously pissed-off, but was too much of a Southern belle to let it show. The "bless your heart" was implied.

Every eye in the throne room—and probably a lot of eyes from outside, as well—focused on Niall to see what he'd do. He studied the crown for a long time, as though trying to decide what would happen to him and whether he could really have been considered a winner. At last, he beckoned to one of the handmaidens and set the crown down on the floral pillow. "The Realm must choose the winner, so it would be inappropriate to crown myself prematurely," he said with a slight bow to Tallulah.

"Yes, there is the final vote," the fairy woman said. "This will decide who wins the crown." She raised her voice and addressed the crowd. "You have seen how the contestants, the crowned queens and the challenger, have fared in a series of tests. These tests measured the skills that are of value to the fae. But no ruler can lead without the acceptance of her—or his—people. The final test will be one of loyalty as the citizens of the Realm choose their new ruler based on what they've seen in this contest."

That sounded to Michael suspiciously like a democracy, which the free fae should like. But who would they choose? Had Sophie and her grandmother done enough to demonstrate that they were worthy of leading the Realm in spite of only having a trace of fae ancestry?

"The two candidates may state their cases to those they would rule," Tallulah declared. "The challenger first."

She gestured to Niall, who came to stand at the front of the dais, directly in front of Sophie's throne, where he blocked her from view. "You've seen the contest and who has won fairly and who has benefited from some perhaps questionable calls." Michael wondered if he even remembered that he'd benefited from at least one of those calls. "But the real key here is that I am fae. Should the Realm not be ruled by one of our own? The human influence on the Realm is already too great. Should we really have a human as a ruler? That would be most irregular. As your king, I would create a truly fae Realm and return us to our former glory."

There was polite applause, with a few who sounded slightly more enthusiastic. Tallulah waited for it to die down, and then waited a few moments more, until the silence grew uncomfortable, before she gestured to Sophie.

Sophie rose from the throne, took her grandmother's hand, and the two of them walked together, stopping halfway down the dais steps, still enough above the people to be seen, but far enough down to not appear overly distanced from them. "To be honest, I didn't really want to take this crown," Sophie said. "I did it out of duty to my ancestor, who thought she was leaving the Realm to flourish on its own. In case the Realm ever needed a queen again, she left the knowledge of how to regain the throne with her descendants, and that is how my grandmother and I came to be here. I awoke the Realm when I took the throne and crown after winning them with my blood and success in the ancient trials. My grandmother has also passed the trials and won the right to wear the crown."

The crowd applauded, and when the applause died, Sophie continued. "The Realm only needs a ruler to keep the land awake and to settle disputes. I intend to change very little. Those of you who want courts may live among them. The free will only notice that they have a ruler if they need to resort to royal judgment. I ask only that all residents of the Realm deal fairly with each other, regardless of who they are—human, or any variety of fae."

That got even more applause. With a glance over her shoulder at Niall, Sophie added. "If I were you, I'd worry about a ruler who first attempted to gain power through trickery, putting an impostor under his control on the throne. Look at what he did in that impostor's name. He used the Hunt to menace his subjects. Is that the kind of ruler you want?"

There was shouting this time, mostly from the wilder fairies. Tallulah stepped in, motioning for the crowd to be silent, and Sophie and her grandmother moved aside. "Who among you choose Niall as ruler?" Tallulah called out.

The more medieval-looking of the rulers came forward and knelt in front of Niall. His consort—probably now "former"—very pointedly did not. A few of the attendees dressed in his 1930s style, the mid-century style of Maeve's old court, or the medieval fantasy-land style moved forward to kneel. Michael didn't notice much action out on the grounds. There were one or two cheers.

Tallulah nodded, then said, "And for the two ladies?"

There was a long silence that made Michael nervous. It was like no one wanted to move first. Jen surprised him by releasing his arm and moving to kneel in front of the Drakes. "I apologize for allowing myself to be used as an impostor," she said.

Taking a cue from her, Michael moved forward and bowed, as did the enchantresses, Eamon, and Emily. A rustling and rumbling rolled through the room behind him, and Michael couldn't resist a glance.

The Hunt, still in their renewed form as a royal guard and dismounted from their steeds, marched down the center of the throne room, bowed to Sophie when they reached the front, and took positions to either side of her. Behind them came the free fae and human army Emily had recruited. Following them was a flood of the wild fae, with a few in courtly costumes sprinkled throughout. It looked to Michael like about as definitive a victory as anyone could hope for. It was a landslide.

Once it was clear where things lay, some of the court members joined in. Even Niall's former consort went over to give Sophie and her grandmother a perfunctory curtsy.

It looked like this would go on all day, but Tallulah raised her hands over her head and shouted, "The Realm has decided. These ladies will now be our rightful rulers."

The cheer that arose was deafening. Michael could imagine

that it echoed throughout the Realm. He was surprised to see that instead of grinning in triumph, Sophie actually looked somewhat humbled, like the acceptance of the people had truly touched her. Her mismatched eyes were bright with tears, and her lower lip quivered.

Her grandmother looked more serene about it. She gave the impression of someone born to this kind of adulation, nodding and smiling to each person who came before her.

With a roar of rage, Niall rushed toward the two Drake women, a sword materializing in his hand as he attacked. Sophie moved automatically to shield her grandmother. There was a flash of light, and Michael couldn't tell if Sophie had managed to block the blow magically or if she'd taken the hit.

He didn't stop to find out before rushing to tackle the fairy. He wasn't sure what he expected to be able to do, but when someone waved a weapon in a crowd, his cop instincts kicked in. Niall easily brushed him aside without laying a hand on him, and Michael went rolling across the dais, barely stopping himself before he went over the edge and down the steps.

From where he lay, it didn't look like Sophie was hurt, but she was having to fight magically against both magic and a weapon that seemed to be physical. Suddenly, Niall yelped. Michael hadn't seen Sophie get in a blow, but then he noticed Beau with Niall's ankle clamped firmly in his jaws.

By this time, the leaders of the Hunt had made it up the steps. "You shall not attack our queens," the lead Huntsman said in his eerie, booming voice. Michael wasn't sure what the Huntsman did to Niall, but the attack stopped instantly and Niall was being drawn inexorably toward the Hunt, fighting every inch of the way. Beau was dragged behind for a few feet before the dog apparently decided the Hunt had it under control and released his grip.

When Niall reached the Hunt, he changed. Gone was his tuxedo, replaced with armor. A helmet covered his handsome face, horns growing out of holes in the helmet. "You will now serve the queens for eternity," the Huntsman boomed.

The Hunt turned and trooped away, back down the middle of the throne room to the great doors. Michael couldn't pick out which one of them was Niall. Even Sophie looked a little stunned by this development.

Jen came over to where Michael still lay and knelt beside him. "Are you okay?" she asked, helping him sit up.

"Yeah. Probably just a few new bruises," he said.

"Good," she said, but her voice trailed off before she could even finish the one word. He followed her gaze and saw the fairy man she'd been clinging to the last time he was here. The man stared at her like a man fearful of losing a great love—the way Michael must have looked his last time in the Realm when he'd been forced to leave Jen behind. Michael turned to look at Jen, but he couldn't read her face. Did she still have feelings for this guy? Had she ever had feelings for him, or had that just been part of the spell she was under as a captive?

Whatever it was, he needed to get Jen out of here as soon as possible. The contest, battle, or whatever this had been was well and truly over. Leonie appeared serene as she gazed out upon her subjects, but Sophie looked utterly exhausted. He met her eyes, and she nodded.

"I suppose it's time to go home," she said, gesturing to her grandmother, the enchantresses, and Emily, who'd picked up Beau's leash. Coming over to Michael and Jen, Sophie said, "Ready?"

"Yes, please," Michael said with great feeling.

"Can I, really?" Jen asked, her voice shaky.

"I think so. We seem to have done all the right things. It should just be a matter of taking you through a gateway. There will be some adjustment, of course, but I should be able to leave the Realm often enough to help you through it."

"You're really planning to stay here?" Emily blurted, sounding dismayed.

"I told you, it's the only way to make sure this doesn't happen again," Sophie said mildly, sounding like she wasn't all that enthusiastic about the idea, herself. "I can't afford to leave the throne vacant."

"But this time, everyone's seen you win the throne, very definitively," Emily argued. "It would be really hard for someone else to claim to be the queen now. You could just show up here to hold court every so often and no one would care whether you lived in a palace here or back home."

"And then how long would it be before someone decides to challenge my rule on the basis that I'm no longer here? Or what if someone sets herself up as my agent, giving orders in my name? If I'm not here, I might never know, and I'd have no way of knowing how much time has passed in my absence." Sophie shrugged. "It may not be permanent. I just need to make sure there's stability. When our ancestor left, it was after centuries of established rule. I can't expect to swan off after five minutes and have everything be okay."

Tallulah came to stand behind Sophie. "She is correct," she said, placing a hand on Sophie's shoulder. Sophie twitched as though to shrug it off, then winced and let out a deep breath, visibly forcing herself to remain still. "Your sister must do her duty."

Sophie managed a grin. "On the bright side, it's not like I'll age while I'm here."

"What about Nana?" Emily asked. "You're just going to take her home and leave her there with Mama while you play fairy queen?"

"Now you sound like Mama," Sophie shot back.

"I'm not saying it's your duty to stay at home with her. I've been the one arguing all along that you need to get out of there. Moving to the Realm wasn't what I meant. But what will happen to her without you? You're the one who's been using that as an excuse all along. But if you wouldn't leave to go be a real dancer, why are you leaving now?"

"Because going off to dance would have been selfish. This is a duty. It's not about what I want, but what all these people need, and keeping our world safe."

"Excuse me, but I believe I get a say in this," Leonie Drake said. "You can't talk about me like I'm not here. I'm just as much a queen here as you are, Sophie. In fact, I believe I'd be ahead of you in line."

"She's right, Soph," Emily said. She turned to Tallulah. "Isn't she?"

"The order of succession is seldom an issue in the Realm, as the fae are immortal and so few are born," Tallulah said. "You woke the crown, throne, and palace. She also won the crown. You, however, can't give it up entirely. You will always be a queen of the Realm."

"And there would still be someone on the throne if I stay," Leonie said.

"But what about Mama? You can't just vanish," Sophie protested.

"You left a changeling," Leonie reminded her.

"She'll notice when it doesn't move or wake up."

"She'll just find a body," Leonie said with a dismissive wave reminiscent of Sophie. "I may have slightly adjusted your changeling."

Sophie gasped. "So Mama's going to wake up in the morning and find your dead body? Oh dear."

"It'll make more sense than you disappearing would have. What kind of cover story did you have handy?" Her eyes softened, and she took both of Sophie's hands in hers. "It's for the best, and you know it. You have a life to live. What kind of life did I have? Here, I'm young and powerful. You wouldn't ask me to give this up to return to the way I was, would you? I can assure you that your mother won't miss me. She may act bereaved at the funeral, but she'll be happy to have me out of the house. About the only person who'll really feel it will be Bess, but ultimately this is a job for her, and I won't be the first patient she's lost. She's already bracing herself to lose me, and then she'll have another patient. You girls will be able to visit me here. I challenge you to find a single flaw in this plan."

Sophie started to speak, but her eyes filled with tears and no words came out. Instead, she threw her arms around her grandmother in the biggest hug Michael had ever seen Sophie give anyone. "Oh, thank you," she said at last.

Leonie patted her on the back. "I'm doing it as much for myself as for you. I want you to get out there and have a life, then come here and tell me all about it. You spent way too much time looking after me." When Sophie finally pulled away from the hug, her grandmother took her shoulders firmly and stared directly into her eyes. "You will get out of that house and go do what you want. Go dance. Fall in love. Be happy."

"Yes, ma'am," Sophie said, nodding.

"Sorry you didn't get to sacrifice yourself," Emily said, squeezing her sister's shoulder. "I know how much you love martyrdom."

"Oh, hush, you." Sophie pulled herself together and regained her usual aplomb. "Okay, so now I need to get everyone home and probably get back to my own home before my mother finds a dead body and has a heart attack. Eamon, do you think you can take care of Emily and the enchantresses? I need to be able to focus on Jen."

"Gladly," he said with a bow.

"If I start a band, I'm totally calling it Emily and the Enchantresses," Emily said. "Good luck, and let me know how things go." Turning to Eamon, she added, "Can you make it still be morning? I want to get a nap before the show. It's been a long night."

They moved away, and Sophie returned her attention to Michael and Jen. "Let's get out of here," she said.

She led them to the now-familiar staircase that led to the kitchen. It felt good to get away from the pomp and the crowds, and Michael noticed a similar easing of tension in Sophie.

Jen, on the other hand, seemed more anxious. "Where are we going?" she asked, her eyes moving nonstop as she surveyed their surroundings.

"We're going out the back way," Sophie said. "There are too many people here, and we'll want some quiet for this. Maybe I should have sent them all back to the valley."

"No, I think you need to let them celebrate here," Michael said. "Symbolism seems to be important in the Realm, and where else would you celebrate a coronation?"

"I don't remember this part of the palace," Jen said as they went down the seemingly endless stairs.

"It leads to the kitchens and service area," Sophie said.

"Oh, no, I didn't get down here. Why did you? You're the queen."

"It's my palace. I figured I'd better know about it."

"And that paid off," Michael added.

Sophie grinned. "Yeah, Niall didn't think to block off the kitchens when he was trying to keep me out."

The kitchen staff were their usual effusive selves when the group arrived there. Sophie greeted them all graciously, not acting like she was at all impatient, but Michael could see her glancing toward the door. "Sophie, we need to be going," he said, raising his voice above the sound of their fawning. He figured he could play the rude bad guy here and give her an out.

She shot him a grateful smile and said, "Yes, we must go. But you have a new queen to serve, and I'm sure she'll be down to see you before long."

They made their way out of the kitchen and across the yard to the hidden gate in the wall. The wooded area beyond the wall was peaceful and serene, a welcome change from the tumult in the throne room. "If I were you and could come here anytime, I think I'd be tempted to come here a lot," Michael said as they walked into the woods.

"Why do you think I'm so well-acquainted with the kitchen staff?" she asked with a wry smile. Coming to a stop, she said, "This should do well enough for a gateway."

Jen cleared her throat and said, "Um, do you mind if I ask what's going to happen?"

"I can open a portal between worlds, connecting the Realm to any point in the human world. We'll come out in Central Park, and then you go home."

"Just like that," Jen said with a little laugh that sounded a touch hysterical. Michael put a reassuring arm around her shoulders.

"Just like that," he said.

"You do this often?" she asked him.

"Only a couple of times," he admitted.

"But what will I do?" Jen asked.

"Whatever you want to," Sophie said. "We can come up with a good cover story for where you've been. When Emily went missing, I managed to keep the police from prying too deeply, and the mystery just made her famous, which she loved."

"Will I age?"

"You'll probably catch up to where you were when you left, but that's only seven years."

Jen looked down at her own hands. "I suppose mid-thirties is a little early for liver spots, so I don't have that much to worry about."

"You know, aging is normal in our world," Sophie said gently.

"How much has the world changed?"

"Not too much," Michael said. "The same sort of things keep happening. Technology moves pretty quickly, but you'll still recognize it. No flying cars or jetpacks, unfortunately. You'll want new clothes, and you might want to redecorate the apartment."

"Definitely, if you haven't changed anything in seven years." Her smile was the closest she'd come to the old Jen since he'd first found her, and he couldn't help but smile back at her with the hope that this really would work.

"You missed the end of a few TV series, but that's what Netflix is for," he continued. "I think you'll be surprised by how easy it is to catch up."

"I wonder about my career. I'm about at the age when parts start drying up for women." With a bitter little laugh, she added, "I guess I'd better get used to playing moms. I'll be demonstrating cleaning products in commercials. I bet they've come up with some new ones I've never even heard of."

"I'm the wrong guy to ask about that," Michael said.

"You're telling me! I can only imagine what that place looks like."

"It's not that bad," Sophie said. "I don't think the health department would even raise an eyebrow at his housekeeping."

"Is anything going to happen to me when I leave? I heard stories when I was a captive."

Michael and Sophie exchanged a glance. "Well, Emily did go through some ordeals that also tested us," Sophie said, "but she was still under Maeve's control then. Michael has already gone through all the trials, so you should be free. You're bound to be affected, as you would whenever you move to a new place after living somewhere else. But don't worry; we know a lot of people who can help with your transition. You won't face this on your own."

Michael remembered what Sophie had done when freeing Emily

and thought of something. "Here, wear this," he said, taking the fairy shawl out of his satchel and draping it around her shoulders. "I traded something of value for it. The plan was to trade it for something else of even more value, but I didn't get around to it. But if I'm right about the way this works, that puts you under my protection."

"Good idea," Sophie said with a nod.

Jen rubbed her palms against her skirt. "Okay, then, I'm ready to go. What do I have to do?"

Sophie moved to stand between Jen and Michael, and he reluctantly separated from his wife, reminding himself that soon he'd have her back home for good. "You each need to hold my hand, and then I take you through the gateway. All you have to do is walk."

She reached out for both of them. He grabbed her hand perhaps a bit too eagerly, then quickly eased up on his grip. He knew she wasn't as delicate as she looked, but her hand felt so small in his. Jen took longer to put her hand in Sophie's, like it was a decision she was weighing. Finally, she took a deep breath, bit her lip, and thrust her hand at Sophie.

"Here we go," Sophie said, and together they stepped forward.

And didn't go anywhere. At least, not that Michael could tell. It should still have been dark in New York, and it should have been a lot colder than this. He glanced back, and the palace was still behind them. "What happened?" he asked.

"I don't know," Sophie said, her voice sounding vague, but she was looking directly at Jen, who was shifting uncomfortably under Sophie's gaze. "I haven't had that happen to me before."

"Well, I didn't pull an Orpheus and look back," Michael said.

"I did," Jen whispered, her eyes cast downward. "I looked back."

"Then we should try again, and don't do that this time," Michael said, trying to keep the irritation out of his voice. He wasn't angry at her, just frustrated at the situation. After all these years, he was so close, and now things were going wrong.

Jen looked up at him, tears in her eyes. "I'm sorry, Michael. I love you, but I can't go back there."

"We can live somewhere else. Anywhere."

"That's not what I mean. I don't think I belong to that world anymore."

Trying not to sound too desperate, he said, "You don't know that."

"I know it's hard for you to believe, but I'm happy here. I have friends here. You may not have moved on, but I did. You're the only thing I have left in that world, and that's why I was willing to try. I know what this means to you." Her voice broke in a sob. "I just can't."

It took him a while to find his voice again, and he fought to sound reasonable because anger wouldn't help matters. "But all that I did back there. I won your freedom so you wouldn't have to stay here."

She placed her palm against his cheek, and her touch was cooler than he remembered. "You won my freedom so I could be myself again. Before, staying wasn't my choice. It was all I could do. I had no options. But because of you, I can choose. I thank you for that, and I will always owe you for that." She smiled as tears streamed down her face. "But this is the choice I have to make." She moved her hand around to behind his head to pull him to her for a kiss. He tried to deepen the kiss, but she pulled back, staying close, but not touching him. "I love you so much, and that's the only reason I'd even consider going back with you, but I can't go, and I want you to let me go and move on. Please."

"I could stay here with you," he said, getting desperate.

"No, you couldn't. I can't imagine you being happy here."

Michael couldn't speak. Getting shot hadn't hurt this badly, and he felt like he must be bleeding out, his life draining from him as the world spiraled away. In desperation, he cried out, "Sophie, do something!"

Forty-Four

Sophie had been trying to make herself scarce and invisible, then realized she really had made herself invisible, which somehow felt worse because it meant she was spying on Michael and Jen, so she toned down the magic. If she was going to eavesdrop on a private moment, they needed to know she was there.

This wasn't at all what she'd imagined happening. They'd done all the right things, so why hadn't it worked? It had never occurred to her that Jen would make any other choice but to go home.

And then Michael had to ask her for help. Was this some kind of cosmic test of her will to do the right thing, regardless of what she wanted?

But then she realized that she wanted what would make Michael happy, and the anguish on his face was killing her. She would do anything to make things work out for him, even if it meant she never saw him again.

"I can't force her to go," she told him. "But Jen, the transition may not be as bad as you think. I could help you."

"Could you guarantee I'd be happy?"

"No one can guarantee that for anyone."

"Here it's a guarantee. There's nothing to worry about—no money, no job, no cares, no responsibilities, no illness, no getting older. Look at your grandmother. She's so much better off here. She's young and healthy, and I assume that wasn't the case in our world. And no one else gets older, so you don't lose your loved ones."

"What about the loved ones in our world?" Michael asked. Sophie thought he was doing a remarkable job of keeping his cool, even as tears turned his eyes a bright green. "Not just me, but your father, your sister. You have a niece you haven't even met yet."

"A niece?" Sophie thought Jen's resolve might be wavering, and she held her breath, afraid that saying or doing the wrong thing might alter the outcome.

"Yeah, she's four, and she looks a lot like you. Your sister says she also acts a lot like you."

"Coming from her, I'm not sure that's a compliment." She shook her head. "I hadn't even thought about my sister."

"Well, until recently, you didn't remember me, or who you were."

"My mom's still dead, isn't she?"

"She died before we met."

"She wasn't much older than I am—than I will be if I go back—when she died."

"That doesn't mean the same thing will happen to you."

"It runs in the family. Do you think you could bear to lose me all over again, and in such a horrible way?"

Sophie forced herself to remain silent, even though she wanted to cry out, "That explains everything!" She could understand Jen's fears, but she didn't understand wanting to stay. She'd been willing to do so out of duty, but her relief from her grandmother taking that burden made her feel like she'd taken a magic potion and gained a new life. Wanting to live in the Realm full-time was beyond Sophie's comprehension, even if death was a looming specter.

But Michael had mentioned that Jen was a dreamer. Dreamers tended to be drawn to the Realm, and they had been, throughout history. "You may find your artistic abilities enhanced," Sophie said, without even thinking first. Jen turned sharply to her, and Sophie spoke rapidly, taking advantage of her attention. "You were an actress, right? Well, Emily's career took off like crazy upon her return. She now has this ability to hold an audience in the palm of her hand. You may not need commercials for cleaning products. When you step onstage, no one will be able to look away from you. That shows up throughout folklore; whenever someone in the arts is taken by the fae, when they return, their abilities are beyond human." Come to think of it, they also tended to drink a lot and die young, but Jen didn't need to hear that now, not when she was already afraid of dying young.

"Really?" Jen looked hopeful, and Sophie mentally crossed her fingers in hope that this would work.

"Em's the toast of Broadway now," Michael said, the hope in his eyes giving Sophie a warm glow.

"What would you do in my position?" Jen asked Sophie. "Would you give up being young forever to live a human life?"

"I just did," Sophie pointed out. "That's why my grandmother is taking responsibility for the Realm, so I can live in the human world. Who knows, when I'm eighty and can't dance anymore and have nothing left in the human world, I might just disappear here for good, but until then, I want to live a life."

After a long, deep breath, Jen held her hand out to Sophie. "Okay, then, let's go, before I change my mind again." Sophie took her hand and Michael grabbed Sophie's before she even had to reach for him.

"Ready?" she said to them. They both nodded, and she took a step. Just as she felt the tingle of passage through a gateway, Jen's hand started to slip from hers. She tightened her grip, for fear the Realm might be dragging her back, but Jen wrenched her hand away. When they emerged in the dark, chilly park, Michael and Sophie were alone.

"What happened?" Michael demanded, whirling on Sophie.

"She let go. I tried to hold on to her."

"Was she still held to the Realm somehow? Is there something more I need to do?"

"I think she changed her mind. She just couldn't do it."

"We've got to go back and get her. Open a gateway now! Aren't you the queen? Can't you make her go?"

Sophie searched herself to determine if her answer was what she wanted to say or the right thing to say. No, seeing him hurt this way was too painful for her. She didn't want this to happen to him, no matter what it meant for her own happiness. "You went through all that—you 'killed' me—to win her freedom. Would you take that freedom away from her? You saw what happened to people forced out of the Realm. Would you do that to her?"

She tried to read his face to see if sanity would prevail, but that was difficult in the early-morning darkness. She wouldn't blame him one bit for being furious at her, for being outraged with the universe in general. When at last he spoke, his voice was soft and rough. "Is there anything I could have done? If I'd found her sooner, if we'd figured out what was going on, if I'd tried to take her home immediately…"

"I don't know. But I think it may have already been too late when you first saw her at the market. You can't blame yourself. She doesn't blame you. She thanked you. You saved her, one way or another, even if it wasn't the way you wanted."

He stood very still for a long moment and she wondered what she should do—hug him, lead him home, talk to him, or let him be. Suddenly, he crumpled, his legs going out from under him as he sank to the ground.

Blinking back tears, she moved toward him. He'd dropped his messenger bag, with his coat draped over it. She picked up the coat and wrapped it around his shoulders, since it was chilly in the park. When he didn't shrug her off or otherwise indicate he wanted her to go away, she knelt next to him and put her arm around him, somewhat awkwardly.

She wasn't at all prepared when he leaned against her like he was drawing warmth and comfort from her. She couldn't tell if he was crying, but she sure was. Normally, she liked to be alone for her cathartic cries after a crisis, but this wasn't entirely that kind of cry. Someone she cared about—loved—was hurting, and the pain was almost too much for her to bear. "I'm sorry," she whispered. "I'm so, so sorry. I wish I could make it be different, somehow. If I could think of something, anything…"

They sat like that for a long time, him resting against her in the circle of her arms. Finally, he gave a long, deep sigh and said, picking up the conversation where they'd left off, "No, I think you're right. She was right. I know what I wanted to happen, but it's her choice, and since I know she was able to choose, I have to accept it. I should have remembered about her mother. I knew she was afraid of what would happen to her, even before she disappeared. That was why she always went after anything she wanted, including me." He straightened, not really pulling away from Sophie, but moving to sit beside her, still leaning against her. She kept one arm around him. "If she'd left me for someone else in this world, I guess I wouldn't be able to do anything more than what I just did, then accept her decision."

"You'd have every right to be angry, in that case. Now, too, I guess."

"It would have been difficult for her, wouldn't it?"

"Yeah, I think so. You might have made it work, but it would never have been the same as before. You're both different people. You went through so much, and you went through it apart."

"I think it was the gray hair that did it," he said, a hint of laughter in his voice. "I got old while she was gone."

"Not that old."

"Yeah, but the wrong side of thirty. It's one thing when the transition is gradual, but getting it all at once must have been a shock."

"I really don't think it was anything to do with you. She found a place she liked, and leaving was too much for her to bear."

"So I guess I should do what she said and move on, huh? Everyone else has been telling me that for years." He got to his feet and extended a hand to her. For once, she took it and let him pull her up.

"You do what you need to do on your own schedule," she said as he put his arms in the sleeves of his coat and bent to pick up his bag.

A noise nearby in the park startled both of them. The park should have been closed by now, so Sophie was leery about what it might be—not another would-be fairy ruler trying to get rid of the reigning queen, she hoped. What she didn't expect to see was a stocky woman pushing an old shopping cart with a woman wearing a prom dress sleeping inside the basket. A wan-looking fairy who appeared to be fading fast trailed behind the woman.

"Oh, you again," the woman said to Michael. "And I take it this is your friend the fairy queen." She bowed her head ever so slightly to Sophie. "Your majesty."

"And I take it you're Michael's wise woman friend," Sophie said. "Pleased to meet you."

"You're not kicking out the humans, are you?"

"No, and I've stopped the ones who were."

"Good. Now, I've got a couple folks who need to get home, if you'd be so kind."

"Of course." Sophie opened a gateway, and the fairy immediately perked up. He lifted the sleeping woman from the shopping cart and disappeared into the darkness.

The wise woman nodded her approval. "So I guess I can send any others I find who want to get back on home now, if I can find a friendly fairy to take them."

"It should be safe now," Sophie agreed. "And if I'm around, I can get them back, but I may be tied up for a few days."

The woman turned back to Michael. "I won't even ask how your quest went. You'd look better if you'd been successful."

Sophie wasn't sure how he held himself together well enough to say calmly, "Actually, I was successful. She just didn't want to go after I freed her."

"Good job, then. I knew you had it in you. But yeah, some people don't adapt too well. Like those two." She gestured with her head toward where the gateway had been. "Nothing I did for her would have made her happy here. And I can tell you're not suited for life in there. Your calling is here. Time for you to get to work, son." She gave her cart a good push and headed off.

"You meet some very interesting people in the park at this time of night," Sophie remarked, mostly to break the uncomfortable silence that lingered after the woman's departure.

"I just wish I knew what she wants me to do," Michael said.

"If it's a calling, you'll figure it out."

He shrugged and shook his head. "How should I even handle this?"

"What do you mean?"

"Do I just let Jen stay missing? I'm at the point where I could declare her legally dead. Or do you do something like you did with your grandmother and make something into a body to be found?"

"I could do that. Is that what you want?"

He was silent for a while, then said, "No, I don't think so. A body would turn it into a murder investigation, and that would send the force on a wild goose chase. I should probably just let her vanish. I'll wait a little while before declaring her dead, and I'll talk to her family about it."

"Yes, jumping on that would just be tacky."

He chuckled at that, and it sounded real, not like borderline hysteria. "I wouldn't want to look too eager."

"So no lining up the wedding to the next wife as soon as you get the papers signed?" As soon as she said it, she wanted to kick herself. Talk about tacky.

But he laughed. "Yeah, I don't think that'll be an issue. It's not like I've established a waiting list."

Sophie felt a pang at that. She reminded herself that whatever they had was entirely one-sided, as he'd been focused on his wife. What did she expect, for him to make a move on her the moment he realized his marriage really was over, even if he had fallen into her arms at that moment?

"Are you going to be okay?"

"Yeah, I think so. Eventually. It's just going to take some time."

"Then let's get you home."

"You don't have to escort me. Don't you have to get home to your mother? She'll be finding a body in her parlor pretty soon."

"I wouldn't want to interrupt her performance of 'Ding, Dong the Witch Is Dead.' Besides, I think you need a friend right now."

"Yeah, I do, if you don't mind." He held out his arm for her to take, and together they headed for the edge of the park. "One great thing about this city is that we shouldn't have any trouble finding a place where we can get coffee even at this hour. Whatever hour this is. You up for a cup?"

"Make it tea and you're on."

After they'd walked awhile, he said, "What about you? What are you going to do now?"

"I don't know. It hasn't really caught up to me yet. I'll probably still pop back every so often to see Nana."

"I meant in real life. That's why you were staying at home. What about now?"

"I don't know. I've been taking some classes up here, and a few people have offered to have me audition, so I may give it a shot. I should still have a few years in me."

"So you'll be around?"

"Yeah, I think so."

"Good."

That single word was enough to make her warm with hope, no matter how chilly the morning was.

⟨Forty-Five⟩

The A sisters headed off to their apartment near their shop, insisting that they were fine getting there on their own. After seeing them in magical warfare, Emily didn't argue with them. She was a little disappointed that Eamon barely said a farewell before going back through the gateway. She'd thought something had happened between them, but maybe it had just been acting, after all. As her sister often said, the fae were difficult to understand. She'd worry about it once she'd had some sleep. Tugging on Beau's leash, she said, "So, whattaya say we go home, buddy, huh?"

The dog wearily pushed himself to his feet with a sigh, but then he trotted eagerly in the direction of her apartment. When she came down her block, she was surprised to find Sophie sitting on the front steps of her building. She looked rather forlorn. Drawing nearer, Emily noted that her eyes were puffy and red from tears.

Beau waddled forward to head-butt Sophie's ankle and flop against her feet. "What is it, Soph?" Emily asked, sitting next to her.

"Jen didn't come back."

"Oh, God. Poor Michael. What happened? I thought he did all the stuff to free her."

"Yeah, that's the problem. He freed her to make her own choices, and she chose the Realm." She shook her head, and her lower lip quivered slightly. "We tried everything to change her mind. I even thought she was coming through with us, but she let go on the way through the gateway."

"What are you going to do?"

"She told him to let her go and move on, and that's what he's decided to do. It may be worth one more try after she's lived awhile in the Realm without being a captive, but I really don't think that's going to make things better."

"At least he knows he did everything he could. Doesn't he?"

"Yeah, I think so. Anyway, I thought I'd hang around to tell you so you'd know to keep an eye on him. He's going to need friends. What kept you, anyway? We went for coffee and talked a while after we got back."

"I guess we came through at a different time. Eamon has that fairy time problem, so he must not have been on your schedule."

"Oh, right," Sophie said with a nod. Her cell phone rang, and she took it out of her bag, then groaned. "I should have gone back earlier."

"Mama?"

"Yep. She must have got up early." She answered the call. "Hello?" Sophie said, brilliantly impersonating the sound of a person awakened from a deep sleep by a ringing phone. "What is it, Mama?"

She winced as she held the phone out so Emily could listen. "She died! Your grandmother's dead. And you were gone! This is what happens when you stay away from home overnight."

Sophie rolled her eyes but maintained her act. "Oh dear. Did you call nine-one-one?"

"They said a death by natural causes wasn't an emergency and to call the funeral home. Sophie, what should I do?"

"It's early, Mama," Sophie said. "Pull the sheet up over her and go back to bed. I'll be there as soon as I can, and then I'll deal with it."

"But if I just leave her there, they'll think I killed her."

"Mama, everyone in town knew that Nana was very old and very sick. No one is going to suspect you of murder."

"Just get here as soon as you can."

"It may take me an hour or so." Sophie turned away from the phone, as though speaking to someone else nearby, and said softly. "It's my mother. Something happened and I need to get home." She chuckled and said, "No, I can't just stay in bed a while longer." Returning to the phone, she said, "I'll be on my way soon. Now, hang tight."

When she'd disconnected, Emily crossed her arms over her chest and asked, "Now, what the hell was that about?"

Sophie looked a little sheepish. "Sorry, I couldn't resist baiting her a bit. I told her I was spending the night with a friend, and I might have implied that the friend was male. She needs something to distract her, and that should do the trick."

"I have been a very bad influence on you," Emily said. "And have you considered getting into acting? After that performance, I'm not so sure that I'm the one in the family with that talent."

Sophie stood and brushed off her skirt. "Now I guess I'd better get home and deal with Mama. Do you want me to schedule the funeral for when you can be there, or would you rather me give you an excuse not to come, since you can't get away?"

"If you could take me through the Realm and find a way to hide that from Mama, then I could look like I moved heaven and earth to get there without disrupting my life much."

Sophie smiled. "That works for me. How about Monday morning?"

"If you can do it. Isn't it weird to bury a log?"

"No one will know otherwise."

"And now you're free. How does it feel?"

"It hasn't really hit yet. I have a lot to deal with first."

"Oh, right, I guess you do." As tired as she was, Emily forced herself to stand so she could hug her sister. "Take care of yourself. When all this is done, you deserve a vacation. Find yourself a beach with some drinks with little umbrellas in them."

"I have a dance career to relaunch, so the vacation will have to wait."

"And that's why you need a vacation. You need a break before you head into the next phase of your life."

"The next phase of my life *will* be a vacation for me." Sophie bent to scratch Beau's neck. "I'll let you know about funeral arrangements. And now I'd better go face Mama."

Emily watched her disappear down the block before she unlocked the front door and went to her own apartment. It was funny that somehow in settling everything, they'd ended up changing everything.

⌒Forty-Six⌒

Maybelle, Louisiana
Friday, 5:00 a.m.

Sophie stepped out of the gateway near her car. The familiar smell of pine needles told her she was home again. She glanced at her dress, which was rather the worse for wear, and contemplated changing clothes before facing her mother. On the other hand, looking like she was making a walk of shame would complete the image she'd suggested earlier. After all, she really had spent the entire night with a man, and then had a very early breakfast with him.

Feeling rather defiant, she threw her bag and coat into her car and got in to drive home. The lights were on in the house when she arrived, so she braced herself to deal with her mother. Putting on the proper air of mourning when she'd last seen her grandmother looking young, healthy, and happy would test her acting abilities.

The really difficult thing to hide would be the joy of knowing she had her whole life ahead of her, with a wider array of choices than she'd ever had before. She parked her car, got out, and prepared to face her future.

The End

Thank you for reading *To Catch a Queen*, the second book in the Fairy Tale series. The first book in the series is *A Fairy Tale*. The series will soon continue with more adventures.

Coming July 2015, Farrar, Straus and Giroux Books for Young Readers introduces *Rebel Mechanics*, a new book by Shanna Swendson.

Please turn the page and enjoy an excerpt.

One

If I'd let myself think about what might lie ahead for me, I'd have been terrified. So, instead of thinking, I lost myself in the book I'd bought at the train station newsstand—the kind of pulp novel I'd have had to hide behind a copy of *The Odyssey* if I'd still been at home in New Haven. Now, though, I could read what I wanted without my father having any say in the matter. My life had improved in that way, at least.

Although the motion of the train made it difficult to keep the paperback book steady, I defiantly held it with the lurid cover clearly visible as I read about a daring gang of bandits terrorizing stagecoaches. I was so engrossed in the story that when I heard a sharp noise and raised voices, I initially mistook it for my imagination bringing the story to life. Then I looked up to see a group of masked, gun-wielding men rushing through the connecting doorway at the front of the car. A thrill shot through me. I had told myself my life would be more exciting beginning today, but I hadn't really believed it. I picked up my bag and dropped the book into it so I wouldn't miss a thing.

"Seal the door!" the tallest bandit ordered, and one of the masked men turned to throw the latch. He held his hands over it, and I thought for a moment that I saw a shimmer beneath them. A shiver went down my spine, making me gasp. Could that have been magic? No, I decided, only the magister class could use magic, and that class held most of the property in the British Empire and controlled the magical power that ran all industry, even here in the American colonies. Magisters shouldn't need to rob trains. When I looked again, the shimmer was gone. I must have imagined it.

While the man who'd sealed the door stood lookout, the tall bandit who'd shouted the order strode up the aisle, heading toward the rear of the car where I sat. Abruptly, he stopped and raised his pistol at a man sitting three rows ahead of me. "I'll take that," he said in a soft but firm voice as he grabbed a slim black leather case the man held in his lap. The man clung to his case, and it looked for a moment as though he might put up a fight, but the bandit cocked his pistol with his thumb and held it closer to the man's face. The man released his hold on the bag. The bandit gave him a disconcertingly polite nod as he lowered the gun and took the case. He then continued up the aisle, seemingly unaffected by the swaying motion of the train as it slowed to round a bend.

He stopped directly in front of my seat, and I gripped the handles of my bag as my heart beat wildly. The bandit stood so close to me I could see his eyes through the slits in his mask. They were an icy, pale blue, hard and cold, with little flecks of gray around the pupil and a band of darker blue around the outer edge of the iris. I had never met a killer, but based on every novel I'd read, that was how I imagined a killer's eyes would look.

When the bandit stepped toward me, I reacted instinctively. I rose to my feet, swung my bag at him, and then felt the shock go up to my elbows when I connected with his head. He staggered backward, and I felt light-headed as my breath came in shallow gasps. I shrank away, fearing retribution.

Instead of being angered by my assault, he smiled wryly and holstered his gun. The smile made his eyes look much less icy and hard. With a slight bow, he said, "My apologies, miss. I did not intend to alarm you."

"They're coming!" the lookout called from the front of the car. "Hurry!"

My bandit glanced over his shoulder to see the railroad guards attempting to open the locked door, then returned his attention to me. "And now, if you will excuse me, I need to make use of your seat to reach that hatch." I followed his eyes upward to see a hatch in the car's ceiling, directly above me. The bandit put the case he'd taken on the seat near me, stepped onto the seat, placed his hands against the hatch, paused for a moment, and pushed. The hatch flew open, sending a gust of wind rushing into the car and jolting me back against the window. I worried that my hat would fly off, but I was too afraid of letting go of my bag to secure my hatpin. "It's open, come on!" the bandit shouted to the others as he climbed down.

The rest of the gang ran toward us, and I clutched my bag against my chest as, one by one, they jumped onto the seat and hoisted themselves through the hatch onto the roof of the car. A couple passed heavy-looking sacks up to other gang members before climbing after them. When the others had all gone, the bandit I'd hit reached for my gloved hand and brushed my knuckles with his lips, whispering, "I hope the rest of your journey goes smoothly, miss," before he climbed onto the seat, passed the stolen case up to a colleague, then pulled himself through. The hatch closed behind him with a clang and the car instantly grew quieter.

Breathless and quivering, I sank slowly onto my seat, resting my bag on my knees. I absently rubbed my left thumb across the knuckles of my right hand, where the bandit had kissed me. It was the first truly romantic thing I'd ever experienced.

The guards finally made it through the door, and they ran down the aisle. The man whose bag had been taken leaped out of his seat to accost them. "I am a courier on official business for the crown, and those bandits took my case of priority dispatches!" he shouted, his mustache bristling in fury. "I expect better protection than this when I travel!" The other passengers joined in, adding their complaints at high volume.

The guards did their best to calm everyone. They interviewed the courier and several of the other passengers. One of the guards climbed onto the seat beside mine—without so much as a word to me—and attempted unsuccessfully to open the hatch. All the while, I kept glancing out the window, wondering where the bandits had gone. The train hadn't slowed down enough for them to jump, and I'd seen no one running away from the tracks.

The connecting door at the rear of the car opened and a well-dressed young man carrying a large brown leather valise entered. He pulled up short and gaped at the commotion. "I say, what's all this?" he asked.

"Nothing for you to worry about, sir," a guard said brusquely. "Please have a seat."

The newcomer glanced around for a seat and took one across the aisle from me. With a sheepish grin, he told me, "There was a baby crying in the other car. I didn't think I could bear it any longer. This looks a lot more interesting." He watched the guards conducting their investigation with great fascination, as though this was the best entertainment he'd seen in a long time. I thought he seemed a little too interested in the proceedings, and his color was heightened, as though he was either excited about something or had just done a great deal of physical activity. Surely one wouldn't get that red-faced merely while making his way through the train in search of a seat. Then I dismissed my suspicions as a flight of fancy. The bandits couldn't possibly have come down off the top of the train, removed their masks and adjusted their appearance in the lavatories, and then dispersed throughout the train as ordinary travelers.

Or could they? This man's height, build, and voice were all wrong for the lead bandit, and I'd paid too little notice to the rest of the gang to tell if this man could have been part of the group. I decided to leave the investigation to the guards. If there was something worth looking into, they'd question him.

The remainder of the journey passed without incident. When the train pulled into Grand Central Depot in New York City, I noticed upon disembarking that the third-class passengers were being searched, so apparently the first and second classes were above suspicion. I was fortunate that my father's last gesture of goodwill to me had been a second-class ticket.

In the depot, I was immediately swallowed by the sea of porters, newsboys, and passengers. After several vain attempts to get a porter's attention, I was finally able to arrange for my trunk to be held. Then I followed the flow of humanity onto the concourse toward the exit, where I paused on the threshold. Seven potential employers had requested interviews based on my letters of application, so I had high hopes of obtaining a position and a place to stay by this evening. Beyond those doors lay my future, and I was ready for it to begin.

I was entirely unprepared for the assault on my senses as I stepped out of the depot onto Forty-Second Street. Horse-drawn carriages and omnibuses and magical horseless carriages clattered up and down the street, their drivers ringing bells, sounding horns, and shouting. Smaller magical roadsters zipped in and out of the traffic, startling the horses. That many horses on the street left a pungent odor that competed with the smell of cooking from nearby restaurants and street stalls and a pall of smoke from coal fires that hung over the city. There were people packed shoulder to shoulder on the sidewalk, all in a great hurry. Scattered through the crowds were the bright scarlet coats of British soldiers.

In spite of my grand ambitions, I now worried whether I was up to the challenge. The city was even bigger, more crowded, and noisier than I'd imagined, and I was so very much alone in those crowds. "I fought off a bandit," I reminded myself as I consulted my map. When I spotted a lull in the traffic I darted across the street in the direction of my first interview.

A few streets away from the depot the traffic and noise were lighter, and once I entered an enclave of fine homes, the stench from horses was gone. Perhaps the city wasn't so intimidating after all, I thought. This wasn't too different from the neighborhood where I'd grown up. It was merely grander.

I soon found the first home on my list, the household that most closely met my criteria. According to my research, they were of the magical class but not titled nobility—probably descended from a younger son many generations back. I hoped that meant this family wasn't so high that they would never consider a relatively inexperienced professor's daughter as a governess. The house wasn't all that imposing, a modest brownstone. *I could be at home here,* I thought.

Feeling confident about my prospects, I boldly climbed the front steps and rang the bell. A moment later, a butler opened the door, and the way he scowled at me sapped my strength. "I'm Miss Verity Newton, here to see Mrs. Upton. We have an appointment. She's expecting me," I blurted, all in one breath.

He said, "I'm sorry, but Mrs. Upton instructed me to tell you that the position has been filled," then closed the door before I could protest.

"But she never even interviewed me," I whispered plaintively to the closed door. To hide my disappointment, I marched down the steps, my head held high, then strode down the sidewalk with a sense of purpose. This was only the first interview. I still had six more, and none of them could go as badly as this one.

At the next interview, I made it into the house before I was informed that I was far too young to be suitable for the position. That was a slight improvement. The next interview went even better, as I wasn't rejected outright but rather told that I would be considered. It was only after I left that I realized they would have no way to contact me if they decided to hire me. They had only my New Haven address from my initial letter of application, and no one there would know how to reach me.

I kept ringing bells and smiling my way through interviews until there was just one name left on the list, a Mrs. Talbot who was housekeeper for Lord Henry Lyndon. Although I had never imagined I might be employed in the home of a titled gentleman, Mrs. Talbot's response to my inquiry had been encouraging. The address was much farther uptown, on Fifth Avenue at Seventy-Seventh Street. I headed toward Fifth Avenue, leaving behind the clean, quiet neighborhood and reentering the clamor of the city.

When I reached the avenue and got my bearings, I realized that my destination was nearly forty blocks away. My feet cried out for mercy at the thought of that long a walk. I saw a horse-drawn omnibus approaching and decided I could spare a few pennies to avoid walking that far.

The bus stopped and I stepped forward and asked the conductor, "Excuse me, but do you go up to Seventy-Seventh Street?"

"Sorry, miss, but horses aren't allowed above Fifty-Ninth on Fifth Avenue. The magisters don't like the mess in their neighborhoods." One of his team proceeded to demonstrate exactly what mess he meant, and I averted my eyes. The prohibition on horses in magister neighborhoods explained the clean streets where I'd just been. "Though, if you ask me," he added more softly, "it's their way of keepin' the likes of us out of their part of town." Back in a louder voice, he said, "There's an uptown bus on Third Avenue that'll go to Seventy-Seventh."

I frowned, puzzled. "But if that bus goes to Seventy-Seventh, why not this one?"

"Only magisters live around the park up there. Farther east, it's just regular people—that is, until more magisters move uptown and shove them out. You can take a cab." He gestured as a magically powered carriage passed, looking rather naked without any horses pulling it. I knew my budget wouldn't extend that far. As the bus rattled away, I allowed myself a weary sigh before gathering my strength to walk to Third Avenue to catch the bus there.

"Hey, miss!" a voice behind me said, and I turned cautiously. A newsboy stood nearby, a stack of papers at his feet and several held so he could display the headlines to passersby. The banner at the top declared it to be the *World*, a newspaper with which I was unfamiliar. He wore a flat cap pulled low over his forehead. Dark hair straggled past his collar in the back, and his thin face was smeared with ink and dirt.

He gave me a cheeky wink as he raised the papers he held and shouted to a passing man, "Parliament renews the colonial tax act! Straight off the ether from London! How will it really affect us? You won't read the truth anywhere else!" The man tossed him a coin, which he deftly caught while handing over a copy of the paper.

The customer folded the paper and tucked it inside the breast of his coat as he walked away. When the customer was gone, the boy said, "You're tryin' to get up to magpie land by the park?"

I assumed that "magpie" was his slang term for the magisters. "Yes, I am."

"What would you wanna do that for?"

"I have an interview for a position as governess."

He raised a skeptical eyebrow. "You want to work for the magpies?"

"I want to work for someone who will hire me." I couldn't help but allow my discouragement to creep into my voice. "Now I suppose I had better start walking or I'll be late for my interview."

"Don't go just yet." He glanced around, then gestured for me to come closer. "You can get a ride from here if you wait. Some friends of mine'll be along any minute now." He flicked a small gear wheel with a red ribbon tied through it that was pinned to his oversize coat and waggled his eyebrows like he was conveying some hidden meaning. I wasn't sure what the significance of the gear was, but I nodded as though I understood. "Ah, I had you figured for one of us," he said with a grin. He stuck out a hand blackened with newspaper ink. "The name's Nat."

I shook his hand, grateful that I'd worn black gloves instead of white. "And I'm Verity."

A shrill whistle rent the air, and Nat gave a satisfied nod. "Here they come, right on time. Wait'll you see this, Verity."

With a screech and a shudder, an enormous metal contraption lumbered to a stop beside us. A horizontal cylinder on huge spoked wheels belched smoke from a chimney on top, and steam billowed from vents on the sides. Two men rode on the machine, one steering while the other monitored a series of gauges. An omnibus like the horse-drawn one was hitched to this monstrosity.

Nat rushed forward and called out to the man studying the gauges. "Hey, Alec! I've got a friend here who needs a lift to magpie land. You can take her, can't you? You're goin' that way anyhow."

I couldn't see Alec's reaction because a large pair of brass goggles obscured most of his face and his attention was focused on his device. "We might not be stopping when we're there," he said as he worked.

A head in a bowler hat emerged from the doorway of the bus. "Did you say this charming young lady needs a ride?" The speaker swept the hat off his head, revealing a shock of bright red hair and a young face spattered with freckles.

"I need to get to Seventy-Seventh Street," I said shakily, wondering if perhaps I'd fallen asleep on the train and had dreamed everything from the robbery until now. This was all so very strange.

Nat added, "Verity's tryin' to be a governess, and she's gonna be late for her interview."

The red-haired young man gave me a look of theatrically exaggerated pity and held his hat against his heart. "Oh, you poor dear. You're too pretty to be a governess. Ah, but I suppose you're the independent type and won't settle for letting a man take care of you."

I couldn't help but smile, and I felt my cheeks warm in a furious blush. I'd never in my life been called pretty. I was admired for my cleverness rather than my appearance. I suspected he was what romantic novels called a flirt, but I didn't think he meant any harm, even if he didn't mean what he said. "You flatter me," I said. "I have no choice but to make my own way in the world."

With a saucy wink he replied, "Well, if you change your mind about finding a man to take care of you, let me know, and I'll submit my application. The name's Colin Flynn, and if ever you want me just ask around, and I'll be there."

While we were talking, a few people who had been milling around on the sidewalk approached the bus. Colin replaced his hat on his head and stepped down. "One at a time, people!" he called out, his tone switching from flirt to officious conductor. "All aboard for a voyage into the future."

As the people stepped up to Colin, they each flicked something on their lapels. A closer study revealed that they were gears on red ribbons, like the one Nat wore. Colin also wore one on the breast of his frayed morning coat, but his gear was much larger and his ribbon much wider. When all the passengers had boarded, Colin turned to address the man tinkering with the gauges. "Have you got Bessie all stoked up, Alec?"

"One minute more, Colin. Look out for some competition."

Colin returned his attention to me. "And now, if you will step aboard my humble conveyance, we will take you on a journey you won't soon forget."

"How much is the fare?" I asked.

"Today we're offering a complimentary demonstration run. It's an experimental project. We're engineering students at the university."

I hesitated. I needed reliable transportation, not an experiment. "That's very kind of you—" I began, but Nat grabbed my arm.

"Go on, Verity. Trust me. Bessie'll get you there."

"I assure you, it's quite safe," Colin added. "All the explosions happened in the lab. We've had no trouble with the full-size model."

The idea of explosions wasn't very reassuring, but I didn't know how else I would make it to my interview on time, and I *had* to get this job. "Very well, then," I said as firmly as I could manage, in spite of my misgivings. "I accept your kind offer of transportation."

He grinned, sweeping his hat off his head and giving me a gallant bow. "Welcome aboard, Verity. And be prepared to make history."

Colin seated me at the front of the bus, next to a girl about my age. "This is Verity," he said to her. "Look after her." To me, he added, "This is my sister, Lizzie. Pinch her if she gives you any trouble."

"Ignore him, I always do," she said with an air of much-tested patience. She shared her brother's bright hair, freckles, and lanky build. A notebook rested on her knee, and she held a pencil. Another pencil was stuck behind her ear.

Most of the other passengers on the crowded bus were young men, and the few women were not at all what my mother would have considered proper ladies. They wore the wildest clothing, a mix of pieces that seemed as though they'd dug them from a rag pile with their eyes closed and then dressed in the dark. The men mixed formal wear with working attire, and some of the women wore their elaborately decorated corsets *outside* their blouses. A few of them wore skirts that fell well above their ankles. There was one woman near the back of the bus who looked out of place in the dull black of a widow in deepest mourning, with a black veil obscuring her face.

The engine made louder sounds, and more steam and smoke billowed from it—so much that I feared it would explode. Alec patted the man at the controls on the shoulder, then tapped on the front window to signal Colin. Colin acknowledged him with a nod, secured his hat on his head, and pulled a pair of goggles from his hat brim down over his eyes. He shut the door, then turned to face his passengers. "Ladies and gentlemen—and the rest of you lot," he shouted above the rumble of the engine. "We are about to embark on a great venture, one that will prove us to be the equal of any thieving magpie. What they do with magic, we have built with our own ingenuity. They think to shut us out of their districts with their laws, but this bus violates no law—yet. I'm sure they'll think of something after today." The passengers chuckled, and one or two shouted obscenities coarse enough to make me gasp.

"If there was any doubt as to why we do this, look to our guest." He pointed at me, and my skin prickled as I sensed every eye on the bus focusing on me. "This young lady here is the perfect example of our cause. She seeks honest employment at a home in magpie land, but how is she to get there for the interview? The cabs that can go there are too expensive for common folk, and the buses that do convey the common folk aren't allowed to violate their precious streets because they're drawn by horses. This is why we've devoted our knowledge and skills toward this momentous day, creating an engine powerful enough to pull a bus without being powered by magic. Now, hang on to your seats, because here we go!"

The engine grew even louder, making *chug-chug* sounds. After a long, piercing blast of the whistle, the engine strained forward, dragging the bus with it. At first it crept, as though moving was a struggle, but then it built momentum. The bus drew up alongside a magical carriage that had the coat of arms of a noble house painted on its door and a driver in livery seated in front. It looked like the passenger compartment was empty. Colin leaned out the bus window and called, "Nice toy you have there. Do you know what it can do?"

The driver turned to look at the engine and the bus, and his eyes grew wide. "What the blazes is that?" he shouted back at Colin.

Colin cued Alec, who pulled a cord, making the whistle sound a shrill blast. The engine moved a little faster, pulling ahead of the carriage. "This is the machine that'll leave your magical toy in the dust," Colin shouted with a laugh. The other young men on the bus joined in with raucous catcalls at the carriage. The driver glared at them, then furrowed his brow and moved a lever, and the carriage increased its speed. The engine soon responded, going ever faster. Colin leaned out the window, thumbed his nose at the driver, and said, "What's the matter, think your master'll turn you into a frog if you actually drive that thing? Or were you a frog to begin with, and he turned you into his driver?" I saw a flash of fury on the driver's face, and the race was on.

The noise was deafening. The engine chugged and puffed and made a great rumbling roar. The bus moaned and creaked alarmingly. I suspected it had not been designed for such speed. Every so often, it bounced when the wheels hit an obstacle, and there was a constant vibration from the paving bricks. Next to me, Lizzie wrote in her notebook, and I wondered how she could manage while being jostled so badly.

As we rattled our way up Fifth Avenue, crowds gathered on the sidewalks. Most merely gazed in curiosity, but there were also cheers as we passed. I was both terrified and exhilarated. Carriages on the cross streets barely stopped in time when the bus plowed through intersections. The bus swayed side to side as it wove its way around slower vehicles. The magical carriage kept up, with the bus occasionally pulling ahead before the carriage caught up again. In the brief moments when we were neck and neck, I saw that the carriage driver was focused intently, a look of sheer determination on his face. Alec and the other man on the engine made frantic adjustments, pulling levers and shoveling coal into what looked like a furnace.

Colin stood at the front of the bus, surprisingly steady on his feet. He sang at the top of his lungs in a strong Irish tenor, "'Yankee

Doodle went to town, riding a steam pony. Led the magpies on a chase and made them look like phonies.'"

The rest of the passengers joined in the chorus, singing, "'Yankee Doodle keep it up, Yankee Doodle dandy. Fight the magic and the Brits, and with machines be handy.'"

My blood ran cold as the meaning of their song struck me and I realized amongst whom I'd fallen. These were the infamous Rebel Mechanics, the underground group that wanted to use machines to overthrow the magical ruling class and break the American colonies away from Great Britain. Just being with them would be considered treason.

My heart racing with the awareness of where I was, I turned to Lizzie and shouted over the noise of the engine and the bus wheels clattering on the pavement, "You're *rebels*?"

She gave me a reassuring smile. "There is nothing treasonous about what we're doing here. Do you think this is wrong?"

I honestly didn't know what to think. I'd heard rumors about this group in New Haven, where some university students had supported the cause, but my father hadn't taken the rebels seriously. He'd said it was merely young men being foolish. I didn't think it wise to say this while I was at their mercy. "We are perhaps going a trifle fast for safety," I suggested, holding my bag with one hand while I gripped the edge of my seat with the other.

She laughed. "Yes, I suppose we are, but we're merely proving that this machine is as good as any magical engine. Usually we'd travel at a more reasonable speed."

There was a shout from the back of the bus, and I looked over my shoulder to see a man positioned at the rear window waving frantically. Colin noticed the gesture, stopped singing, and nodded. Then he leaned out the front window and signaled Alec, who frowned and adjusted a lever. The bus picked up speed, making even more alarming noises. I was afraid it would fall apart around us. "What's happening?" I asked Lizzie.

"The police are giving chase. You were right about us going too fast."

"The police?" I squeaked in horror. With a criminal record, I could never find a position in a good home. I wondered if the authorities would believe this band of dangerous rebels had kidnapped me.

I glanced anxiously over my shoulder again and saw the rear lookouts grinning broadly. "They've given up!" one shouted. Colin raised his arms over his head in triumph.

His sister shook her head. "They'll signal ahead and cut us off!" she warned. "We should stop now!"

"The race is still on!" he cried out. "We don't stop until we've won!"

About The Author

Shanna Swendson is the author of the Enchanted Inc. series of humorous contemporary fantasy novels, including *Enchanted, Inc.*, *Once Upon Stilettos, Damsel Under Stress, Don't Hex with Texas, Much Ado About Magic, No Quest For The Wicked,* and *Kiss and Spell.* She's also contributed essays to a number of books on pop-culture topics, including *Everything I Needed to Know About Being a Girl, I Learned from Judy Blume, Serenity Found, Perfectly Plum,* and *So Say We All.* When she's not writing, she's usually discussing books and television on the Internet, singing in or directing choirs, taking ballet classes, or attempting to learn Italian cooking. She lives in Irving, Texas, with several hardy houseplants and a lot of books. Visit her Website at http://shannaswendson.com or find her on Facebook at www.facebook.com/shanna.swendson.

CPSIA information can be obtained at www.ICGtesting.com
Printed in the USA
LVOW10s1947301015

460458LV00020B/588/P

9 781620 511398